Susan Sallis is one of the most popular writers of women's fiction today. Her Rising family sequence of novels has now become an established classic saga, and *Summer Visitors, By Sun and Candlelight, An Ordinary Woman, Daughters of the Moon* and *Sweeter Than Wine* are well-loved bestsellers.

Water Under The Bridge

Susan Sallis

CORGI BOOKS

WATER UNDER THE BRIDGE
A CORGI BOOK : 0 552 14318 9

Originally published in Great Britain by Bantam Press,
a division of Transworld Publishers Ltd

PRINTING HISTORY
Bantam Press edition published 1995
Corgi edition published 1995

Set in 10/11pt Galliard by Kestrel Data, Exeter.

Corgi Books are published by Transworld Publishers Ltd,
61–63 Uxbridge Road, Ealing, London W5 5SA,
in Australia by Transworld Publishers (Australia) Pty Ltd,
15–25 Helles Avenue, Moorebank, NSW 2170,
and in New Zealand by Transworld Publishers (NZ) Ltd,
3 William Pickering Drive, Albany, Auckland.

Reproduced, printed and bound in Great Britain by
Cox & Wyman Ltd, Reading, Berks.

For my father. A gentle man.

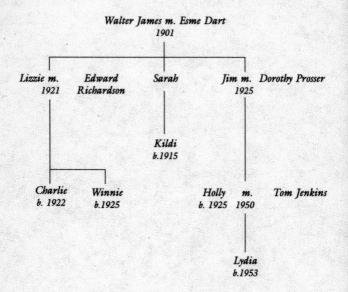

ONE

1953

Emmie James woke at four as usual and lay for some time thinking she must get up, riddle the ashes for the kettle and get out to the hens. Then perhaps she would fetch a knife from the kitchen and go up on the high ground above the river towards the Grange and look for mushrooms. She could smell it was summer; the darkness was soft and insubstantial. No rain, but a low sky all the same. Good for drying though; she might light the copper and do the towels. If Kildie came she had a way of looking through the drawers and picking out things that were slightly less than clean.

And as Kildie's name formed in her head, so realization dawned. She was no longer at the cottage in Dymock. She was at Jim's. She was lying in her granddaughter's bed and the sheets were pristine in spite of there being no proper copper here. And she had not seen Kildie for three months; but she might come today. Yes, they might all come today, though for a long moment she could not think why. And then she remembered and she closed her eyes. It was 21 July 1953. Today she was ninety years old.

At five o'clock, Jim stifled the alarm and eased himself away from Dorothy. He was on early turn at the old Great Western office in Gloucester, now called the Western Region of British Railways.

He spent a few seconds sitting on his side of the bed, arching his back, rubbing his eyes. He had felt it was a good omen, his mother's birthday falling during his early turn. It meant he would be home for the celebrations.

9

Now he was not so sure. Towards the end of the week he needed an afternoon nap to get over the early alarm. No hope of that today with the whole family rolling up.

He shuffled his feet around until they found slippers, and stood up stretching mightily. Dorothy muttered something and he said, 'It's all right, Doll. Go back to sleep.' And she sighed and murmured, 'Poor Bob.'

For some reason that made him think of Kildie. He wondered whether she'd turn up this afternoon and hoped not. She was supposed to be ill, unable to come and see Gran. He knew she was staying away for other reasons. To punish him? He slung his dressing-gown around his shoulders and crept to the bathroom. He had another niece besides Kildie; she was no problem. But then . . . Kildie was different. They were more like brother and sister than uncle and niece. He ought not to look on her as a burden.

He ran water and splashed his face. He would shave in the kitchen, one kettle of water made tea and filled his shaving mug. He sat on the lavatory fruitlessly; he needed hot tea. Then he went along the landing and stuck his head into Holly's old room.

''Morning, Ma,' he whispered. 'Happy birthday.'

She did not stir. When she had come here first, her stillness in the early mornings had frightened him. Now he was practically certain she was awake and determined not to delay him.

'D'you need the commode, Ma?' he persevered. Dorothy found it heavy work getting her on to the commode.

There was no reply. He crept downstairs.

Holly James, who was now Holly Jenkins, turned her head on the pillow and looked at her husband. After two and a half years of marriage it still seemed odd to her to find herself in bed with someone else. Odder still that the man who had been her friend for so long was now her husband in all ways. She grinned at that unspoken turn of phrase.

10

'Her husband in all ways.' What had she expected? Had she honestly believed they could have shared a celibate marriage?

He did not open his eyes but muttered, 'What are you staring at?'

'You. And it was not a pretty sight.' She moved closer and nuzzled his cheek. 'Your mouth was open and you were dribbling.'

'Oh God.' He squinted at her. 'Has it put you off?'

'Not really. Ten years of nursing acclimatizes one to the full physical horrors of *Homo sap*—'

He squinted worse than ever and growled at her.

She giggled. 'Tom, stop. You'll wake Lydie.'

'Our whole lives are ruled by that tiny scrap,' he protested. 'I've got a day off for Gran's birthday and I'm still not able to make love to my wife.'

'No, but I could make love to you.'

She kissed him and he surfaced to say, 'I don't know where you get it from!'

She smiled into his nice brown eyes.

'My mother,' she said. And was surprised that she could say that with a kind of pride.

Later they drooled over Lydia.

'Who's Daddy's good little girl then?' Tom asked, holding her to the ceiling so that she could look down on him. 'Who's going to Gran's ninetieth birthday party and is not going to cry once?'

'Well, it won't be Lydia Jenkins,' Holly said realistically as she made a big bundle of nappies and baby food to put in the car. 'Margaret Lashford said it's quite usual for them to be a bit tetchy when they start solids.'

'Margaret Lashford . . . Marghanita Laski!' Tom mocked the health visitor. 'My God, Hol, you've made her into a little tin goddess! You probably know more about babies than she does!'

'Well, I was on the maternity ward of course. But they weren't *my* babies.' Holly was determined on this point. 'Margaret Lashford can bring an objective eye to Lydie.

11

And, Tom, she knows you call her Marghanita Laski!'

'Well, of course. I call her that whenever I see her.'

She was going to tell him off properly then because not everyone could take Tom's incessant teasing, but the phone rang and it was the hospital for him.

He was quite calm about it.

'Look, they don't need me until twelve. Plenty of time to run you and Lydie to the Green. And I'll be back to see the cake cut. Never fear.'

'I do hope so,' Holly said. 'Gran is so pleased about you, Tom.'

'Pleased about me? What does that mean exactly?'

'Well, you know. That I landed up in a safe harbour. Someone with roots in Dymock . . . that sort of thing.'

Tom frowned. 'I don't think I like that. Safe. Secure. I like to think I'm dangerous. Mysterious. Bit of a devil—'

'We've got enough of those in the family. You are what we all need!'

He put Lydia into her carry-cot and she began to cry.

'Don't touch her, Tom!' Holly said. 'Margaret Lashford says she's got to learn to—'

He grabbed her. 'I'm not doing this for Marghanita. I'm doing it for me!'

'Tom! Stop. We've already . . . and we're in a hurry—'

'I'm dangerous and unpredictable, woman!' He lifted her almost as high as he'd lifted Lydia. 'And, officially, it's my day off!'

Gran's rough country voice had a rasp in it. Dorothy told herself it was because of the stroke, but of course it did not help.

'I'll have the blue nightgown and matching shawl. And I want Holly to do my hair. On top.'

Dorothy fumbled in the chest of drawers. She extracted the blue nightgown.

'There's a pink shawl here. I can't see—' Dorothy knew very well the blue shawl was waiting to be washed. Gran knew it too.

'It'll be in the laundry basket. I hope it's washed!'

'It is,' Dorothy lied. 'It needs airing. Why don't you have the pink one?'

'Blue shawl, Doll. To go with the blue nightgown.'

Dorothy kept her head down and swore under her breath. She still had to wash Gran, before starting on the sandwiches for tea. Thank God Lizzie was doing the cake. Lizzie had changed so much; and all for the better.

'OK. I'll make sure it's aired.' She laid the blue nightie on a chair and went to the washstand, smiling determinedly. 'And you know I don't like being called Doll.'

Gran made no comment. She took the warm flannel and washed her face slowly and carefully. Dorothy rinsed it and she did her neck. The nurse would come and give her a bed bath tomorrow. Holly wanted to do it, but Gran wasn't having her own granddaughter seeing her private parts.

Dorothy towelled her gently.

'Well, Gran, ninety today. You always said you'd see your ninetieth.'

'Made a promise, I did.'

'Yes. We know, Gran.' Dorothy thought if she had to hear that story again she might scream. 'It seems strange that you can remember two world wars . . . the Boer Wars . . . Queen Victoria's Golden Jubilee—'

'I'm old, Doll,' Gran interrupted firmly. 'But my life didn't really begin till the old Queen died.'

Dorothy did not protest again about being called Doll. She looked at Gran's faded grey eyes so like Jim's. The old Queen had died in 1901 on the very day that Walter James had asked Esme Dart to marry him.

Dorothy said softly, 'Oh Gran . . .'

There was a silence. Then Gran said suddenly, 'Will you go back to teaching after?'

Dorothy could have asked 'After what?' But she did not. She just shook her head.

Gran said triumphantly, 'There! I knew you didn't give

it up just 'cos of me! You were probably glad of the excuse to stop home!'

Dorothy looked at the old lady who was her mother-in-law. After all, it was her birthday.

She smiled. 'D'you know, I think I was,' she said. 'Now come on, let's change your nightie, then you can have a rest before Holly and Tom come.'

'I expect that baby will have grown some more.'

'I expect she will.' Dorothy slid the clean nightie over the wispy white hair and struggled to get the arms through.

Gran emerged looking battered.

'D'you think Kildie will come this afternoon?'

Dorothy was not to be drawn. 'I don't know.'

'Three months I've been here. She hasn't been round yet.'

'I hear she's not very well.'

Dorothy began to move away but Gran took her arm.

'If she comes, Doll . . . just remember the blood tie. And more than that too. They was brought up together, like brother and sister.'

'Of course, Gran.' Dorothy looked at those grey eyes again and wondered how much Gran knew.

Holly and Tom roared around the Green and drew up outside the cottage with a squeal of brakes.

'What's the rush?' Dorothy went out to them noticing that Tom had his sign in position, 'Doctor on Duty'.

'Tom's been called in. He'll be back later.' Holly lugged the carry-cot off the back seat and looked at him. 'He hung around unnecessarily. No need for all that rush. If we'd left when I was ready—' He leered at her through the window and she moved away hastily before he could say something embarrassing. 'How is Gran?'

'As usual. Tom, do drive carefully,' Dorothy leaned down to peer at him fondly. They all liked Tom. It had turned out best in the end.

He grinned at her. 'Of course. Take no notice of Holly. She's a congenital liar.'

'Takes after me, I expect.' Dorothy spoke without thinking then hoped Holly hadn't heard.

But Tom's grin widened. 'In that case, no grumbles. I don't mind what she inherits from you.'

There was obviously a double meaning there. Holly was blushing and Tom drove off laughing like a hyena.

They put the cot on its wheels and looked at Lydia. She lay on her back, her legs lifted high, her face serious.

'I think she has just found out about her toes,' Holly said. 'She's trying to count them.'

'Darling Holly!' Dorothy laughed. 'She is three months old! And don't you think she should have a cover over her legs? I know it's July but it's so dull today.'

'The health visitor said she should have all the air she can. She put on six ounces last week!'

'That's brilliant. Who's the cleverest little girl in the whole wide world?' Dorothy leaned over the pram too, and succumbed to Lydia's charm.

'Actually, it's a bit too much.' Holly was taking modern motherhood very seriously. 'I had started on solids but the health visitor said—'

'Oh, what does she know?' Dorothy laid her hand on her granddaughter's midriff and squeezed. It was delightfully cushiony. Lydia gurgled appreciatively. 'You see? She's content. If you cut down on her food, she won't be!' She straightened. 'Honestly, Holly. We had no such things as health visitors in my day, but we knew that much! I gave you as much food as you could take and you were always such a happy little girl.'

'That was just luck,' Holly insisted. 'Since the War there's been lots of research into child welfare. I mean, just look at what cod-liver oil and orange juice have done for the deprived children in the slums!'

Dorothy wheeled the perambulator beneath the ancient plum tree within sight and hearing of the kitchen door and began to joggle the handle soothingly.

'Never mind them. How are you?' she asked.

'I'm fine. And don't try to rock her off to sleep. I just tell her what is happening and leave her to it.' Holly leaned over the pram again. 'Off to sleep now, darling. Mummy is going to do Gran's hair.'

They moved back to the kitchen and Dorothy reached down cups and saucers from the dresser. 'Have a cup of tea before you face Gran. And can you take up that shawl?' She indicated a blue crocheted square on the airing rack. 'The old so-and-so knew very well I hadn't washed it, so of course that was the one she required! I've had it drying on the oven door – I wonder she couldn't smell the wool singeing!'

'Oh Mum!' Holly laughed but looked distressed. 'Is she getting on your nerves?'

'Not that much. Don't worry, we do very well,' Dolly said quickly. 'You've got enough to worry about without your Gran.'

'When I think you had to give up teaching—'

'Darling, I didn't mind. I told you that. When the wretched comprehensive education hit even the Forest of Dean schools, I knew it was time to go.'

'Nevertheless, she has two daughters and Kildie.'

Dorothy poured tea and raised her brows in mock surprise.

'Now you know very well, Lizzie is up to her eyes with Chas and the Grange and everything. And Sarah's only just back from America and hasn't even surfaced yet.'

Holly said quietly, 'And Kildie? Apparently it was all arranged for Gran to go to Kildie.'

'Yes. I know that Kildie blames me for Gran coming here. She thinks I practically kidnapped the old girl.'

Holly laughed.

'Actually, Hol . . . it's strange. Gran did not want to go to Kildie.'

Holly raised her brows and was going to ask more. But then did not. After all, Kildie was a delicate subject. And anyway, outside, Lydia started to cry.

16

'Leave her, Mum. Don't you dare pick her up when I go upstairs. She has to learn to be independent.'

Dorothy smiled. 'All right, all right.' Then she looked at Holly searchingly. 'Are you all right?' she asked.

Holly sipped her tea. It was an ambiguous question. It invited confidences without applying any persuasion.

She said at last, 'Yes. I am.' She returned her mother's look.

'Are *you* all right?'

And Dorothy gave her question consideration too, then answered, 'Yes. I think I am.'

Holly wanted to say, 'In spite of Kildie?' but her mother was clattering her cup in its saucer and laughing.

'D'you remember Blanche Cooke? I was looking at the beans this morning. They're right at the top of the sticks. I wondered whether Blanche might be down there waiting for you!'

Holly smiled, remembering. 'She did not rely on the bean sticks, Mum. I could take her with me wherever I went. That's the best of an imaginary friend!'

'But it was in the bean sticks that you used to read your poetry to her.'

Holly was aghast. 'You listened! How could you?'

Dorothy held up her hands. 'Not guilty! Your father used to tell me.' She paused then added bravely, 'And Bob.'

Holly held her breath, stared into her cup.

Dorothy said, 'Bob had an *alter ego* too. Did you know?'

Holly let her breath go tremblingly. She said, 'Oscar. He was called Oscar.'

'So he was. I'd forgotten.'

There was a pause. Lydia was still crying.

Dorothy said, 'You were in love with Bob.'

Holly tried to laugh. 'I was sixteen!' She looked up at her mother, noted her blue eyes and the golden hair that was only a little faded. She was beautiful. That had hurt once. 'I was in love with Charlie. And with

Bill too. But now I am in love with Tom.'

Dorothy smiled. 'I know that. I'm very glad.'

Holly climbed the familiar staircase slowly. She had not lived in this house since 1942 when she was sixteen but it was still home to her in a much deeper sense than the flat in Cheltenham. Perhaps because of the garden. All the cottages had the same sized garden but each was completely different. Mabs had laid hers down as lawn and put a tennis net across the middle. The Crabtrees were still digging for victory, and the rows of summer cabbage, broad beans and peas were absolutely parallel. But their own was as it had always been, the square lawn just outside the back door dotted with fruit trees, then the thicket of gooseberry bushes which screened the kitchen garden beyond. Until Dad went to the War she had always helped him plant the kidney beans, and then for two years she had done it herself.

She looked out of the landing window. Yes, there they were again, flowers like red bunting, sticks symbolically crossed at the top making a tunnel of wigwams. Maybe when Tom arrived she would take him down there, tell him about Bob and what Bob had said to her. He already knew about Blanche Cooke, her imaginary friend. Whenever she broke a cup or lost a library book he would open his eyes innocently and say, 'I bet it was Blanche Cooke all the time!' She smiled and could have wept with love for him. And not only him: she could have wept for Mum . . . and Dad . . . Winnie and Charlie . . . even Kildie. Especially Gran.

She shook herself mentally for being maudlin. Margaret Lashford had told her that at the end of breast-feeding there was a tendency to be weepy. Not that Margaret Lashford knew about Gran and gardens. Because all gardens were symbolic of Gran. She came into her own when she was outside, always bent double, routing out weeds with one muddy finger, picking mushrooms, tending her fern garden. Sometimes she thought Gran must have sprung from the earth like a knotty old dandelion, so tough and hardy was she.

Holly counted the last two steps automatically in her head and felt with her sandalled toe for the loose stair-rod. Yes, it was still there, comfortably movable like an over-worn slipper. She knocked on the half-open bedroom door and then peered round in sudden fright when there was no reply. Gran was asleep, her head falling off the pillow, her mouth sagging. She stirred immediately and opened her eyes.

Holly said gently, 'Hello, Gran. Sorry to wake you.'

Gran opened and closed her mouth like a fish, swallowed and seemed to click into place.

'You didn't wake me, maid. It was that baby. Why d'you leave her to cry like that?'

'She has to learn to be left alone sometimes, Gran. The health visitor says—'

'Drat the health visitor! If I have to hear what that woman has to say much more, I'll write to Mr Bevan myself! That man has a lot to answer for!'

'He's not even in the Government any more, Gran! Mr Churchill's back again!'

'I know that! And the new queen bin crowned! I'm not daft, maid!'

'Sorry, Gran.'

Holly laid the blue shawl on the bed and went for a brush and comb. She glanced through the window and saw that her mother was jiggling the pram. She almost knocked on the glass, then didn't. After all, Mum had not actually touched the baby. And anyway Lydia had stopped crying.

Gran said, 'What's the time?'

'Half-past two. Shall we just tip you forward . . . ? A pillow here . . . that's fine. Comfortable?'

'As comfortable as I ever am. You sound like your dratted health visitor!'

Holly grinned. 'Tom calls her Marghanita Laski. You know, like the novelist.'

'No, I don't know. And you shouldn't have time for novels now, my girl. A baby and a husband, cooking and cleaning and sewing and washing. If there's any time left over you can start a garden!'

'I was just thinking about the garden, Gran. We haven't got one. But when we get a house I shall enjoy doing the garden. D'you remember how we used to do the garden at Dymock?'

'You don't have to wait for that, Hol. Get out in the fields. Nature's garden.'

Holly had visions of herself hunting for mushrooms and berries over on the college playing-field.

She sat at the top of the bed and propped Gran against her knees.

'D'you remember going out together very early when we were on holiday?' she began. 'The dew would still be thick – I remember somewhere or other we used to see the milkman starting out in his float.'

'Best time of day,' Gran said contentedly. 'Go on, our Hol. What else do you remember?'

Gran's thin hair was in a queue down her back. Holly unplaited it slowly and with infinite care, then began to brush. And all the time she talked. It was as if she were piling up Gran's life for her to see. The Station House at Dymock, and then the little cottage at the top of Middle Lane with the fern garden against the wet brick wall at the bottom.

'D'you remember the veranda?' she said, brushing carefully. 'How we'd sit on that lovely wooden lavatory and leave the door open so that we could do our business and see the garden at the same time?'

'That I do, my girl. When we were looking for a retirement house, I said to Walter, we must have that one 'cos of that veranda.'

'And what about the farmhouse on the Fens? Uncle Edward and Mum going up in the aeroplane?'

'You wouldn't go.'

'No.' Holly paused. 'But Charlie went.'

'Aye. That he did. Just to show off in front of Kildie.'

There was silence in the bedroom except for the sweep of the brush.

Then Holly said, 'What about the really old days, Gran? Before you met Grandad. Back in the eighteen-hundreds?'

If she hoped to lead Gran into more reminiscence, she was disappointed.

'Nothing happened then that's worth recalling, Holly. And when something isn't worth recalling, it's best forgotten.' She twisted her head like a tortoise and looked up. 'Jest you remember that, my girl. Some of the water what goes under the bridge is much best forgotten.'

Holly nodded and resumed her brushing. She knew that Gran was referring not only to her own past.

Holly said quietly, 'I don't really agree with you there, Gran. Because if things go wrong it makes you more grateful when they go well.'

Gran thought about that and Holly waited philosophically to be contradicted. But then the old lady said, 'I reckon you're right about that, Holly.'

Then she changed the subject.

'You was always gentle. Sometimes too gentle.' She dropped her head forward to allow the brush to sweep up the hairs on her neck. 'You used to pretend to be stupid sometimes, just so that I'd be able to tell you something. Something you already knew!' There was a smile in her voice. 'Little minx!'

'I don't remember *that*.' Holly scooped up the hair behind the ears and began to brush it all over her hand. There was hardly any of it. It was silvery white, the scalp pink beneath it. She brushed rhythmically, roots to ends, roots to ends.

'What's the time now?' Gran asked.

'Let me see . . .' the rhythm stopped. 'Almost three.'

'Your dad will be back any minute now. Pin me up, Holly, there's a good girl. And go down to that baby.'

'All right, Gran.'

Holly laid out the old-fashioned hairpins, scooped the

21

pathetic tail of hair into her hands and began to twist it towards the top of the bony skull. Little wisps frayed out and she stopped to tuck them in. At last everything was neatly in place and she pinned carefully.

'You should have let Kildie do this,' she said without thinking. 'Don't you remember how she did your hair for her wedding?'

'Aye. I do now. I had forgot.' She put up a hand and touched her topknot. 'That's nice. Kildie couldn't have done it better. Anyway, she hasn't been to see me since I was in the workhouse.'

'Dear Gran.' Holly went to the window to check on the pram. Lydia was asleep. 'You weren't in the workhouse. You know that very well. And I told you, Kildie has been ill.'

'D'you think she'll turn up this afternoon, our Hol?'

'Of course.'

Gran subsided among the pillows. 'That's a pity.'

'Gran!'

'I only meant . . .' Gran could not think what she had meant. She said, 'She should be resting. If she's ill.'

Lydia woke with a jerk and lifted her legs to eye level.

Holly said hastily, 'And so should you. Close your eyes until they arrive, Gran. You've got the bell if you need anything.'

Gran watched the door close after her granddaughter. It was true, she was tired. Well, at ninety years old it wasn't surprising. She drew her blue shawl around her and sniffed it suspiciously. Doll had had it drying on the oven door, that was obvious. Not that it mattered. She herself had dried enough stuff on the oven door in the past.

The past. There was so much of it at ninety. And some she hadn't been able to look at for years. Perhaps now was the time to remember one or two things. It might be quite important to gather her thoughts together in case Kildie did come. She ought to have a word with the girl . . . not that she was a girl any longer, almost forty. She did not act like forty, or even think like forty, but that's what she was. Almost. And maybe all she needed was a good talking-to. Or perhaps just someone to listen to her troubles . . . If only Walter were still alive. What a listener he had been! She remembered the first time they had talked – really talked. Confession-time he had called it.

Gran felt her eyes beginning to close. She wanted to remember just the happy things; only the happy things. But some of the water that had gone under the bridge was muddy. She would have to see through that first, clear it away, before she could watch the clear river streaming by.

1874

When she was eleven years old Esme Dart was sent into service. She knew she would not see her parents again; her father did not like her and her mother spent a lot of time and energy in keeping her out of his way. It would be a blessed relief to her not to have Esme around any more.

Unrequitedly, unrestrainedly, Esme loved her mother. She soon learned not to show this love; in fact to recognize it as something wrong. She did not expect her love to be returned. From that early age, Esme never ever expected her love to be returned.

She spent two fairly uneventful, even happy, years at the farm. It was in the lush Herefordshire countryside. It was called Valentine's Farm because Jack Valentine owned it. He was a burly man who had once got drunk during the Three Choirs Festival and lurched down the aisle of the Cathedral singing a bawdy song. He had been imprisoned for six months because of it and became belligerent and surly. Nobody liked him. His wife was frightened of him and his children had all left home as soon as they could.

Esme, as the maid of all work, saw little of him for those first two years. She scrubbed the dairy and scalded the milk churns. She saw to the fires and did the vegetables for the missis. She hung out the washing and pressed it with a flat-iron. Mr Valentine sent five pounds each year to her mother and called her a lazy good-for-nothing. And then she was thirteen and in a long, awkward, gawky way, she was beautiful.

He took her to bed almost casually and when she cried he hit her across the head so that she thought she had dreamed the whole thing. The next night he hit her again and when she wept as she did the grates, Mrs Valentine thwacked her with a broom.

For two more years she endured stoically. She became quieter so that by the time she was fifteen she rarely spoke. But she grew. How she grew. She was taller than Jack Valentine, and when he hit her she went with the swing of his fist so that the blow never really connected.

Twice she became pregnant and twice Mrs Valentine took her into Hereford to an old midwife she knew. When Esme emerged from these ordeals she went to sit in the cathedral and on the second occasion she saw her father.

She stood up, holding the pew in front because she was still dizzy, and curtseyed. He was cleaning the candlesticks at the end of every row of pews and stared at her in amazement.

' 'Tis me, Father, Esme.' She spoke in a soft, guttural voice, husky from the excess of laudanum she had been given. She would not have spoken at all if she had been herself.

He was completely taken aback. 'Esme? Little Esme?' He had to look up to her just as did Jack Valentine.

She whispered hoarsely, 'I've growed.'

'Aye. That you have!'

His hands continued automatically to rub the candle sconces. He had been a farm labourer in a tied cottage; she wondered what had happened.

'Your mam be dead, Esme,' he said, glancing around to see if the verger was watching. 'She bin dead this three year.'

Esme gave a low moan. The one person she loved, gone.

24

He whispered, 'Now don't take on, girl! You'll get me put out, you will!'

She covered her treacherous mouth with one bare hand. She possessed a pair of cotton gloves but Mrs Valentine had told her they might well be bloodied and to leave them at home.

He said, 'I'm doubled with the rheum, as you can see. The rector got me this sittyation.'

She saw why he was so short. He was, in fact, bent right over.

She forced words out. 'You shoulda sent for me.'

'She wouldn't do that. I said to her – there's our Esme who would look after you . . . but she wouldn't have that.'

Esme was not surprised. Right to the end she had to be kept away from her father. This man. It was almost five years since she had seen her mother. She ached for just one glimpse.

'Where is she buried?' she whispered.

'Leominster cemetery.'

He moved down a row and began on another candle holder.

'All these years you've had your comfy life, our Esme. No worries. Plenty to eat, by the look of you. It's time you paid something back, I reckon.'

'How? The Valentines send my money home.'

'Haven't seen a penny piece this last two and a half years!' he came back sharply.

'Oh!' She moved her hand to her heart. Her money must have stopped when he took her to bed. He saw no reason to pay for his whore.

He said, 'I en't going to be able to do this work much longer. I reckon you should come home and look after me and earn enough to keep us both!'

She stared at him, unable to believe her ears. He was offering a haven as if it were a punishment.

She moved out of the pew holding on fiercely to whatever support there was. She came up to him.

25

'I can come now,' she said.

'Dun't talk so loud, girl!' He glanced round again. ''Ow can you come now? Your things—'

'I 'aven't got no things. I can come now.'

He had not reckoned on this.

'I only got one room. In the Back Yard. Over a bookshop. I keeps an eye on the place at night—'

'I can do that while you sleep. I'll cook and clean then too. And I can find work in the mornings and sleep in the afternoons—'

'Hang on,' he became suspicious. 'You bin thrown out? You bin thieving?'

'No! Mrs Valentine will be along to collect me any minute! She brought me in the trap.' She had found a new voice, new words. She had found hope.

He would not take her that day, but he promised she could come to him when he had arranged for another room for her. And he was as good as his word. On her sixteenth birthday, Esme moved into a small flat above the Cathedral Bookshop. There was a tap and a privy in the yard outside, and a tiny range with a trivet and a side oven in her room.

For nearly ten years she cooked and cleaned for her father. He gave himself up to invalidism almost immediately so that she was forced to take on more and more work to pay their rent and buy food. She cleaned the bookshop, taking down each volume and dusting it carefully. Sometimes she would open it and read a few pages with laborious care. When she was discovered, the owner was delighted and encouraged her in her reading. She read Dickens and was thankful for her present lot. And then she read *The Return of the Native* by an author called Hardy.

She found more work, cleaning, in the house of the organist. He lived in Chantry Cottage which was, in fact, a narrow Georgian house in the Close. He kept a cook-housekeeper and Esme did the rough. When he passed Esme, usually on her knees wielding a scrubbing brush,

he was polite enough to say, 'Good-morning, Miss Dart.'
She liked being called Miss Dart. What she required above
all else was respect from her fellow men and women. It
meant more to her than almost anything else. As she
found her new niche so, very gradually, the five years at
Valentine's Farm faded in her memory. She was tough and
resilient. Her father told her she was as hard as nails. She
was thankful for it.

She dared to make plans. When her father died, she
would use his room as a sitting-room. It overlooked a
pleasant courtyard where, on a winter's afternoon, she
might watch the world go by as she did the mending for
the housekeeper at Chantry Cottage. The cathedral was
so protective. She could grow old here, old and secure
and almost revered like one of the stone monuments in
the gardens.

Then, on the day that General Gordon was murdered
in Khartoum, her father called her into his room after
supper. His eyes were fever-bright. He pushed back the
bedclothes. He was naked.

'Get on me, girl,' he rasped. 'Come on. I know you
did it for Jack Valentine. I 'eard all about it! If you could
do it for 'im, you can do it for me!'

She stared at him, horrified.

'He – he forced me!' she gasped.

He cackled horribly.

'I've heard that one before! They all says it! Now come
on. Do as you're told. Take off them drawers and get on
me!'

She wanted to be sick. She whispered. 'My own father!
My own father!'

'I en't your father, girl! Where d'you think you got
that long body and brawny arms? The Squire paid me
to marry your mother and make you legal-like. 'E
was going to pay me more but never did. So we sent you
away.'

Esme backed towards the wall and pressed herself hard
against it. Below she could hear the bookshop being

closed up for the night. She should be down there, dusting, polishing the shelves.

His voice changed suddenly to a whine. 'I bin good to you, en't I, Esme? Daft name for a daft girl but I still bin good to you, en't I?'

She nodded somehow.

'Well then. I'm not long for this world, Esme! You can see that. An old man's last wish—'

She stumbled from the room and went to fetch the dustpan and the broom. She told herself fiercely she would forget this too; push it away from her physically. He would have forgotten all about it by the morning. He hadn't meant it – he hadn't meant it.

But he was downstairs, behind her in the shop doorway. He was bent over, wizened, his skin hanging on his frame.

'No-one else would want you! You'm no oil-painting – you know that! You should be pleased to think there's someone in this wide world—'

'Go away!' she screamed. 'Go away and leave me alone!'

She ran for the stairs and began to climb, two at a time. He was behind her like a ragged shadow.

'I'll tell everyone about Jack Valentine! See if I don't! They won't want you at the Chantry no more. They'll turn you out of here—' He seized her heel and she let fly with the other. It connected. She never knew with what. She was free and taking the last few stairs and he was bumping and rolling and flailing and screaming to the bottom of the flight.

He was quite dead when she got to him.

Although she was urged to stay on over the bookshop she could not. There was no hope of forgetting her dark and awful secrets there. She moved into the Chantry and when the organist married and moved into his wife's neat cottage behind the Cathedral Close, she stayed on to look after the widower who took up residence. He was a minor canon at the Cathedral, heart-broken after the loss of his wife. He did not call her Miss Dart, but there was no doubt about his respect. Over the years they managed together. They grew into each other's ways. His son came to visit and actually changed Esme to Emmie. She did not mind that either. He was only *two* years younger than she was, but she treated him as if he were her son too. And she thought once again, This is where I will die. People will remember me as a good housekeeper to Canon James, a good friend to Master Walter, and a respectable Church-goer. They will never know that on the day General Gordon was murdered, so was my adoptive father.

And then, as the cathedral bell tolled sonorously for the old Queen and the snow lay thick on the city, Master Walter put a proposition to her and once more her plans were knocked sideways.

TWO

1930

In November of 1930 Holly and Kildie stayed at the
Grange in Dymock for three days with their cousins,
Charlie and Winnie. They all knew that although Charlie
and Winnie were mysteriously related to Squire and Lady
Richardson, none of them were welcome. They were
confined to an upstairs room called the nursery and
the parts of the garden that were not visible from the
drawing-room windows. In the evenings Uncle Teddy and
Aunt Lizzie joined them and put Charlie and Winnie to
bed and then went down to the dining-room to eat supper
with the Richardsons – only it was called dinner. Kildie
put Holly to bed and then read aloud until it was time
for Kildie herself to climb into her nightie and kneel by
the window to say her prayers. Holly tried to stay awake
during this process. She wanted desperately to know how
long Kildie knelt there. How long it took for God to hear
her. But she always fell asleep before the fifteen-year-old
got into bed.

Jim or Dorothy popped in during the day, always in a
hurry, always brightly cheerful on top and anxious underneath. Holly hated most of it. She hated being what her
mother called 'a poor relation'. She hated the absence of
her parents and grandparents, but mostly she hated the
reason for it all. Kildie had told them that Grandad was
dead and Gran was going mad with grief.

Holly did not immediately believe her.

'If Grandad was dead, there'd be a funeral,' she said
with all the knowledge of someone who had just buried
a favourite cat.

'There is, baby.' Kildie still treated Holly as if she were two instead of five years old. 'That's why we're here.'

'But that's wrong.' Holly looked at Winnie who was the same age as herself and was crying yet again. 'Winnie, cheer up. If there was a funeral, we'd be going. I went to Fluffy's funeral and he was only a cat.'

Kildie tried to put her arms around everybody. She had left Newent Grammar School that summer and had been working in the bank in Gloucester for two whole months. The children had been entrusted to her.

'I expect we *would* go, my darlings. But poor Gran . . .' She heaved a melodramatic sigh. 'I don't know how she will live without Grandad. She was so in love with him, you know. She was just a maid in his father's house and he married her and made her the happiest woman alive.'

Holly, thinking of Gran, so sturdy, so strong, so indomitable, said, 'Grandad told me she made *him* the happiest man alive.' She smiled, forgetting that Grandad was dead. 'He says he was a nardiell and he wanted to be a proper man and she told him to become the station master at Dymock and he said he couldn't unless she came with him—'

'A what?' Kildie asked, diverted from blowing Winnie's nose.

Charlie said gloomily, 'She means a ne'er-do-well. It's what Ma do call our Pa.'

Kildie's eyes widened. She had heard that Uncle Teddy and Aunt Lizzie had moved to Suffolk to escape the gossip.

She swallowed her avid curiosity and said, 'Well, I don't think we should call Grandad or Uncle Teddy a ne'er-do-well—'

'Grandad called himself that,' Holly maintained stubbornly, determined to get the facts straight. 'And he called Gran an angel. And . . .' her voice suddenly shot up a register, 'I want to see Gran.'

'And you shall, darling. Once this is over,' Kildie comforted, still young enough to believe that it *would* be

31

over and everything would return to normal. 'Now let's go for a nice walk down to the pond and feed the ducks, shall we? Then after dinner we'll play Snap and then Jim – your daddy – will come for tea and then—'

Charlie said, 'Let's go to the funeral. It's tomorrow, isn't it, Kildie? Let's go.' Charlie Richardson was almost eight, morose and over-exuberant by turns. He had tried numerous ways to impress his cousin Kildie without success. This was just another bid for her attention.

'We've been sent here, Charlie, to keep us away from the funeral,' Kildie said, rather exasperated. Surely she had been a little more sentient at his age?

'I know that!' he came back scornfully. 'But he was our grandfather. We should be there. Let's go – let's just go. Don't you want to go?'

She did. He saw immediately that she did. Her huge dark eyes filled with tears and she looked over Winnie's head longingly. She was fifteen and earning her own living. If it weren't for her duties with the little ones, she would be there, all in black, like a foreign princess.

He said quietly, 'We could stand behind the yews, at the top of the churchyard. They'd never see us. Bit like Tom Sawyer.'

He had her. He had forgotten her penchant for living inside books.

She said, 'They'd see us go. The Squire would send old Matson out after us—'

'We'd just go for a walk in the orchard. Like we're going to now. And anyway, they'll all have gone to the funeral themselves. No-one will be here.'

He was thrilled. It was a secret adventure, shared with Cousin Kildie.

Dorothy came that evening and put Holly to bed. Holly hung around her neck almost desperately. Her mother always told her the truth, she had only to ask. But she was not absolutely sure she wanted to hear the truth.

'What is it baby?' Dorothy smoothed her daughter's

short brown hair into the little hollow of her nape. 'Has Charlie been horrid to you again?'

'No.' Holly found her mother's ear and breathed into it to make her laugh.

Dorothy laughed and protested. 'Come on now. I know you're trying to put me off. What is the matter?'

Holly whispered, 'Is Grandad dead?'

Dorothy was still.

'Kildie told you. Well, why not? Yes, darling Holly. Dear Grandad is dead. He was so lucky, Holly. He just went to bed, cuddled up to Gran and went to heaven. He wasn't ill. He didn't have a pain. Don't you think that's rather wonderful?'

Holly thought of cuddling up to Gran and going to sleep. It was a lovely feeling. Gran's arms were so strong. She smelled of lavender or damp earth. But she would not let you go. Not even to Jesus.

'Mum, why can't I go to the funeral? I went to Fluffy's.'

'I know, darling. But that was just you and me and Daddy. There will be so many people there. And sometimes they cry a lot. And I don't want you to think of the sadness of this. I want you to think of Grandad being happy.'

Holly let her mother put her back on the pillow. She smiled upwards. Dorothy was a silhouette in front of the night-light glow, but Holly knew her so well she could fill in every detail. The intensely blue eyes, the golden hair, the snub nose and full mouth – which was now smiling down at her. She wanted to tell her about coming to the funeral and hiding behind the yew trees.

Dorothy said, 'No more talking, dearest. After tomorrow we can go back home and you can go back to school—'

Holly surprised herself by interrupting fiercely, 'I want to stay with Gran!'

Dorothy was shocked and a little hurt. 'Gran has Kildie. She can't be looking after you.'

Holly had always known in her bones that Gran did not

33

love Dorothy. Now she had the first inkling that perhaps Dorothy did not love Gran.

She said nothing more about the funeral or staying on in Dymock.

'Tell me a story,' she whispered instead.

It was raining, which Kildie said was good luck. They stationed themselves behind the enormous family tomb of the Richardsons which fronted the yew trees, and watched everyone filing into the church. The villagers came almost to a man; then the railway contingent – porters, engine drivers, inspectors, permanent waymen, signalmen, clerks from the Gloucester office, even the lady telephonist. And then the hearse arrived and the family got out. Gran did not look mad with grief. She was as stiff and straight as a ramrod beneath the big black umbrella her son held above her black hat. She did not look as big as she had earlier in the autumn; her black sleeves met the black gloves without the usual glimpse of stringy wrists.

Kildie breathed names.

'Your mummy and daddy, Hol. Yours, Winnie. The Squire and Lady Richardson. Mr and Mrs Milsom-Parker from school. That's the manager at the cider farm. And I think . . . I think that's Mr Edwards himself!' Mr Edwards was an old friend of the James family. He had originally got Grandad his job on the Great Western. He was also from London: a very large shareholder.

'Mummy's told me about him,' Holly whispered back. 'Mummy says he's a really good sport.'

Kildie nodded. 'He was the man on the velocipede.'

Winnie clamoured for the story. But Charlie shushed her.

'That's Grandad.' His voice broke. 'That's our grandad in there!'

Kildie hissed, 'Shut up, Charlie!'

Holly quavered, 'In the box? The big box?'

Kildie, suddenly as affected as the children, sobbed,

'What did you expect? You wanted to come! All of you wanted to come! What did you expect?'

They held one another and heard faintly through the misty rain, 'I am the resurrection and the life, saith the Lord . . .' Then the doors of the church closed.

By the time everyone emerged, they had cried themselves out and were sitting on the soaking grass, exhausted, their backs against the giant slab of granite guarding the Richardsons' tomb.

Charlie, standing, his arms resting along the wing of a stone angel, looked up and said, 'They're coming out of the church!'

'Get down then!' Kildie reached up and dragged him back. She was regretting the whole trip. Winnie and Holly had probably already caught terrible colds and their faces were swollen with weeping.

'They can't see,' Charlie protested. 'Not unless some-one has brought a telescope. It's important – this is the part that is important!'

So they stood up and looked over the edge of the granite and watched as the procession stumbled between the tombstones towards the open slit in the wet green grass almost immediately beneath them on the sloping ground. The family groups had reformed themselves now. Edward and Jim were either side of Gran, holding an elbow each, Lizzie and Dorothy flanked them. They stood very close to the edge of the grave and watched as the coffin was lowered.

'. . . hath but a short time to live . . .' the Revd Dempster intoned, '. . . cut down like a flower . . .' One of the bearers threw a handful of dry soil into the grave. It clattered onto the wood of the coffin. Gran immediately leaned forward and threw something which also clattered.

'Her wedding ring,' Kildie whispered, tears dripping heedlessly from her chin. 'To show her heart is with him in death.'

Holly put a hand over her mouth to stop herself from crying out.

'Forasmuch as it hath pleased Almighty God of his great mercy to take unto himself the soul of our dear brother . . .'

Kildie could barely see the group of black-clad mourners; what between her own tears and the rain, the churchyard seemed waveringly under water. But she did hear the car that came roaring through the gates and stopped with an almighty squeal of brakes. And she did hear the shout as someone leapt from it.

She dashed away her tears and stared hard.

'. . . commit his body to the ground; earth to . . .' continued the vicar indefatigably.

'Hol . . .' Kildie seized her small cousin by the sleeve. 'Hol – it's my *mother*!'

The three children blinked hard and straightened until they had a better view. Leaping between the tombstones came a small slim figure clothed in what appeared to be multicoloured chiffon scarves. In the dim, grey, damp morning, bracelets and ear-rings flashed their diamond brilliance; a vivid face beneath a magenta scarf was dominated by enormous black eyes. The figure resembled an exotic gypsy from Hungary, or an escapee from an Eastern harem. It was so completely out of place, it was at first simply unbelievable.

'Mum—' Kildie would have shouted, but her voice cracked and was blessedly drowned beneath the cries from below.

'Ma – Ma – it can't be true! Tell me it's not true!'

Sarah arrived behind the little group next to the grave and broke through it to stare downwards. She must have seen the earth and the ring and the brass plate engraved with her father's name. Whatever it was, she gave another great cry.

'Pa!' And she jumped into the grave and disappeared.

Kildie shouted, 'Mum!' again, and broke cover, tearing down the slope until, unable to stop her momentum, she too plunged into the grave.

The little ones, horrified by her sudden disappearance,

followed, bawling at the tops of their voices, even Charlie. They slithered down on the wet grass, the state of their clothing completely indescribable.

The adults split into two camps, each one pandemonium. One camp turned to the children, the other to the mother and daughter atop the coffin.

Through it all, the Revd Dempster shouted, '. . . that we, with all those that are departed in the true faith of thy holy Name, may have our perfect consummation and bliss, both in body and soul, in thy eternal and everlasting glory; through Jesus Christ our Lord.'

Gran, alone, untouched by the events around her, looked up into the low grey sky and said, 'Amen.'

As Edward remarked much later, 'It was all over then, bar the shouting. But there was plenty of shouting!'

1901

Walter James asked Esme Dart to marry him on 22 January 1901. It was the day the old Queen died, though neither of them knew it at the time.

Esme was shocked to the core. She was thirty-seven, a lanky raw-boned woman, so-called housekeeper to Canon James – really general dogsbody – at his house in the precinct of Hereford Cathedral. She had long ago given up thoughts of marriage and could only hope that when the Canon died he would remember her in his will.

Walter was the only child. When his mother died he was still at university. He came down immediately and never went back. For the next fifteen years he lived mainly in a flat in London, supposedly writing a history of the Church from the Reformation. In reality he wasted his life and his allowance. It was rumoured he was living with a woman, but then a letter would arrive from somewhere far-flung, somewhere completely unsuitable for females. He would turn up now and then, charm everyone in the Close, scotch any rumours of a *mésalliance*, check that things were all right at home, tip Esme a sovereign, and disappear again.

He came home for that Christmas of 1900, and seemed in no hurry to leave again. While his father wrote sermons, he wrote letters. They dined at four and the Canon went to Evensong afterwards. Walter sometimes went with him; oftener he sat with Esme by the kitchen fire which was the only warm room in the house. He talked to her about anything and everything. About his mother whom she had not known. About some of his travels. About his search.

'What are you looking for, Master Walter?' she asked.

'I won't know till I've found it, Emmie.' he replied. Then he asked her about her 'inner life'. She thought he was questioning her church attendance and said sharply, 'I go three times on a Sunday. No-one could ask for more than that!'

He laughed then – she often made him laugh – and said, 'Ah . . . how wonderfully you simplify things, Emmie. You know exactly what you are doing at every minute of the day. Even if sometimes you don't know why.'

'I don't need to know why!' she came back sharply. 'I'm too busy to wonder why! And it's the best way!'

'I agree. Oh I do agree, Emmie.' He was younger than her by two years and sometimes she spoke to him as if she had been his nanny.

'Why don't you get yourself a job, Master Walter? Settle down and live properly.'

'What would I do, Emmie? I'm not trained to earn a living.'

'You could go into the Church like your pa, surely?'

'I'd have to take up studying again. Besides . . .' He grinned. 'I'm no churchgoer, Emmie. I tend to fall asleep during the sermons!'

That raised an unwilling smile. Esme started Sundays at the seven o'clock Communion and finished it with Compline. It was a long day, the busiest of the week.

She said, 'Well, there are other jobs. What about the railway? Your pa's got shares in the Great Western

Railway. He could find you a job with them.'

He laughed. 'I'd be welcome if I had some mechanical knowledge. Or money to invest.' He sobered and leaned forward. 'Emmie, I need a job where I can be by myself. I need to be my own boss.' He grimaced. 'Actually, I don't really like work. But there again, I've been idle too long. I need . . . something.'

She frowned prodigiously. 'I shoulda thought . . . a nice little station somewhere. One of they country stations around Symonds Yat. You'd be your own boss all right. Some of those real small stations only got a booking clerk and a porter to keep them going.'

She thought he'd laugh at that. Canon James's son a country station master – it was laughable. But he didn't.

'It's a thought, Emmie.' He looked into the fire. 'It's a thought. And that's what I'll give it. Thought.'

A month later he was still in Hereford, though there had been considerable going and coming during that last week. It was 22 January and he caught her up as she was returning from the shops. It was bitterly cold; there had been snow the day before and hard packs of ice ridged the gateways where people had swept a pathway to the road.

'Watch yourself, Emmie. It's dangerous along here.' He took the heavy basket from her hand and held her elbow. Nobody had ever done that before and she felt so embarrassed she could barely think straight or hear properly. The cathedral bell was tolling – there had been prayers all week for the Queen. He said something.

She slipped and half fell against him.

'I didn't mean to knock you flat, Em!' He held her up, laughing. 'Surely it's not that much of a shock? We've always been friends.'

The bell tolled sonorously.

He said, 'I wouldn't bother you, Em. But I think you should come and help me. As I took up your suggestion and have been offered Dymock station.'

She stopped on the icy pavement and shook herself free of him.

'Are you teasing me, Master Walter? Cos I won't have it! I might only be your pa's skivvy but I'm a human being, you know. And a Christian! And it ill becomes you to—'

The bell cut her short. He looked at her while the reverberations brought down the icicles on the trees around them. His eyes were blue and he had a long nose ending in a full moustache. Beneath the moustache his lips were not smiling.

As soon as the frosty air stopped quivering, he said quietly, 'Let's go home, Em. Close the door on this racket. And talk.'

They went back between the tall Georgian houses with their bright brass door knockers and letter boxes. He opened the front door of Chantry Cottage and pushed her ahead of him. She never used the front door and scurried down the hall like a frightened rabbit.

He followed and stood watching her while she threw off her shawl and riddled the fire frantically.

'My father is over at the Lady chapel,' he said. 'We've got the place to ourselves.'

She said, 'I didn't think you were like this, Master Walter. I'm a respectable woman. I'm not young and I need to be respected – I need that—' She was almost weeping.

He said, 'I respect you, Esme Dart. Just because I call you Emmie and ask you to marry me, doesn't mean I don't respect you. I respect you more than anyone else I know. Otherwise, why would I ask you to be my wife?'

She took the poker out of the fire and replaced it neatly alongside the other fire dogs. She said pathetically, 'I don't understand.'

He came to her and took her mittened hands in his gloved ones.

'I'm going to be a station master, Emmie. There's a station house. It needs a family. I think you would be a very good station master's wife. And an excellent mother.'

Her voice quavered all over the place. 'I'm almost forty!'

'I need someone older. Someone mature. Someone who will understand.'

'Understand . . . what?'

'Me. I need someone who will understand me, Emmie.'

He drew her to her usual armchair and pressed her into it. Then he drew up a footstool and sat on it, his hands in her lap, his eyes on her face. His low, persuasive voice spoke to her at some length, telling her things about himself which no-one else knew.

He whispered, 'Can you bear this, Emmie?'

And she said, suddenly certain, 'Yes, I can bear it.'

'Then . . . will you marry me? Make me a respectable man and father?'

She did not answer immediately.

He said, 'What is it? You can bear what I am telling you, yet you are still disgusted? Still shocked?'

'No. How could I be when . . . no, I am not disgusted. Nor shocked. Sorry perhaps—'

'Sorry for me?'

'Aye. And the others.' She looked down at his hands in her lap. 'And for myself.'

He waited, then said, 'Go on, Emmie. Tell me.'

So she too began to talk and to tell him things that no-one else knew. When she had finished he let his breath out in a long sigh.

'A-a-h. Emmie. Oh my dear.'

She whispered, 'I'm that sorry, Master Walter. I would not be a fit wife—'

His voice was stern. 'Do not talk like that! I would be honoured . . . I am not worthy of you, Esme Dart, but I would be so honoured if you would marry me. Will you do that, Emmie? Keep my counsel as I will keep yours, yet share both.' He leaned forward and looked up into her face. 'Emmie, please let's go into partnership – would a partnership be easier for you to accept? Will you come with me to Dymock and be a station master's wife?'

41

She looked into his eyes and after a long while she nodded. 'Yes. Yes, I will do that, Master Walter.'

His smile was gentle . . . so gentle . . . She would remember that smile as long as she lived.

'Thank you, dear Emmie. I will be faithful to you till I die.'

It was unnecessary to respond to that vow; obviously she would be faithful to him because she would never have the chance to be anything else.

He waited, holding her rough hands on her lap. Then he said, 'Can you not promise yourself to me as well, Emmie? I do not ask it – I have no right to ask it—'

She said fiercely, 'I will be faithful to you till you die, Master Walter. And beyond death also.'

His blue eyes held her grey ones for a second longer, then he said humorously, 'And could you drop the Master? Call me plain Walter, Emmie.'

She smiled back. Suddenly she was so happy, so wondrously happy, she felt she might levitate from the old chair by the range and float to the ceiling.

'All right, Walter.'

They had been at Dymock Station House for only four months when Canon James died. It was murmured at the funeral that his son's marriage and job had caused the old man's death, but Esme James was heard to say stoutly, 'More like his new housekeeper! She can't boil water, can't that one!'

Walter said sternly, 'Emmie! That is slanderous!'

She glanced at him, surprised. It was the very first time he had reprimanded her. She rather enjoyed it. It made her feel . . . mastered.

The Canon's house belonged to the diocese, and apart from papers and photographs there was very little to take back to the Station House. The furniture was too big, the curtains too long, the linen was all 'on its last legs', as Esme put it. She packed some tea towels, a shaving mug and all the antimacassars she could find and they left the

42

Cathedral Close for ever, sitting on two tea chests in a wagon, photographs and pictures stacked around them, a box of baking tins rattling at their feet.

'We're the older generation now, Emmie,' Walter said. He smiled at her almost sadly, as if he thought this was the end of his life. 'Do you feel old?'

'No.' She shook her head stoutly. She had felt old until she married Walter James. So much had happened. So much past pressing her into the earth. This was a new life for her. She grinned. 'I'll always be older than you, Walter. While I'm here you're still young!'

He managed a laugh and one of his friendly hugs.

'I'll remember that,' he promised.

He had said he would not 'bother' her and he had slept in the second bedroom of the cosy Victorian house ever since they moved in. But she had certainly not reciprocated that particular promise. That night she went to his room.

It was a hot night and she wore a cambric nightgown which tied at neck and wrists and covered even her toes. Her hair, an uninteresting brown colour, but very prolific, hung around her face softening the long straight lines of jaw, nose and chin.

He was lying on the bed, still in his shirt and trousers, hands clasped behind his head. He started up at the sight of her.

'Emmie! What's the matter? Can't you sleep?'

'No. 'Tis too hot. An' I knew you wouldn't be sleeping either.' She sat on the edge of the bed. He did not move away. ' 'Tisn't your fault your pa died. His heart was broke when your ma died. You couldn't break it no more by marrying me.'

He turned his head from her.

'It had nothing to do with marrying you. And you know that, Emmie. Let there be no pretence between us. I wronged him and I wronged you.'

'Hush . . .'

She put her fingers across his mouth and turned his head back to hers.

43

'You said we would not speak of it again, and we will not. But any wrong that was done is right now. We have made it right, Walter.' She stopped and took a breath. 'I think it might make it easier, however, if . . .' Again she stopped and breathed deeply but this time could not go on. He had taken the hand that covered his mouth and held it fiercely.

'Speak, Emmie! Please! There must be nothing between us that might fester!'

She could not look at him. 'You asked me to make you a respectable husband and father.'

'And you have done that.'

Her eyes flicked up then down.

'If I . . . if we . . .'

He was silent, staring at her through the late dusk. She was so conscious of his hand clamped on her wrist she wondered if she would faint.

'Emmie . . . is it likely . . . ?'

In sudden anguish she said, 'I know I am nearly forty! I know that!'

He sat up and held her rigid body to his. 'Ah, Emmie . . . I'm sorry . . . sorry . . .'

'Do you think I don't have no feelings?' she sobbed into his shoulder. 'Do you think – because I am your wife – I don't look at you on the station in your gold-braided uniform and think – and think . . .'

He murmured to her, kissing her neck, moving her hair until she burst out again, 'I'm that hot, Walter! I don't know what to do with myself!'

And with gentle fingers, he began to undo the tapes at her neck and wrists.

Their baby was born nine months later. Emmie James, who had been Esme Dart, knew that no woman in the world had been as happy as she. She loved Walter with such a passion and force that sometimes it frightened her.

But, of course, she knew that he did not love her.

THREE

1938

The best thing about sleeping with Gran was that she was an early riser. A very early riser. As soon as Holly sat up in their double bed on the sixth day of their holiday, Gran said in her toothless lisp, 'Time for our walk, maid. Use the gosunder and wash yourself.'

Holly looked at the moon face of the alarm clock and said, 'It's not six o'clock yet, Gran.' Dad had insisted the night before that no-one stirred before six because of disturbing their landlady, Mrs Gibbons.

Gran said, 'Will be by the time we're ready to go out.'

Holly knew, at the age of thirteen, that Gran's word was law, even above Dad's, but the bed was warm and the air felt cold.

'It might be raining,' she said.

Gran made a sound of impatience.

'Go and look, maid! You'd argue the hind leg off a donkey, you would!'

By the time Holly had tugged the stiff and reluctant curtain along its wire, she was used to the air anyway. She put her nose against the glass pane and peered through. The small garden was a jungle of sunflowers, kidney beans and tall Jerusalem artichokes. Below it were other houses and gardens and then the sedate bay of Swanage. It was a typical grey July morning. The sky and sea were the same colour, the trees and houses slightly darker. Rain had fallen in the night and one or two slate roofs gleamed sleekly. Holly thought she had never seen a sight so beautiful.

'Oh, it's lovely, Gran,' she breathed. 'Where shall we go?'

Gran was already getting out of bed. Holly watched the shining swollen legs and the bulbous feet feeling for slippers and rushed forward to fit them over yellow, broken toenails and horny heels.

'We'll go up on the downs.' Gran reached for the glass containing her teeth, fiddled expertly, and spoke clearly at last. 'I'll take that little kitchen knife I brought. You can pick mushrooms for breakfast. I want some ferns for the back patch.'

The back patch was in the walled garden at home in the cottage at Dymock. The wall there held back an ancient earthwork of sorts and constantly oozed water. Gran had made it a fascinating area of ferns and moss.

Holly scrambled for the gosunder and lifted her nightie carefully away from its rim. As soon as she had finished, Gran took her place, while Holly poured water into the basin and rubbed soap on to her face-cloth.

'Neck and arms too, maid,' Gran reminded her, pushing the chamber-pot back beneath the bed. Holly had asked her once why she called it the gosunder. ' 'Cos it goes under the bed,' Gran had replied briefly and without humour. It was obvious at times that Gran considered her fourth grandchild a little below par.

By the time Holly was in her vest, knickers and treasured khaki shorts, Gran had dealt with her straggly white hair and was hooking up her stays. Holly topped her shorts with an aertex shirt and pulled on ankle socks and sandals. Gran struggled with petticoat, stockings, thick knickers, black skirt, black blouse, black jacket, black shoes and black hat.

'Ready, maid,' she said, anchoring the hat with a six-inch pin and picking up a shopping bag. She checked for the kitchen knife and a handkerchief and glanced at the clock. 'See. Five past six. I told you.'

Holly smiled and opened the bedroom door and they crept downstairs.

*   *   *

The air to the west of the small seaside town was damp and soft. Gran hated roads and pavements so they climbed the first stile they came to and cut through a field of cows to the edge of the woods which led up to Durlston Head. Gran wasn't frightened of cows and chided Holly for edging away from them. 'Proper townie,' she scoffed. Holly waited for a reference to her mother but thankfully none came. The world was still perfect, the Garden of Eden without a snake in sight. Already Holly could see the great bay of Poole, with Wight rising from the grey mist. She knew from her mother's indefatigable teaching that the valley of the Frome was beneath her, the Purbeck Downs all around her. It came as rather a jolt when Gran said prosaically, 'There goes the milk float. That wretched milkman is still drunk!'

On the road above them a pony high-stepped along between the trees pulling a float. The float was taken up entirely with churns and dippers; the milkman stood on the step beneath them and flapped the reins across the churns.

'How do you know, Gran?'

'He isn't a-driving that float. Them reins is slack. See? The pony knows where to go.'

'Has he been drunk ever since we came last year?' Holly asked.

'Prob'ly. Milkmen usually are.'

Holly questioned no more. Gran knew these things. Her mother would have said, 'I really don't know, darling. We must try to find out.' Gran would call that pre-varicating.

As if Gran had tuned in to her thoughts, she said, 'Your ma might give 'im the benefit of the doubt, I s'ppose.'

Holly heard the rustling from the first snake of Eden.

But all Gran said was – and she said it darkly, 'Her benefit and her doubt, of course!'

And while Holly was mulling that over for the scathing criticism she knew very well it implied, they emerged from the trees on to the sheep-cropped grass of the South

Dorset Downs. Tiny white snowballs showed in the emerald green. Gran handed over a paper bag.

'Right. Off you go, my maid. Reckon the sun will break through in half an hour. Get them before the dew can dry.' She turned and re-entered the woods, knife at the ready. Apparently there were to be no more snake-rustlings. At least for the time being. Holly reassembled her Garden of Eden speedily and stared around her.

This was the part she liked best. She really did own the world now; or rather she owned England. She scuffed through the wet grass until her ankle socks were soaked with the English dew, and wondered whether she should summon her *alter ego* as dear Mum insisted on calling her imaginary friend. She smiled because Mum was the only one who accepted that there *was* an imaginary friend. Dad ignored poor Blanche Cooke, and Gran thought she was talking to herself. Holly's smile spread to a grin. She didn't need Blanche at this moment; everything was just perfect as it was. She began to pick the English mushrooms.

Dorothy woke as the front door of the holiday digs closed after Gran. She lay quite still listening for them to open the gate but there were no more sounds. Trust Gran to make a successful getaway.

She leaned on one elbow and looked down at Jim. With his mouth slightly open and his facial muscles apparently dissolving he looked unfortunately like his mother. She couldn't bear it and poked him in the back.

'Wha' 's it?' he asked through his slack lips. 'Early turn?'

Immediately she regretted her action. This was his holiday. No earlies, lates or nights for two whole weeks.

'Sorry, baby-honey,' she whispered. 'Go back to sleep.'

But he wouldn't, of course. He came to life with a series of grunts, registered the early-morning greyness and turned to envelop her.

'We're at the seaside!' he said with childish delight and kissed her chastely on the forehead.

She felt her usual rush of protective love. He might be

48

under his mother's thumb but he was also under hers. And his mother couldn't do what she could with him. She proceeded to prove this to herself and then afterwards scolded him for being 'Awful'.

'Oh Doll! Doll, I love you so much – I worship you!'

She knew that Jim was at the very core of her being but she did not like the word 'worship'.

'I love you too, darling. There, there. Put your head on my shoulder . . .'

She tucked him comfortably into her arm and kissed his thick brown hair. 'Your mother woke me. She's taken Hol out for one of her walks again.'

He chuckled. 'I thought Hol wouldn't want to do that again this year. After all, she's almost grown-up now.'

'She's thirteen!' Dolly said quickly.

'When I was thirteen, I started at Brimscombe as lad clerk,' he reminded her.

'Oh Lordie! Not that again!' she groaned.

'Well, it's true.'

'I don't care. Holly is thirteen and she is still a little girl. She wakes up early. She would go back to sleep but your mother gets her up and takes her for long walks—'

'Doll . . . don't get cross!' His voice was pleading. 'It helps Ma to be out early. She doesn't sleep at all since she lost Dad.'

'Nonsense! She goes to bed at eight o'clock so naturally she's had her sleep out by dawn the next morning!' Dorothy changed tactics suddenly. 'Other people don't have to take their mother-in-law on holiday with them!'

'Other people don't even have a holiday, Doll.' His tone was sad now. He knew where this road was leading. 'And besides, Ma wouldn't go anywhere if we didn't take her.'

'She's got two daughters as well as you! *And* she's got Kildie!'

They had reached the usual impasse. Sarah, Lizzie and Kildie. His sisters and niece.

'Kildie is working—'

'Like you. And – like you – she gets two weeks annual leave.' Dorothy wondered why she was pursuing this. It always ended in the same brick wall.

'Oh Doll . . . she's young. She's got friends . . . be fair, she has Ma every day.'

'She *lives* with Gran, for goodness' sake! She was adopted by Gran when she was three weeks old and your sister left Dymock! She lives at home with her grandmother who looks after her! She doesn't have to do a damned thing!'

'I know, I know. But if she didn't live there, it would be very awkward for us.'

'I really don't see why, Jim! Gran is perfectly capable of looking after herself.'

'But she shouldn't – we couldn't let her – be alone—'

'In that case she could stay with her daughters. Both Lizzie and Sarah have . . . er . . . establishments—'

But Jim could not bear to discuss his sisters. He visibly clamped his lips together. Dorothy sighed and would have gone on but she saw his grey eyes suddenly flash with fear. Like a hunted rabbit.

She kissed his neck.

'Sorry to badger you, old boy.' She lifted her head and smiled at him. 'It's just that . . . I do worry about Hol with your mother.'

Jim relaxed his mouth with a little puff of relief and said eagerly, 'They get on famously – you know that, Doll!'

'Your mother thinks she's backward.'

'Well, what does that matter? We know she isn't. Holly herself knows she isn't.'

'She might say things to her . . . I know she goes on and on about Pa. Holly cries sometimes and tells me how much "poor Gran" is missing Grandad.'

'Holly can take it, Doll.'

'Holly is terribly like you, Jim.' Dolly was very serious now. 'She's much too sensitive.'

'But . . .' Jim turned from her again and said in a muffled voice, 'She's not a coward.'

Dolly wanted to say fiercely that neither was he. And of course he wasn't. He was soft sometimes, that was all.

She agreed quietly. 'No. Holly is not a coward.'

Gran said, 'Did you count 'em?'

'Twenty-five.' Holly peered into the paper bag. 'Some are bigger than others. But that's five each.'

Gran stared at her. 'Fours into twenty-five, is six each, maid.' She shook her head. 'Don't teach you proper tables any more, do they?' She opened her handkerchief. 'See what I got.'

Holly did not bother to tell her that she had included Mrs Gibbons in her calculation. The fern displayed in the handkerchief was a magnificent specimen.

'What's it called, Gran?' she asked, awestruck.

'Horsetail. But that there acorn thing, that's the spores.' Gran had other specimens in moss at the bottom of the shopping bag; a hart's tongue, royal fern, and adder's tongue. Holly thought the latter particularly appropriate when Gran immediately said, 'Remember them names, maid. Recite 'em to your ma. She's completely iggorant about plants.'

Holly said defensively, 'She told me that it's ferns from millions of years ago that make coal.'

'She did, did she? Tommyrot. Coal has to be dug out the earth. Ferns grows on top of it.'

'Yes but—'

'Your ma thinks she's a darn sight cleverer than she really is. Don't let her fill your head with rubbish, maid. Now, tell me the name of this one.'

'Horsetail,' Holly said angrily.

'And this?'

'Lady's.'

'Lady's? Where d'you get that from? I never got any lady's fern this morning.'

'I meant royal.'

Gran settled the moss back in the bag, her lips compressed. They were halfway through the wood when she said, 'You knew the names of all these ferns already, didn't you?'

'Well . . . not all. But we've just been doing ferns in Bots and—'

'Bots?'

'Botany, Gran. It's like nature-study in the Junior School only—'

'I know what botany is, maid!'

They stumped on silently until they emerged into the field of cows.

'You been making a mock of your old Gran all this time, Holly. That's something my Kildie wouldn't never do.' Gran shook her head sadly and took a route very near a bunch of cows.

Holly kept close to her. 'Gran . . . I wouldn't ever . . . Gran, don't smack them like that. You frighten them!'

'They're in our way, maid. Take no notice of them kicking up their heels like that. Gran wouldn't let them hurt you.'

'I know, Gran. But—'

'My Kildie used to come walking with me. Down into the forest we'd go. She's got all her young men now but I thought I'd still got my Holly-maid—'

'You have, Gran! You have!' Holly felt almost distraught, what with the galumphing cows and Gran's funereal dirge.

'No-one else'd come out with you early mornings – go to bed with you early—'

'I know, Gran! Honestly—'

'An' me so lonely since poor Walter died.'

'Oh Gran . . .' Holly felt her eyes filling up. Her heart threatened to burst in her chest. The world was so beautiful. And so empty.

'There now, girl. Don't grieve. Give your old Gran a kiss and let's take a smiling face in for Mrs Gibbons to see!'

They were past the cows and Holly cast herself at the gaunt figure. The thought that she might have hurt poor Gran was too much to bear.

Gran sighed and led the way up the garden path.

'She doesn't know no better,' she said as if to herself.

Mrs Gibbons was good at high teas but not so good at breakfasts. They each sat down to a cold plate covered with fast-congealing bacon fat, an orange-eyed egg and a rasher of very thick, underdone bacon. The mushrooms had shrunk to tiny hard buttons. Luckily the sauce bottle, with its austere illustration of Westminster on the label, was almost full and there was plenty of bread. Jim took Holly's bacon and she made herself an egg sandwich puddled in sauce. She was very hungry.

Gran said, 'She should have that bacon fat, our Jim. Keeps the cold out.'

This ensured that Dolly would let the bacon go. In fact, she went one better and grinned conspiratorially at Holly.

'We'll let Blanche have it, shall we?'

Holly glanced at Gran and blushed. Gran thinned her lips to nothing. 'Encouraging the child in those silly fancies,' she grumbled when Jim smilingly cut the bacon into small pieces.

'It's only Mum teasing!' Holly protested. And then she realized she had played into Gran's hands and added, 'Mrs Cooke came and took Blanche away just after Christmas, didn't she, Mum?'

'I believe she did.' Dolly frowned as if in thought, then smiled brightly. 'But of course we made it clear that Blanche can come and stay with Holly any time she likes!'

Jim laughed and shook his head at Dolly so bright eyed and provocative. Holly tried to smile, then felt positively traitorous towards Blanche Cooke, who had, after all, been her invisible friend since she was old enough to walk down the garden where Blanche lived in the shed.

'Cheer up, Hol!' Dolly manhandled the teapot vigorously. 'The sun is coming through – look. We'll be able to spend all day on the beach!'

Holly and Gran cheered up instantly. Jim, looking at the three smiling women, felt his usual mixture of adoration and anxiety. They were his responsibility; he wanted to keep them safe, make them happy. He knew it was impossible.

He controlled a sudden shiver.

1908

Walter James woke up on an August day in 1908 and knew, with absolute certainty, that he was a deeply happy man. At forty-three he felt like a young man again without any of the uncertainties of being young. His marriage to Esme Dart had seemed like a rebirth. At first it had seemed like a rebirth into a lower order of things. His father had almost cast him off, his remaining relatives, distant uncles and a cousin or two, had done so completely – there were no Christmas cards from any of them. And he had traded his idle life as a kind of dilettante academic, for the treadmill of being a public servant. Certainly he had always let it be known that he spent time researching esoteric material for a book he was supposedly writing on the history of the English Church since the Reformation. Actually he had two small notebooks filled with references. He had written 'Chapter One' at the head of a manuscript book, but got no further.

In his new life he was bound to spend a little more of his day attending to matters on behalf of the Great Western Railway. But it was not onerous work and he had always had a boyish enthusiasm for trains. His father's old friend, Leslie Edwards, was on the Board of Directors and had procured the sinecure of Dymock station for him much as his father might have got him a living had he so desired. And no-one knew him down here. They recognized that he was 'different', but other men took menial railway jobs because they were in love with trains.

And between the trains he could pursue his own interests. He liked to fish the waters of the little River

Leadon, read detective novels, play with his children, and, above all, get to know his wife.

And Emmie was just as a station master's wife should be. She could grow fruit, make jam, keep chickens, kill them, pluck them and cook them to just that right shade of brownness that made his mouth water even before he could smell them. She could care for her family and still find time to dig the garden and see to her hens.

He had known she would be a good wife and mother; that had been her part of the bargain. But he had not been able to guess at her sheer versatility. In one way she was an open book, the kind of woman you would expect to find in service. In other ways she was a mystery. He had known she would be good for him. He had not known that she would make him so positively happy.

That particular morning he woke early because it was his day off and they were going to the Three Counties Show at Gloucester. Normally Emmie had to shake him several times before he rolled, groaning, out of bed. Contrarily, on his day off he woke up naturally and refreshed at six a.m.

He turned his head on the pillow and looked at her. She was not beautiful. At forty-five, her hair was already greying, her skin lined and her big bones seemed very prominent with the muscles of her face relaxed in sleep. But his heart cramped with sudden tenderness for her. Her love for him was so unexpected and wholehearted; he saw it as a gift from heaven, as a personal salvation. Sometimes he remembered his practical proposal to her and almost blanched at his sheer effrontery. He had honestly thought he was doing her a favour by marrying her. And probably he had continued to think like that until the night of his father's funeral when she had come to him to offer comfort and stayed night after night to give him love.

She opened her eyes suddenly in a way she had and was instantly awake.

'Don't look at me, Walter. I don't like you looking at me.'

She spoke clearly, her voice unblurred by sleep. She had never understood what it was to droop with tiredness. 'When I'm awake I'm awake. And when I'm asleep I'm asleep,' she said when Walter asked her if she was tired.

Now he put his hand to her cheek and whispered, 'Why not, Emmie? You never stay still long enough for me to get a good look at you.'

'I'm old and ugly. That's why not,' she replied. But she did not move beneath his hand and her gaze did not falter.

'You're fishing for compliments. All right, you shall have them. Forty is not old—'

'I am forty-five, as you well know! And my mother died at forty. I am old, Walter.'

'Don't speak of dying, Em. I could not live without you.'

She turned pink as she so often did at his remarks. She said quietly, 'I am not going to die till I am ninety years old!'

'Thank you, dear Em.' He leaned over and kissed her nose. 'You are still young and you are not ugly.'

She smiled briefly. 'I am not beautiful though, am I?'

He kissed her mouth. 'What is beauty, Em? It is what pleases the eye most of all. My eye is most pleased when it beholds you.'

She drew a trembling breath. 'Oh Walter James! The things you say!'

'I mean them, Em. Oh, I do mean them.' He kissed her insistently between his words. 'Everything we planned has happened. But we did not plan on such happiness, did we?'

She held his face away from hers and smiled right at him.

'I did,' she said simply. And then she returned his kisses with the passion that always surprised and delighted him.

They caught the eight o'clock into Gloucester. Lizzie and Sarah were dressed in identical gingham frocks although they did not look in the least like twins. Emmie had made their sun-bonnets to match and sewed broderie anglaise around the brims. Jim wore a suit of fine grey worsted, with an Eton collar on the short pea-jacket and wide breeches tucked into his socks. They looked a handsome family and when they turned into Northgate Street and made for the Cross, heads turned to watch them walking sedately along the pavement. It was a long tramp down Westgate Street to the causeway and the showground beyond, but the children did not lag or whine once. Walter pointed out the Cathedral and the monument of Bishop Hooper who had been burned as a martyr by the Catholics but whose body had remained unconsumed by the flames.

Jim, in particular, enjoyed these stories.

'Tell us about King Edward,' he demanded as they passed Llanthony Abbey.

'Oh no you don't!' Emmie said sternly. 'None of them got any sleep last time you told that one!'

'Maybe tomorrow,' Walter promised, smiling at his children, knowing the pleasure of family pride.

The show was an enormous affair with a show ring and innumerable side shows and a big fair for the children. Roundabouts and helter-skelters were not for Emmie or Lizzie and they held caps and bonnets while Walter took Sarah and Jim around the various attractions. Sarah adored the Flip-Flap. As the enormous paddles soared high into the air she screamed with delight. 'I am lord of all I survey!' she yelled in a most unladylike manner. 'I can see everything – the whole world!' Jim, on the other hand, felt diminished and isolated and frightened. 'There's your mamma!' Walter shouted above the noise of the air and the music. 'Can you see her? And Lizzie? Look, Sarah – look, Jim!'

Sarah continued to scream delightedly, but it was the final straw for Jim. His womenfolk looked like ants far below him. His mother was far too small. And he didn't like that. He liked his mother to be big and strong and capable. He looked up at his father and clutched at his hand.

'Ma's small,' was all he said. But Walter knew exactly what he meant and held him very tightly until they reached the ground.

'Did you enjoy it, Jim?'

Emmie smiled down at her favourite child who shook his head.

Walter said, 'Neither did I.'

'I loved it!' Sarah screamed. 'I was better than anyone up there – better than you, Lizzie! Better than the Richardsons even!'

'Hush, child!' Walter looked at her. 'We're not talking into the wind any longer!'

Then he fell into step with Emmie and said, 'We were too far away from you, my dear. That's why we didn't like it.'

Jim was not surprised to see his mother's face turn pink. He wondered why his father's small comments had that effect on her. He'd noticed it before.

They shouldered their way to the show ring and watched a farmer from Apperley win the rosette for the best milk Jersey. And then it was time for the bulls to be paraded and Joe Matson, the cowman from the Grange, led on the Richardson Black.

One of the things that surprised Walter about his wife was her knowledge of farming. She had had a 'place' at a farm when she was eleven years old, but as far as he knew her duties had been mostly indoors. It seemed to be in her blood. Nearly all the village women kept hens, so that was nothing unusual, but she always fattened a pig for the winter and did not turn away when the butcher came and the Station House was filled with its frantic squealing.

Her opinion on stock rearing was often equal to Joe Matson's and she had drawn down her mouth when he said that the Richardsons were certain of winning this year's Three Counties. As the bull entered the ring, side-stepping for a moment until he felt the pressure of the ring on his nose, Walter glanced at her.

'He's a good-looking beast,' he said.

'So would you be if you'd had your hair oiled twice a day for the past week!'

He grinned and was going to make some spirited repartee, when she added, 'Where's our Sarah got to?'

She wasn't there. Lizzie stood meekly by Jim, watching Joe Matson twitch his leading stick deliberately to make the Black snort.

'Where did Sarah go, Lizzie?' Walter leaned beneath the brim of his daughter's sun-bonnet.

'Sarah?' Lizzie looked around vaguely and at the same time the bull lowered his head aggressively and lunged for old Matson. The stick held him at bay and he bellowed pain and rage. Lizzie yelped and cowered against her father, dragging Jim almost to the ground.

Emmie reached down and picked him up. He was not small by any means but she swung him into the crook of her elbow without difficulty.

'It's all right,' she said above the excited noise of the crowd. 'Mr Matson is doing it purposely.'

'But he's hurting the Black!' Jim protested.

Walter said loudly, 'Lizzie, pay attention. Where has Sarah gone?'

Emmie murmured close to her son's ear. 'Not really. They're both putting on a bit of a show. And it won't do the Black a bit of good because the judges will see how bad-tempered he really is.'

Lizzie tried to climb up her father's trouser leg.

'He's going to come over the rails, Pa! He's going to kill us!'

Walter felt his family pride ebbing fast. He pulled the whole lot of them to the back of the crowd.

'Now come on, Lizzie. You were holding Sarah's hand.'

Lizzie wept. 'It wasn't my fault! She said she would sing

59

for him. In church. I would have gone with her only he didn't ask me.'

Walter sat on his haunches and forced her to look into his eyes.

'Sarah has gone off with someone? A man?'

'A vicar, Pa. He was a vicar!'

Emmie spoke soothingly from above. 'She will be safe then, Walter. Don't worry.'

He said grimly, 'They're the worst. The very worst.' He stood up. 'Hold your mother's skirt, Lizzie, and do not let it go.' He touched Emmie's shoulder. 'Stay put if you can, Em. I'll know where to find you.'

She said sharply, 'Be careful – Walter—'

And as if in response to her belated alarm, Sarah's high voice came from above. 'That's my ma and pa! And my little brother!'

And far above them on the platform of the Flip-Flap, Sarah's bonnet was waved from its strings like a flag and then, as the wind took it, it floated gently down to them.

The crowd, relieved of tension for a moment, laughed, several people waved.

At last Emmie was angry.

'Showing us up like this!'

Walter laughed louder than anyone. 'Who cares! That little minx! She was determined to have another turn on the Flip-Flap! How did she inveigle anyone to take her?'

Emmie looked at him. 'By using her woman's wiles,' she said drily.

He returned her look for a moment then went forward to rescue Sarah from her 'vicar'.

In the event, it turned out to be a reunion, and not a happy one at that.

'My good God!' Walter held Sarah's hand in a vice-like grip. 'It's – surely – it's Passmore-Williams?'

The man in question wore a black cape around his dog-collar and a round black clerical hat like that of a French priest.

His blank expression, covering what was evidently

considerable confusion, wavered for a moment as he recognized Walter.

'It's James, surely? Walter James? My dear man! How long is it? Just after Oxford? Must be all of twenty years!'

'Longer than that.'

Walter shushed Sarah who was jumping up and down like a puppet on a string. Emmie arrived with the other two children, she placed Jim carefully next to his father and went to Sarah.

'You naughty child!' She bent down to replace the retrieved sun-bonnet and tuck away the blowing black hair. 'You look like a gypsy! Be still while I tie your sash – now pull up those stockings.'

Above her, Walter said, 'Why did you take my daughter away, Williams? We were terribly worried.'

'My dear James! I hardly took her away!' But the round face was flustered now. 'The child came to me and said she was frightened of the bull and she would sing for me if I would take her away from it—'

'You made no attempt to find her parents?'

'She seemed alone. And frightened. She wanted to go on that . . . contraption.' He pointed to the giant arms of the Flip-Flap. 'It seemed the best way of removing her from the source of terror.'

'I see.' Walter stared at this man and wondered whether he should call his bluff. Then Emmie straightened and Passmore-Williams held out a pink hand.

'My dear lady, I do not think I've had the honour. And I am such an old friend of—'

'Passmore-Williams,' Walter said curtly. 'We were fellow students for a time, my dear.' He glanced at the chubby face, smiling ingratiatingly. He was unwilling to introduce Emmie but there was no way out.

'My wife. Esme.'

'*Enchanté!*' Passmore-Williams placed his other hand momentarily beneath the brim of Emmie's sun-bonnet in benediction. She started back. 'Like mother like

61

daughter.' He turned his beam on Sarah. 'You are very like your mother, child.'

Sarah laughed excitedly, looked up at him and then down, letting her thick black lashes rest on her cheeks.

He laughed richly. 'Very like,' he repeated.

Walter said, 'We must go now.' He turned so that he was between Passmore-Williams and Emmie. 'We have brought a picnic and it is time for the children to eat. I am a family man now, Passmore-Williams. As you see.'

There was something in his voice that made the other man bite back his next remark. Instead he said, 'Then I will make my adieus.'

'Yes. Goodbye.'

Sarah was regretful. 'I want—' she began.

Emmie gripped her shoulder. 'Say goodbye to the gentleman, Sarah. And thank him for taking you on that thing again.'

'Goodbye, sir. And thank you,' Sarah trilled obediently.

He had a special smile for her. 'Goodbye, little lady. Perhaps we shall meet again one day.' He did not shake Walter's hand. 'Goodbye, James. I was sorry to hear of your loss.'

They watched the portly black figure disappear into the crowd. Jim said, 'What loss, Pa?'

Walter said, 'He was speaking of the death of my father a long time ago, son.'

Sarah said, 'He was nice.'

Lizzie said, 'You're a naughty girl.'

The crowd roared as the Black was led off.

Sarah said quietly, 'He bought me lots of sweets. And you can't have any.'

'Then I'll tell.'

'All right. Just one.'

They began to shove their way out of the crowd and towards the open reaches of the water meadows.

Walter said, 'Emmie . . . I'm sorry. So sorry.'

She smiled at him. 'What for? Making me the happiest

woman in the world?' She looked back. 'Ah. There's the winner. That Guernsey from Northleach.'

'How do you know?' asked Jim.

'I know. Wait and see.'

He was not surprised that she was right. She always was.

FOUR

1938

Holly walked up the beach as slowly as she could without actually coming to a halt. She knew exactly what would happen when she reached the three deck-chairs lined up within easy distance of the toilets. Mum would want her to go swimming and Gran would want to walk along the shoreline looking for large shells she could set about the ferns in her garden. Dad would want to sleep.

Holly narrowed her eyes against the sun which had grown fierce since midday and surveyed her family. Gran looked like an ancient and rather tattered crow in her rusty black ensemble; Mum's shingled hair and black regulation swimming-costume made her look like one of the boys splashing about in the sea. And Dad looked like . . . Dad. Holly smiled indulgently. Dad had a life none of them shared, concerned almost entirely with those magic words 'rolling-stock'. He was the rolling-stock clerk in the control office and it was his proud boast that he could trace any wagon or engine wherever it might be on the Great Western system within half a day. But how he did it, or even why he did it, was a complete mystery. Holly wondered sometimes why he could not turn that phenomenal memory to games of bridge or chess. But all he wanted to do was to pinpoint his rolling-stock.

She turned her attention to Mum, already fidgeting in her deck-chair. Mum was interested in so many things. Holly's education came top of the list, but she would try almost anything. She had been up in an aeroplane, she had played tennis for the city club which was the local equivalent of Wimbledon, she had a signed photograph of Errol Flynn and, on certain occasions, she wore not only lipstick but rouge and mascara as well. The girls at school envied Holly her mum. But life would have been much easier if Mum had liked making jam and digging the garden. Gran would have approved of her then.

Holly turned her gaze on the occupant of the third chair. Gran was very still, very sombre in her funereal clothes. Sadness surrounded her like an invisible shroud. Holly liked that phrase and tried it out again inside her head. An invisible shroud. She wondered if she could write a poem about Gran and her grief and her love for Grandad. But Gran would be ratty and Mum would laugh and Dad would look anxious and it wasn't worth it.

She turned her toes over and dragged them through the sand. Her euphoria of the morning had disappeared into a tiredness; afternoons were her least favourite time of day. It was a Monday. If she'd been at school it would be double physics. She thought of Miss Joliffe whose enthusiasm for the subject was only surpassed by her complete inability to teach it. Holly always had a terrible job to stay awake throughout that one-and-a-half hours. The thought of it now made her eyelids heavy. She knew what to do about it; Blanche was there for the sole purpose of cheering her up and helping her to see things straight. But Holly was now thirteen; it had been all right to have an imaginary friend when she was a child. She was no longer a child. Gran thought she was a penny short of a shilling because of Blanche Cooke. And maybe Gran was right.

And then, quite suddenly, Blanche was with her.

'Come on, Hol, brighten up!'

The voice was unmistakable. It had a slight London twang with a husky undertone as if emerging from a sore throat.

Holly glanced sideways, trying not to grin. After all, Blanche's visits were becoming less and less frequent.

Blanche grinned back. 'I'll always turn up,' she said, 'like a bad penny.'

65

'A good penny,' Holly murmured, trying not to move her lips just in case Mum's sharp eyes were watching her. 'And you always come at just the right moment.'

'Course. That's what I'm here for!'

Blanche wasn't deep. That was what was so great about her. She stated the obvious and was infinitely reassuring.

'Blanche Cooke,' Holly murmured like a mantra.

'Blanche Cooke, can't read a book.' Blanche recited as she had done when they were both four years old. 'Your first poem.'

'Not at all, Mrs Ball,' Holly said mincingly and they both laughed aloud at this recollection of Holly's first realization of a joke. Mrs Ball lived next door to Gran and had been taking afternoon tea when she dropped a cake.

'Oh I do apologize, Mrs James,' said Mrs Ball, becoming very flustered as Gran was well known for being houseproud.

And Gran, automatically, replied, 'Not at all, Mrs Ball.' Blanche had enjoyed that joke even more than Holly herself.

'Written any more stuff lately?' Blanche asked now, controlling her giggles with some difficulty.

'Lots. I was thinking about Gran just now.' Holly narrowed her eyes again at the black crow in the deck-chair. 'What do you think of grief wrapping round her like a shroud?'

'It would rhyme with cloud,' Blanche said helpfully.

'It doesn't have to rhyme any more. It has to be sort of rhythmical instead. It comes to you gradually. Like listening to music. It can sound nothing at first, but the more you hear it . . . think of the *Moonlight Sonata*.'

'Mmm.' Blanche did her best. 'You mean those three notes played over and over again?'

'Well, sort of. I mean, it could be her grief is like a cold, cold shroud, wrapping her in its misty arms . . .' She floundered helplessly and Blanche supplied, 'Like a cloud! There! I told you. Her grief is like a cold shroud, wrapping her in a misty cloud!'

She stared at Holly and they began to laugh again. Holly knew with horrible certainty that she would never apprehend poor Gran's lonely grief now without seeing it as a wet cloud. She felt guilt as well as amusement and decided she would forego a swim with Mum and go looking for shells with Gran.

But Dolly had other ideas. She came running down the beach, laughing too as if she had heard the whole conversation with Blanche.

She obviously knew Blanche was there.

'Hello, hello! Who's your lady friend?' she carolled as she reached Holly.

'Oh, Mum!'

'I'll give you oh Mum!' Dolly ruffled Holly's mouse-brown bob. 'Go and jump into your costume and let's have a swim. Gracious, it's hot!'

Afterwards, as she and Gran combed the tide-line for shells, Holly could not control her shivering.

'You shouldna stayed in so long,' Gran chided, stopping to rub Holly's spine quite painfully. 'All that cold water isn't good for you. Course, your mother was always one for water. I well remember our Kildie coming home and telling us . . .' And off she went into one of her tales that made Dolly sound unbalanced and very selfish.

'Course that Percy, he died of pneumonia only a year later. And Billy Matson's children are all simple.'

Holly controlled her shaking body with difficulty. If only she had gone to play cricket as Mum had wanted she would have warmed up in no time.

'Here's one, Gran.' She picked up a razor shell nearly six inches long.

'That's a good one, our Holly,' Gran congratulated. 'Ah you're a real James. Not a bit of Prosser in you anywhere.'

Holly felt cold and miserable beyond belief. She looked round for Blanche who obviously couldn't be there.

Gran held her shoulder and leaned over to pick up a shell.

'D'you know what this one is?' she asked. 'You were so clever with the plants this morning!'

Holly knew very well it was a cowrie but she said, 'I think it's a dog whelk.'

Gran put it to her ear. 'Right, my girl. Can you hear any barking?'

Holly looked at the old grey eyes and smiled. 'No, Gran.'

'What do you hear?'

'The sea.'

'Then what is it?'

'It's a cowrie, Gran.'

'That's better.' Gran listened herself, smiling. 'Your grandad loved to listen to the sea in shells.'

'I know. He taught me how to do it.'

Gran's face lit with pleasure. 'So he did, didn't he? What else did he teach you, our Holly?'

'He taught me . . . he taught me . . .' She had been going to say that Grandad told her it was not the sea she could hear at all but her own blood coursing through veins and arteries. She stopped herself in time but fumbled for an alternative and finally blurted, 'He told me how you met and fell in love.'

'He did, did he?'

Gran was silent, trudging over the firm sand in her black shoes, staring down. Holly could see that her face was suffused with colour.

She said timidly, 'Do you mind, Gran?'

'I don't mind for you to know, our Holly. But no-one else. No-one else at all!'

'Not even Kildie?'

'You an't told Kildie, 'ave you, maid?'

'No.'

'Then don't.'

'What about Dad?'

Gran stopped walking and lifted her head to stare out to sea.

'There were a time . . . he would have understood. But now . . . he'd tell her.'

Holly did not need to ask who 'her' was.

She said in a small voice, 'I told Blanche Cooke, Gran. I'm sorry.'

'Blanche who?' Gran looked down, startled, then laughed. 'Oh, my maid. You kin tell your Blanche Cooke! I dun't mind her a-knowing!'

And chuckling, she resumed the beachcombing. And Holly said inside her head, 'Thank you, Blanche.' It was good to know Blanche still had her uses.

Dorothy returned from her game of French cricket, glowing with well-being. Jim still slept in the deck-chair, lower jaw sunk almost into his neck, looking like his mother again. She couldn't bear it and shook her damp hair over him so that one or two drops fell onto his face.

'Wha' the—' He opened heavy lids, obviously unable to orientate himself. 'Oh . . . Doll . . .'

She crouched by his chair and smoothed his hair over the part of his scalp that was becoming visible.

'You should have worn a hat,' she chided. 'And do *not* call me Doll! Dolly is quite bad enough!'

'What's the time? Where's our Hol?'

'It's four o'clock. Time to put the primus on and make tea. And Hol is with your mother. As per usual.'

'I thought you and she were going for a swim?'

'We went. And I wanted Holly to join in some French cricket on the shoreline. To warm her up.'

'Doll . . . please . . .'

'I'm allowed to have a grumble now and then.' She rubbed her nose against his and said seriously, 'I don't know anyone else who would share their annual holiday year after damned year with their mother-in-law!'

He pleaded with her. 'Dearest Doll. Only since Dad died.'

'And he's been dead eight years! Eight years, Jim!'

'It's the only holiday she has—'

'And as I reminded you this morning, she's got other children besides you! Lizzie and the scarlet Sarah!'

'Dolly! If Ma ever heard you mention Sarah like that—'

'Don't be potty, Jim! Am I likely to invite Gran to cut my throat? The fact remains—'

'Dolly, don't start again. You know the situation with both my sisters.'

'You mean Lizzie trying to keep one husband and Sarah trying to get through as many as possible?'

'Doll . . .'

She kissed him briskly. 'Sorry, darling. It's like squeezing a boil. Poison's out now.' She kissed him again. 'But I'm warning you. Once Kildie gets married and sets up home, I shall expect a break now and then!'

He laughed comfortably. 'Kildie's a child, Doll.'

Dolly was standing up but paused, hanging on to the back of the chair to stare down at him in surprise.

'She is twenty-three, Jim! When I was twenty-three Holly was already two years old!'

His colour darkened and he would not meet her eyes. 'Yes but . . . there were reasons for that. And Kildie hasn't been to college like you . . . she's still . . .'

Dolly's intense blue eyes widened. 'Innocent?' she asked.

He laughed, missing the real point. 'I jolly well hope so!' he said bluffly. 'Otherwise I shall have to unhook Pa's old horsewhip!'

Dolly said nothing. She straightened her back and went into the beach tent to take the primus out of its wooden box.

1914

When Jim was twelve he could leave school.

Walter said, 'After this blasted war is over, son, there will be an outcry for men with qualifications. Engineering. Teaching. You could go into Gloucester and take your School Certificate then go on for a State scholarship to one of the universities.'

Jim was astonished. 'I want to go on the railway, Pa. You know that.'

'I know you've always said that, Jim.' Walter smiled at the round face so like his own but dominated by enormous grey eyes like Emmie's. 'But you can see from my experience, it's not a career for an ambitious man.'

'But you love it, Pa! You've always said it was the best thing you ever did!'

Emmie was sitting by the range darning socks. She smiled down at the large hole stretched over the bottom of a teacup, but she said nothing.

'I am not ambitious for a career, Jim. There were other factors which guided me along this path.'

Jim grinned. 'You mean track, Pa.'

'Of course. Track.' But Walter did not smile. 'I find, however, that I am ambitious for you. I cannot imagine you being content with a country station offering the odd afternoon's fishing—'

Emmie laughed aloud.

Jim said earnestly, 'Oh no, I wouldn't want that either.'

Walter was disconcerted at this. He lifted his straight brows which overhung his blue eyes these days and stared at his son. Jim leaned forward earnestly.

'I *am* ambitious, Pa. I want to work on the railway. I want to know where the trains are going and when and what they carry – people or goods. What goods. How much tonnage of coal from Pembroke Dock. Iron ore from—'

Emmie could not stop laughing.

Walter said, 'What have we done? It's no laughing matter, Emmie. It's all right for me, I've got my own escape routes. But railway servants are just that. Servants.'

Emmie stopped laughing. 'I had a good life as a servant, Walter.'

'Is it what you want for your son?' he asked directly.

Jim said, 'Dad – please listen—'

'No, you listen. You're twelve, Jim. You're too young to know your own mind—'

Emmie said, 'He is his own man. As I was my own woman. We choose to do what we want to do.'

Walter was unusually annoyed with her.

'You had little choice in the matter, Emmie.'

'But I chose how I went about it. The kitchen was mine. Your father ate what I decided. He had rules, of course, but so did I.'

'I noticed little of your rules. You had to go to church three times every Sunday. Get up at six to do the grates and carry coal. He should have had extra staff but you did it all so—'

'Why did you think of me when you needed a wife, Walter?'

Walter glanced at Jim. 'I loved you, of course.'

'No. It wasn't that. You wanted a *suitable* wife. Did you choose me because I would be a good servant?'

He turned his back on Jim and confronted her angrily. 'You know it was not that! It was because you were efficient. You were neat and clean and – and you could listen and understand when I talked. And you replied with common sense and dignity and . . .'

His voice died and she took her hand out of the cup and sock and held it up to him.

'Jim has dignity too, dearest. He has understanding and common sense. And ambition too, it would seem.'

'And he argues just like his mother!'

Jim spoke almost shyly, 'Pa – I love the railway. And I know everyone in the Division. It . . . it's like working for a family concern.'

Walter was still unconvinced. He said eventually, 'Look. I'll have a word with the Staff Office in Gloucester. If there's an opening for a clerk and you can get it, then I'll give you a year. But I shall want a good report from your station master. And if that's not forthcoming . . .'

It never occurred to Jim that he might not get a good report. Everyone liked him, just as they liked his father.

He was sent to Brimscombe on the Stroud line. He lodged with Sidney and Ella Coles in the station house, had as much as he could eat of wet potatoes, cheese and cabbage, and Mr Coles kept two shillings of his four shillings wage each week. He sent a shilling home and kept a shilling for himself. He made some extra by sticking up the pins at the local skittle alley and collecting the empty beer mugs for the landlord.

Mr Coles treated him with studied indifference but did his duty by him. Jim learned how to tap a message along the line in Morse, to do Pitman's shorthand; he learned the Rules and Regulations and started to study for the Signalling examination.

Mr Coles was determined young Jim James should not be a special case, even though his father was a personal friend of one of the directors, who was a personal friend of the Assistant Manager, the popular Sir Archie McKinnon. Everyone knew that Walter James himself was unusual – some kind of gent. Disgraced, or so they said, by his marriage to his father's servant. He hadn't worked himself up to the position of station master as had Sidney Coles. No memorizing the Rules by candlelight for Walter James. No exams taken in the boardroom at Gloucester Divisional Superintendent's Office, invigilated by the Chief Clerk, who had a way of looking over the examinee's shoulder and snorting at every spelling mistake.

In fact, Walter James had it easy. His porter had been with him ever since he took on the station; Jack Bowie acted more like a family retainer than a porter. As well as carrying luggage and finding horses and traps, he was checking on the windows and door handles of incoming trains and covering for Walter who had gone fishing in the Leadon. Walter could get away with it; he was well liked because of his easy-goingness. His son was another kettle of fish entirely.

Jim sensed Mr Coles' disapproval immediately and hoped it would disappear with time. But the year wore on and Jim knew he was not going to get a good report at the end of it. He tried to ingratiate himself by asking about Sidney's career but the hectoring way Sidney spoke of his beginnings as a lamp boy made Jim's heart sink.

Once started, however, there was no stopping him. He told Jim about the time he had averted an accident by levering some frozen points with a garden spade.

'No credit given, lad. No credit at all. Taken for granted. Me duty. I did me duty. And that was that. Never mind I lost the senses in me finger from frostbite and ricked me back something cruel.'

Jim's large grey eyes looked at the sixty-year-old veteran respectfully. When the points froze at Dymock, his mother brought out kettles of boiling water and thawed them without difficulty. His father might then pull the lever, or more probably Jack would do it. His father was probably reading by the fire in the station master's office. The comparison did not upset Jim in any way. He knew – as did everyone – that his father 'played' at working for the GWR. Nevertheless, Dymock was one of the best-kept stations on the line and one of the most efficient. Emmie did the flower-beds and the hanging baskets and Walter James hobnobbed easily with the local squire, the manager of the cider works and anyone else who might need to use his station. Sidney Coles did not play. He worked 'every hour God sent', as he told Jim. Brimscombe took more revenue than Dymock, but only just and only because the Stroud Valley was teeming with small industries, all needing transport. Sidney never had to woo customers, which was just as well because he tackled every job as if he were levering frozen points with a spade.

Jim already knew himself well enough to realize he must find a middle course between Sidney Coles and Walter James. He was as committed to the railways as was Sidney; but he would definitely use boiling water for frozen points. And – and this was the real difference – he would find every minute of working for God's Wonderful Railway absolutely absorbing.

He said, unwisely, 'Shouldn't you see the Company doctor, sir? Get something for your back?'

'What you getting at, young James? I don't need no checking up on! Trying to get me retired early with no pension? Is that what you're after?'

Jim was appalled. 'Of course not, Mr Coles,' he stammered. 'I just thought . . . you deserve compensation and I know Dr Stalley is the one to go to . . .'

'I never run to a doctor in me life!' thundered Mr Coles. 'An' I'm not about to start now! You get your 'ead down, lad and don't interfere in matters what is of no concern to you whatever.'

'No, sir.' Jim got his head down and began on the monthly return of coal wagons for the Divisional office. Each wagon had a number and in theory should be easily traceable. A train of empty coal wagons had been stabled in the sidings overnight. Twenty-four of them. There were now twenty-two. He would enter this on his return and the Rolling-Stock Department would then go to work to find the missing wagons. It was like detective work. He finished the job and began to copy out the correspondence, correcting Mr Coles' grammar and spelling as he went. The letters were all reminders about previous bills. Jim noted that payments from the Valley Wool Mill for their monthly consignments of yarn to London were six months overdue. The manager drank at the Black Boar on a Saturday evening. Jim nibbled the end of his pen and wondered if he could do what his father did and approach the man informally. He needed to do something to please Mr Coles, that was certain.

Saturday afternoon arrived. It was raining. It seemed to be always raining at Brimscombe.

'Thought you was catching the seven o'clock to get 'ome?' Mr Coles mentioned, surprised to find Jim still working by the light of the single gas jet in the booking office.

'I'm sticking up tonight, sir. At the Black Boar,' Jim said, pushing his floppy hair back from his face.

'Oh you are, are you? Suppose you expect your bed and some supper at the Lord knows what time o' night?'

75

'Well, sir, I thought my room was for the whole—'

'You bin home every weekend so far.'

'Well, sir, I thought—'

'You does too much thinking, lad! Don't think I didn't notice what you put on that there wagon return in the week!'

Jim pushed back his hair again. If he had expected praise for his perspicacity he was going to be disappointed.

'It's just that those two missing wagons would have disappeared when they were full, sir. So the likelihood is that they've turned up at Fishguard by now and—'

'And how do you know they went missing when they were full then? Because that's what happens at Dymock station? Not content with getting logs and coal on the cheap, the James family slip off a couple of wagons of coal when it suits them! Is that it?'

Jim flushed. His father had never taken advantage of railway 'perks'. But he knew that most station masters with their own sidings did just that.

'Good job you wrote that piece of information in pencil!' Mr Coles stared down at the boy angrily, quite certain he knew that the wagons had been shared between Brimscombe and Chalford station houses. 'I rubbed it out. Saved your bacon for you again. An' I suppose my wife, being the soft-hearted woman she is, will save you some bread and cheese for tonight. But no later than nine mind!'

'No, sir,' said Jim crossing his fingers surreptitiously under the desk because Mr Fordham of Valley Wool Mill did not drop in to the Black Boar until nine-thirty.

By eight-thirty that evening Jim had almost given up. He was going to miss his Saturday-night supper at home with Lizzie playing the piano and the prospect of Church the next morning. Whatever he did would not please Sidney Coles, that was obvious. He was going to get a bad report and his father was going to insist he went into Gloucester to school. He jumped down into the strawbed at the end of the skittle alley and hoisted the heavy pins back into position and wished he'd gone home as usual.

At nine-thirty he took a tray of mugs into the bar and peered over into the lounge. At last, there was Mr Fordham with his usual glass of whisky on the table in front of him. Unfortunately tonight of all nights he had someone with him: a fat cat of a man in black, his podgy white fingers around the stem of a sherry glass. Nobody drank sherry at the Black Boar. Jim grimaced with frustration.

And then the man looked up and met Jim's narrow stare for a long moment. Jim knew him. He couldn't remember where but he had met this man before.

And the man recognized the boy. He put out a hand as if to detain him and called across the lounge in a consciously modulated musical voice.

'By all that's holy! Is it Walter James's son?' He paused and when Jim did not move or reply he smiled. 'It is. The likeness is amazing. Come here, boy. We need some service.'

Fordham also recognized Jim and remembered the outstanding bills. 'I don't want any more, Francis. Time I was—'

'Heavens, man, we've only just arrived! And if I have to stay in this God-forsaken place overnight, then you can at least stay with me!'

Jim ducked under the flap and stood by the table. He was not tall for his age and his silky hair and large eyes gave him the appearance of a choirboy.

The fat man kept smiling.

'Well . . . so it's Walter's son. You do not remember me?'

'No, sir.'

'My name is Francis Passmore-Williams. And your name is – what?'

'James, sir.'

'That I know. Is it Walter James Junior, as our American friends put it?'

'No, sir.' Jim hesitated. 'I am called Jim.'

'James James, eh? Typical of Walter!' The man's smile widened. He looked exactly like an illustration of the Cheshire Cat in Lizzie's copy of *Alice in Wonderland*.

'And what are you? Pot boy?' He enjoyed this and the smile developed into a wheezy laugh. 'Well, well, well. How *are* the mighty fallen! Indeed.' He leaned forward and Jim realized that he was 'the worse for wear', as his mother described tipsiness.

'Tell your honourable papa . . . did I say honourable? It's not an easy word for me to enunciate at the best of times . . . but yes, honourable . . . tell him, Jim, that I too have been cast out! I too have been chewed up by Mother Church and spat in all directions!'

Jim was lost. He still could not place Passmore-Williams as an acquaintance of his father's. He glanced at Mr Fordham who was staring glumly into his whisky glass. A comment was obviously called for. Jim said sympathetically, 'Oh dear.'

As far as Passmore-Williams was concerned it was the riposte of the year. He flung back his head and roared with genuine laughter. Fordham tried to smile but made a poor job of it. Jim stood there, bewildered.

Stanley Meadows, who was the freeholder of the Black Boar, appeared around the bar.

'Everything all right, sirs? Jim, fetch another bottle of sherry for the gentleman. Mr Fordham – whisky?'

Passmore-Williams spluttered into coherence and held up a hand.

'No. No more sherry for me, I thank you. Landlord, I'll have a light supper in my room, if you please, and perhaps you will accompany me, Jim. We have a lot to say to each other.'

Jim glanced anxiously at the big clock suspended from beneath the boar's head on the wall. It was ten already.

Mr Fordham said quietly, 'Francis . . . Jim James is

clerk at Brimscombe station. He doubtless has duties to attend to—'

'The railways?' Passmore-Williams was struggling to stand up. He turned in a crouched position and stared again at Jim. 'So . . . you're following in Father's footsteps, are you? Don't blame either of you. Next to the Squire. House, position . . . Walter was always his own man . . .' He stumbled and would have fallen had not Jim leapt practically beneath his armpit.

'Thank you . . . thank you, boy. See me upstairs then. Won't take a minute. Fordham – I'll see you in the office tomorrow morning.'

'It's Sunday, Francis!' Mr Fordham protested.

'So it is. So it is.' The grin returned. 'Sunday was always a working day for me, Fordham. And it shall be for you.'

Using Jim like a crutch he moved towards the door. The landlord got there first and opened it wide and then came behind. The three of them negotiated the stairs with great difficulty. Below, Mr Fordham called a surly farewell.

Passmore-Williams sat on the edge of the bed in one of the rooms overlooking the valley and hung his head, getting his breath with difficulty. He kept a hand on Jim's shoulder and glanced up at Stan Meadows.

'Supper,' he wheezed. 'Veal and ham . . . some cheese . . .'

'Certainly, sir. Jim,' he looked meaningfully at Jim, 'you can come down and bring it up when Mr Passmore-Williams tells you.'

'Very well, Mr Meadows,' Jim said resignedly. If Sidney had locked the door he would have to sleep in the booking office.

Passmore-Williams waited for the door to close then sat back and surveyed Jim while his breathing slowed down and the smile grew back into place.

'So . . .' he said at last when Jim began to squirm. 'Not for you the joys of Oxford's dreaming spires.'

'No, sir.'

'No brains? No inclination?'

'Yes, sir.'

'What does that mean exactly?'

'Not enough brains. Not enough inclination.' Jim was fed up with the whole evening.

His reply pleased the fat man and there was another bout of laughter, this time rather high and whinnying.

Jim said, 'I'll fetch your supper now—'

'Not yet. I want to know things. I want to hear how your father fares. You know I was at Oxford. Like him. He was older than me, but he was destined for the church and so was I.'

Jim said stoically, 'He is very well, sir.'

'And his daughter. Sarah, was it? How is she?'

Jim frowned. 'My sister is away from home.'

'Is she indeed? Your mother sent her packing, eh?'

Jim flushed. 'She is with a concert party.' It sounded raffish. He added, 'It's to do with the Church.' Well, Hope Chapel and her uncle were Methodists which was practically the Church.

'I see. I see. So . . . when – if – things go wrong, she will come home?'

'Yes,' Jim's eyes opened with surprise.

'To Dymock?'

'Yes.'

'Good. Excellent. Still a happy little family. That is good.'

'Yes, sir. I'll fetch—'

'And you . . . are you one of the family, James James?'

Jim thought the man must be mad. He nodded.

'Yes. I thought so. You are very like Mrs James, are you not? I glimpsed her briefly when we were introduced. Grey eyes. You must have been about five years at the time. She was holding you. I never forget a face.'

And suddenly Jim remembered. The Three Counties Show on Gloucester's water meadows. Sarah and Lizzie frightened of the bull. This man had taken Sarah onto the Flip-Flap. So he was good and kind.

Jim smiled at last and his face was such an amalgam of Emmie's and Walter's that the man sitting on the bed drew in a breath.

'You rescued Sarah!' Jim said. 'I remember! She was scared of the Richardson Black when Joe Matson put him through his paces. She ran off – and you took her on the Flip-Flap!'

'Is that what they told you?' Passmore-Williams' grin was going from ear to ear.

'I think so.'

'Then that is what must have happened. It's so long ago I quite forget.' The grin was moderated slightly. 'Now, James. Tell me about yourself. Come. Sit down. I can see mine host keeps you busy here, you must be completely done up.'

No-one had suggested before that Jim might be tired. His mother never felt tired and considered it a sign of mental weakness.

He sat on the bed thankfully.

'I don't usually come here on Saturdays. I go home instead. But I was hoping to have a word with Mr Fordham,' he said somewhat woefully.

The smiling man was all concern.

'And why would that be?' he enquired.

Jim found himself confessing his plan.

'Father won't let me stay on the railway if I don't get a good report from my first station master,' he concluded.

'Oh dear . . .' Passmore-Williams mimicked Jim's tone as well as his words. 'Oh dear, oh dear, oh dear. What are we going to do about that?' He smiled and patted Jim's knee. 'All is by no means lost, my boy. When I . . . er . . . left Mother Church, I bought several thriving enter-prises. One of which was the Valley Wool Mill.' He squeezed the knee gently. 'Tomorrow morning, your Mr Fordham will be settling his account with the Great Western Railway. And I will make sure the credit is yours. How does that sound?'

Jim stared at him in amazement. It was the sort of thing that happened in books, never in real life.

He stammered, 'Thank you, sir . . . thank you very much . . .'

'And in return . . .' the hand squeezed again, 'I would like you to let me know when your sister comes home.'

Jim swallowed. 'She may not, sir. She wants to be a famous singer and travel the world—'

'She will be home, Jim. Never fear. Just a note care of the Mill will find me.'

'But—'

'You are anxious about my intentions? Jim. Your father and I are old friends. And then we quarrelled. Over other friends. He finds it difficult – impossible – to forgive me. I was younger than he . . . hot-headed, I suppose. I have been looking for a way to make amends. I could help Sarah, perhaps.'

Jim was puzzled. Why Sarah and not Lizzie?

As if he picked up the thought Passmore-Williams swept on. 'I realized that day she had a voice. She sang to me, you know. And I feel . . .' His smile became humorous. 'You are old enough now, perhaps, to understand . . . Sarah is what is known as a handful. I think it would be good if she found a career . . . elsewhere.'

Jim knew just what he meant. His sister was as wild as a gypsy.

And then the door opened and Mr Meadows entered with a loaded tray.

He took in the scene and said, 'I thought you was never coming down, boy.'

Passmore-Williams released Jim's knee and stood up.

'It has been interesting to renew our acquaintance, James.' He ignored the tray and the landlord and reached beneath Jim's cowlick of hair. 'I will bless you, my child. I think I still have a right to do that.'

With his thumb he made a cross on Jim's forehead while the boy turned bright red.

Then he turned briskly to his supper.

'Excellent. Excellent, Landlord. And perhaps some apple pie . . .'

He had apparently forgotten Jim, who made good his escape and stood outside the inn, cooling down and wondering whether the strange man – after all a friend of Walter's at one time it seemed – would forget everything by the morning.

But he did not.

The trouble was, Mr Coles still did not approve of Jim James, and was heard to tell his wife to cut down on the 'young upstart's dinner'. But after a long and serious debate with his father, it seemed all was going to be well in any case.

'I can see how it is, Jim. Coles resents me – many railwaymen do, of course. Stick it if you can son. You will win him over in the end.'

Walter had listened to Jim's tale with an intensity of concentration that had worried Jim considerably. Now, piloting the boy from his office into the waiting-room, he added quite casually, 'You will, of course, never speak to Passmore-Williams again, Jim. As for his request – it is beneath contempt.'

'But, Pa—' Jim's grey eyes were full of questions.

'Ask no more, Jim. The man is obviously evil. I could not allow him near any of my family.' He paused and looked across the line to the up platform where Jack was lighting the oil lamps. 'And I think the whole episode should be between the two of us.' The hand on Jim's shoulder was rigid and Jim could see his father's neck muscles hard above his high, starched collar. 'You will not mention any of this to your mother. Is that understood?'

'Of course . . .' Jim almost stammered his assurance.

At last Walter's face relaxed.

'And of course, you will stay on the Great Western. As you wished.'

They went into the cold winter evening and around the ganger's shed to the Station House. Jim did not remember his father mentioning Passmore-Williams' name again. But somehow he always associated his job on the railway with the big fat man. Though he did not know why.

FIVE

1938

Kildie said, 'Dearest Hol! You must come and stay at the cottage! I can't possibly get married without you!'

Holly laughed, infected as always by Kildie's intensity. It had been such a shock to return from Swanage and hear that Kildie was getting married! Kildie, so beautiful, in age midway between Holly and Dorothy, like an actress in a play by Noël Coward, enslaving the young men, captured by none of them.

Holly said, 'How can I, Kildie? Of course I want to be your bridesmaid. But there's school starting in two weeks' time and anyway you've got your job at the bank—'

'Darling – Marcus wants me to give it up before we're even married! He doesn't believe in women working! He says I am a flower which must be cultivated with enormous care . . .' She bubbled into delighted laughter and was joined by Holly.

'But you won't give it up, will you? After all, there's the band and Bill and – and everything!' Kildie sometimes sang with a sextet of musicians, organized by one of her flames, Bill Masters, who worked at the bank. Bill was Holly's favourite of all Kildie's beaux. He might have lost Kildie's hand but surely not her co-operation with the band?

'Hol! What are you saying? Of course I must give up Bill! It's a shame, I know, but Marcus wouldn't stand for that!'

'Oh Kildie! That lovely black dress. And "Smoke gets in your Eyes"!'

Kildie looked better than Hedy Lamarr in her

off-the-shoulder black dress cut on the cross and swathing her slender figure like a caress.

'I know . . . I know . . .'

For a moment, Kildie's huge dark eyes stared unseeingly across the lawn to the bed of ferns and shells near the bottom wall. Marcus Villiers was a catch; there was no doubt about that. Partner in the five-storey department store which dominated Gloucester's old Cross, he had been too busy making money to do much in the way of socializing. There were rumours about him, of course. But she was practically certain she was the first girl to whom he had made a proper proposal of marriage. She couldn't let him slip through her fingers. And yet she knew it would mean giving up her old life entirely. Just for a moment she felt a terrible pang of regret and nostalgia. Then the excitement bubbled through her again and she hugged Holly convulsively.

'But I'll have a house in Cheltenham, darling! It's halfway up Leckhampton Hill with views right across the valley! And I'm allowed to furnish it just as I like! And I'll have my own car! Marcus is going to teach me to drive! Can you imagine it!'

'No.' Holly thought of their own modest villa in Hatherly Green, a peppercorn rent because it shared a septic tank with the whole terrace, but within cycling distance of Gloucester so that she and Dad could get to school and the office without incurring the expense of the bus. No-one in the family had ever possessed a car.

'I'll be able to meet you from school and bring you up for tea! Won't it be the greatest fun in the world?'

Holly stared down the garden in her turn. They were sitting under the glass veranda because a light rain was falling. The veranda had been one of the reasons Gran had wanted the cottage in the first place. It sheltered both outside lavatory and coal house and provided storage space for bikes and bags besides a good-sized henhouse. Above Holly's head hung the tin bath Gran used every Saturday night although she had a bathroom with a perfectly good geyser. To the left of the bath hung the wicker clothes basket and a peg bag lumpy with pegs. The veranda was criss-crossed with washing-lines for days such as this. It was completely private from the windows of the house and when Holly was small she had left the lavatory door open so that she could see the garden. As long as she could remember Kildie had been in this cottage with Gran. Grandad and Gran had bought it when they'd had to leave the Station House. First Grandad had gone, and now Kildie. Gran would be on her own.

She said, 'Gran will miss you.'

'I know.' Kildie sighed deeply. 'But life has to go on, darling.'

'That's what everyone said when Grandad died.'

Kildie sighed again and said, 'I know.' She hugged Holly a little less enthusiastically. 'Don't worry about Gran, sweetheart. She'll be all right here – Mrs Ball is next door and will let us know if she is ill. Not that Gran is ever ill.'

'What will happen if she is?' Holly asked fearfully.

'She can come and stay with me, of course!' Kildie brightened at the thought. 'My goodness, there are five bedrooms in Hill House! And Marcus says we can afford a maid! It will be like a hotel for her!'

Holly tried to imagine Gran in a hotel. She failed completely.

She said, 'Anyway. How did you meet Marcus Villiers? He's supposed to be a recluse, isn't he?'

'Darling, it was the most romantic thing. It was the first Saturday you were at Swanage. I'd gone into Villiers' to buy something for the tea-dance at the Cadena. Bill was playing and I was doing just two numbers. I knew exactly what I wanted: black, of course, with a really low waist and a tiny, tiny skirt.' She sketched a boxy shape in the air. 'I was going to wear my pearls – matching ear-rings – you know.'

Holly pursed her lips. 'Understated,' she commented knowledgeably.

'Exactly!' Kildie laughed. 'How wrong I was!'

'You mean—'

'I mean, Marcus came on to the floor just as I was doing a twirl in front of the glass. He just shook his head and told me I was in show business and should dress accordingly.'

Holly was round-eyed. 'I didn't know men were interested in clothes—'

'Oh he is. After all Villiers' started as a dress shop in Westgate Street, you know, long before they bought the department store.'

'Yes, Gran told me. So he must have known you?'

'Said he'd heard me sing twice, and I was the best thing about the band and shouldn't melt into the background.' Kildie pulled her mouth down. 'I'd never have worn what he suggested if he hadn't been Marcus Villiers. But, of course, I had no choice. I felt a bit . . . I don't know . . . odd. But it was quite a jazzy song. 'Anything Goes' – d'you know it?'

Holly sang a few bars and Kildie nodded.

'I finished with some dance steps and then sort of flung out one hand.' She demonstrated and the hens squawked a protest. She laughed and sat down again. Then she went on soberly, 'Well, he just stood up and took my outstretched hand and whirled me across the dance floor – it was the most amazing thing. I mean he's a man of the world, Hol. Older than me. Like John Barrymore actually. And he's so *rich*!'

'Yes,' Holly agreed.

'And he asked me that night. That very night! Can you believe it?'

'And you said yes?'

'Of course. How could I resist him? He wouldn't take a penny for the dress—'

Holly gasped. 'Does Gran know that?'

'Of course not! Don't you dare tell her!'

'I wouldn't! She'd kill you!'

'Especially if she saw the dress!' Kildie giggled.

'Why? What's it like?'

'I'll show you after tea. But don't you think it's the most romantic thing you've ever heard?'

'I suppose so. But Bill's asked you to marry him and you just laugh!'

'But he doesn't ask properly – I don't know if he's serious! He says things like, "When we're married we'll join a proper band" . . . you know Bill.'

'Yes.' Holly thought of Bill Masters. He had taught her to dance by letting her stand on his patent leather pumps all around the edge of the dance floor at the Cadena. She thought of his blond curls and his dark blue eyes and his fair Errol Flynn moustache and the way he played the piano, pumping the loud pedal and crossing his left hand over his right at every opportunity. She knew that he wanted to marry Kildie more than anything else.

She said, 'Does he know about Marcus?'

'Of course, darling! I've been engaged for three whole weeks now! Everyone at the bank knows about it! I've flashed my ring around like a hurricane lamp!'

'Oh Kildie . . .' Holly had to laugh in spite of poor Bill Masters.

'Come on, Hol. Let's go and make ourselves pretty for tea!'

Holly said gloomily, 'You mean, for Marcus Villiers! And I can't make myself pretty!'

Kildie kissed her swiftly. 'No. Because you're pretty already!' she said stoutly. And Holly loved her.

Marcus Villiers was as dark as Kildie, but where her eyes and face seemed mobile as if seen under water, his were set and still. His eyes were almost black but you could not see into them and they reflected no light at all. However, Holly had to admit that he was handsome. His black hair was brylcreemed into a shining cap, his moustache seemed painted on his upper lip, his jaw was firm, his nose wonderfully aquiline, his cheek-bones high and prominent. He was tall, his hands beautifully manicured and his manners impeccable.

'So this is the bridesmaid.' He took Holly's hand and bent over it as if he might kiss it. 'Perfectly charming.' Bent like that his eyes were on a level with hers and he smiled right at her. She glimpsed very white teeth and a very red tongue and felt herself flushing. 'Ah. A real English rose.' He squeezed her hand gently. 'May I choose a dress for her, Kildie?'

Kildie was unusually flirtatious. 'Are you trying to make me jealous?'

He straightened but he did not take his eyes from Holly's nor release her hand.

'If admiring your bridesmaid makes you jealous, then jealous you must be,' he said.

Gran said repressively, 'The teapot will be boiled dry if you don't come to table quickly! Holly, did you wash your hands?'

'Yes, Gran.'

'Then tell your mother to bring in the scones.'

Holly escaped thankfully to the kitchen where Dorothy was buttering scones and Jim was trying to wash away the grime of the office under the cold tap. Jim had just arrived on the three-fifteen from Gloucester: he had not wanted to come. He disapproved strongly of the sudden engagement and thought by ignoring it, it would go away.

Dorothy said irritably, 'I'm hurrying as much as I can! Trust your Gran to give me this job! She probably knew the damned things would crumble immediately they spotted a knife coming at them!' Jim turned blindly for a towel and knocked the offending knife to the floor. 'Honestly! Jim! Turning up at the last minute and getting in everyone's way—'

Holly handed her father the towel and looked at her mother tragically. 'I don't like him. Mum, if Grandad was here he'd tell him to clear off! I'm sure he would!'

'Darling, for goodness' sake!' Dorothy picked up the knife, wiped it furiously on the corner of Jim's towel and

90

set to again. 'You're as bad as your father! Kildie is twenty-three and capable of making up her own mind! Now carry these in and try to be nice. And as for you—' She turned to Jim, reached up to straighten his tie. 'Make up your mind that Kildie is no longer your baby sister. Come on, the pair of you! Best feet forward! He's the catch of the century! Be pleased for Kildie even if you hate him!'

And she herded her family into the dining-room.

In the event the tea party went swimmingly. Marcus Villiers had come from humble beginnings and was well able to talk to Gran about her hens and what she was saving on the price of eggs. He feigned an interest in subjects about which he knew very little, drawing her out about the fern garden and asking her to show him around and identify each specimen. One of the reasons he was so successful in business was his ability to 'cultivate' the right people. And to be utterly ruthless. He cultivated the James family with excellent results. If some of them, especially Holly and Jim, felt the iron hand behind his soft velvet glove, they decided it would be good for Kildie. She had always been protected; Marcus Villiers would continue that pattern. There was more to it than that, of course. As Dorothy said, quoting from some book or other, 'Perhaps it's simply that the rich are different.' Gran, placing her best china carefully into hot soda-water, agreed for once with her daughter-in-law. 'An' if our Kildie can have a bit of that difference, good luck to her!' she added.

Jim, retiring to the bathroom as soon as he could, watched Kildie making her fond farewells at the gate. Marcus Villiers' car, a dashing Morgan, waited in the lane and he was obviously recounting to her its finer points. Kildie arranged herself by the gatepost, probably for Mrs Ball's benefit, and smiled up into the dark face with just the right amount of tilt to her head.

Marcus said something and she straightened out of her pose and glanced anxiously backwards. Then she shook her head. Jim felt warm. The bounder had asked his sister to kiss him. In front of all the neighbours!

Marcus laughed, white teeth flashing beneath the small moustache. Then he extended one gloved hand, put it casually around Kildie's throat and drew her head to his. She struggled momentarily, then, quite suddenly, relaxed against him. Jim could almost hear her small gasp of surrender. He hated it. He hated it so much he trembled. And when the kiss went on and on he clenched his hands around the pipe of the cistern till he felt the whole contraption move.

At last Villiers released his hold and Kildie almost staggered back against the gatepost again. He did not wait to see whether she was all right. He was laughing like a blasted hyena as he climbed into the low car, fished out some goggles from somewhere and adjusted them. The car roared away in a cloud of dust and still Kildie stood there, one hand to her throat, the other to her mouth. Jim was horrified. It was as if he had witnessed her rape.

Kildie would not put the red frock on to show it off to Holly.

'I don't want you giving me your disapproving look like Aunt Lizzie,' she said, laughing but stubborn. 'It doesn't look too bad lying there on the bed.'

Holly surveyed it doubtfully. 'It's a bit like a lampshade,' she commented. 'Just a tube of frills.'

'Yes, darling. It's where the frills begin and where they end, that's what makes it so unusual.' Kildie kept on laughing. It was as if she could not stop.

Holly said, 'You were ages saying goodbye. Gran said Mrs Ball would have a grandstand view from her front room!'

'We gave her something to watch . . .' Kildie sat down suddenly on the bed. She picked up a handful of the satin material and hid her face in it. 'Honestly, Holly, Marcus is . . . so possessive! You should have heard what he said to me out there!'

'What? What?' Holly asked avidly.

'Oh, nothing really. You wouldn't understand. Just things like . . . he wants to own me body and soul . . . you know.'

'Oh.' Holly looked doubtful. 'Like the song, d'you mean?'

Kildie took a deep breath and controlled her giggles.

'Yes, of course. Just like the song,' she agreed.

1915

If Sarah and Lizzie James had not been twins it would have been difficult to believe they came from the same family. Sarah was the beauty; dark eyed with jet-black hair, she could sing like a lark and dance like a gypsy. When she was fifteen she begged off cleaning and cooking for the vicar and joined a concert party for a summer season. As the aptly named choir-mistress, Hope Chapel, also joined as the pianist, it was permitted. Miss Chapel's uncle ran the concert party. It was practically a family affair. And as Esme said to Walter, 'If we don't let her go with them, she'll go somewhere else without our permission.'

Lizzie was like her parents; 'a nut-brown maid' Walter called her. She was adept with knitting needles, crochet hooks, and embroidery frames. She played the piano for the Sunday School and took soup to sick old ladies in the winter. That year of 1914, she played and sang at the Grange for the Christmas party and fell in love with the Squire's nephew.

It was known in the village that Edwina Richardson, the Squire's sister, thankfully now dead and gone, had – many years ago – formed an unwise attachment to an itinerant poet. The son of that brief and unfortunate union had been brought up in the Grange, but had been kept very much in the background. There were all kinds of rumours about Edward; the only one that could be confirmed was

93

that he had recently been sent down from university and was in disgrace again.

Lizzie, of course, knew that he would never look at her and she prepared to contract consumption and die as quietly as she lived.

And then Sarah came home with a swollen abdomen and – so she said – an absent husband.

'He's had to go to France, Ma!' she wailed. 'I'll die without him! I know I'll die!'

Lizzie wondered if this was one thing they could do together like proper twins. Die.

'Is he a good man?' Emmie asked.

'Can he afford a wife and child?' Walter demanded.

'He's a saint, Ma. And his family owns a theatre in Margate, Pa! But more than that, he's so . . . so . . . oh, you know!' She began to weep. 'I'll wait for him for ever!'

Lizzie took her sister's hand and put it to her lips. At last she had the soul mate she had always felt cheated of.

But a week later it was all over the village that Gaffer Jenkins had caught Sarah in Red Marley churchyard with Alf Matson. Walter should have taken a strap to her, but he had never been that kind of a father. Instead, far more frighteningly, he blamed himself and would not speak to anyone, not even his wife.

'Pa . . .' Sarah sobbed. 'He made me! Honestly, he asked me to go and see the stone they've had made for his mother – two angels guarding a heart—'

Emmie glanced at Walter and when he said nothing she spoke up herself.

'How dare you concoct such lies—'

'It's true, Ma! I swear it! It's the third on the left past the pump—'

'And didn't it so much as cross your mind that it was a strange request at nine o'clock on a March night?'

'I was so bored! There's nothing to *do* here! And he reckoned he'd seen a ghost—' She stopped weeping and became defiant. 'Anyway, where's the harm! I can't get into trouble twice, can I?'

The silence was aghast. Into it came an audible groan from Walter.

'Dearest,' Emmie moved swiftly to his side and tried to put her arms around him. He would have none of it.

'I knew!' he spoke at last, not looking at Sarah. 'I knew the risk! And still I let her go off with that blasted concert party!'

'Hush, dear. Hush now . . .' It was as if Emmie was comforting a child. 'You *couldn't* know – and you put her in the charge of Miss Chapel. She would have gone anyway.'

'It's true, Pa!' Sarah herself was frightened now. Pa was making terrible sounds as if he might even be weeping. 'I would have gone. You couldn't have stopped me!'

Emmie knelt before Walter and held his two hands between her own.

'That is not the real trouble, Sarah, is it?' She looked past his head at the girl's face, tear-streaked but still defiant. 'You came home swearing undying love for your husband. Now it seems he is not your husband at all! And you care so little for him – whoever he is – that you allow yourself to be seduced for – apparently – a second time—'

'Ma, I'm sorry . . . I'm sorry, Ma . . .' Sarah sobbed, remorseful at last. Walter had always been a critical father, Emmie had been unusually indulgent with them. This criticism hit home.

Emmie said, 'Go upstairs now, please, Sarah. Don't speak to your sister or your brother. Sit in your room and think very carefully about what has happened. We will talk later.'

Sarah tried to say something to her father but Emmie would have none of it. 'Go upstairs. Now, Sarah,' she repeated. And, more chastened than she would have thought possible, Sarah went.

Emmie whispered, 'Come now, my dearest. You mustn't take it so much to heart. She's young and foolish and—'

He put his forehead on her shoulder wearily. 'It's in the

95

blood, Emmie,' he said in a low voice. 'In the blood. My father spoke the commandments every Sunday and I laughed at him, Emmie. Now . . . do you remember how he told us that God is a jealous God, visiting the iniquity of the fathers upon the children? Do you remember? She is without morals – just as I was—'

Emmie stroked his head to quieten him.

'What rubbish you do talk at times, Walter. We have brought the children up to be God-fearing and good. Do you really believe that God is a jealous God? I *know* he is not! Otherwise, I would not be so happy!' She raised him and sat him in his favourite chair by the fire.

He managed a smile and whispered, 'Emmie, I'm sorry. Sometimes, it is such a burden.'

'Listen, dearest. Give me that burden. I will carry it. Gladly. And lightly.'

'Oh Em . . . I have asked too much already—'

'Wasn't that the bargain?'

'Em – you are so good – so very good . . .'

She kissed him and soothed him and later made tea and toast and Lizzie and Jim came in and they ate it together. Nobody mentioned Sarah's absence. Lizzie's face was long and shocked; she must have heard something in the village. It was hard to tell whether Jim knew anything. He had already joined the Great Western Railway as a lad clerk and lodged at Brimscombe in the week. Emmie looked at his enormous grey eyes so like her own, and his long fingers, fine like Walter's. And then she looked at Walter who, in spite of still being a humble station master, was real gentry. Sometimes she felt so full of love she could hardly bear it. It did not matter that what he felt for her was gratitude.

Lizzie was shocked for two reasons. The first was because the bowl of soup she had taken to the witch-like Miss Protheroe, who had done sewing at the big house, had been thrown on the back of the fire with the statement that Miss Protheroe refused to eat any food prepared in a

96

house of ill-fame. The second was because Miss Protheroe performed this histrionic act before another visitor to her tiny cottage. The visitor was Edward Richardson, the young man for whom Lizzie was dying of love.

Lizzie stammered, 'I don't know what you mean, Miss Protheroe! I thought you had influenza and my mother had some good beef stock and I—'

'Like mother like daughter, I shouldn't wonder!' Miss Protheroe was thoroughly enjoying herself. She cast a sidelong glance at the young man who was as red as Lizzie. 'Sixteen and expecting a baby! And then found half-naked with that awful Alfred Matson – himself married with half a dozen children—'

Lizzie waited no longer. Clapping her palms to her cheeks she rushed outside into the March rain and leaned against the wall of the cottage. And it was there she heard all about her young man.

Miss Protheroe must have turned immediately to him because she was saying ingratiatingly, 'I do apologize, Master Edward, for that unpleasant little scene—'

And then he interrupted. His voice was very deep for one so young. It had a rough Gloucestershire burr to it. It sent shivers down Lizzie's spine. The actual words sent further shivers. She shook as if with the ague.

'You enjoyed that little scene almost as much as you enjoyed telling me of my parentage when I was just a child, didn't you, Proth?'

Miss Protheroe said, 'I don't know what you mean, Master Edward! The truth will out and I think I was the best person to tell you—'

'And the best person to tell little Miss James about her sister?'

'They all think they're almost gentry! It won't hurt her to be sent packing for once. Her and her soup!'

'Compared with you, the pigs are gentry, Proth! And don't you forget it! You're a gossip-mongering old bitch! Self-righteous too! Just because no man ever wanted to tickle you in Kempley churchyard—'

'I wouldn't let Alf Matson near me, let alone . . .' She stopped speaking as Edward Richardson barked a laugh, then said, 'It was Red Marley. Not Kempley.'

'Never mind where it was! Just forget it! D'you understand? If I hear that anyone's been spreading this around the village, I'll know who to blame!'

She said sulkily, 'Everyone knows already. Nothing to do with me.'

Lizzie hung her head and hot tears joined the raindrops coursing down her face. The shame of it! The bitter shame!

Edward Richardson then said something very rude, so rude that Lizzie's hands, which had been covering her ravaged face, automatically slid to her ears and stoppered them. She did not hear Master Edward slam out of the cottage until he was standing by her and actually pulling one of the hands down.

'Miss James, isn't it?' He sounded quite different. Courteous . . . formal. As if they had just been introduced at a garden party in the vicarage.

She could not reply. Her mortification was complete as a very large raindrop ran down her nose and hung on its end.

He said, 'I am Edward Richardson. Son of Miss Edwina Richardson and Adrian Frost.' He sagged at the knees so that he could peer under the brim of her hat. 'I expect you have heard what they say about my mother. And me. And you are embarrassed. Please don't be. Try to understand and forgive.'

Lizzie had the strangest feeling he was referring to Sarah's disgrace as well as his mother's.

She whispered, 'Of course. I would not dream . . . please . . .'

'Then prove your forgiveness by allowing me to walk you home. See? I have an umbrella.' He produced it and began to open it. Without knowing how or why she found herself walking back down the muddy lane towards the Station House, holding his arm, listening to his deep, deep voice telling her the most amazing things.

'You see, I am not responsible for the behaviour of my parents, any more than you are responsible for the behaviour of your sister. But I will say this much, Miss James: I am not ashamed of my mother. She gave herself to the man she loved. What is wrong in that? Unfortunately she was seen to do it, and that is where the shame came in. Garden of Eden all over again, don't you think?'

She made a sound. She was quite unable to form words.

He went on meditatively, as if thinking aloud. 'The mistake she made was in accepting her brother's patronage. If she had moved away – or even had me adopted – it might have been better. As it was I came home for the holidays and was neither one thing nor the other. People like that frightful bitch Miss Protheroe—' He paused at her gasp and then laughed. 'She really is, isn't she? You know, she doesn't deserve your soup. Now I'd simply love it. Would you make me some?'

She made another sound which he took for assent.

'Thank you. Bring it to the stable loft tomorrow, will you? That's where I live now I've finished university. I help Jem with the horses and earn my keep in the stables just as my mother earned hers as unpaid housekeeper.'

They arrived at the gate of the Station House. The lamp was lit in the kitchen and she could see Sarah sitting at the table, her head on her arms. She shivered again.

Edward Richardson opened the gate and armed her into the porch.

He smiled at her. He was very English, with a round face and slightly bulldog jaw. It was his conventionality that had attracted her at Christmas. Now it was his unconventionality. She simply adored him.

He put his mouth to her ear and whispered, 'Don't be too hard on your sister, little Lizzie. And come to see me tomorrow. Six o'clock. Without fail.'

She watched him hurry down the path, his umbrella resting on his shoulder. His Norfolk jacket was heavy with water around the hem and his breeches soaked. She wished she could take him some soup tomorrow; it was out of the question. She wondered whether Sarah, pregnant and in double disgrace now, would do it for her.

When Kildie was born it was Lizzie who suggested the adoption. She remembered what Edward Richardson had said to her that wonderful night in March. If his mother had gone away or had him adopted, it would all have been easier.

'If you stay here, everyone will remember what happened. If you go away and let Ma and Pa adopt her, people might forget. And anyway they won't blame Ma or Pa, will they?'

Sarah laughed lightly. 'Anyone would think poor little Kildie is illegitimate!'

Lizzie tightened her lips and when Sarah continued to smile tauntingly, she said, 'You have no wedding certificate. That ring is turning your finger green—'

'Lizzie, it simply does not matter! Well, only to you! You want me to go away for your own reasons, don't you? Are you afraid I shall seduce your bastard lover? Is that it? You know I could get young Master Edward by clicking my fingers at him! I should think you'd have more pride – he's been with every girl within a ten-mile radius of the village—'

She stopped on a loud squawk because Lizzie's nails were raking her face. Emmie, entering with clean napkins, separated them with difficulty.

'Stop it at once, you girls! What on earth is the matter with you? If you're going to live under this roof you must learn to stop your incessant arguing.'

'She called my baby illegitimate, Ma! Then when I told her about some of the antics of her Master Edward, she—'

'That's enough, Sarah. I dare say you started it.'

'I did not—'

'Actually, Ma,' Lizzie looked pious, 'I suggested that she should let you and Pa adopt Kildie.'

Emmie looked startled.

'Adopt the child? We're too old to start again, Lizzie. Besides, Sarah would never agree to it.'

'I didn't disagree,' Sarah said slowly.

Emmie stared at her, then down at the baby. Kildie was like her mother, dark and already exquisite. She would need a good family, protection, great care. Emmie felt her heart leap at the prospect of another child. A girl baby too.

She whispered as if afraid of being heard. 'I don't know what your father would say, girls.'

But they both knew that Emmie wore the trousers.

They all adored Kildie. Jim, home at weekends, nursed her tenderly through teething. At twenty years of age he was accepted into the Control Office at Gloucester. Kildie was seven years old and she made him a cake to celebrate his promotion. He talked to her as if she were grown up.

Lizzie had enjoyed wheeling her out in her high perambulator. It gave Edward lots of ideas and he tried time and time again to lure her into his room above the stable. Even after the war, when he had 'done his bit' in the War Office for a couple of years, she still held out. He was forced at last to ask her to marry him.

Squire Richardson sent for Walter.

'I couldn't ask better for the boy,' he said bluffly, shaking Walter's hand and offering him the best port in recognition of his clerical background. 'I've been his guardian, as you must know. Wanted a good match for him – respectability at least. But it wasn't going to be easy. Your little girl is just the ticket!'

Walter had never given the Squire much thought; suddenly he disliked him. Lady Alicia was not in the room and Emmie had not been invited.

The Squire said, 'There's a cottage on the estate – the boy is a decent enough farmer – your girl can help in the house.'

Walter said smoothly, 'I rather thought a farm of their own might be a good start. I believe in self-sufficiency, as

101

you know. Lizzie would be an excellent housekeeper and she could see to the poultry. I think it would be good for Edward to be independent of all . . . this . . .' He swept his arm around the drawing-room, exquisitely furnished by Lady Richardson.

The Squire's colour flamed. 'I don't think you can expect me to provide for my sister's by-blow, James old man—'

Walter hung on to his temper. 'Leave it with me,' he said. He turned immediately and made for the door. 'I have some capital and will need to talk to my wife.'

He left the Squire speechless.

It was Emmie who suggested contacting Edward's father, the now famous poet, Adrian Frost. Together – from sheer curiosity – they had read some of his poetry, and were surprised to find they both liked it.

'He understands the countryside,' Emmie stated definitely. 'And he knows about kindness . . . gentleness. Write to him, Walter.'

There was no reply to Walter's letter, but amazingly, the man arrived at Dymock station two days later and found Walter in the station master's office.

'My name is Frost, Adrian Frost. I am Edward's father. You wrote to me.'

Walter stood up but still had to raise his eyes to this enormous man. With his long hair, thick beard, and voluminous clothes it was as if he were in some kind of disguise.

He said, 'I did. I've read your stuff. I thought you would want to help.'

'Very perspicacious of you, James. Especially as I've had nothing to do with Edward since his birth.'

'Squire Richardson's conditions, so I understand,' Walter said.

'Aye.' The large loose-limbed man sounded gloomy. Then he smiled so that his whole face emerged from the surrounding growth like a sun. 'However, it sounds as though things have changed. So how can I help the young couple?'

Walter said, 'There is a farm for sale on the Kempley Road. Mostly fruit, but I think pigs and poultry would do well too. It would be something of an investment. I can manage fifty pounds—'

'My dear sir—' Adrian Frost took Walter's hand in both of his and proceeded to pump it vigorously. 'My dear sir, only too pleased . . . Teddy would never let me set her up in her own home – clung to her brother like a limpet to a rock. This is my chance to make reparation.'

'Teddy?' Walter asked.

'Edwina. The boy's mother. I couldn't leave my own litter – but they're all off my hands. Have been for years now. About time I did my duty to the other one! Only too pleased . . . glad you got in touch.'

'It was my wife's suggestion,' Walter said smiling.

'She sounds sensible. Hold on to her. I lost mine,' he looked around the small parlour, '. . . somewhere or other,' he added vaguely. 'Anyway, let's meet the happy pair and go and inspect this farm. Hey?'

Walter beamed. Emmie's instinct had been right as usual. They walked round to the garden of the Station House where Emmie was seeing to her hens. She rose to meet them, flustered because she had her morning apron on and a sun-bonnet that had seen much better days. Walter made the introductions and she could tell that he was happy.

'If you'd let us know you was coming . . .' Her grammar always went wrong when she needed to make a good impression.

But he bent over her hand so that his long hair swept her work-worn knuckles.

He murmured, 'Ah . . . the original earth mother.'

'Beg pardon?' she said glancing down at her pinafore which was not – after all – that dirty.

He stepped back and surveyed her and there was no missing the appreciation on his large-featured face.

'You are truly beautiful, madam,' he announced.

And then Emmie realized he was one of those Bohemians who were all as mad as hatters.

She said tartly, 'Well, I think you need to get your hair cut!'

He laughed inordinately and, through it all, Walter said, 'I think Lizzie is going to be all right, Em.'

And Emmie, staring at the laughing madman before her, nodded.

SIX

1938

Kildie's wedding was to be the first week in October.

'It's absolutely crazy,' Jim said to Dorothy as she pinned a row of tucks down the bodice of Holly's dress. 'Six weeks ago they barely even knew each other!'

Dorothy took the last pin from her mouth and inserted it with great care. This particular taffeta seemed to puncture when she pinned it. She wondered whether the pins were blunt. Or perhaps she should have insisted on silk. She frowned; dressmaking was one of the things she couldn't do. If only Lizzie hadn't gone to the other side of the country, she could have taken this on. Trust Jim's sisters not to be around when they were needed.

Jim said, 'I spoke to Villiers. Let him know that since Pa died I'm Kildie's guardian—'

'You're what?' Dorothy stared at him in astonishment. 'Kildie's guardian? She's twenty-three, Jim!'

'He just laughed. Said they couldn't wait.'

'Dear Lord! You're lucky he didn't punch you on the nose! Of all the cheek!'

'I don't see it like that, Dorothy. The man is old enough to be her father—'

'So long as he'd had her at sixteen!' But she did not go back to her sewing just yet. Jim never called her Dorothy, always the hated Doll. He was serious.

'I don't see how you can treat it so lightly. As you say, she is twenty-three. But she's never done anything – never been anywhere – since Pa died she's been closeted with Gran—'

'For goodness' sake, Jim! What did *we* do? Where did

we go? She's had a good job at the bank – she's gone out and about with that band—'

'I tried to squash that. It was very like her mother.'

Dorothy let her breath out in a gasp of exasperation.

'Jim, I know you feel responsible for her. But surely you can see that a slightly older man such as Marcus Villiers—'

'He's forty.'

'Not till next year. And because he is older he is in a good financial position—'

'Money doesn't matter.'

'It does to Kildie. She doesn't just like nice clothes, she needs them.' She went to him and put her arms around him. 'Darling, surely you can see it was simply not on to talk to Marcus like that. He'll see you in the wrong light and that might make it difficult for Kildie. Later on.'

'He'll take it out on her, d'you mean? Yes – you're right, by golly! That's the sort of man he is!' Jim would have liked to have told Dorothy about the kiss, but he could not find the words. 'I should have spoken to her.'

Dorothy dropped her arms and went back to the table. She had always been very fond of Kildie James. But Jim's attitude was much too possessive. She started on another tuck.

'Anyone would think we were talking about an imminent disaster instead of a wedding,' was all she said.

'That's how I see it, Dorothy. A disaster.'

'How you can talk like that after the Munich business, I do not know. *That* is a disaster!'

'But that doesn't affect us. This does.'

She could have warmed to him again; he was such a deeply family man and one day he would care as much – more – about Holly's future. But then he moved past her to the door and commented, 'That tuck isn't straight by the way.' And he was gone. She could have screamed.

He was on early turn and when he left work at two, he went to the Cadena with the guest list and placings. He should have got on his bike and gone straight home after that, but instead he hung about outside the bank until Kildie emerged and suggested a cup of tea before her train to Dymock.

She glanced over her shoulder to where Bill Masters was arming one of the young female tellers towards his ancient car.

'He's trying to show me he doesn't care,' she said to Jim. 'Honestly, he's so childish.'

She was delighted to have tea with Jim. They walked up George Street and chatted to the ticket collector who had known Walter James well, and then they went into the refreshment room. Jim surveyed the rock cakes beneath the glass bell without favour.

'Reminds me of the summer Doll came to Dymock,' he said glumly. 'I used to have tea here so that I could go straight to school and meet her.'

'I remember that. I must have been about nine. I adored her.' Kildie hugged his arm in the impulsive, little-girl way she had. 'Wasn't it fun when we were all together, Jim? D'you remember the spider? And the velocipede?'

Jim smiled at last. 'Of course. How could I forget?'

'But why a few fly-blown rock buns should remind you of that time, I can't imagine!' Kildie was laughing. She was laughing too much these days. Probably nerves.

'The weather too.' They sat down and waited for their tea to be brought to them. 'It's another Michaelmas summer.'

Kildie said eagerly, 'For my wedding. That's a good omen, isn't it?' She took Jim's hand. 'It couldn't be more romantic, could it, Jimbo? How one's life can be turned upside-down in such a short time—' She shook her head, laughing again.

'Kildie, are you sure you want it turned upside-down like this?' Jim leaned back to make room for the tea tray. The waitress held out her hand for the money and he counted out four silver threepenny bits. All the time Kildie did not release his fingers. Her childishness was utterly endearing.

He leaned forward again. 'Don't you think it's all rather sudden? Why can't you wait and have a spring wedding next year? What's the mad rush?'

'It's Marcus. I think he's afraid of losing me.' She laughed again but looked slightly embarrassed. 'He keeps saying he can't wait much longer . . . you know . . . silly things like that.'

Her face was pink. Jim tightened his hold reassuringly.

'Listen, Kildie. If you think it's too sudden you must *make* him wait.'

There was a pause. He realized suddenly that she had indeed tried to delay the wedding. She picked up the metal teapot and her new engagement ring grated on the handle.

She said in a small voice, 'I might lose him then.'

'Ah.'

Jim watched the dark brown liquid fill the teacups. He helped himself to milk. They both sipped sedately. It was very awkward to do everything with one hand but neither of them made a move to release the other.

He said quietly, 'You know he's blackmailing you in a way, Kildie.'

'Only because he loves me so much.'

'Do you love him just as much?'

'I don't know, Jim.' Her voice was deliberately childish now, and pathetic. 'I know I love you. But this is something different.' She put her cup down with a clatter. 'This is exciting. And dangerous.'

'Yes.'

Jim, forced to consider the nature of love, felt himself in very deep water. He said slowly, 'I love you too, Kildie. And I would never use my love to force you into something *I* wanted. Do you see what I mean?'

Obviously she did not because she said in a high voice, 'You don't love me, Jim. Not really.'

'Yes, I do.' He kept his voice completely steady somehow. There was a strange burning in his chest from drinking the hot tea. She was so vulnerable. So much like her mother in many ways; so much like Pa in others.

He went on firmly, 'We are more than uncle and niece, Kildie. More than brother and sister even.'

'You have always looked after me, Jimbo.' Tears formed in her beautiful eyes. 'I was so jealous when you married Dolly. But you went on looking after me.'

'Were you?' he was sidetracked momentarily.

'You never shut me out. We were always a threesome. D'you remember?'

'Yes. Of course,' he repeated. 'The spider . . . the velocipede.'

'It'll go on being like that, won't it, Jimbo?' she was pleading now. 'That won't change?'

'Do *you* think it will change?'

'No! No, I don't! Marcus is at business all day and I'm going to learn to drive so in the day I can come to the Green and we can go bluebell picking . . . or we can all go to Dymock for the daffs . . . Gran can come and stay . . .' She gripped his hand really hard and shook it gently. 'Nothing will change, Jimbo! It will be wonderful – even better!'

He looked into her eyes and knew that she was frightened. He said urgently, 'Don't do it, Kildie! Please don't marry Marcus Villiers. He's too old – too experienced—'

She said tensely, 'Shall we run away, Jim? Shall we run somewhere abroad? Just the two of us?'

He felt suddenly as he had felt years ago when he met Dolly first. As if he'd come suddenly upon a precipice and might easily tumble into its depths.

'Don't be silly, darling! How could we do that? What about Doll? And Holly?'

She laughed again. 'I was only joking! Silly! Of course I'm going to marry my darling Marcus! And we're still going to have such fun! Just you wait and see!'

Holly sat among the bean sticks and told herself she was being absolutely ridiculous to conjure up Blanche Cooke, when all she had to do was to sit and think about the wedding as if she were running a film through her head. But that wouldn't be quite enough; she badly needed a confidante and though her school friends were avidly interested in the wedding it was all for the wrong reasons. 'Where are they going for their honeymoon?' and 'D'you think they'd actually done it already?' were just two of the questions Holly found utterly irrelevant.

Blanche cut through all the prevarications and was suddenly there, settling herself down, chewing a tough left-over bean. Holly waited no longer; she went into an immediate description of the dresses, the hats, the flowers, and Kildie's stunning beauty.

'How did Gran take it?' Blanche asked very relevantly indeed.

'Well, not too bad.' Holly frowned, thinking back. 'For one thing she wore grey. It was such a shock to see her out of her funeral clothes—'

'Funeral clothes – the funeral was eight years ago!' Blanche reminded her.

'Well . . . not funeral clothes. Just black. She always, always wears black.'

'I know,' Blanche said gloomily.

'But she was in grey. It was a kind of silvery grey.' Holly paused, narrowing her eyes against the autumn sun coming through the practically bald sticks. 'D'you know, Blanche, she looked . . . beautiful.'

'*Gran?*' Blanche sounded incredulous.

'Yes. Gran. She looked regal. She reminded me of Queen Mary. And she wore a hat like Queen Mary.'

'Toque,' Blanche said.

'Yes. A toque. With veiling and things. And her hair sort of fluffed around it.'

'How did she get it to fluff up?'

'Tongs. Kildie did it for her.'

'Why didn't Aunt Lizzie do it? She was staying with you, after all.'

'Yes.' Holly straightened and sucked her lower lip. She

wasn't quite sure whether to tell Blanche about Aunt Lizzie and Aunt Sarah because she was not quite certain of her facts.

Blanche went on inexorably, 'Aunt Sarah turned up in the church and everyone thought she was going to stop the wedding!'

Sometimes Holly forgot that Blanche knew everything she knew herself, and just for a moment she looked up, surprised. Then she laughed.

'Yes.' This was something she definitely could not tell her school friends. 'Mum reckons Uncle Edward and Aunt Lizzie have had to do a moonlight flit! From the farm in the Fens, you know. She says Uncle Edward should be a poet not a farmer. He loves the land but he can't do his accounts properly. He owes a lot of money to a lot of people. So he loaded all their stuff on a lorry and drove them all through the night and they arrived on Friday morning. I'd already gone to school. Mum said Winnie was crying and Charlie hardly spoke a word. They wanted to stay here, with us, but Uncle Edward had to go and see the Squire, *his* uncle.' She shrugged her incomprehension. 'Anyway Aunt Lizzie said she couldn't face Gran till after the wedding. So she and Winnie stayed with us and Uncle Edward and Charlie went to Dymock to Gran. Poor Kildie nearly died! All this happening when she was getting ready for her wedding!'

'Are they all staying with Gran now?'

'Yes. Uncle Edward says his real father disowned him and his uncle is ashamed of him—'

'Is that true?'

'I don't think so. His real father gave Uncle Edward lots – all – his money, but Uncle Edward lost it. Adrian Frost is a famous poet but it said in the paper he died a pauper.'

'Poor man.' Blanche spat out the bean and edged closer to Holly. 'Now tell me about Aunt Sarah, Kildie's mum.'

Holly too changed position on the hard-baked earth. She drew her school cardigan over her chest; the sun was already on the tops of the elms in the bluebell field. She should have changed out of her school uniform, but Mum wasn't at home and she'd taken her milk and biscuits straight down to the bottom of the garden to talk to Blanche. Her head positively seethed with the events of the past few days.

'Well . . .' She tried to remember what she knew about the mysterious Aunt Sarah. 'After Kildie was adopted by Gran and Grandad, I think Aunt Sarah went to London and became a singer. And sometimes she is in plays – in the theatre, you know. But her heart is still in Dymock. When Grandad died she came back for the funeral and did a lot of crying.'

'Remorse,' Blanche said tersely.

'She was still really beautiful. I remember her. Just. I was five. Kildie was fifteen . . . Oh it was so sad.'

'Well, of course. Grandad dying—'

'Yes, of course. That. But it was more than that. Aunt Sarah did not hear about Grandad dying till it was almost too late to come to the funeral. She drove all through the night and when she saw Gran throw her wedding ring into the grave . . . oh, she was broken hearted. Kildie wanted to go and live with her mother. Aunt Sarah has a big house in London. But no-one has seen it. And Kildie said she'd go back with her—'

'But Kildie had started at the bank then.'

'I know. She said she would be able to get transferred.'

'Poor Gran,' commented Blanche.

'She never knew. I'm sure she never knew. Aunt Sarah turned the whole idea down, so Kildie never told her.'

'Oh dear. Poor Kildie.'

'She cried and cried. And Gran kept crying about Grandad. It was awful – just awful. But then Kildie got to know Bill Masters and they started the band. And I used to stay with Gran a lot . . .'

'Poor Holly.'

'Not a bit of it,' Holly said stoutly. 'We went on making the fern garden. And Gran taught me to knit and things.

And we'd sit by the grave and she'd tell me stories about Grandad. He was a very learned man was my Grandad.'

'So you've told me. Often,' Blanche said rather gloomily. 'Go on about Aunt Sarah, is she still with everyone else at Dymock?'

'She had to get back to London. She wanted me to go with her. She said she'd fallen in love with me!' Holly giggled selfconsciously.

'What about at the *church*?' Blanche insisted.

'Oh. Well. Of course Kildie sent her an invitation. But there was no reply so we all thought she was touring with a play. Anyway, Kildie and Dad and me arrived at Dymock Church. Dad looked as if he was going to die at any moment. Kildie looked just wonderful. Like a Spanish princess. You should have seen Marcus' eyes light up when he turned to watch her come down the aisle. Dad wanted to kill him.'

'How d'you know that?'

'I just do. Anyway when we got up to him, she turned to give me her bouquet and I saw her eyes go all big and black – you know how they do – she must have seen Aunt Sarah then. I bent down to arrange the train and then I saw her too.'

Holly paused and Blanche said, 'Go on!'

'She looked wonderful. More beautiful than Kildie even. She had a hat like Robin Hood's only in white silk. And a white silk coat over a powder-blue dress. And powder-blue shoes with heels like this—' She measured off at least twelve inches with her hands. 'And huge silver bracelets and . . . and . . . everything.'

'Sounds as if she wanted to make an impression. Did she forbid the marriage or something?'

'No. But I could tell that's what Kildie was thinking. When the vicar said, "Therefore if any man can show any just cause, why they may not lawfully be joined together, let him now speak or else hereafter forever hold his peace" Kildie's back was rigid. Absolutely rig . . . id.'

'Golly,' said Blanche.

'But of course it was all right. And she said she'd sent an RSVP and it must have got lost in the post. But of course she didn't. It didn't matter. She's like a whirlwind. Like a beautiful, beautiful whirlwind. Like a princess. Like a gypsy. A gypsy princess.'

'You ought to write a poem about her.'

'Oh, I have. It starts, "Queen of my Heart from whence camest thou. Where goest thou? From mist-morning to dusk-evening I will remember—" '

'Sounds good,' Blanche interrupted.

'It stresses her mystery.'

'That makes two of them.'

'Aunt Lizzie isn't mysterious.'

'No, but he is. Uncle Edward. Fancy having a father who was a famous poet.'

'We're doing him at school actually. Adrian Frost, pastoral poet.'

'Did Aunt Sarah fall in love with him too? Uncle Edward?'

Holly blushed. It had crossed her mind once or twice that Aunt Sarah was making up to Uncle Edward. And he had just loved it too. But she hadn't voiced those thoughts. They were adulterous thoughts and you could be punished for thoughts as well as deeds.

'There's Mum. I'd better go.' Mum's arrival on her bike made Holly realize all over again how absolutely childish she was being. She stood up briskly and shook the dry dirt off her school dress. Even so, Blanche – quite unbidden – spoke.

'OK. Sweet dreams.'

Holly ignored her. For one thing she wasn't really there. And for another Holly didn't like to be reminded of her dreams. They were indeed sweet and quite numerous too. Previously they had concerned Bill Masters. Now they somehow included her cousin Charlie, who, according to Aunt Lizzie, took after his paternal grandfather; Uncle Edward, who was so sweet and kind it melted her heart completely; and now, of course, Aunt Sarah. Life was getting complicated. But wonderfully fascinating. Holly just hoped she wasn't going really mad before anything could come of it all.

She glanced over her shoulder as she struggled out from the wigwam of bean sticks. Thankfully, Blanche wasn't there.

1915

Edward Richardson learned of his mother's shamelessness when he was sixteen, by which time Edwina was dead and therefore forgiven. In fact, Edward had always been treated as the son of the household. His aunt and uncle were childless and would have adopted him legally except that Edwina chose to defy convention and claim him as her own. But when Edward discovered what had happened, he played up to it for all he was worth. He was a natural actor and rather enjoyed the idea of being the bastard son of the Squire's sister. He took to spending a lot of time with the gamekeepers and stablemen, letting it be known that the Squire thought that was all he was fit for. He let his imagination run freely on the scenes of his conception. When Miss Protheroe told him that his father was a famous poet, it was grist to his mill. He visualized Edwina and Adrian together in a field, stark naked. Adrian Frost with his gaggle of children and his two wives, holidaying in Dymock with the American poet Robert Frost, meeting the aristocratic artist who was also the Squire's sister, seducing her without difficulty, then tossing her aside like a soiled glove.

When he confronted his uncle for the facts that Miss Protheroe did not know, he was told that the 'bounder Frost' had tried unsuccessfully to set Edwina up in yet another of his households, but she had declined.

Uncle Charles was bluff about the whole thing.

'When you go up to Cambridge, you'll realize, old chap, life is not the simple affair we make of it down here. Life throws up some strange characters and you will meet many of them at university. Adrian Frost was a law unto himself. I believe he imagined he was a latter-day Byron. Not so much immoral as amoral. He would have cared for you had Edwina wished it. But she did not.'

Edward did not wait to go up to Cambridge. He was the son of a poet and a wanton and he experimented sexually throughout Dean Forest. By the time he went up to King's he had sown a number of wild oats and was looking for something else. Something different. Something that would give meaning to his strangely empty life – because he had inherited neither his father's talent for 'versifying' nor his mother's love of painting. He was full of vague longings which were not satisfied by clandestine eroticism. He had started to dream of a pure woman; a pure love; family life.

He was sent down after a year and was in disgrace at the Grange. During his absence the Squire had received two visits from irate farmers in St Briavels and Coleford respectively. They both maintained that their daughters had been interfered with and had produced sons. Edward was named.

The Squire placated them with sums of money and told them that Edward must have been still sixteen at the time of the seductions. They left and did not return, but Squire Richardson was by now thoroughly disenchanted with his nephew.

Rather than kick his heels in the cold and unfriendly Grange, Edward again took to more menial tasks, enjoying the sense of martyrdom and injustice by turns. He helped on the home farm; he went out with the gamekeeper and fed the pigs.

And then came the Christmas party of 1914. He had always managed to get out of these 'family' affairs, but he was considering joining up in the New Year and this Christmas could well be his last.

He spotted the pianist immediately. She was dark; her hair pulled back like one of the Brontë sisters. The collar of her blouse was very high, making her neck look positively swan-like. He noticed her hands; long and thin. She looked far more aristocratic than his aunt. He enquired her identity.

His aunt said dismissively, 'That's one of the twins from the Station House. Lizzie James.'

'She plays well.'

'Yes. The sister sings. She's gone off with some concert party. They're like two sides of a coin: wicked and good.'

He was fascinated. He imagined having them both. A life of the mind and the body.

His aunt said sharply, 'Don't get ideas, Teddy! Her father might be just the station master, but he is an unusual man. A scholar. A gentleman. They are no ordinary family.'

That made the situation more fascinating than ever. When they played Oranges and Lemons he made sure he was standing right next to her. He could see the line of her chin and her black lashes moving up and down between the music and the keys. He wanted her so much he thought he might explode there and then.

His aunt must have had a word with his uncle, because after Christmas when he was still trying to face the prospect of the trenches, he was sent to Hereford to study farming methods at a dairy farm just outside the city. He obeyed his uncle; he could join up at any time.

But even at the farm, with the attractions of the dairy maid right under his nose, he could not rid himself of the image of Lizzie. He went to the Cathedral one day and saw Canon James's name on a brass commemorative plate in one of the niches. He made enquiries. Canon James was Lizzie's grandfather. Lizzie's mother had been Canon James's housekeeper. He was more intrigued than ever.

When he returned to the Grange the village was buzzing with the news of Sarah James's behaviour.

He waited until his uncle and he were in the smoking-room after dinner.

'Are you going to sack Matson?' he asked directly,

bypassing the questions he really wanted to ask. 'Because if so, I'd like to apply for the job.'

'My dear boy, Matson is one of the gamekeepers—'

'I've got to start somewhere, Uncle. Are you going to sack him?'

'Of course not. His lechery is nothing to do with me.'

This was almost laughable. Everything had something to do with the squire of a village. The truth was Alf Matson was good at his job and could not be spared.

Edward raised his brows. 'But I understand it was the station master's daughter. I understood from my aunt that the family are gentle folk.'

'This one – Sarah – is a throw-back. Wanton. Utterly wanton. She comes home pregnant, and the next thing we hear is . . . this. In the cemetery too, would you believe.'

Edward almost smiled at the way he had inveigled the story from Uncle Charles without asking any direct questions. He wondered whether Sarah or Alf had chosen Red Marley churchyard. He had used it himself in the past. It was a very theatrical setting for a seduction. Alf Matson had no imagination; it must have been Sarah's idea. He almost smiled again.

He went to see Miss Protheroe because he wanted to know how the two unlikely lovers had been discovered. For one thing, he might need to know for personal reasons if the sexton had taken to making regular rounds with a storm lantern. For another, he had a curious wish to find a parallel between Sarah James and his own delinquent mother. Had Sarah and Alf Matson been stark naked as had Adrian and Edwina? Was there some kind of pattern that was being repeated and would be including him, Edward Richardson at some point? During his brief time at Cambridge he had taken up with a group of fatalists who called themselves the Predestines. He found himself constantly testing out their theories of predestination. After all, if they were right, there seemed little point in making much of an effort to do anything. It would happen whatever he did or did not do.

So Lizzie's arrival and expulsion from Protheroe's cottage was at once a shock and yet all of a piece. He had never liked Proth – she had relished telling him the truth about his parentage during his puberty – and he thoroughly enjoyed the excuse to get into a tearing rage and rout her completely. When he left the cottage and found Lizzie cowering under its eaves in the rain, it was another piece of the puzzle which he hardly needed to affix. It was simply happening. Here was his shining light; his symbol of goodness and purity. And, waiting in the station master's cottage, was 'the other side of the coin'. Someone, like his mother, talented and passionate and – what had Uncle Charles said – amoral.

When he suggested to Lizzie that she should meet him in the stable loft with some of her soup, he had not really expected her to come. He had not wanted her to come. Someone who was really pure would not take soup to a man in a stable loft. But he had painted a picture of himself as the complete underdog, despised by his family, bereft of a mother, deserted by his father. So there was a possibility her heart would melt sufficiently to force her into bringing him the soup. He went down to the stable block at six o'clock the next evening and told Jem to take the evening off. When the bell leapt on its spring, he ran back down the steps, suppressing a feeling of faint disappointment, already curious as to how he would tackle this particular seduction.

He might have thought for a moment that the muffled figure near the third stall was Lizzie James, except for the large abdominal lump obtruding through her old-fashioned cloak. His heart leapt as the bell spring had leapt. It was Sarah James who was carrying the soup and making excuses for her sister.

'She thought it not quite the thing . . .' The dimples were different – Lizzie did not have dimples. Or perhaps he had not seen her smile. 'After all, I am a married woman. As you see.' The dimples deepened and she laughed. It was a wonderful full-throated laugh. He felt immediately relaxed and happy.

He said, 'Will you step into my parlour?'

She pushed back the hood of her cloak and mimicked, ' "Said the spider to the fly".'

'I assure you, Miss James, I have no intention of eating you!'

They were both laughing. They both knew this game well. She went ahead of him up the splintery wooden steps. When he joined her she was putting a saucepan on the Aladdin oil stove and pouring soup into it from her jar. He thought, startled, that she must have been here before to know where Jem kept the saucepans.

She said, 'Two spoons—' and went to the box of old iron cutlery unerringly. 'As soon as the steam rises, we start to drink it. You this side. Me the other.'

And so it was. And, replete, warm, with dripping chins and tears of laughter, they kissed.

The more he saw Sarah, the more he revered Lizzie. He wanted it to go on for ever, but she told him it must stop once the baby was born.

'Why?' he asked like a sulky schoolboy.

'Because I'm never, ever going to go through this again.' She touched her abdomen with loathing.

'I wouldn't let it happen again. I'm a man of the world – I know what to do.'

'I've heard that before,' she put a hand over his mouth. 'And the answer is no.'

'Sar—'

'No.'

He said, 'I'm not going to beg. I can get other whores.'

She wasn't angry. In fact, she smiled as if at an inner secret. She was sixteen and he was twenty and she made him feel like a schoolboy.

He went outside with her. The banks were choked with primroses and long catkins hung from the trees. Still she did not speak and finally he was forced to apologize.

'I didn't mean it, Sarah. I love you. You know that.'

Her smile was almost maternal. 'You love Lizzie, not me. But Lizzie will never do what I do. And I look like her. That's what it's all about, isn't it?'

He was going to deny everything, but then couldn't. 'I'll talk Lizzie into bed eventually,' he said instead.

She laughed. 'You won't, you know. You'll have to cough up a wedding ring before Lizzie will go to bed with you. And then . . .' She kissed him. 'It won't be like me.'

'It'll be better,' he maintained, angry again. 'I'll be the first. The only one.'

She laughed again infuriatingly and patted his cheek.

'Goodbye, Teddy. I'm not coming here again. Lizzie is getting suspicious.'

She moved across the stable yard like a galleon, smoothly, magnificently. A month later she gave birth to Kildie. He went to see her and he and Lizzie took the baby for a walk in the high perambulator brought from Gloucester. It made him feel rather special. This was how it would be if – when – he married Lizzie.

He said, 'You are the eternal mother figure. I had forgotten how beautiful you are, Lizzie. Your neck—'

'Oh Edward . . .' She blushed exquisitely. 'You do say such things. We hardly know each other—'

'We've been going out since March, Lizzie! How can you say that?'

She laughed. 'It's only May now, Edward!'

Her laugh was quite unlike Sarah's. It was a gurgle. Not a torrent. He covered her hand with his and she moved away. He longed suddenly for Sarah.

She said, 'Actually, Edward, I have something to tell you. After what you said – in March – I think I have persuaded Mother and Father to adopt little Kildie. Poor Sarah cannot give her a proper home after all—'

'But will Sarah permit that?' he interrupted quickly. He knew she would. She wanted nothing to do with the child.

'Oh yes. She has been wanting to get away again ever

since Kildie was born. Father has a great friend who might have heard of something suitable for her.'

He did not enquire what that something might be. He simply knew she was going out of his life and he could not bear it.

He did not even have a chance to say goodbye. If she had wanted to punish him she could not have thought of a better way. Lizzie stubbornly refused to be kissed or hugged. It became the accepted thing that they would marry one day. 'We must wait till then, Edward,' she said primly.

So in the end he let his uncle buy him a commission in the War Office. After all, it was his best chance of seeing Sarah again.

SEVEN

1939

Holly did not realize how important Dad was to her until the War came and he joined up. She knew she could not live without Mum. But Dad was different. She and Mum managed without Dad when he was at work, they were used to it. She thought.

He was later than usual that October afternoon. Usually after his early turn he was home before Holly, but that day she had been home and had tea with Mum and they had gone into the front room for a piano lesson and then Mum went on 'playing for pleasure' as she put it. They never worried when he was late. So many things happened with the rolling-stock now that they were at war. Dad was heavily involved with assembling trains for troop movements down to the coast. His knack for remembering exactly where coaches were stabled and available made him very useful indeed in the control office.

They heard his bike grate along the side wall of the house, then the back door squeaked on its hinges, and Mum stood up and called, 'We're in the front, Jim.'

He did not push his head around the door and say as usual, 'How are my beautiful women?' Instead he came into the room, stood in front of Mum and made his announcement like an excited schoolboy wanting approbation.

'I've done it, Doll. I've joined up.'

He had his arms open as if he thought she might fling herself into them. She did not. She held on to the back of the armchair and stared at him as if he had announced a death.

'You've . . . joined up?' she repeated and then opened her mouth and began to breathe through it quite quickly.

His smile was nearly tremulous.

'The Air Force. I have to begin training. Tomorrow.'

There was quite a long pause during which Mum's colour drained away and she began to shake. Then at last words burst from her.

'This is the most selfish act you have ever perpetrated, Jim! I'll never forgive you! I mean that!'

Holly knew she meant it because she used the word perpetrated which was definitely out of a book and not from real life. Holly crouched lower under the piano, where she had been sitting while Mum played the *Moonlight* – not accurately but with a great deal of feeling. Mum seemed to have forgotten Holly was there. Dad probably did not know. In spite of cramped legs Holly did not dare move in case they remembered her.

'Doll—' Dad's voice was pleading but by no means desperate. 'You know how I feel about you and Holly—'

'It's Percy Jenkins and Billy Matson all over again, is it?'

Holly peered up at her. The short autumn day, though fine, was ending quite suddenly as the sun disappeared behind the elms that guarded the village. She shivered. Mum's body was bent backwards like a bow as if she meant to spring and hiss, or even spit.

Dad said, 'Doll, please. I had to go—'

'You did not have to go, my lad!'

Mum was breathing much too fast. Miss Joliffe had told the Upper Fifth that sudden intake of oxygen could cause faintness. Holly bit her bottom lip and wished she could summon Blanche.

Mum panted twice and went on. 'You are in a reserved occupation! And you know it! You are far more important to the war effort helping to keep the trains going than stuck in some awful camp somewhere keeping records! Because that is what it will mean, Jim! You do realize that, don't you? If you think they're going to train you to fly

124

an aeroplane you've got another think coming! You're a clerk. So they will use what skills you already have! You'll be writing all day long!'

'I'm going to train in aircraft maintenance.'

Dad spoke quietly then. Not with pride but to contradict what Mum was saying without actually contradicting her. He did that often and it should have poured oil on troubled waters, but it never did.

Mum shouted furiously, 'As I thought! Billy Matson and Percy—'

'Doll. Please.'

'Let me tell you something, Jim James! There was no need to rescue me that day at Applecross Farm! No need whatsoever! Percy and Billy had come to escort me to school! It meant they got up early and arrived at school in plenty of time for once! That was all!' She seemed to be gasping for air. 'And it's the same now! There is no need to rescue Holly and me from the Hun! For God's sake! We've been at war over a month and nothing has happened!'

Her words had the strangest effect on Dad. He stared at her for a long moment while she panted and waited like an animal at bay. Then he said in a defeated voice, 'Don't you see, Doll? That just about sums up the situation, doesn't it? There's nothing I can do for you and Holly – nothing I can do for my mother – nothing I can do for my sisters, or Kildie. So I'm going somewhere where I might be able to do something. Something positive. Something that's not . . . idiotic.' He turned, put a hand out behind him which she did not take, and then left the front room and went straight out to the garden.

And then, when it was too late, Mum fainted.

He left the next day, travelling on one of his beloved trains to Swindon where he was taken with a hundred others to Corsham to begin their square-bashing.

Dorothy refused to go to Gloucester to see him off and Holly said she would say goodbye at the garden gate. Jim kissed his wife on her dry, cool lips as she lay on the sofa.

'You're all right?' he asked.

'Of course. I fainted from an excess of oxygen. Holly will explain.'

He hesitated. 'You're not pregnant or anything?' He remembered that her morning-sickness had precipitated fainting attacks.

'No, Jim, I am not pregnant. I am the same as the rest of your family. We seem to slip up quite quickly for the first one, and then nothing.' She spoke bitterly. She had wanted a large family.

He whispered, 'Doll, don't let it be like this. Only last year – at Swanage – we were so happy. What has happened?'

'I think you know what has happened, Jim.'

'You mean the War. Yes, I suppose so.'

'I mean Kildie getting married. That's what I mean, Jim.'

He straightened, staring down at her, honestly bewildered.

'That had – has – nothing to do with us, Doll. It's a tragedy, as I knew it would be. And poor old Ma left on her own out at Dymock—'

'Gran is perfectly all right. And so would Kildie be eventually. She is, after all, her mother's daughter—'

'Doll!' he said warningly.

'Oh . . . botheration!' Tears rimmed the glorious blue eyes and she reached up for him. 'Jim, never mind all that. You're going away! Just be careful! If you don't come back in one piece I'll kill you!'

He laughed aloud his relief and dropped on his knees beside the sofa. They hugged convulsively. Then she tore away and turned into the cushions.

'Go. Go quickly,' she commanded.

'Goodbye, Doll,' he said with a catch in his voice.

'And don't call me Doll!'

'All right, my darling. I'll see you in six weeks. Take care of . . . everything.'

She said, 'As always.' But her voice was muffled by the cushions and he did not hear her. He went outside and put his arm around Holly who was waiting by the gate.

'Look after her, Hol.' He spoke the time-honoured words as if they were original, and Holly, at fourteen, thought it was the most romantic moment in her whole life, superseding Kildie's wedding day which, in its turn, had superseded Aunt Sarah's leap into Grandad's grave.

She said, 'Oh Dad.'

'Don't worry, flower. It will all be over by Christmas.'

'I know. But you going off by yourself—'

'I'd prefer it. Honestly. I hate goodbyes.'

He looked so ordinary on his bike, just as he'd always looked when he left for work, his little GWR case strapped on the carrier at the back, his cycle clips revealing his thin ankles . . . She waved until he rounded the bend by the pump, then went back inside to sit on the sofa with Mum and cry.

But Jim was not to have his lone departure after all. When he reached George Street, where he was to leave his bike in the office yard, his mother awaited him, clutching a bag already oozing grease.

'Ma. You shouldn't!' He took the bag, half-laughing, but half-crying too. It was true he hated goodbyes, but it was dreadful to leave without them.

She said briskly, 'It's that piccalilli I made last year. Matured well, it has. And some of the Applecross cheese. And there's cider here if you want it. They still keep me supplied.'

In his railway days, Walter James had made certain the big Herefordshire cider firm had always had wagons at the ready for their despatches. In return they had kept him supplied with cider. Jim was touched that almost nine years after the death of his father, the tradition was kept up.

He declined the cider with thanks. It was strong and he did not want to create any wrong impressions at Corsham.

'Let's get up to the station then,' Emmie said. 'I think

my train goes just before yours.' She glanced at him then away. 'Unless you want me to go out to the Green to look after your girls?'

He hesitated for a moment. Ma would cook a proper meal and make sure they ate it, and force them into some kind of routine. But Doll was in such a strange mood and if she started on about Kildie, Ma might retaliate and then Holly would be upset and have to resurrect that damned Blanche Cooke again.

He said, 'The buses are so irregular, Ma. And Holly will be up to her eyes in homework – she does her School Certificate next summer remember.'

'A year earlier than everyone else,' Gran said with great satisfaction. She lengthened her stride to fit in with his. 'Funny. I always thought she might be a bit backward.'

'She's a dreamer, Ma. That's all.'

'And that imaginary friend of hers—'

'That all finished a long time ago.'

'She was with us last summer at Swanage,' Emmie said gloomily, remembering how Holly had walked up the beach, her head turned sideways, listening to someone invisible.

'Doll says it's very important for an only child to have someone her own age to confide—'

'Dorothy always had funny ideas. Remember the spider.'

'Yes, Ma.' Jim sighed, wondering whether he wanted to be seen off after all. But then, contrarily enough, he hated it when she got on the railcar and left him standing there without any words to give him comfort. He even asked her for some.

'You've seen it all, Ma. You're on your own all the time now. How do you manage?'

But she shook her head with uncharacteristic helplessness.

'Don't know, son.'

He said, 'I suppose . . . you just have to.'

They stared at each other, both looking for something

they could not find. The guard walked down the train checking the door handles.

'Morning, Jim. And it's Mrs James, isn't it? How are you these days?'

Emmie suddenly tugged off her black cotton glove and reached through the open window. Jim took her hand and held it oddly, as if he might be going to kiss it.

The guard said, 'I heard you were going into the Air Force, Jim. Your pa would've been proud of you.'

'He is proud. He is proud of you, son.' Emmie's voice shook ever so slightly and Jim gripped her knuckles.

''Course he is. Real gentleman he was. Never an angry word. Courtesy, that was his hallmark. Courtesy.'

He raised his green flag and the engine whistled acknowledgement. The single car began to move and Jim walked alongside it, still holding his mother's fingers. Behind them now, the guard swung himself aboard.

Emmie said above the hiss of steam, 'Remember, son, you are of the same blood.'

He smiled at her. Was she frightened he might forget his manners in his harsh new world?

'I won't forget, Ma.'

Her hand was wrenched away and she immediately withdrew her head and pulled up the window. It was then he turned and saw Kildie at the ticket barrier.

Kildie was hysterical. She wept uncontrollably into his neck and when he managed to get his fingers beneath her chin and smile at her reassuringly, he saw there were black streaks all down her cheeks. He hated mascara. There was no need for it with her dark eyes and lashes; she had only started to wear it when she married Marcus Villiers.

'Jim, you didn't tell me! You would have gone without saying goodbye! How could you be so cruel?'

It was what Doll had said. And he had simply thought he was doing what every sensible father and husband should do.

'Kildie – stop it, Kildie. People are looking. Let's get

over the bridge. My train will be in at nine forty—'

'Let me come with you, Jim. D'you remember how we planned to run away before? It was on this station – just before the wedding. D'you remember? Let's do it now – please, Jim! I can't live without you—'

'You have been doing very nicely without me.' He tried to sound humorous but she took it as a reproach.

'Oh my dear, is that what you think? How could you possibly imagine I would prefer Marcus to you? He is an animal and you are a gentleman.' She stumbled on the steps of the bridge, recovered, laughed and said, 'Gentleman Jim! My very own Gentleman Jim!'

He was struck again by the coincidence of her description. Doll had called him cruel, old Guard Jackson had said he was a gentleman like his father. And Kildie had used both those words. Cruel and a gentleman. He meant to be neither.

Kildie was still babbling on as they reached the far platform. Marcus expected too much of her, he was demanding and . . . she hesitated . . . not gentle. No, he was not gentle.

Jim knew that his mother would have been unable to explain anything to Kildie; Lizzie had complained bitterly of her initial ignorance of marriage. Sarah might have told the girl something on her wedding day, but there were nuances she could not understand unless someone spoke of them. And Doll had given him a vocabulary, and told him there was no shame in speaking of sex.

He cleared his throat. 'My dear, be sensible. You must surely have realized that married couples show their love for one another in a variety of ways—'

She turned her stained face up to him.

'I knew about bed. Yes. The girls at the bank were always talking about that kind of thing. But I thought it was for having babies.'

'Well, of course. But . . . not always. It – it's a display of affection, it's a wish for closeness—' His mouth was completely dry.

His train was being shunted in. The coaches were a jumbled lot of first, second and third. Nobody cared these days about assembling a smart train. The chocolate-and-cream livery was filthy.

She said something and he bent his ear to her mouth to hear against the hissing of steam and grinding of wheels.

'Do you and Doll . . . I mean . . . often?'

'Yes.' He refused to qualify the monosyllable. Doll would have been proud of him. He could have explained that Doll was a very liberated person who nearly always instigated their love-making . . . on second thoughts, he could not have explained that.

She said in a smaller voice still, 'I see.'

The train drew to a halt with a hideous clanking of buffers and then snorted passively.

Kildie said, 'What does Holly think?'

He was shocked. 'Kildie! The privacy of our room is sacrosanct!'

She looked at him uncomprehendingly for a moment, then said, 'Your room? You mean your bedroom! Oh. But that's at night. In the day—'

He returned her look and then turned away afraid she might see the horror in his mild grey eyes. Did Marcus really make love to her night and day? Did she really think he and Doll would make love in front of Holly

She knew he was appalled and said quickly, 'Jim! Don't hate me! I know I shouldn't talk like this. But there's no-one else. Gran would be shocked. And Holly is still too young. And anyway I've always talked to you. It's just that I get so – so *tired*!'

He almost laughed. Her naïvety was redeemed by her ingenuousness.

A whistle shrieked its warning and he opened a door and got into the corridor.

He said, 'None of this would be helped by anything I could do, Kildie,' he began, like the solemn uncle he was.

She said, 'I don't care! I just don't want you to go. And if you're going I want to come with you!'

131

'You know that's impossible, Kildie. Now stop crying and listen.'

'Jim – I can't – I can't—'

Another shriek and the train began to move. She climbed onto the running board.

'Get off, Kildie! And promise me one thing.'

'What? Anything!'

'Go and talk to Doll. She will help you. Will you do that?'

'Jim!'

She had her arms around his neck. She put her mouth on his.

It was the kind of kiss that he had never experienced before. Doll did not know about such kisses. He knew with terrible certainty that she had learned it from Villiers. His heart pounded.

When she dropped away he saw she had stopped crying. Her tears had gone, quite suddenly and miraculously. In fact, she was smiling. And with her coat falling off her shoulders, and the mascara on her face she looked . . . wanton.

He opened the door of a compartment and sat down. He was shaking. Villiers and Kildie. Villiers corrupting Kildie. And his own heart pounding with excitement.

His mother's words came to him. 'Remember you are of the same blood.'

She had not been talking of his father after all. She had seen Kildie behind him and she had been warning him.

He sat and shook and was deeply thankful that ahead of him lay six weeks of monastic existence.

1915

When Jim came home for a weekend in mid-March, his pleasure at seeing Sarah was not altogether wholehearted. He had missed her a great deal because she made him laugh – she made everyone laugh. But although he had

132

no intention of disobeying his father, he could not quite forget the glib promise he had made to Francis Passmore-Williams. As far as he knew the man had left the day after their meeting at the Black Boar, but he had made certain the bill from the wool factory was paid up; he had kept his side of the bargain and Jim felt a qualm about the fact that he himself had no intention of keeping his. So he had rather hoped that Sarah would, in fact, find a permanent career on the stage and not return to Dymock for any length of time.

It seemed – though no-one actually told him this – that she was married. She must be because she was obviously expecting a baby. And her husband was in France. It was odd; neither she nor anyone else in the family seemed to think he would come home again. Jim knew that the casualty lists were catastrophic, but to write a bloke off before his time seemed heartless to say the least. Worse than heartless. Sinful. They were depriving the unborn child of a father quite deliberately.

He arrived on the Friday evening and they spent the cold drizzly evening comfortably by the fire. And then, suddenly, the next afternoon, the household was in uproar. He was sent out with Lizzie as if he were a child again and they walked down to the Post Office in another typical March drizzle, bought six penny stamps and walked back without exchanging a word. It was good to get indoors, but in spite of the fire in the living-room, the Station House was somehow cheerless. Sarah was in the kitchen with Ma and Pa. He and Lizzie sat together knowing they must not interrupt whatever was going on. Lizzie fiddled with the big pot of soup on the range.

'I'm going out again,' she said suddenly. 'I'll take some of this to Miss Protheroe. She's had flu.'

Jim's new-found confidence was ebbing fast. He might be a Great Western man, he might be cunning about collecting debts, he might even be getting on better with Mr Coles; but everything seemed to be falling away quite suddenly.

'I'll come with you,' he said, standing up almost eagerly as if the idea of taking soup to old ladies was exciting.

'No you won't,' Lizzie replied flatly. 'You might pick up a germ.'

'You want her to yourself,' Jim accused. 'Just 'cos she was the seamstress up at the Grange. You're a snob, our Lizzie!'

It was only half true. Lizzie wanted to find out more about the young man who had been at the Christmas party.

'You might hear something . . . unpleasant,' she prevaricated.

It opened a way at last for Jim to ask questions.

'What do you mean? Has something happened?'

'It's our Sarah . . . What did you think?'

Jim was immediately Sarah's champion.

'I don't know why everyone is so strange in this house now!' he exploded. 'Sarah's husband is fighting for our freedom – and everyone acts as if—'

Lizzie turned suddenly. Her face was bright red from the fire. She said, 'Oh Jim – you are fourteen now, for goodness' sake! Sarah's not married! The father of that poor child is probably Hope Chapel's uncle!'

Jim was aghast. He had been prepared to defend Sarah to the death. He put his hands on the arms of his chair, half levered himself up, then sat down again.

'Mr Chapel is practically a man of the cloth!' was all he could find to say.

Lizzie reached for a basin and put it on the table. She shrugged almost irritably. 'Well, I don't know about that for sure, of course—'

'It's wicked gossip!' Jim protested angrily. 'Just because Sarah is pretty and a bit – you know – she laughs a lot—'

'It's not that, you silly boy! Everyone has to believe her whether it's true or not. But this—' she jerked her head at the kitchen door, '—this is nothing to do with whether she's married or not!'

'What is it then?' he asked helplessly.

There came a cry from the kitchen. He was out of his chair immediately. The voice was Walter's.

Lizzie was behind him dragging him back.

'For goodness' sake, Jim! Don't interfere! Sarah was out last night with Alf Matson! They were seen together—' She sobbed and went back to the fire, covering her face. 'Oh it's so shameful! I don't know how I went into that Post Office! They were all talking about it! Didn't you notice how quiet it was as we went in?'

Jim was frozen by the kitchen door.

'Alf Matson? The gamekeeper?'

'Yes. He's got half a dozen children. It – it's disgusting!'

'You mean, Sarah and Alf Matson . . .'

'Yes.'

'He – he's dirty!' Jim protested.

'Yes. And common.'

Jim sat down slowly. After a while Lizzie took the basin to the fire and filled it with the good beef stock which Emmie kept simmering all through the winter. She covered the basin with grease-proof paper, then tied a cloth over it.

'I won't be long, Jim,' she said. And went into the hall.

She was indeed only about half an hour. It was raining properly when she returned and she was accompanied by a young man who held an umbrella over her head and shepherded her up the garden path as if she were made of porcelain. Jim watched through the parlour window without interest. Sarah and his parents were still in the kitchen. The sound of sobbing filtered through to him now and then. Mostly they were Sarah's sobs; but he was almost certain that he had heard his father weep too.

He felt sick and very frightened.

Mr Coles said jovially, 'Another weekend down here, young James? What's the attraction? Eh? Eh? Farmer Ellersley's daughter?'

Jim kept his head down, hoping Old King Cole wouldn't notice the colour creeping up his face from his collar. Rosie Ellersley came down with her father on the big old haywain once a week. The tall wagon could hold up to a ton of cabbages or swede collected from the farms on the steep sides of the Stroud Valley. It was sent by special vegetable trains up to London for Covent Garden. Rosie was fourteen and a big strapping girl who could carry a sack of vegetables to the weighing shed without so much as a grunt. She was tongue-tied and smelled always of onions. But that wasn't what made Jim colour. It was the thought of his sister in Red Marley churchyard with Alf Matson. His sister, pregnant by a man of the church who had no intention of marrying her. Then going to Red Marley churchyard with . . . Perhaps Rosie Ellersley was like Sarah; he could not risk trying to find out. The whole idea of girls put him off.

Mr Coles laughed ribaldly and clapped Jim's cringing shoulder.

'Good on you, young James! I wondered where you got to this summer. Missis says you takes your bread and cheese and disappears most of Sundays. Now we know where and why, eh? Eh?'

Jim felt bound to protest at last.

'I go hiking, sir.'

That did it. The station master guffawed uncontrollably for at least half a minute. Then the bell rang from the signal box and he turned to stagger out on to the platform for the midday from London.

'Never thought we'd get on, young James. But I reckon I've whipped you into nice shape. Boy after me own heart now.'

Jim watched him settle his cap over his ears and stride down the platform towards the first-class coaches. He must know about the fiasco at Dymock. Surely everyone up and down the line must know. Sarah's total disgrace was the one thing which had won Mr Coles over to Jim. It was crazy, but it was so.

Jim sighed and closed the ledger. It was the first Saturday in May and the finest day of the year so far. At

136

midday the sun was sitting almost over the chimney pot of the booking office and the donkey which pulled Mrs Coles to and from Stroud in a tiny trap called a jingle, had his long chin resting on the gate of the station house waiting hopefully for a few carrots or an early lettuce from one of the passers-by.

Jim did not enjoy missing his weekends at home. His father would be sitting on the banks of the Leadon right now, trailing a line over the eddies. His mother would be spiking tomorrow's lamb with rosemary from the garden. Lizzie's young man would be hanging around somewhere, supposedly courting Lizzie but really fascinated by the fecund Sarah. It occurred to Jim suddenly that Sarah might have . . . done something . . . with Edward Richardson. He flushed again, hating his sister, knowing he could not go home again while she was still there.

Out on the platform Mr Coles was touching his hat to Sir Arthur Devereaux and palming a tip. That would annoy Jefferies, the porter. The guard was checking the door-handles, blasting his whistle to get people away from the train. Jim caught a glimpse of the green flag, then the train began to move towards Gloucester. And the morse tapper began to chatter anxiously.

Jim moved over to it and began to write automatically on the pad. His father had told him never to try to read the message as it came through. 'Let it be automatic, Jim. Simply write down each letter and each space and read it afterwards. If you try to do both at once, mistakes are made.'

So it was not for some time that Jim read the words in front of him.

'To James. Lad clerk. Brimscombe. Niece born midnight Friday. Both well.'

Jim stared at his own block capitals hardly taking it in. Sarah's pregnancy had somehow become divorced from this result. A girl. He now had a niece and was therefore an uncle.

Mr Coles opened the door.

'Was that the tapper?'

Jim palmed the paper. 'Yes. But it stopped. Must have been for Chalford.'

'Right. That's all right then. I'm off. Expect you at tea-time.'

'Yes, sir. Thank you.'

Jim waited until he heard the gate slam and listened as the old man's voice talked to the donkey. Then he crumpled the paper and threw it in the tall waste-paper basket. He did not wish to be an uncle. The baby merely confirmed all the sordid physical horrors that had gone before. He shuddered. Then he got out a map from the desk drawer and began to plan tomorrow's hike.

It was June before he went home to see the child. He would not have gone then but the parcel of laundered collars and shirts, which usually arrived on Friday, failed to put in an appearance. It was his mother's way of ensuring he would come home. He could read her like a book.

The station was empty when the Gloucester train pulled in. Jack Bowie appeared from the ganger's hut and ran to take the mail off the brake van, but there was no-one to open doors and help old ladies and carry luggage. Jim hastened up and down the train doing his best. Obviously Walter was fishing.

The Station House appeared to be deserted. He went upstairs to Sarah's room, determined to swallow the pill immediately. The room was empty, the curtains blowing gently in the June breeze. There was a sound from the garden below. He looked out and saw Lizzie and Edward Richardson apparently making a daisy chain.

'Hullo!' he called. 'Are you the only ones at home?'

They looked up, startled. Lizzie gave a crow of pleasure and Edward Richardson smiled politely. Jim did some quick calculations. Richardson must be twenty at least. Why wasn't he at the Front? Was he a coward like Jim himself? Boys of fourteen were joining up all over the

138

place, lying about their ages. Jim shivered and hoped that the War would be over before he was eighteen. He had been brought up not to lie.

Lizzie shaded her eyes. 'Ma and Pa have taken Kildie for a walk,' she called back. 'Come on down. We'll make some tea.'

'Where's—' he began, then stopped. Sarah might well be out with . . . anyone. At least it could not be Edward Richardson.

But it seemed Sarah had gone again.

'Such a lot to tell you,' Lizzie said, setting out the tea tray like they did at the Grange. 'You haven't been home for ages. Not since I started my job.'

Jim gaped. Lizzie was wearing a pin-tucked lawn blouse, the sleeves cascading in frills on to her narrow hands. Surely she had not agreed to go into service?

'I only started last week actually,' she giggled, glancing out of the door where Edward was sprawled on the grass smoking a cigarette. 'Teddy isn't keen, of course. Though his uncle has bought him a commission. A nice safe one in the War Office, thank goodness!' she rolled her eyes.

Jim nodded. He did not blame the man. And as far as Lizzie was concerned it was the best possible move.

'Well, what are you doing?' he prompted her.

'I'm on the railway! Like you!' She spooned tea into the warmed pot. He made to lift the heavy kettle from the gas but she shook her head. 'Pot to kettle, never kettle to pot!' she reminded him. He watched her tilt the kettle so that the water still bubbled as it hit the tea leaves. He could not help but admire her. After Sarah she was so . . . decent. So ordinary.

'They were taking on two women to replace the men who had joined up. Pa put in a word and the next thing I knew—' She put the teapot on to the tray, serious now. 'Actually, it's really difficult, Jim. I wanted to see you before Monday. I have to coagulate these monthly returns of stock—'

'Collate,' he corrected her. 'You have to take each piece of information from each station and enter it in the red book.'

'That's *right*!' She stared at him with new eyes. 'Oh Jim – can you go through it with me?'

'Of course. It's easy when you know how.' He grinned at her. 'Golly, Sis. Congratulations. I bet you raise a few brows going round the offices with your hair up and that long skirt swishing.'

'I don't wear this,' she replied. 'I've got a navy coat and skirt. It's jolly hot actually, but I keep it buttoned right up to the neck.'

His grin spread across his face. 'Anyone would know you were a real . . . lady,' he assured her. And it was true. Sarah would get the knowing grins and stares. Lizzie would get respect.

As if reading his thoughts she said solemnly, 'Sarah has gone, Jim. She almost joined up. Once she knew Kildie was all right she nearly drove everyone mad – pester, pester all the time. She wanted to have her hair cut and join the Army – you know what she's like. Anyway, Pa was talking to Mr Edwards and he had heard of this small group of artistes who were performing for our boys in barracks up and down the country.' She glanced at him furtively. 'And in France. She wants to go to France.' Jim drew in his breath. Lizzie and Sarah doing men's jobs. And he and Edward Richardson . . . Lizzie went on, 'Don't mention that to Pa. Probably it's Sarah romancing again. Anyway, she's gone.'

'And the baby?'

'She's called Kildie, Jim. She's going to be christened tomorrow. That's why Ma wanted you here. You are to be godfather.'

'Christened? Kildie?'

'After St Kilda.'

'But Sarah's not here? How can they have a christening without the mother?'

'Jim! Surely Ma has told you? She and Pa have adopted

Kildie. I don't know whether it's official or not, but she belongs here now.'

He was astonished all over again and made noises while they carried the tea things on to the lawn and settled themselves by Edward.

He grinned amiably and rolled onto one elbow.

'It's a popular move, old man. Everyone adores the kid. You should see Lizzie wheeling the perambulator.'

Lizzie blushed prettily.

'It's giving me ideas, I can tell you!' Edward continued robustly. Then, when Lizzie made no response, he let his face droop pathetically. 'Not that anyone takes me seriously. No real job, no real family. I'm . . .' He knew he could not use the word bastard in front of Lizzie. 'I'm a real half-breed, aren't I? I'm not a whole anything!'

She responded to that all right.

'You are the best man I know, Edward Richardson. And don't you forget it!' she said, sounding exactly like Ma.

Jim smiled. Sarah had gone and there was no fear of disgrace from Lizzie. He could come home again at weekends.

He was never to forget his first sight of Kildie. She was already six weeks old, her eyes had changed from blue to a kind of navy. Her head was darkly downy beneath its sun-bonnet, and her whole body was constructed of curves; there was not a straight line to be seen.

He met the perambulator at the gate and kissed his mother sedately on the cheek, then shook hands with Walter.

'We're glad you're back home, Jim,' Emmie said as if she knew exactly what Lizzie had told him and how he had reacted.

Walter retained his hand.

'We want you to meet your niece,' he said, beaming proudly. 'Miss Kilda James.'

Jim looked. The tiny girl child smiled gummily.

'That's just wind,' Emmie said, watching his face.

He put a tentative thumb against her reaching palm and immediately she gripped it.

'She's so strong,' he said wonderingly.

'Simply a physical reaction,' Walter said, glancing at Emmie with a smile.

Jim knew better. He lowered his head and looked into her eyes.

'Hello, Kildie,' he said.

The baby gripped harder still and opened her mouth on a chortle.

Jim said, 'I'm your brother. Did you know that?'

He glanced over his shoulder. 'That's right, isn't it, Ma? If you've adopted her, I must be her brother.'

'Yes, son,' Emmie said quietly. 'You must be, mustn't you?'

Walter said, 'Pick her up, Jim. It's time for her bottle of milk. You can be the one to give it to her.'

Jim reached for her, clumsily, reverently. She seemed to leap from the pram into his arms. He held her aloft between him and the sun and shook her gently until she laughed again.

He loved her.

EIGHT

1940

It seemed perfectly logical to Holly that when Aunt Lizzie decided that her family were in danger in Croydon and should be evacuated instantly, she and Winnie came to the Green, while Uncle Teddy and Charlie went to Dymock, just as they had after their sudden departure from Suffolk on the eve of Kildie's wedding.

Even so, Aunt Lizzie had to explain it all very carefully.

'Your mother would be forced to do war-work or take in any old evacuees – she would hate that. And she certainly does not want my whole family plonked on her. That would be extremely selfish of me – though I miss them, dear Holly, more than I can say.' She wiped away an invisible tear and continued bravely. 'In a way it would have been better the other way round – me with my dear mother and Edward . . . But of course that cannot be.'

Holly said, 'You could have all come here, Aunt Lizzie! Mum and me could have—'

'Your uncle wished to see his dear family in Dymock,' Aunt Lizzie said firmly. 'He does, after all, come from a very good . . . There is no question whatsoever of us parting. If you should hear any such rumour I trust you will squash it immediately, dear Holly!'

That had not crossed Holly's mind. And, in any case, who knew her aunt and uncle in the village? Who cared? So she laughed as easily as she could. Winnie, sporting an incredibly pendulous dewdrop in spite of the glorious summer of 1940, did not smile. Winnie was desperately homesick for Croydon. She was a mere four months older than Holly, but in her opinion that made her old enough to be in love, whereas Holly was not. Holly would have liked to tell Blanche just how wrong Winnie was on this score; but Winnie's presence made Blanche's impossible.

Mum, coming into the living-room with a tray of tea, wore a smile that looked painful.

'Now come along, everyone – no tears please! We're not going to beat old Hitler by sitting around like dying ducks in a thunderstorm!'

'Oh, Aunty Doll!' Winnie adored her aunt and tried to get her own hair pinned up at the sides in imitation of Dorothy's golden locks.

'Well? The only way we can do anything is to keep up our spirits! Now, let's have our tea. I've made some watercress sandwiches – Holly, could you fetch them? And I've got the best table-cloth . . .' She proceeded to flap it over the table while Holly went into the kitchen and stared down the garden at the bean sticks all ready for the beans which she had planted assiduously on May the first just as Dad always had. She wondered about Dad. And Gran. And . . . her cousin, Charlie.

Mum was saying, 'How did you find life in the big city, girls? It must be such a complete change after Suffolk.'

This was bordering on the tactless. When Uncle Teddy's debts had been settled up after Kildie's wedding, he had spent a lot of time at the Grange, trying – as Jim had put it – to 'get in' with his uncle, the Squire. It hadn't worked and finally, early in 1939, a friend of his father's had got him a job as a sales representative for a publishing house. They had rented a nice little house in Croydon and never mentioned their farming days.

But Aunt Lizzie did not seem to mind the direct question.

'I'll always be a country girl,' she said, equally frank. 'But the children . . . they enjoyed it in Croydon. Didn't you, dear?'

Winnie thankfully wiped her nose before nodding vigorously.

'Why was that, Winnie? Tell us about it,' Mum suggested encouragingly.

There was a long pause. Aunt Lizzie opened her mouth and Winnie just managed, 'The shops and that.'

Aunt Lizzie followed up swiftly, 'And, of course, the wonderful sights. We did the maze at Hampton Court one day, didn't we, Win? And your father took us to see the Tower.'

'There was a picture house just down the road,' Winnie suddenly volunteered. 'I saw Tyrone Power there. Three times in one week. The manager said I was a good advertisement for the film and he let me in for noth—'

'People are very kind to children in London,' Aunt Lizzie interrupted firmly. 'And of course we entertained a great deal. Edward had to make a good impression with clients.'

Mum said, not entirely innocently, 'Did you do a cookery course or something then, Lizzie?'

But Lizzie laughed. 'Oh my dear, it did not involve much food! Perhaps a few sandwiches to go with the drinks. You know the sort of thing. The men would play cards and talk—'

'We had to dress up and smile. And Charlie had to go out!' Winnie laughed, coming out of her shell properly. 'Dad said if you got them drunk, they'd sign anything!'

'Now, Winnie!' But Lizzie was not really embarrassed. 'Secrets of the trade!'

Mum was genuinely curious. 'You mean, you had to butter these people up?'

'Exactly!' Lizzie laughed too. 'You know my Edward! When his father got him the job he said he could sell fridges to Eskimos!' Everyone laughed at this. Lizzie shook her head indulgently. 'He enjoyed it immensely. And we never minded helping him, did we, Win?'

Winnie, already fed up with cotton summer frocks, ankle socks and sandals, turned to Holly. 'Dad bought me a little two-piece. A skirt and bolero. Do you know what a bolero is, Holly?'

145

'No.' Holly was amazed at her cousin's transformation. Without the dewdrop and with a smile, she was really attractive.

Mum's eyes started to darken.

'You don't mean, you had to . . . *vamp* . . . these people?'

Lizzie spluttered helplessly.

'Well, I suppose, if you put it like that . . . ' She obviously liked the idea of being a Mata Hari. Even her long dark face brightened a little.

Mum caught Holly's gaze and Holly very gently closed one eye. There was a pause then Mum too laughed helplessly.

'Well, yes,' she said. 'I suppose it is funny!'

Holly breathed easily and smiled at Winnie. She admired her mother's strong principles, but it was so much easier to be what Gran called 'happy and chatty'.

Winnie let her try on the bolero suit that very evening. Holly's gawkiness was merely emphasized by the smartness of the clothes. Winnie rummaged in her mother's suitcase and found some black suede court shoes which she donned with the suit. She spat on her fingers and pushed the silky hair by her ears into little kiss curls and pinned the other longer bits on top of her head.

'You look rather marvellous, Winnie,' Holly admitted.

Winnie mimicked her voice. 'Rather marvellous, Winnie!' She laughed. 'You don't half sound posh at times, Hol. Not a bit Dymock.'

'Well, I'm not Dymock.' Holly was surprised by the accusation.

'No, but your dad is. My dad always calls your dad, Hickory Jim. Or Jim the Hick.'

Holly flushed angrily. 'How dare he! Just because he's some distant relation of the Richardsons, he thinks he's—'

'He's only joking, Hol,' Winnie said hastily. Already she could see her only consolation now would be having Holly as an audience. She could not afford to antagonize

146

her. 'Listen. Did I tell you about the manager at the picture house?'

Holly was always ready to be mollified. 'You told me you were in love. Is that—?'

'He says I'm like a film star. I wear all this stuff when I go there. He says I look like Hedy Lamarr.'

'Does your mother let you wear her shoes?'

'She doesn't know! And I borrow one of her hats.' Winnie started to giggle again. Holly was bored and fascinated at the same time. She listened while Winnie ran through exactly what he said and what she said and then what he said and then what she said. And she tried to put herself into Winnie's high-heeled shoes, and substitute Charlie for the cinema manager. Not that Charlie ever said anything . . . silly. And he could never do anything indoors like being a cinema manager. But he could climb a tree like a panther and his dark eyes were full of mystery.

Dorothy told herself she was 'fed-up' about having Lizzie and Winnie parked on her, apparently for the duration. But she knew deep down in her soul she was more than just fed-up. She had been married to Jim James for over fifteen years and it seemed to her that nothing else was going to happen in her life. She was thirty-five, right in the middle of her three-score-years-and-ten, and everything had been so exciting and promising, and now it was not. Marriage meant that she had to subdue all her personal ambitions to her husband's. And Jim had no ambitions beyond being married to her, being a father to Holly and tracing GWR rolling-stock all over the West Country. Sometimes she could not believe that this was all there was to life. And then Jim looked at her with those gentle grey eyes and his perennially schoolboy face split in a grin, and her heart melted just as it had melted back in 1924 and she forgot that she had expected so much more.

But the War had confirmed her uselessness beyond all doubt. Jim was not there to melt her heart any more.

In fact, Jim was able to go away and do something else because of the War. She was more of a prisoner than ever.

Probably that was why she suggested the trip to Dymock the following weekend. For one thing her curiosity was aroused about the possibility that Lizzie really had left Edward. For another she was no good at wheedling extras from her local grocer and thought Gran might top up her larder with some eggs and local butter. And thirdly, if Edward was 'getting back in' with the Richardsons, she saw no reason why Holly should not have that advantage too.

Thinning her full lips with determination she overrode Lizzie's reluctance and put it to the vote. Winnie, of course, was keen to go; she was thoroughly 'fed-up' with an exclusively female household. Unexpectedly, Holly was delighted. Her cheeks became pink and her grey eyes, so like Jim's, positively blazed with excitement.

'You can wear the cornflower dress,' Dorothy said kindly. 'And your open-toed sandals.'

Holly would have loved something less schoolgirlish, but the dress buttoned on the shoulders rather fetchingly and the sandals made her legs look good.

'No socks?' she bargained hopefully.

'Oh . . . all right.' Dorothy knew Gran would disapprove of bare legs very much and gave her permission because of it.

They borrowed a bike for Winnie; Lizzie rode Dorothy's and Dorothy rode Jim's with much clowning about the crossbar. They put all the bikes in the guard's brake van and settled down for the half-hour trip with some anticipation.

'It's doing us good to get out, you see, Lizzie,' Dorothy said.

'Yes.' Lizzie nodded. 'I just hope . . .'

'What, dear?'

'Nothing. It's all right. I wish we could have let them know we were coming, that's all.'

'A nice surprise for them. And I've brought bread and milk.'

'Oh . . . good.'

The guard came round and asked how Mr James was doing with that training of his but of course Dorothy could not tell him where Jim was stationed or anything because she had to 'Be like Dad and Keep Mum'.

'I 'eard as 'ow he was up in Scotland, Mrs James. Servicing the Sunderland flying boats, I did 'ear.'

Dorothy flushed, annoyed. Lizzie said hastily, 'It's all a secret, you know. You mustn't say anything about his whereabouts to anyone else, Mr Lewis.'

'I wouldn't dream of it, Mrs Richardson – wouldn't dream of it!' The guard turned to Holly. 'My goodness, girl, but you're like 'im. The very spit, eh, Mrs James?'

Dorothy could only thank her lucky stars Jim wasn't there to be nudged and winked at. But then Mr Lewis redeemed all by adding, 'More beautiful young lady I haven't set eyes on in a month of Sundays!'

And Holly, her grey eyes almost blue because of the cornflower dress, turned very red indeed.

Gran showed no sign of being pleased to see them.

'Our Sarah turned up just, and Kildie last night,' she told them after the briefest of greetings. 'Seems like it's a proper family reunion apart from poor Jim.'

Dorothy said nothing with great difficulty; poor Jim, indeed! Holly and Winnie were also silent, not knowing what such a crowd might entail. Lizzie screamed with delight; in the mêlée of a family party it would be difficult for anyone to notice whether she and Edward were estranged or not. Difficult for her even.

'They've all gone for a walk down by the Leadon.' Gran turned to the gas stove and took off the boiling kettle. 'Where your grandfather used to fish.' She was lost in the steam. 'D'you want a cup of tea?'

Lizzie was already through the kitchen door on her way to the river, the girls trailing after her.

Dorothy said, 'I don't want to take your tea ration, Gran. But if you're making a pot . . .'

Gran emerged from the steam, her grey hair in tendrils around her face.

She said, 'You all right on your own?'

Dorothy said, 'Yes. And anyway, I'm not on my own, am I?'

'You're without your husband. That's what I meant.'

Dorothy looked at the bowed back and wondered what Gran's life had been like. Nothing without Walter, or so she said. And she had been older than Dorothy was now when she married him.

'I'm fine, Gran, honestly. And now, with Lizzie and Win, I don't really have time to miss him.'

'They won't stay long, don't worry.'

'I'm not exactly worried.' She wanted to be frank and say straight out that she was bored. Bored into the ground. Instead, she took a cup from Gran and went ahead of her into the living-room. 'You know, Gran, you should have let Adrian Frost dedicate that last book of poems to you.'

Gran was honestly surprised, her wrinkles concertina'd out of control for a second before she said, 'What made you say that?'

Dorothy laughed. 'I don't know. It would have given you immortality. That's all.'

Gran frowned impatiently. 'Oh you and your fancies, Doll. Drink your tea before the rows start.'

'For goodness' sake, Gran! Don't call me . . . oh never mind!' Dorothy sipped and said, 'What rows?'

Gran said laconically, 'Lizzie will find Sarah kissing her Edward half to death, they'll fly at each other like they always do, then Lizzie will realize she can't live without Edward and she'll move here for the rest of the War.'

For a moment Dorothy stared at her, startled. And then she began to laugh. Then she said, 'But what about Kildie?'

This time Gran pulled a face. 'She says she's left Marcus

for good. She'll be letting poor little Charlie kiss her, I dare say. He's mad for her.'

Dorothy stopped laughing. 'Left Marcus? Oh . . . never mind poor little Charlie. What about Holly?' And she left her tea and ran out of the cottage.

Aunt Lizzie had outstripped the girls and was out of sight by the time they reached the churchyard. They were halfway up the steep slope to the stand of elms at the top when Winnie spotted her father below them on the river bank. Her mouth was actually open to call to him when she realized he was not alone. Someone in a bright orange dress and a hat the size of a cartwheel came swinging down the slope towards him. He opened his arms, caught the flying figure and whirled her around as if she were a child. But she was not a child. And Winnie knew enough about her father to push Holly to one side and continue the tramp to the top of the slope where they had hidden all those years ago.

And then luckily there was a diversion because she saw Charlie's unmistakably long legs dangling from a branch of one of the elms. He was staring down at Grandad's grave.

'I can see you, Charlie!' Winnie called out, running beneath him. 'Come down and say hello!'

'Bugger off!' Charlie returned.

Winnie was outraged. 'How dare you speak to your cousin like that, Charlie Richardson! You make me so embarrassed! Holly is a nice girl – she thinks you're nice actually, though I can't think why – and you tell her to . . . I'm disgusted with you!'

Charlie scrambled down, crestfallen.

'Holly! I didn't realize you were there. Sorry. I didn't mean—'

'You just meant me!' Winnie was working herself up into a Hedy Lamarr state. 'Right! I will bugger off then! And go and find Ma and Dad and tell them exactly what you said—'

She flew down the slope in a rage that had little to do with her brother and a great deal to do with her father.

Charlie watched her, surprised.

'What's up with her? I've told her to – to clear off before—'

Holly, red-faced, dug into the dry turf with the toe which protruded from one sandal.

Charlie turned his dark eyes on her. 'Aren't you getting on too well?'

'Oh yes! Fine. Absolutely fine!'

Charlie, trying hard to make amends, said, 'D'you want to climb this tree? It's easy. I've been up there ages.'

Holly was thrilled. She swung herself up after her cousin, grabbing his hand whenever he offered it, thrilling to his touch and wondering whether he thrilled to hers.

'Sit here—' He was astride a long branch which reached over the slope, so seemed very high indeed. 'Hold on to this and this. See? Safe as houses.'

'Oh, it's wonderful!' Holly liked climbing trees more than anything. To be part of a trunk or a branch, surrounded by leaves, high above the ground, was the most exhilarating feeling she knew. Apart from being in the sea at Swanage.

She stared down and saw that they were in a direct line with Grandad's grave.

'Oh Charlie!' she said.

'I know. We should have got up here that day of the funeral, shouldn't we?'

'It was too misty. We wouldn't have seen anything.'

'Except Aunt Sarah flinging herself into the hole!'

Charlie gave a schoolboy snigger.

'It wasn't funny. Not really.' Holly narrowed her eyes, remembering. 'Poor Kildie got into such trouble. And Winnie was really ill after. It was awful.'

There was a silence. Then Charlie said abruptly, 'Kildie was down there just now.'

'Kildie? Gran said she'd gone for a walk with Aunt Sarah and your father.'

'Well, she was down there. She just sat by the stone and cried and cried. It was terrible. I didn't know what to do.'

'What did you do?'

'Nothing.'

Holly was distressed. 'Poor Kildie. Where can she be now?' She shifted along the branch towards the trunk. From the other side of the tree there would be a view of the river.

'Don't know.' Charlie sounded glum. 'I couldn't do anything, you see. Because I love her.'

Holly paused, startled. Then edged further and said, 'So do I. We all love Kildie.'

There was a pause, then Charlie said, 'Yes.'

Holly felt the bark of the elm branch tear at her skin just inside her left knee. She was glad of the stinging pain. It stopped her feeling too shocked at what she saw far beneath her on the river bank. It was Uncle Teddy and Aunt Sarah. They were kissing. Rather like Charles Boyer and Hedy Lamarr kissed in films.

And it stopped her thinking about what Charlie had said too. Because when she said 'we all love Kildie' he had waited before he agreed with her.

1916

The Albion Entertainers were a group of well-to-do amateur actors who seized the War as an excuse to do their bit and enjoy themselves in a way that they could never have done – respectably – before Kaiser Wilhelm attacked little Belgium. Mr Edwards had attended two of their 'evenings' at the Café Royal and had no hesitation in recommending them to Walter James. By this time Walter had few illusions about his daughter, but, as he said to Emmie, there was always the forlorn hope that if she mixed with idealistic people, she might herself absorb some idealism. Emmie smiled and shook her head and said, 'Oh Walter.' He said, 'What?' She said, 'Our Sarah certainly never lacked ideas.' He smiled too and said, 'Ideals, Em. Stick an "l" on the end of your word.' She looked blank for a moment then shook her head more vigorously. 'Ideals. Them she'll never have.'

But Sarah could not wait to leave the Station House again. She knew there was no future for her with Edward Richardson; indeed, although the situation amused her immensely, she had no wish for a future with any one man. She wondered whether she would mind leaving Kildie who was such a placid and endearing baby. But when it happened, she hardly gave her a second glance. Emmie and Walter would be much better parents for the child; Lizzie would have free rein with her young man; everyone would be better off.

Strangely, it was the thought of Jim that disturbed her most. Jim had not come home since she had disgraced herself with Alf Matson. She knew that she was an embarrassment to him. She told herself she did not care, but the thought of his large grey eyes avoiding her dark ones made her squirm inside. She had odd dreams about her brother; more than simply erotic dreams. Dreams in which he had a child, a child who looked like him; and she took the child from him. She thought she woke from these dreams, shivering, surrounded by fear. She did what she had always done as a child, she conjured up visions of her mother to banish the aftermath of the dream. Emmie would stand between her and the darkness; big-boned, slightly sardonic, as if she did not believe in the dream or the terror. She never spoke. She looked from Sarah to the transluscent blackness around her and then she gave that tight, reluctant smile of hers and the darkness always gathered itself into small coagulations and shrank away.

Sometimes Sarah would speak to her mother.

'I know I've sinned. I know there is no redemption. This is hell, isn't it? Only it will be for ever and you won't be there.'

The tight smile widened and more reassurance seeped into Sarah's soul.

'All right,' she would whisper. 'But I shall go on sinning. Oh Ma . . . Ma . . . I *am* a sinner! Nothing can change that!'

And then her mother laughed. As if it didn't matter. And Sarah would wake up properly and lie quivering still, but in possession of herself again.

Her father never featured in these dreams. It had been terrible to see his anguish when she disgraced herself, but her own responsibility for that did not distress her as it did in Jim's case. Her father had his books and his fishing and a separate life of his own connected to the children through Emmie. Sarah knew – they all knew – that Emmie was the only person who really mattered to Walter. He loved his children, but it was his wife who gave him what he called 'the spark of glory'.

In spite of the dream, she fully intended to turn over a new leaf when she joined the Albion Entertainers. But the small group of would-be artistes were not her 'cup of tea' at all. They combined their own upper-crust image with what they saw as a Bohemian lifestyle into a mix of total hypocrisy. Sarah was many things but she was not a hypocrite. She found their lack of talent and their snobbishness not only obnoxious but eventually just plain boring. The only young male was Bertram Trenchard the pianist and though she made the very most of him, she could not help wondering why someone did not send him a bouquet of white feathers.

However, the 'Albions', as she called them, were better than any other viable alternative. And unfortunately when the War ended so would they. She did not think the War would last much longer. She had heard her father declare that the Schlieffen Plan had failed; that Germany had reached the nadir of international disgrace by using poison gas and the world would not put up with it; that Italy was only the first to protest by joining forces with the Allies. Germany must surely capitulate by Christmas; and then what would happen? If she hadn't managed to get some other work, she would be back in Dymock, engaged to some worthy farmer. It was almost as bad as her other dream.

But the War had dragged on into 1916, and as the casualty lists soared the Albion Entertainers suffered from the introduction of conscription. At first it was unmarried men, which meant they lost Bertie. By this time Sarah was sleeping with him on a regular basis so that she could share his charming flat in Bloomsbury and she viewed his departure with mixed feelings. He was the most boring man she knew and made her long for Alf Matson's rough hands or Edward Richardson's gentle ones, but she would miss his flat terribly. However, when he turned up trumps and said she could live there for the duration, she was entirely happy and saw him off with crocodile tears and adjurations to keep the flag flying. Then she returned to the flat and began to rearrange the furniture.

The next day was a Sunday: no performances. She was still in bed when the Fairchilds called. They were nominally in charge of the group and it was George Fairchild who knew Mr Edwards.

Sarah answered the door in Bertie's silk dressing-gown and Mrs Fairchild immediately turned and went back to the hansom waiting at the pavement. Mr Fairchild mumbled something about inconvenience and suggested that she should call that afternoon to see them at their hotel to discuss their future.

She smiled happily. She had no misgivings at that stage.

They had a permanent suite at Brown's Hotel. She arrived for afternoon tea, expecting the rest of the group to be there. When she was the only guest and there was no tea, she realized she was to be dismissed. She glanced at Mrs Fairchild, who was still avoiding her eye as a sign of disapproval, then at George Fairchild, who was also looking nervously around the room, and hated them both. And then her resolution hardened. She might not have a doublebarrelled name, but her father was more of a gentleman than any of them, and she was the best of the Albions anyway. She could sing and dance and tell jokes and flirt with the audience in a way none of the others dared.

George Fairchild cleared his throat. 'This is a terrible time, Miss James. A really terrible time.'

They both wore grey as if in mourning. The dark brown panelling of their private drawing-room absorbed the watery spring sunshine from Albemarle Street. Sarah's red military-style costume was the only colour in the room. She knew they considered it the extreme of bad taste.

She kept looking at him, willing him to meet her bold dark eyes. 'It is indeed, Mr . . .' She had been about to call him Mr Fairchild. But he was Mr Edwards' friend and had taken her on as a personal favour to that gentleman. She said, 'It is indeed, Uncle George. A terrible time. I understand the latest figures are worse than ever. It makes our work even more important, don't you think?' That would stymie the miserable old devil.

It certainly did. He looked at his wife who took up the batting angrily not knowing whether the Uncle George was usual or not.

'We were thinking of the loss of dear Bertie, Miss James. That was why we wished to see you.'

Sarah felt a real pang. 'Bertie? Dead? Already?' The words came out like pistol shots. He had barely reached Aldershot let alone France. He could not be dead yet.

'Of course not, girl!' Mrs Fairchild abandoned her distaste and became impatient. 'I speak of our loss. We now have no pianist!'

Sarah stared directly at her. She had pale blue eyes. Fishy eyes. Sarah could have hooted with joy. Neither of them knew that she played the piano.

She put her head on one side and said thoughtfully, 'Yes. I can see that might be a blow to Miss Crombie-Smythe. She doesn't play herself, I believe. Perhaps I could accompany her? If I play for myself . . . of course, that means I cannot dance. But there is a certain intimacy to self-accompaniment, don't you agree? And I can simply stay on stage for Miss Crombie-Smythe's song.' She gasped and put a hand to her throat. 'You weren't thinking of dismissing Miss Crombie-Smythe? It would be a great blow to her, I'm sure. I too have realized that her top C is not quite *there*, but I feel sure that with a little coaching . . . perhaps I could help with that too? We must all pull our weight in these dreadful times. Our dear family friend – Uncle Leslie – told me when he suggested I should join you, that I must be willing to turn my hand to . . . anything.'

Mr Fairchild was clearing his throat desperately. Mrs Fairchild's gaze was baleful. But there was nothing they could do. After all, this young upstart had connections, though neither of them was quite certain how strong these were.

So Sarah continued with the Albions and became more and more bored, and by the autumn of 1916 thought she might atrophy unless something exciting happened quite soon.

It was then, when the German casualties were reported to be much heavier than the English ones, that the Albions entertained for a soirée in the drawing-room of a large house in Pimlico overlooking the river.

Sarah wore a red satin dress, very *décolletée*, with matching fingerless gloves which ended past her elbows. She stuck an ostrich feather in her black hair and frayed a few curls around her forehead. The audience consisted mainly of officers on leave from the Somme. They had the strange withdrawn look Sarah recognized now. She heaved her bosom and sang about Picardy. At the end of the song, she sat with her hands resting on the piano keys, head thrown back, eyes closed. Then she turned on the stool, stood and curtsied deeply.

The applause was polite.

A portly man stood up with difficulty from one of the sofas and advanced to take her hand and lead her forward. She looked at him, surprised. George Fairchild approached fussily.

'Sir . . . may I present . . .'

The man said smoothly, 'I know Miss James, thank you, George.' He turned to the audience and said, 'Ladies, gentlemen, I am going to ask Miss Sarah James for an encore. Have I your approval?'

It was such a theatrical ploy that Sarah was certain it had been prearranged and she raised her brows humorously before she sat down again on the piano stool. Obviously she was in favour.

She sang a song from the Boer War, sickly with sentiment from an era just as indecisive and hopeless as the one they were in now. And then she did something she had never done before. She interrupted the soulful gaze directed towards the cornice, and glanced – just momentarily – at the audience. The women were all smiling bravely; some of the younger ones sporting cigarettes in long holders, others fanning themselves gently with the embossed programme of tonight's performances. They were unimpressed. The men were sitting well back in their comfortable armchairs, almost as if they were pushing themselves into the upholstery. The sickly poignancy of the song had done nothing for them either. It distanced them even further from the other people in the room. For the first time, Sarah wished she had a 'proper' voice. She thought of the terrible song of Orpheus – 'what is life to me without you' – it offered no consolation except its acceptance of a universal plight.

She could not sing opera, but she could offer . . . diversion. As she finished on the word 'heart', she forebore the usual dropped head and silent pause.

'Shall we finish with a rag?' she suggested brightly, looking towards George Fairchild. 'What about "Harlem Rag"?' She did not wait for approval but broke into the syncopated rhythm from America, pumping the pedal with her foot and flashing a broad smile around the room. It was like a glass of cheap gin offering momentary forgetfulness; after a second's startled silence, the tension was broken. The youngest officer in the room pushed himself out of his chair and seized one of the girls. They began a crazy one-step more or less on the spot between the scattered furniture. Someone began to push chairs to the side of the room. Within two minutes half a dozen couples were jerking frantically like puppets; everyone was laughing almost hysterically and Sarah was banging out the rhythm as hard as she could.

The portly man asked her to stay to supper.

'Just supper?' she asked, provocatively.

'I will send you back to Brown's in a cab afterwards,' he replied very solemnly.

She smiled proudly, 'I have my own flat. In Russell Square.' She thought of Bertie with gratitude. She wondered who would get his flat when he was killed and then cut that thought off.

The owner of this mansion led her into a small morning-room. A fire glowed in the grate. Red velvet curtains were pulled against the autumn evening. Silver covers gleamed on the sideboard.

'A cold collation, Miss James. Will it do?'

She thought of toast and cocoa at the flat.

'It will do nicely.' She swept to a chair by the fire. 'Now. How do you know my name?'

'You do not recognize me? We met many years ago.'

She was certain he was lying. He had been interested enough in her to ask George Fairchild for her name. She smiled and played along with him.

'My memory is not what it was,' she said roguishly.

He laughed. 'My dear Sarah! You cannot be more than seventeen and your memory – like everything else about you – is razor sharp!' He brought some dishes to the table. Cold ham, some kind of pickled fish. Her mouth watered. 'Perhaps if I remind you that I wore a dog collar then . . .'

She frowned. He was serious. Would it have been at Hereford on one of their rare visits to the Cathedral?

He helped her to ham. 'Our meeting also involved a fairground. You were addicted to a certain contraption. I believe it was called the Flip-Flap.'

She paused, her fork held above her plate. Then she laughed.

'Of course! Gloucester! The Three Counties Show! I've never forgotten it! And you are—'

'Francis Passmore-Williams at your service. Very much at your service.'

She was completely intrigued. This was the most interesting and surprising thing that had happened to her.

'How did you recognize me? I must have been only eight or nine years old!'

'You were like your mother then. You are even more like her now.'

Sarah pulled her mouth down. She adored Emmie but had never considered her to be in any way attractive.

'I have dark eyes, she has grey. I am on the small side, she is . . . not.'

He laughed then. 'Ah. Well . . . there is an essential quality she has which you have. Let us leave it at that, child. I could never forget you. Never.'

She paused still, caught by something in his look. She had seen it before, of course. Lascivious, Lizzie would call it. Most men looked at her lasciviously. But there was something more in this man's gaze. A kind of yearning.

He held her gaze for a moment, then smiled.

'Eat your supper, Sarah. You worked very hard tonight and must be hungry.'

'I am.' She spoke with her mouth full. 'Aren't you having any?'

'I think I'd prefer to watch you. I very much enjoy watching you, Sarah. Please don't allow it to put you off.'

'Oh it won't.' She grinned. 'I am used to being watched. It is part of the job.'

He nodded. 'I want to know so much about you, my dear. But first, supper. I will pour you some coffee and have some myself.' He went to a coffee pot above a small spirit lamp. Two cups were set out. So he had been expecting her. He poured and brought the coffee to her. 'This meeting is as much a surprise to me as it is to you.

I had asked the Albion Entertainers to arrange a soirée for purely business reasons. One of my interests is a woollen mill in Brimscombe.' He smiled at her wide eyes. 'Yes. Where your brother is at present training on the Great Western Railway. We met there. A while ago. In fact, I asked him to let me know when you were back at home. I was certain you would be.' He smiled over his coffee cup. 'I will teach you how to avoid last year's unpleasantness, child. There is no need to bring any more babies into the world. I take it you came home very pregnant?'

She flushed darkly and stopped chewing. She could be brazen herself, but this was different. Did he intend to read her a sermon for disgracing her family? She swallowed fiercely and began to gather up her bag.

'Stay where you are, Sarah. Finish your ham. And then there will be some trifle. My housekeeper invariably provides trifle when I am entertaining.'

She paused yet again. Trifle.

She said aggressively, 'You said this meeting was accidental. Yet your housekeeper knew you would be entertaining!'

'I always entertain after one of my business meetings,' he replied smoothly. 'I rarely know who it will be, of course. But tonight I knew instantly.'

'I don't understand.'

'Then let me explain while you continue to eat. And then you can do the talking. How does that sound?'

She picked up her fork again but said sullenly, 'My private affairs are nothing to do with you. I was married when I had Kilda and—'

'Rubbish! The child could have been fathered by anyone in that concert party! I knew you would get into trouble. You take after your mother in that too! And then, I knew, you would go home. So I asked your brother to let me know when that happened. He did not.' She was utterly bewildered. She took after her mother in . . . that? What on earth could he mean? And Jim – honest, grey-eyed Jim

162

– dragged into . . . what? She said, 'Jim is a good boy. He would wish to protect me.'

'But I wanted to help you. I told him that I would be able to help you to go on to the stage.' He looked at her. 'You have a flare for entertaining, Sarah. Tonight was a triumph. And it enabled me to secure a very lucrative contract. Officers' uniforms, don't you know.'

She laid aside her plate and waited for the trifle. She might as well eat as much as possible. And if he wanted to help her she was more than willing to be helped. But why would he want to help her? And what kind of payment would he exact?

He seemed to read her mind. 'I left Mother Church some time ago, Sarah. We did not really suit each other. I have a head for business and they needed that up to a point. But when I diverted some of the profits I had made into my purse, it was a different matter.'

She looked at him and suddenly laughed. And he laughed too and reached for a cut-glass bowl on the sideboard. The trifle was not quite what she was used to. It smelled very strongly of sherry.

He said, 'You see? We are two of a kind. I am what is known as an opportunist, Sarah. Do you understand me?'

'Oh yes.' What had Hope Chapel, Alf Matson and Edward Richardson been if they had not been opportunities to be seized?

'Your father disagreed with my . . . methods. We knew each other quite well a long time ago. He would not approve of this meeting of minds.'

'No.' She crammed her mouth with fruit.

'But your mother . . . that would be different, I fancy.'

She thought of Emmie. Yes, perhaps he was right. Emmie, after all, had seized the opportunity of a marriage far above her station.

'Yes,' she said through some cranberries.

'I have a wish, Sarah, to become a patron of the arts.' He looked at her and once again they both laughed.

Then he leaned forward. 'I could teach you so much,

Sarah. I could set you up with your own house. You could entertain. You could live life to the full. You could do exactly what you want.'

She felt juice running down her chin and handed him her napkin. Very gently he dabbed at her face.

She said tipsily, 'Shall I stay with you tonight?'

'No, my dear. Perhaps one day. But not tonight when you are drunk. And not to pay me either. You will sleep with me when you want to. Not before.'

She could not imagine wanting to sleep with someone whose stomach pushed at his waistcoat and was almost as old as her own father. But she smiled anyway.

He kissed her chastely and whispered close to her ear, 'And when that time comes, Sarah *mia*, we will go to Dymock. Together. And you can present me to your father so that we can renew our acquaintance.'

She looked up, intending to protest. But then her gaze was caught and held by his. His eyes were as dark as hers but quite opaque. She could not see what he was thinking or feeling at all. But, paunch or not, she was attracted. She blinked hard and stared again, questioningly. But he had straightened and was leaning back in his chair, smiling benignly. And a small bell tinkled a warning somewhere in her head.

NINE

1940

Dorothy's hurried departure from Gran soon slowed into an aimless stroll. She could not find Holly and Charlie – or, indeed, any of the scattered James clan – and was wandering back to the house when Kildie joined her at a run.

The girl – even Dorothy thought of her as still a girl – had obviously been crying and it occurred to Dorothy that perhaps Charlie *had* kissed her and, just possibly, gone further than that. How old was he now – seventeen? Surely Kildie could cope with a boy of seventeen?

Kildie caught her arm. 'Dorothy, I'm so *glad* to see you! You're like an answer to a prayer! I've been at Grandad's grave, praying like mad. And now here you are!'

Dorothy leaned her head away and stared in astonishment.

'You were praying for me to turn up?'

'Well . . . I didn't know I was, of course. But I was praying for something!' She pulled Dorothy close again. 'Dorothy – please! I'm absolutely desperate! I can't stop here! Please let me come home with you! Please!'

Dorothy tried for a small laugh of normality.

'Of course you can come back with me, my dear. But why? If you want a little break I should have thought the company of your mother—'

'You don't know what's going on!' Kildie seemed near hysteria and her face was horribly streaked with crying. She used far too much mascara. 'Mother sucks up to Uncle Edward and Gran doesn't seem to take any notice!'

Dorothy pulled the clinging arm through hers and drew

Kildie along as companionably as possible in the circum-stances.

'It's Gran's policy to let people work out their own salvation,' she said, discovering this for the first time. 'Yes, that is what she does.' She smiled and added wonderingly, 'Of course, Sarah will be much too much for poor old Edward. He will come running back to your Aunt Lizzie as fast as his legs will carry him!'

Kildie was checked momentarily. 'Do you think so?'

'It's what Gran thinks.'

'Is it? She is so . . . so . . . wise. But she could be wrong this time. Mother told me – on my wedding day actually – that she only had to crook her finger at a man and he would come running.'

Dorothy was shocked but tried not to show it. She laughed. 'I doubt that now. We are none of us in the first flush of youth, Kildie. I think you should remember that.' She put a slight emphasis on the 'you', but Kildie said nothing.

They were walking down Middle Lane. Dorothy stopped suddenly and looked around her.

'What?' asked Kildie.

'This is where Jim rescued me from Percy and Billy.' She turned down her mouth. 'I wish I hadn't told him that I did not need rescuing.'

Kildie's eyes filled with tears again. 'I wish he was here now. I need rescuing. Desperately.'

Dorothy looked at her curiously. Kildie was now twenty-five, almost twenty-six. Was she really as ingenuous as she seemed?

She said coolly, 'I really don't see what Jim could do, Kildie. I take it you are referring to your marriage to Marcus? I don't think Jim would interfere between a husband and his wife.'

Kildie drooped and wept openly.

'I know you're cross about Jim—'

'I am not "cross" as you put it, Kildie—'

'You only sound like a schoolteacher when you're cross!

166

He asked me to talk to you. Ages ago he asked me. But you won't let me come near you. You won't even let me come and stay with you!'

Dorothy made a sound of exasperation. 'Kildie, I have just told you . . . You are very welcome out at the Green. But I cannot actively encourage you to leave your husband, my dear. And I can assure you that your Aunt Lizzie and Winnie are no better company than Edward and Sarah!' She tried to laugh at that. Then she shook the girl's arm gently. 'Come on now, stop that crying, it will get you nowhere. And when did Jim advise you to talk to me. And what about?'

'About sex! And he told me the day he left for his training! Nearly a year ago! A whole year!'

Dorothy stared at Kildie's centre parting. Jim had said nothing of seeing Kildie. He had been home for his Christmas leave and said nothing except that he was to be posted to Scotland. She pushed it all to the back of her mind.

'And you want to talk about sex?'

'Marcus is vile! Three — four times a day! And I have to dress up in things — and he puts make-up on me – he makes me look like . . . look like—' She dissolved into frantic sobs.

Dorothy's mind did several leapfrogs. No wonder Jim had fended off the questions of sex.

She put her arms right round the heaving shoulders.

'All right. Come back with me. We'll talk properly and try to work something out.'

'Oh Dorothy – do you mean it? Oh, this is an answer to my prayer! I sat by Grandad's grave and prayed and prayed and then you came along – he sent you – he sent you, Dorothy!'

Dorothy said, 'Gran sent me, in a way. I wanted to find Holly.' She had wanted to find Holly to console her about Charlie. But if Kildie was not with Charlie it did not matter. She hugged the girl again. 'You are the next best! Now come on, cheer up, chicken!'

'Oh Dorothy . . . I always loved you – before Jim even!

D'you remember the pump? And poor old Percy Jenkins dying?'

Dorothy said indulgently, 'The two weren't connected, you know, dear.'

But Kildie said, 'Well . . . It was pneumonia. Gran told us.'

'She did, did she?' Dorothy compressed her lips. 'Actually, Percy Jenkins contracted pneumonia a whole year after I left the school, Kildie. He was out all night, poaching, with his father in those dreadful storms of 1925—'

'Well, it doesn't matter now. I was just trying to remember those happy, happy times . . .'

'I know, dear.' Dorothy tightened her hold. 'It was quite a time, wasn't it? Walter was such a wonderful man . . . so different . . . so unusual . . .'

'He explained to us about arachniphobia—'

'He knew I'd set the points for the main line quite deliberately that Boxing Day. And he understood.'

Kildie was momentarily diverted. 'Did you? Gran said your coat must have been caught in the lever.'

'She did, did she?' Dorothy repeated with some grimness. 'Well . . . actually, I rather resented the way those men were treating Gran that day.' She guided Kildie past the gate of the Station House towards the cottage. 'Walter understood that. He appreciated that.'

'Nothing has been the same since Grandad died,' Kildie mourned. 'Gran sits by his grave for hours and she seems grumpy and never sticks up for me any more.'

'Gran lived for your grandfather.' Dorothy led the way around to the back garden and paused. 'Every meal she cooked, every egg she collected—'

'I know, I know. But life has to go on,' Kildie inserted with slight impatience.

'Yes. That is the tragedy. It should have stopped for her when he died. And it didn't.'

Kildie began to cry again. 'Oh God – it's all so hopeless, isn't it? Everything.'

Dorothy thought of the future. Lizzie and Kildie mooning about the house at the Green while she tried to cope with rations and meals and getting in enough coal to last the winter.

She said bracingly, 'Don't worry about it now, Kildie. We'll talk it all out. And you can help me – I certainly need some help just at the moment.'

And Kildie, also seeing her immediate future, wailed, 'I can't cook, Dorothy! Gran always did all that. And now . . . Marcus sees to the shopping – he can get anything on the black market! Oh Dorothy!'

Someone came out of the back door and Kildie stopped crying abruptly. It was Marcus Villiers.

Sarah watched Edward button his waistcoat, and said with some amusement, 'So you propose to stay in Dymock with Ma, do you?'

'Why not?' He looked up at her defiantly. She was still darkly beautiful, but the wild gypsy look had hardened over the years. He had seen such faces at the servants' entrance of the Grange; their owners had been selling pegs and lucky heather. 'Your ma never criticizes me. And she's good to Charlie.'

'And Lizzie is going to stay with Dorothy, is she?'

He frowned. 'I don't know. We can't all stay here with Gran. We need a home. If only I could get old Matson's job at the Grange . . . Dammit all, I should get it, I'm the old man's nephew when all's said and done!'

'You'd get bored again. You know you would. You were better off in London.'

'Only because you were around. And if I came to live down here you'd be sure to visit your ma now and then! We could see each other almost as often as—'

Sarah tipped her head and laughed full-throatedly.

'I see. So you and Lizzie would have the Gatehouse at the Grange, and you'd pop down to see your mother-in-law like a good boy, and it would just so happen those visits would coincide with mine—'

'You make it sound so – so cynical,' he interrupted sulkily. 'If Lizzie would behave herself there'd be no need for—'

'For me?' Sarah was not offended. 'But I hate Dymock. Always did. Got out as soon as I could. Come back to London.'

'Can't. The children . . . bombing . . .'

Sarah laughed again and threw a stone idly into the Leadon. They were at the spot where her father had liked to fish while Jack Bower kept an eye on the station.

She said suddenly, 'It's not the kids, is it? You're scared.'

'Don't be absurd, Sar—'

'You're scared!' Her voice rose to a crow. 'Scaredy cat! Edward Richardson, son of Adrian Frost, is scared of the Jerries!'

'If you're going to be childish—'

'I'll stop being childish if you'll undo all those buttons you've just done up and . . .' She put her arms around him and tried to draw him down on to the bank. He resisted.

'Don't be a fool, Sarah! Charlie's around somewhere—'

Her voice hardened. 'There's always an excuse lately, Edward dear! I have to seduce you each time—'

'Well, you're good at that!' They were struggling, both enjoying it up to a point.

Behind him, Lizzie's voice screeched like an owl.

'What's going on? What are you two up to?' She was standing just below the clump of elms on the hill and she came running down to them while they released each other and turned to face her, smiling. Neither of them had the courage to tell her of their plans and they both prepared to lie fiercely.

'What are you doing here, darling?' Edward opened his arms and scooped her up just before she launched her handbag at his head. He swung her around dizzyingly. 'Is our little Winsome with you? How are you? Surely Dorothy hasn't thrown you out?'

Sarah said brightly, 'Kildie's here as well, you know! A

real family party again! I thought it might be her come to join us just where Pa used to—'

'Put me down, Edward! This instant!' Lizzie was half sobbing. She clung to her husband's lapels and lowered her head in an effort to orientate herself. 'I know you two were up to something – don't pretend—'

And quite suddenly Edward knew he could never live with Sarah James. He might not love his wife, but he certainly did not love Sarah.

He said, 'Actually, you're right, darling. There's just a chance we might be able to get the Gatehouse at the Grange. Old Matson is past it and Uncle Squire is going to pension him off.' He looked hard at Sarah over Lizzie's head. 'The thing is, Sarah has offered to have a word with my uncle.' He laughed. 'You know . . . one of her special words!'

Lizzie turned her head and stared blearily at her sister.

Sarah hesitated, fuming inwardly. Then, as usual, she saw the funny side of it all. And it might be quite a challenge to vamp the old squire.

She laughed. 'I'll make a list of them – you can help me, Lizzie. Starting with "you silly old buffer". And concluding with . . .' She said a word that the girls had picked up from Poacher Jenkins when they were very small indeed.

Lizzie gasped. And then, unwillingly, began to laugh.

Gran said, 'Well, if you're staying here now, our Lizzie, I don't know what we're going to do with all them bikes!'

Everyone was in a giggly mood. Kildie had departed in Marcus' car, run on black-market petrol. She had stood on the running-board, flung one arm wide and declaimed, 'I cannot resist him,' before Marcus had dragged her beside him, laughing helplessly. She had adored being 'reclaimed', though she had said loudly she was not a piece of luggage at a lost property office.

Winnie and Charlie had joined their aunt and parents on the banks of the Leadon and rejoiced that Dad kept his arm around Mum the whole time and told them they were going to live in the Gatehouse and Aunt Sarah would be returning to London. Winnie had visions of dining at the Grange and meeting someone as nice as the cinema manager at Croydon. Charlie thought that at least Kildie would visit Gran sometimes and he might see her.

Only Dorothy and Holly were subdued. It had crept over Holly that Charlie was really, truly and properly in love with Kildie. And Dorothy had a most peculiar sense of anticlimax. She had hated the thought of returning to the Green lumbered with Kildie as well as Lizzie and Winnie. But to return without them was – in some ways – worse.

Lizzie said, 'Ma – as if that mattered! Dorothy can make two trips before the summer is over and take them back.'

'You're hysterical, our Lizzie,' Gran said. 'Anyone'd think you and Edward had been parted for years instead of days!'

Lizzie giggled again and Sarah, looking at Edward, said, 'I wonder if we shall hear the patter of little feet in nine months' time?'

If she hoped to shut Lizzie up, she was disappointed. Lizzie lifted her face to Edward and murmured, 'I wouldn't be surprised, would you, dear one?'

Edward lost his forced gaiety on the instant and looked down at his wife with deep concentration. This, from Lizzie, was a statement of intent. Suddenly he could not wait for bedtime. Sarah might be the wanton twin with plenty of tricks up her sleeve, but he knew that Lizzie was solely his.

Dorothy said briskly, 'Well, we might as well go on the four o'clock, Gran. Thanks again for the butter and bacon.'

Gran came to the station with them and stood by, while they loaded two of the bikes into the brake van.

'You'll look after each other, won't you?' she said. 'If you need me send a message to the office and they'll ring the station here.'

Dorothy said, 'You've got enough to do. Five extra.'

'They might think they need me, but they don't.' Gran looked at Holly. 'And them who thinks they don't need me, prob'ly do.'

Holly stared over Gran's head at the wall which sheltered all the ferns at the cottage. Maybe Charlie was sitting under the veranda even now.

Dorothy said, 'If you're worried about Kildie, don't. If anything goes wrong again she's going to come and talk to me.'

Gran gave a scornful laugh. 'I'm not worried about Kildie! She's got what she needed in life. I wish Sarah had found a Marcus Villiers!'

Dorothy let her incredulity show through. Gran was the hardest woman she had met.

'It's you I worry about, Doll. You and your maid there. You got too many brains for your own good.'

Dorothy puffed a small laugh. 'I thought you had quite a low opinion of my intelligence, Gran!' she said, only half jokingly.

The guard blew his whistle and Gran stepped back a pace.

'Never doubted your brain-box, Dorothy! Just your common sense!' she called through the steam.

Dorothy looked at Holly who was grinning broadly.

'Come on,' she said. 'Let's go and sit down! What a day! I don't know about *my* common sense, but I reckon your father's sisters are definitely lacking in that department!'

Holly hugged her mother's arm and when they reached Gloucester she handed the bicycles down to her with exaggerated care.

'Don't go too fast, Mum! You might lose what's left of your common sense!'

'Cheeky young madam.' But Dorothy's spirits were lifting all the time. She thought of the easy meals she and Holly could now have for the rest of the summer. They could collect wood for next winter and salt

173

down the kidney beans and make plum jam.

They reached home in good spirits and found two letters waiting for them. One was from school to say that Holly had got her School Certificate. The other was from Jim. He was coming home on leave before going to Canada.

1921

Lizzie had consciously to stop herself from curtseying to Uncle and Aunt Squire as Edward called them. She would always address them as 'sir' and 'm'lady'.

Edward said, 'When we're married, you'll have to stop all that kowtowing, Lizzie. I won't have it. We're as good as they are and don't you forget it!'

Lizzie had been wearing an engagement ring into the office since Edward was demobilized at the end of 1919. After two years she was beginning to think Edward should have saved enough money to buy a farm.

'If they really looked on us as in their class, they would help us to get somewhere,' she said. 'We shall always be the poor relations, Edward. I wish you would accept it and not feel so much bitterness. It cannot do you any good.'

Edward looked down at her smooth brown hair and the high collar she always wore. His love for her made him think he would have to go to London and find Sarah. Either that or marry Lizzie as soon as possible. It was the only way he was going to get her to bed.

He said, 'I hate them! I shall always hate them, Lizzie. You don't know what it's like being dependent on their good will like I am!'

She said gently, 'Dearest Edward. They have been so good and kind to you. University. That farming course in Hereford. Getting you the commission in the War Office—'

'I would have preferred to take my chances in the

trenches!' he said untruthfully. And what was the good of teaching me to farm then not giving me a farm?'

'Perhaps when they know we are engaged—'

'Uncle Squire would just call me irresponsible yet again!'

It was a slight bone of contention between them that Edward wanted to keep their engagement secret. He had no wish to be reminded of his past peccadillos. He still sowed a few oats now and then but he was quite certain his heart was pure. He was obsessed with Lizzie and thought of her even when he was flirting with the girls from Dean. When he saw Lizzie's smooth virginal face bending over Kildie, he wanted to weep worshipfully.

She said, as if reading his thoughts, 'It's almost time to meet Kildie from school, my dear. Will you come with me?'

'I wouldn't miss it for anything.'

Lizzie was a throw-back. With her smooth brown hair and transluscent tea-coloured eyes, she was quite different from her twin. Yet there was a look of Sarah about her and, combined with her personal neatness and precise, old-fashioned ways, she set Edward aflame. But her natural innocence was strengthened by a strait-laced attitude which, as yet, he had not comprehended. She lived near enough to the land to know all the mechanics of procreation. She could see with her clear eyes what a disgusting act it was, yet how necessary in order to continue the species. She gathered, from the shining example of her parents, that when true love was involved, it became possible, even perhaps bearable. She knew that was how it would be for Edward and herself, because they both respected each other.

Sarah's behaviour with her unknown 'husband' and with Alf Matson in Red Marley Churchyard was inexplicable and shameful to Lizzie. She had laid plans immediately to rescue baby Kildie and to rid the house of Sarah herself. This had been accomplished most successfully and she began to feel in control of her fate.

It did not upset her when Edward went into the Army. After all, his uncle had procured him a commission and his uniform was very smart indeed. He was comparatively safe in the London offices – as safe as she was herself. Meanwhile she went into Gloucester each day and learned to be – with Jim's help – a reliable clerk. She saved her money carefully, began a bottom drawer and became even more rigid in her ways.

She was now twenty-two. According to her plan she should get married soon and take on the role of farmer's wife. Then, a year after the wedding, she would give birth to a son. Perhaps after a suitable interval there would be a little girl like Kildie. She was not quite certain about that as yet. But she knew that she wanted to get married. Now.

She had heard the rumours about Edward – not only from Sarah – and knew that young men did behave in a wild fashion before marriage. So for Edward's sake too, they should be married quite soon.

She visualized a small farm quite close to the Station House. It would have a dairy which she would keep spotlessly clean. She would keep poultry like her mother did, and Edward would see to the cows and pigs, and in the early summer there would be strawberries because pigs and strawberries always went together. In her bottom drawer she had accumulated no less than two dozen antimacassars, crocheted by herself during the long winter evenings. These would go on the backs and arms of the easy chairs. There would be a doily beneath the fruit bowl on the sideboard and probably one beneath each of the family photographs flanking the fruit bowl. She would look after Edward; soothe away all the bitterness of the past; cook him delicious meals and mend his socks and sit on the arm of his chair occasionally, and kiss his forehead. She might well heal the breach between Edward and his family too, though that was a long-term plan. For the present, the next step was definitely the wedding.

She talked to her mother about it. Emmie was the practical one and would understand without having to go into the kind of philosophical discussion to which Walter was very prone.

'I think Edward *wants* to get married, Ma,' Lizzie said earnestly, pausing in mid-stitch; she was monogramming pillowcases with a curly R. 'But he thinks his uncle should help him. How can his uncle help him when our engagement is kept a secret?'

Emmie said tactfully, 'I think your intentions are well known, my dear. After all, Edward has been courting you since you were sixteen.'

Lizzie smiled and resumed her work. 'It was love at first sight, really. I noticed him at that first Christmas party of the War. And he has told me that he could see no-one else there.' She blushed very prettily.

Emmie bent down to sweep up the hearth. This was going to be difficult.

'I rather think, my love, that Squire and Lady Alicia are wanting Edward to stand on his own feet over this.'

'You mean, they are not going to help us?' Lizzie said, dismayed.

'How can I know that? It did cross my mind that they have done a great deal for the boy and I sometimes wonder whether he has ever thanked them for it.'

Lizzie knew very well he had not. He resented their help almost as much as he resented their lack of it.

She cast down her work. 'Oh Ma! Edward needs me! I can make sure he fulfils their hopes for him! But on his own . . .'

Emmie put the hearth brush carefully on the fender.

'I think, perhaps, if your father has a word with the Squire, the position may be clearer.'

Lizzie said eagerly, 'There is a farm – no more than a smallholding really – just off the Kempley Road. It would definitely support us. I'm sure we could make a go of it.'

'I know you are a very hard worker, Lizzie.' Emmie retrieved the pillowcase and examined it admiringly. 'But you have little idea how tiring children can be. I know Edward wants a family—'

'So do I, Ma! Of course!' Lizzie's face was alight with enthusiasm. 'But not for a year at least. I would not want to start a lot of gossip again. And in that year I can establish us in a good routine—'

Emmie smiled. 'Dear Lizzie. How can you decide these things? Babies have a habit of arriving when they're ready!'

Lizzie too laughed. It was good to laugh with Ma like this. Two women together, 'happy and chatty' as Ma said.

'Well, dear Ma, if we could just look at the farm. And then, when Pa had a word with the Squire he would have some concrete proposals.'

'You never said things like that before you worked on the railway,' Emmie noted smilingly.

'No. That is a railway phrase. Concrete proposals. It did me so much good, those few years of work, Ma. Broadened me.'

Emmie knew that in fact the office work had narrowed Lizzie. But she had great hopes that Edward would change all that. So she put it to Walter and they all went to look at the farm.

They did not tell Lizzie how hopelessly the interview went at the Grange. But Emmie was concerned.

'If they don't get married soon, that Edward Richardson will go on the loose again,' she prophesied. 'He'll do something Lizzie will not be able to forgive.'

'I have almost half the asking price of that little farm,' Walter told her. 'And if he takes up a mortgage—'

Emmie threw up her hands. 'Edward Richardson with a mortgage!'

Walter said, 'Are you sure this is a good match, Em? He is close to being a wastrel.'

'He is the only one for Lizzie, Walter. What will happen to her if this falls through?'

'She will be safe. She will stay with us.'

'And become an embittered old maid.'

He thought about it and nodded.

She said, 'Walter, let us write to his father. If he could be reconciled with Edward, it might give the boy some kind of reassurance. And he might help him too.'

'He probably hasn't got two coppers to rub together. These Bohemian poets are always the same.'

'Let's see,' she insisted.

Edward wanted to take his bride to Paris for the honeymoon.

Lizzie was bewildered. 'Why? It would cost a great deal of money which could be used to build up the stock!'

Edward looked into the depths of those brown eyes and could have drowned. 'I want our wedding night to be the most romantic wedding night in history! I want to walk with you by the Seine then carry you into a small hotel on the Left Bank and make love to you till the dawn—'

She shook her head at him indulgently. 'Edward, you talk such nonsense. A strange river, a strange hotel . . . when we can be in our own home and walk by the Leadon if we wish.'

'Oh you're right, of course! Darling, darling Lizzie. As if it matters where we are! So long as we are together!'

She was used to his ardour; it was meaningless, just part of his male gallantry. She lifted his thick hair and kissed his forehead.

'You would make anything anywhere romantic, Edward Richardson!'

He looked at her and his eyes filled with tears. She was his. His alone. And she would always be his alone. He knew that just as he knew the sun would come up each morning and go down each night. He said hoarsely, 'Sarah—'

She misinterpreted both his tears and his use of her sister's name. She picked up his hand and kissed it.

'You should know by now, Edward. I am not Sarah. I will be faithful. Completely faithful.'

He gathered her to him and stared over her head wondering if he were indeed going mad. He wanted everything . . . and surely that was what he was getting: his natural father turning up and determined to help him at last, Uncle Squire with his nose right out of joint, the demure innocence of Lizzie and – it must be – the passion of Sarah. No wonder he was going mad. It was enough to drive any man crazy with ecstasy.

It was a proper country wedding with trestle-tables along the up platform and the station canopy garlanded with flowers. Mr Edwards was there and the Assistant General Manager almost put in an appearance but was detained at the last minute. Adrian Frost wrote a poem for the occasion and declaimed it while standing on a parcels trolley. The Squire and Lady Alicia smiled graciously and allowed Lizzie to kiss them. Kildie made the prettiest bridesmaid anyone had ever seen. And Jim was a beaming best man. Sarah's absence was welcomed by everyone there. Passengers stepped off the trains to toast the health of the young couple. Emmie moved among the crowds, passing sandwiches and filling glasses, and Walter, in his best uniform, made the perfect host. 'I am giving away my daughter and receiving back one of the happiest couples in this country,' he said at the end of his speech. Everyone cheered and hurled rose petals indiscriminately. It was a wonderful year for roses.

Adrian Frost carried a tray of glasses into the kitchen of the Station House and found Emmie up to her elbows in scalding water, washing-up for the next round.

'I'll polish,' he said immediately, stripping off his jacket. 'I've polished glasses in public houses up and down the country. I'm quite good at it.'

She smiled briefly but said nothing.

'There is a quality of stillness about you, madam. Especially now, in this hurly-burly, when you are hostess.'

'I'm no good to anyone if I get flusterated,' Emmie told him.

'It's more than that.' He lined up the glasses on the table next to the cask of cider. 'I am reminded of the saying, Still waters run deep. You are a woman of mystery, Mrs James.'

'Me?' she laughed. 'Not me, Mr Frost.'

He picked up something from her tone and opened his hooded eyes. 'So. There *is* a mystery?'

She had outstripped him with the glasses and took another tea towel from the drawer.

'Here's another saying for you, sir. Water under the bridge.' She rubbed vigorously. 'There's always something behind every face. You should know that. But once it's past, it's past.'

He looked through the window to where Edward had a possessive arm around Lizzie's waist. He sighed. He was almost sure the girl was frigid.

'Not always,' he said sadly. 'Not always.'

Edward closed their own front door at last and locked it carefully. He could hear Lizzie – his wife – humming to herself upstairs as she got ready for bed. She had been almost excited about it.

'I'm longing for you to see my nightgown, darling,' she said almost within earshot of her mother. 'It's really too good for bed. I smocked the whole of the bodice and the hem has four broderie-anglaise frills!'

'I'll be very careful with it,' he said, hardly able to take his eyes off her.

And now he was going to see it. He was going to remove it very carefully as he had promised and there would be Lizzie's slender body beneath it, waiting for him.

He took the stairs two at a time and then paused in the doorway of the bedroom just looking. Sure enough she was in the nightgown which was far prettier than her muslin wedding dress, which had reminded him of a Rudolf Valentino costume. Her hair, normally flat to her head, was lying abundantly around her face and over her shoulders and she was brushing it with long regular strokes, scalp to ends, scalp to ends, with the regular motion of clockwork.

He took the brush and threw it onto the dressing-table, lifted the hair and buried his face in it. He encircled her throat with his hands and felt for the buttons of the nightgown, discovered they were seed pearls and tore them open.

'Edward! What are you doing?' Her voice was muffled by hair and the wodge of smocked material.

He could not speak. He left her strait-jacketed by the bundle of cloth and ran his hands over her body. She was wearing drawers! He pushed them down and she squeaked with horror.

He lifted her and put her on the bed. He could wait no longer. He put his mouth over her protesting one and had his way with her.

Long after he was asleep, snoring horribly and stinking of cider, she lay wide-eyed in the summer darkness, rigid with the horror of it. Her plans were in ruins. She would now have her son nine months from her wedding day which would be the talk of the village. Already she felt sick and realized what her mother had meant about pulling her weight with the farm work. She would not be able to do a thing!

Towards dawn she managed to turn her head and look at her husband. He looked as bad as he sounded and smelled. His mouth was open and he was dribbling on to her monogrammed pillowcase. Tears filled her eyes. What had she done? She could not go home and admit it was a failure. He had secured her loyalty by making sure she would be immediately pregnant.

At that moment she hated him.

That afternoon, after he had scrambled through the chores, she said to him, 'I thought you knew I did not want our first child immediately, Edward.'

'Child?' he was honestly bewildered. He had slept late

so that the six cows had been over-full and irritable. The pigs had upset their swill on his feet. And he had a ghastly hangover. The thought of being with Lizzie again had kept him going.

'Last night,' she said in a suffocated voice.

She was sitting in a chair liberally patched with antimacassars. He'd have to get rid of them – they made his eyes blur. He came up behind her, leaned over and cupped her breasts.

'Oh darling. Do you believe *that* will make you pregnant?' He laughed into her hair. 'My little innocent. You were too far gone to notice that I withdrew.' He moved his mouth to her ear and nibbled the lobe delicately. 'Trust me, darling. I know what I am doing.'

Her enormous relief was quickly followed by fresh revulsion.

'Why did you do it, then?' she said sharply, moving her head away from his mouth.

'Because I love you. Because you are irresistible. Because you are my wife. Because I am your husband.' With each phrase he was moving his mouth along her neck, to her chin and finally to her lips.

'Please, Edward!' She jerked away. 'It is mid-afternoon and I have to see to the hens and you have to do the evening milking—'

'There is time, darling—'

'There is *not*!' She stood up and he almost fell down. He grabbed the arm of the chair and the antimacassar slid to the floor. 'Look what you've done now!' She moved right away. 'Edward, I am thankful there can be no child from last night. But I do not intend to simply . . . play around . . . like that! It's not right! It's sinful, in fact!'

He still did not realize the full extent of her feelings and laughed as he picked up the antimacassar and put it on his head.

'And you are my wife, my pretty one . . .' He pretended to advance menacingly. 'And you have promised to obey me and worship me with your body and—'

183

She turned to run but he was too quick for her. He rather enjoyed the struggle on the new hearth mat, he had never had to fight with a girl before.

Afterwards, he whispered, 'I certainly worship you with my body, Lizzie.' He kissed her trembling mouth with great tenderness. 'Why do women always cry afterwards?' He laughed. 'That was not sinful, my Lizzie. I think this time I might well have made you pregnant.'

She turned her head to the wall. Her clothes were all over the floor. Her body was bruised and sore, inside and outside. Her precious antimacassars were askew, one of them like a piece of rag lay under her cheek. She picked it up and dried her tears with it. Edward had said things that made her realize his past flirtations had gone further than she had imagined.

But there was a ray of hope in his last words.

She said, 'If I'm pregnant you will have to be careful Edward. Otherwise I might miscarry!'

He knew then – although it was a long time before he would acknowledge it – that Lizzie was very, very different from Sarah. In every respect.

TEN

1940

Miss Joliffe gave the whole Upper Fifth a tea party in the Cadena – the girls could hardly believe it. She was pink with pleasure at the excellent results. Holly James, who appeared to go into a trance during the long double period in the stuffy lab, and who had twice been caught by Miss Joliffe talking to herself in the cloakroom, had won a distinction in General Science. Four others had done the same. Miss Joliffe thought of those long hours when she had tried to instil her own enthusiasm for the physical make-up of the planet into the rows of puddings in front of her, and felt perhaps her time had not been wasted. Enthusiasm they did not have, but knowledge they must have acquired. And from her.

She said to the Cadena manager. 'Yes, I know there's a War on, miss. But it's being fought for these girls. Surely they deserve the best you can do. I'd like cream cakes all round and as much tea as they can drink.'

The girls cheered. No longer did their round white faces remind her of puddings. They were bright and full of intelligence. Miss Joliffe positively loved them.

'I'd like to think,' she said sonorously above the giggles and chatter, 'that some of you will consider staying on and taking sixth form courses next term. I realize that you have an enormous choice of jobs, but there is a world of difference between a job and a career . . .'

They'd heard it before. Holly sat there, beaming, knowing that she would be staying on at least until she was sixteen next summer. But then . . . if the War was still on, she might be able to lie about her age and get into

185

the WAAF and maybe join Dad in Canada. The thought of Dad made her heart jump. He could arrive at any time depending on the trains from Scotland. She had already gone twice to Dymock to collect the spare bicycles and hang around on Gloucester platform in the hope she could meet him. She glanced surreptitiously at Granny Prosser's watch which Mum let her wear on special occasions. There was a train from Birmingham due in at five-thirty. Dad might change at Birmingham, in which case . . .

Miss Joliffe boomed, 'Eat up, Holly! It's ersatz cream but it might put some flesh on your bones!'

She spoke kindly enough, but Holly flushed sensitively at this reference to her skinniness. She was so different from Kildie who was certainly slender but also beautifully curved. Thoughts of Kildie made her heart jump harder than ever. Kildie represented something other than the humdrum routine of wartime. Kildie was rich and lived a life of luxury and had stepped outside the family somehow. She also lived a life of danger. Not from bombs. From other things. And Charlie knew this. That was one of the reasons Charlie loved her.

She bit into her cream bun and let herself think of Charlie. He and Winnie and Aunt Lizzie were moving into the Gatehouse with Uncle Teddy next weekend and then Holly would be able to go and stay with Gran sometimes and perhaps see her cousins. If Mum didn't mind. Holly licked cream from her chin. Mum said she hadn't had time to be lonely yet. But this second winter of the War promised to be harder than the first.

'Good girl,' said Miss Joliffe, looming over her. 'I have to admit I was a little surprised at your results, Holly. Delighted, of course, but a little surprised. I had no idea you were so interested in physics.'

Holly nearly explained that it was Blanche who liked the sciences. Luckily she remembered that Blanche was supposed to have moved to pastures new. She smiled and licked at the same time.

Miss Joliffe looked unusually sympathetic. 'No napkins,

186

child. I was reminded about there being a war on! It's the excuse for everything these days.'

'They have lovely linen ones for the *thé dansants*, Miss Joliffe.' Holly saw the fish-blue eyes hardening and hastened to explain. 'My cousin used to sing here, you know. She told me.'

'Ah, I see. Good.' Miss Joliffe leaned closer. 'I realize you are one of our scholarship girls. And none the worse for that,' she added bravely. 'And, as you doubtless know, you could sit the Higher School Certificate and have a chance of being awarded a State scholarship on the results.'

Holly nodded. Mum was an expert on this.

Miss Joliffe patted her hand conspiratorially and went on to the next table, and Holly drank her tea and joined in the chatter which was mainly about General Sikorski and his Free Poles who had marched through the city at the weekend. Miranda Parker was wondering what a 'free pole' was. Janet Baldwyn, whose father was mayor so should know better, was telling her. Everyone was choking with suppressed laughter. It was almost five-thirty. Holly grinned and slid towards the door.

Kildie arrived back from her afternoon walk feeling hot and cross. Mrs Davis, who was the best they could do since the maid joined the ATS, was engaged in her usual battle with the vacuum cleaner. Marcus had instructed her carefully on its use, but in her hands it had a mind of its own, crashing into table and chair legs, scraping the paint off the skirting-boards and even attacking her personally at times.

She switched off with evident relief as Kildie came in through the french windows.

'Gawd. I thought you'd gone for ever,' she greeted her. 'I'll put the kettle on and leave this for a bit. Mind you, don't trip over the—' Kildie untangled the cable from her silver anklet and limped to the sofa. 'Sorry, ducky. Damned thing isn't worth the space it takes up. Give me a dustpan and brush any day of the week.'

'Well use one then,' Kildie said irritably. 'And don't bother with the kettle. There's some gin left in the cocktail cabinet. Let's have a proper drink.'

Mrs Davis went to the glass and veneer cabinet with alacrity and used the soda siphon with expertise. The two women sat and sipped, and Kildie let her head fall back on the cushion and closed her eyes and wondered when Marcus would be home.

Mrs Davis said, 'Oh. That there phone rang too.' She sounded aggrieved. 'Kept ringing and ringing. I had to pick it up in the end.'

Kildie opened her eyes. 'I've shown you a dozen times how to answer it. And there's a pad and pencil for messages.'

'I couldn't get it, lovie. Something about a crew.'

'A crew? Sailors, d'you mean?'

'How do I know?'

'It was a man was it?'

'Yes. Said as how you could pass on the message if you would.'

'What message.'

'About the crew.'

Kildie gave up and returned her head to the cushion with unnecessary force.

'I'd better get on,' Mrs Davis said.

'Just put the damned vacuum away and finish off tomorrow.' Kildie lifted her head and reached for her bag, trying to sound a bit more gracious. 'Here's your half-crown anyway. What have you left for supper?'

'One of Mr Villiers' salads. And there's the rest of the pork in that cold cupboard—'

'Refrigerator!' Kildie reminded her sharply. She was the only person for miles around to have a cocktail cabinet and a refrigerator. And a vacuum cleaner.

'And tomorrow is fish day. So you're all right.'

'Yes.' Kildie thought of trailing after Gran around Eastgate market for fish on a Friday. She had, after all, hated it. But now . . . 'Perhaps I could pop into town and get some parsley?' she suggested.

Mrs Davis looked surprised. 'Sprouting everywhere in the garden,' she said. 'I'll soon chop some up in the morning.'

'I'll do it, Mrs Davis.' But Mrs Davis was singing 'Run Rabbit, Run Rabbit, Run, Run, Run' and did not hear.

Kildie sat for a while then got up and climbed the stairs very slowly. She felt like an old woman. There was a mirror on the landing which was meant to reflect light down the stairs. She studied herself in it. Marcus had said she was putting on weight so she had decided to force herself out for a walk every afternoon. Was she putting on weight? Might she be pregnant? She stood sideways and let her muscles sag. She looked pregnant. And lots of women went on seeing their monthlies for a while when they were expecting. She felt a surge of excitement pierce her discontent. It would be absolutely marvellous to have a baby. She would stop feeling guilty about her non-contribution to the war effort and Marcus would have to stop . . . doing it. She flushed at the thought. But he would, all the same. It was dangerous to make love when you were pregnant, she'd read it somewhere.

She went into the bathroom and had a wash. It would have been nice to have a bath but Kildie had not yet outgrown her wariness of total immersion too often. Especially if you suspected you were pregnant. A bath once a week was quite sufficient.

She towelled herself vigorously and went into the bedroom with a lighter step. Already she felt like an expectant mother. She riffled through the wardrobe and came up with a kimono in a willow-pattern print. She unplaited her hair and brushed it out into kinky waves. Then she went through the house, singing under her breath, swinging from room to room seeing it all anew: the nursery, the playroom, the music room – for later. Gran could move in and help her. That would be just marvellous. Gran would be so proud of the baby. If it was a boy they could call him James. Like Jim. Jim would be a wonderful uncle. After the War he would teach little Jim how to fish . . . he would take him around the engine sheds and let him sit in one of the cabs and watch the fireman stoke the box and eat bacon fried on a hot shovel and . . .

The telephone was ringing in the hall. She did a foxtrot out to it, holding on to Jim's shoulder and bending backwards like Ginger Rogers and singing, 'Heaven . . . I'm in heaven . . .'

The phone roared like a gale into her ear. 'Press button A, caller,' she advised in the voice she'd used in her bank days.

The gale stopped abruptly and the operator's voice said, 'Long distance for you . . .' Then Jim's unmistakable Dymock burr came across the line. 'Hello. Is that you, Kildie? Did you get my message?'

'*Jim!*' she squealed delightedly, certain she had conjured him up with sheer mind power. 'Where *are* you?'

'Same as before, Kildie. Crewe. There's a train running from here at midnight. Change at Birmingham. Heaven knows when I'll get home. If you could just tell Doll when you go down—'

'You're coming home *tonight*?'

'Tell her I'm sorry about all the confusion. Not to meet me on any account – don't know when . . . take a taxi out to the Green . . . thinking of you all . . .' The voice seemed to be moving away with each phrase. Kildie yelled, 'Jim! Don't go! Just tell me approximately what time you—'

The operator's voice said firmly, 'Your three minutes are up.'

'Just hang on one second, operator. Jim—'

'Goodbye, Kildie.' His voice was faint and she strove to bring him into her mind again and hold him there. But it didn't work. He was gone.

She stood there, holding the phone under her chin, grinning crazily. Marcus would drive her down to the

Green. She could tell Dorothy about the baby. Holly would be so pleased. So very pleased and excited.

Holly waited on the platform from five-thirty until ten to nine when a troop train arrived and disgorged five hundred men in khaki uniforms. Not one airforce blue.

When they had clambered into trucks and left for Innsworth Camp she stood up and wheeled her bicycle along to the ticket collector at the gate. It had been a beautiful day, but a small chill wind blew through the station as the sun dipped lower and Holly felt a sense of doom which she knew was completely unreasonable and silly.

She surrendered her platform ticket and began the three-mile ride back home. The extra two hours of British summer time meant that it would not be dark until eleven, so she could have probably met another two trains before having to obey Mum's rule to be home before dark. But, after all, Mum was there on her own, waiting and wondering, and Holly's absence was not going to help matters. So she stood on the pedals and tore along the Tewkesbury Road in an effort to 'snap out of it' as Mum would say.

She skidded past the pump at nine-thirty and was surprised to see the house lights blazing in a very unpatriotic way. It might not be blackout time for another hour but it was most unusual for Mum to light up without drawing the heavy bombazine curtains. It was a measure of her anxiety and Holly felt guilty that she had hung around for so long in Gloucester.

She pushed her bike into the shed and went to the back door and slipped into the kitchen. Then she paused, her grey eyes wide. The sound of voices raised in laughter came from the front room, then applause, then a chord on the piano and someone – a male – began to sing 'There'll always be an England'.

Just for a second Holly thought it was Dad. Then she knew it wasn't because Dad never sang, and in any case this voice had a nasal twang that came from the other side of the Atlantic.

Holly waited until the end of the song when there was much laughter – as if it were funny instead of deeply moving – and heard Mum's voice saying, 'Any more requests, gentlemen?'

Holly was shocked. Mum wasn't a bit worried about her daughter's late arrival home. She wasn't sitting biting her nails wondering when Dad would arrive. She was entertaining visitors! And Canadian visitors by the sound of things.

Holly opened the door and looked around it. There was not room for her to go inside because every chair and most of the floor space was taken up by young men sprawling about as if they owned the place. They wore the smooth blue serge of airforce officers, they were all very young and – she had to admit it – they were all extremely good-looking. Standing by the piano turning the music was Mabel Crawshay from the other side of the Green who was Mum's fellow fire-watcher, and her husband was sitting on the arm of the sofa – which Mum never allowed – sharing a map with one of the young men – which was also against all the security advice from the Ministry of Defence.

Mum screamed with delight at the sight of Holly.

'Darling! Have you got him with you?'

Holly insinuated herself inside and closed the door behind her back. Mum's face fell.

'I was so certain you were meeting Dad at the station, Hol. Oh what a shame! These three officers are from Edmonton, where Dad is going.'

Holly looked again. It was true, there were only three young men. They took up so much room.

Mum said, 'Mr Crawshay found them wandering about in the village completely lost! He brought them here as it was Mabs' night for fire-watching and we've been having a bit of a singsong.'

Holly felt slightly reassured. She managed a small smile.

'Gentlemen. My daughter, Holly.'

The young men leapt to their feet as one and made a great fuss of shaking her hand. The youngest grinned at her.

'Dolly and Holly, huh? Sounds as if we're in good company, guys!'

So they were already calling Mum Dolly.

'Yes, Hol. You'll never guess. They're all called Bob! The three Bobs!' Mum laughed as if it were the biggest joke in the world. Mabs Crawshay started stacking music on the piano top.

'Time we did our patrol, everybody!' She had a high trilling voice, rather like Miss Edwards at school when she was calling her teams on the hockey field. 'Charles, dear, why don't you put our Canadian friends on the right road for the camp. Dorothy and I will just whip around the Green and leave it at that for tonight. I don't think we're a prime enemy target, do you?'

Everyone laughed again. The three Bobs picked up their caps and gas masks and broke into a chorus of effusive thanks.

'I thought you Britishers were meant to be reserved! You've given us a welcome tonight—'

Mum was murmuring something about hoping her husband would be accepted into Canadian homes. Mabs Crawshay trilled, 'Cast your bread upon the waters, boys, and it often comes back as hot-buttered toast!'

More laughter. More movement. And Mum reappearing in her tin hat saying, 'I'll be ten minutes, Hol. Are you all right?'

'Yes. Of course.'

'Tea with Miss Jollybags go all right?'

'Yes.' It was ages since the cream bun. Holly wondered what was in the pantry.

'Any news of troop trains arriving from the North?'

'No.'

'Damn. I wonder what's happened.' She shouldered her gas mask. 'Make some cocoa, darling. And there's a crumb of cheese and loads of tomatoes if you're starving.'

'Come along, Dolly dear!' Mabs Crawshay trilled from the hall.

'Oh, better draw the blackout curtains too, darling.' And she was gone.

The views from Hill House were superb. Kildie languished in the conservatory and watched as, far below, a herd of cows was brought across the road for milking. The cows' splashings would doubtless foul Marcus' car again and he would frown and tell her something ought to be done about the blasted animals. And then she would tell him her news and he would stop frowning and . . . and . . . maybe he would go down on his knees in worshipful gratitude to her and she would cup his face and plant a chaste kiss on his forehead. Maybe after an early supper he would drive her down to the Green and she could give Jim's message to Dorothy. Or maybe he would put her to bed and go by himself. Or maybe he would send a wire. Or something.

She let the front of the kimono slip open so that her legs were exposed. He loved it when she dressed up for him. He would throw his hat across the hall and gather her up and their evening meal would have to wait, sometimes for over an hour.

It would be different now, of course. He would still gather her up, but it would be to lie her on the sofa while he did the drinks. He believed completely in the dominant male role, and would come into his own absolutely now. She leaned back in the basket chair and languished more.

The last tiny cow was chivvied through the toy gate and the ribbon of road was deserted. Sometimes a car fitted with a gas bag would toil up and take the Cirencester Road; or a farm wagon would rock from side to side behind one of the working shire horses that were making a comeback these days; or a convoy of army lorries camouflaged past recognition might chug up on its way to Brize Norton. Otherwise the quilted landscape could easily be dead already. Kildie, used to plenty of company in the bank, was frequently horribly lonely up here. The car promised by Marcus had not materialized because of the War. There was a bicycle in the garage, but though she loved coasting down towards Cheltenham, it was a long, four-mile walk back.

She narrowed her eyes and sat up slightly. The sun flashed on something moving fast along the road. A belt of trees interrupted it then the flashing began in earnest. Gradually, a minuscule shape behind the flashes was visible. It was Marcus in his precious car. Doing about fifty by the looks of it. She watched it slow judiciously where the cows had crossed, then pick up speed again. He would be here in under five minutes. She forced herself to lean back again, to control her breathing. Marcus had this effect on her.

He saw her as he swept around to the garage and he ran across the gravel and stood at the open door gazing down at her, not frowning at all, smiling that slight smile of his which seemed to claim her as his each time it was turned on.

He said, 'God, you're beautiful.' He threw his hat towards another chair and came at her like a panther. She had told him once he was like a black panther and he had made himself more so, crouching and reaching for her as if he might tear her limb from limb.

She gave a high-pitched laugh as she always did but held tightly to her kimono when he would have removed it.

'Darling – darling, please! I want to talk to you – I've missed you so – I've been waiting and watching—'

He moved his mouth down her neck, slid his hands to her buttocks and pressed her to him frantically.

'I love that,' he told her. 'The thought of you here all day – just waiting for me – it's what I've always wanted, Kildie. You come alive for me, darling, don't you?'

'Oh Marcus.' She gave up the struggle with the kimono

and let herself collapse into his arms as usual. 'Oh darling, I do, I do. But I have something so wonderful to tell you, sweetheart. Oh Marcus—'

His hands were all over her. It occurred to her that if Mrs Davis had a telescope and stood on the seat of her lavatory directing it towards Hill House, she could probably see her employer standing there naked.

'Marcus, no. Stop, darling. Please. Please, Marcus—'

He was laughing, thinking it was one of her games. 'Are you going all shy on me again, Kildie Villiers? Do you think I should only make love to you in the bedroom? Because your Uncle Jim says so? Is that what this is all about?'

She was diverted. 'How did you know that was what Jim said?' she asked, moving her head back so that her brown eyes could stare into his black ones.

He stopped laughing. 'I was joking. Do you mean he actually said—' He gripped her bare shoulders painfully. 'That means you told him – that I couldn't wait. Is that what you said? That I couldn't wait?'

'Marcus – please—'

'You bitch Kildie. You disloyal little bitch!' He released her and struck her across the mouth. She screamed quite unnecessarily. It wasn't hard and he had hit her before now in a pleasurable way.

'It wasn't like that,' she sobbed, covering herself with her arms as best she could. 'Not like that at all. I suppose I was sort of – well – boasting, really. They *have* to wait. 'Cos of Holly.' This whole thing was going wrong. She hung her head and sobbed again.

At once he became the comforter. His arms were warm around her. She had been pushed out into the cold, now she was welcomed back into the sunshine. He carried her into the lounge and put her onto the sofa and dried her tears and murmured to her, and she wept properly with gratitude and returned his kisses and whispered, 'Forgive me,' though she did not know why.

Marcus said, 'I forgive you, my darling. My poor baby.

Was I angry with you then . . . ?' He stood up and began to undress.

She held up her hand. 'Darling, do stop. I have to tell you something terribly important. We mustn't – we really mustn't–' He did not stop and she took a deep breath. 'We're going to have a baby, darling. I think I'm pregnant.'

He paused and looked down at her. There was no smile on his face.

'How can you be?'

She was astonished. 'Well . . . I'm so surprised I haven't . . . before. I mean . . .' She blushed. 'Every day, Marcus. Sometimes half a dozen times–'

'But I told you, that first time, there would be no babies.'

'Well . . .' She smiled persuasively. 'You were wrong, darling.'

'No I wasn't, darling.' The endearment sounded like a curse. 'If you're pregnant it's by someone else, not me.'

Her smile died. 'What are you saying, Marcus? You know – you must know – I wouldn't look at another man!' She could have said she was too tired.

He continued to stare down at her. 'What makes you think you're pregnant?'

'Well . . . you said yourself I was putting on weight.' She put her hands on her abdomen and pushed it up towards her chest.

'You're always telling me it's your time of the month. Were you lying about that?'

'No! Of course not! I do not lie to you, Marcus!' She sobbed helplessly. 'Darling, I thought you'd be so pleased! I'm so pleased!'

'So you are still seeing your monthlies?'

'Yes! But that doesn't mean a thing. There was a girl at Dymock–'

'I've heard about those sort of girls.' He continued to undress slowly. 'I suppose there's an outside chance . . . but I don't think you're pregnant. If you were, half the

197

girls in Gloucester would have my kids. But . . . if you are, it makes no difference to this.'

'Oh but, Marcus, it does! I read somewhere—'

He was on her. And it was not a pleasant experience. He pinned her arms to her side and there was no tenderness anywhere. His black eyes were . . . soulless.

It must have been midnight before she remembered Jim. Marcus had been asleep for some time, bored with her sobs, satiated with her body. She felt sore all over, even inside her head. She thought of going to Gran. But she'd gone there before and he'd come for her. He didn't even have to speak. He'd just appeared and she'd gone to heel like any puppy dog.

And she couldn't face Gran; she was too ashamed. Gran would know about half the girls in Gloucester. Probably everyone did. That was why Jim had been so against the marriage in the first place.

And there was the thought. Jim.

She slid out of bed, desperate to be quiet, and fell over her slippers. Even so Marcus did not stir. The kimono still lay on the floor of the conservatory so she gathered up an armful of clothes from the back of a chair and crept on to the landing and down the stairs. She switched on no lights, the moon gave a ghostly outline to all solid objects. She pulled on knickers and petticoat and a flimsy dress that was not warm enough in spite of the heatwave. In the lounge she picked up Marcus' discarded trousers and fumbled for car keys in the pocket. The thought of what she was doing made her shake with fear, but she continued to do it, creeping out of the back door and around to the garage with tortoise-like determination. The garage doors creaked as she pulled them open; and there was the car, Marcus' pride and joy, smelling slightly of cow dung but as sleek and shining as ever.

He had let her take the wheel just twice. She found the reverse gear and backed out with a roar of exhaust that would wake the whole countryside. Sure enough the bedroom light leapt on as she was wrenching the wheel around and, as she took the driveway at a tyre-spitting fifteen miles an hour, the front door flew open and Marcus was there, his nakedness silhouetted against the hall lights.

She found the lights with difficulty and only just missed the ditch as she turned into the road. She was sobbing and shouting aloud, 'Oh God! Oh damn and blast – oh God!' But the car was moving along the road down towards Cheltenham and she was going through the gears and guiding properly and . . . she had escaped!

1924

Dolly Prosser came to Dymock School in September 1924, from the teachers' training college in Bristol. She would have to do a year's probationary teaching before receiving her certificate, but if the local inspector was satisfied with her during his unannounced visits, the certificate was a foregone conclusion. Such was the shortage of teachers since the Great War that even the young probationers who collapsed in tears at the sight of the black-clad Schools' Inspector crossing the playground usually ended up fully qualified, and Dorothy was of sterner stuff than that, though she might not look it. At twenty years old, the only child of elderly, bemused parents, she fooled a lot of people. Her strawberry-blond hair and enormous blue eyes made her appear infinitely biddable. Until you came to her forward-thrusting chin.

Kilda James, nine years old, adopted by her grand-parents and as spoiled as Dolly, came home that September afternoon unable to talk of anything or anyone except Miss Prosser.

'She's the most beautiful lady in the world,' she stated, which put Gran off straightaway. 'She's like a golden princess. Her skin is like milk and her fingernails are like pearls and her hair—'

Jim, arriving on the two-thirty after his early turn in the

freight train control office at Gloucester, laughed heartily. 'She won't stay like that for long! Old Millie Parker will have her helping the boys with his garden.'

'Mr Milsom-Parker adores her!' Kildie said, her dark eyes glazing romantically. 'He has told the big boys that if there is any trouble he'll thrash the hides off 'em!'

Jim made a face. He had had experience of Milsom-Parker's thrashings in the past.

Gran said, 'Go and wash your hands, the two of you. Then you can cut the beans.'

She invariably coupled Jim and Kildie together. Jim was twenty-two, but he was still her baby.

The two of them went into the wash-house and continued the conversation while Jim pumped water into the stone sink. Jim had been deeply thankful when his parents had adopted his sister's child. She directed some of the parental attention away from him.

'I reckon Billy Matson and Percy Jenkins will find ways and means of playing up your new teacher, strap or no strap,' he commented, lathering her hands between his.

Kildie said gloomily, 'That's the thing.'

Jim looked down at the dark hair parted in the middle and drawn into two tight plaits. Kildie made him feel almost grown-up. As if he could go out into the world and take on a dragon or two.

He said tentatively, 'Let me know how it goes. I might be able to help.'

Kildie knew this was an empty promise. She said dispiritedly, 'How?'

'Well. They can't do much in school under Millie's nose. But they might hang around outside when she goes to her digs. Where are her digs?'

'Mrs Thrupp's. Applecross Farm.'

'They might try something down Middle Lane.'

Kildie went to the roller towel behind the door and dried her hands. Her dark eyes looked liquid in the gloom of the washhouse.

'Poor Miss Prosser,' she mourned.

Jim made no reply. She was probably right. The only time he might have mounted any kind of guard on Middle Lane was when he was on nights. But even then he left at seven in the morning which was too early for Miss Prosser to start for school, and though he might get up in time to take her home, his mother didn't allow him to set foot outside the Station House until five-thirty when he had had his eight hours rest. School finished at four.

However, Dorothy Prosser was made of sterner stuff than her appearance suggested. She was over-protected, just as Jim was, but instead of sapping her confidence it had nurtured it over-weeningly. Dorothy had never been frightened of anything in her life except spiders. When she was only a little older than Kildie, she had seen a man whipping a horse. She and her mother had been shopping at the time, her mother in gentle conversation with some friends while Dorothy, in the pall of boredom that so often wrapped her, see-sawed two of the wooden blocks that paved the street at that time and watched the man. The horse was pulling a cart laden with junk; a tin bath reared itself from a tangle of wire, flower pots, a cast-iron fireplace and some rusted bins. It was too heavy a load for the frail horse, but the driver plied his whip as if to Dorothy's spinning top. The horse hung its head submissively.

At the sixth stroke Dorothy could bear it no longer. She detached her gloved hand from her Mother's, leapt across the road and snatched the whip from the man's brutal fist. It was 1914 when people were subjected to a great deal of jingoistic propaganda, and the man looked at the small golden girl as if she were Albion herself.

Dorothy would have fought the German army single-handed had she been old enough, so one man was easy meat. She swung the whip expertly and it curled around his neck.

'How do *you* like it?' she asked in her high, carrying voice. 'See how *you* like it! Just see how *you* like it!'

The story, told so often since, lost its thread at that

point. But Dorothy remembered with shame that her mother had paid money to the man before sending him on his way. He had uttered threats concerning magistrates and prisons which had terrified Ellen Prosser. Dorothy had protested in vain that he would be the one who ended up in prison.

Since then there had been other escapades known and unknown to her parents. If Dorothy had had more money and less conscience she would have been an outrageous flapper. She could have married money, or at any rate acquired it through an adorer; there had been plenty of them since she was fourteen. But underneath it all, she was what was known as a good girl. She had sublimated her enormous energies into teaching. Her college professor had made his usual speech to the entrants of 1922: 'Teaching is a profession second only to the Church.' He had looked down at the gaggle of seventeen and eighteen year olds and wondered how much was getting through. The recruitment surge since the end of the War had thrown up some most unsuitable material. 'The clergy minister to the soul. We minister to the mind.'

He had got through to Dorothy Prosser.

She knew only too well that the Matson boys had a reputation for intimidating new teachers. The girl before her had stayed just her probationary year. Billy was the last of a tough breed who considered schooling ill-fitted them for a life on the land. Similarly Percy Jenkins scorned all book-learning. His father was a poacher. Dorothy had known as she saw him watching her during school prayers, that he was kin to the horse whipper of so long ago.

However, one of the college texts – used as maxims for all kinds of problems – had been 'Sufficient unto the day is the evil thereof'. Dolly would face Billy and Percy when she had to and not before.

Unfortunately that day arrived during her second week at Dymock School.

She took the five-to-tens in the second schoolroom and had won them over instantly with her combination of chocolate-box beauty, enthusiasm, and new-broom organization. By that second Wednesday she felt they were all her family and when she saw Kildie James cornered in the playground by the loutish Billy Matson she went immediately to Mr Milsom-Parker.

'Let us observe,' he pontificated, standing by his window holding his cup over its saucer judiciously, and leaving his plate of Bath Olivers to the flies.

Dolly stood impatiently to one side.

'He actually herded Kildie behind the coke pile,' she said, wanting to push Mr Milsom-Parker into the playground. 'I don't think it's to hold a conversation with her!'

'Exactly so,' murmured Mr Milsom-Parker. 'Nevertheless, in this country we deem a person innocent until proved—' Billy Matson appeared to be leaning over Kildie shaking his head mournfully at her. He then turned and strolled into the main playground, smiling broadly. Kildie followed him. She too was shaking her head and looking distinctly unhappy.

'There, you see?' The headmaster turned, smiling himself. 'Obviously no harm done. Probably asking Kildie James the times of the trains to Gloucester.'

'Trains?' Dolly moved away from the window, unsatisfied.

'Kildie's grandfather is the station master. She can memorize the train times for practically the whole of the Great Western Railway.'

Dolly continued to frown. 'She looked very worried. And why was she shaking her head like that?'

'In despair at Billy's obtuseness, I dare say.' He became avuncular. 'I don't want you to worry about the big boys, Miss Prosser. I have warned them that if there is any trouble from any of them, I will make it my business to—'

'Yes, I know,' Dolly said hastily. She could not bear to think of straps descending on trousers; she had had her fill of corporal punishment that time in Gloucester. 'I just wish . . .' she trailed off because what she wished was that she could have everyone in the school loving everyone else, which sounded dreadfully sentimental.

'Would you like a biscuit, Miss Prosser? I take it the Whittle girl has made you some tea?' The Whittle girl had officially left school the year before but the place was home to her. She stayed on as cleaner and general dogsbody.

'Yes. No thank you . . .' Dolly would be full all day from Mrs Thrupp's breakfast. She managed a fleeting smile. 'I'm sorry to have bothered you.'

'Not a bit.' Mr Milsom-Parker held the door for her then closed it. Playtime was for teachers as well as children.

Dolly went back into her classroom and began putting out scissors and crayons. The bell went for the last morning session and Kildie James came in alone ahead of the line.

'Kildie? I thought you were the playground monitor today?'

'I've lined them up, Miss Prosser. I don't want to stand too close to them though.'

'Why on earth not, Kildie?' Dolly looked at the girl's adoring face and saw it marked with tears. 'Billy Matson did hit you then?' She felt one of her monumental rages building. 'How dared he!'

'No, miss. He didn't lay a finger on me.' But Kildie's face was very long. 'But he shook his head on me.'

Dolly shook her own head. 'He didn't hurt you?'

'Oh no, miss. He just shook his head.'

The tinies began to file in and Dolly had to let the subject go. But the next day there was a note from Mrs James who was the local dragon. Kildie had lice.

'He did it to me, miss,' Kildie whispered, her shame making her cheeks flame. 'Don't tell anyone, will you? Gran will get rid of them ever so quick.'

Dolly stared at her, horrified. 'Do you mean it is a well-known fact that Billy Matson has fleas?'

'Oh yes, miss. And Percy Jenkins.'

'Does Mr Milsom-Parker know of this?' Dolly asked unwisely.

Kildie nodded vigorously, though she had no idea whether the headmaster knew or not. Dorothy looked over the girl's beautiful dark hair to where the little ones were settling themselves into their desks with their usual fuss and bother.

'Will all my class be quite silent, please!'

The children stared at her, surprised. A pin could have been heard falling and indeed as they continued to stare, one of Amy Pearce's hairgrips fell to her desk with a tinny clatter. Miss Prosser had never used this voice before.

She indicated Kildie.

'You are in charge. Just for ten minutes, Kildie,' she said and marched to her bag behind the door where she kept a slab of carbolic soap for her personal use.

She went out of the side door, closing it behind her, and stood in the playground. The boys were filing in, late as usual.

'Billy Matson! Percy Jenkins!'

Her voice was like a whiplash and both boys turned simultaneously, as surprised as her class had been.

'Come with me, please!'

She did not wait to see if she was to be obeyed. Her anger was palpable. She strode to the back of the school where the pump still dripped from drawing up the well water for the privies. She immediately began to work it furiously and a spout of water gushed into the drain.

'You first, Percy!' she commanded. 'Just your head please!'

Percy stared at her, goggle-eyed.

'What for, miss? Why?'

She reached with her unexpectedly long arm and yanked him unceremoniously towards her. He was taller than she was and twice as broad, but was so startled he made no resistance.

'Come here, Billy! Keep this pump handle going!'

Billy began to see the funny side of this. Percy Jenkins usually had all the Matsons well under his thumb. Now it was the other way round. Grinning sheepishly he grabbed the handle. Dolly withdrew Percy's head long enough to lather it thoroughly.

'Why you have been permitted to come to school in this state, is a complete mystery,' she panted as she worked the soap into the scalp. 'If the School Inspector knew . . .' She left the implied threat in mid-air. No School Inspector would be brave enough to face up to old man Jenkins and his Great War rifle.

Percy was stupefied. His humiliation was momentarily forgotten in the exciting pleasure of having long female fingers massaging his head. He spluttered and made a fuss.

'What the heck—? No woman never washed me afore—'

'There's always a first time, Percy,' Dorothy said grimly, pushing the soapy square head beneath the gushing pump and holding it there.

When he emerged, Percy thought he might be half-drowned. He stood there, head hanging, dripping but no longer spluttering.

'Excellent, Percy,' Dorothy said, her anger sublimated into satisfaction. 'Now you take the pump handle. Come on, Billy!'

'Not me, miss. You don't get me under that water!' Billy said, more alarmed than defiant.

But Percy wasn't going to be alone in this. He shoved his cohort beneath the spout and pumped vigorously. Billy squawked and squawked again. Mr Milsom-Parker rounded the corner.

'I'll 'old 'im, miss! You get started!' Percy offered. So Dorothy did.

She was very wet herself by this time but managed to look over her shoulder and say one word to the headmaster.

'Infestation.'

It worked like magic. Mr Milsom-Parker disappeared.

The three of them stood in the playground, dripping and cold. Percy took command.

'Billy, nip in and get the roller towel off the roller. You all right, miss?'

Suddenly, Dorothy loved them both. She surveyed them, two hulks who would always be infestations on the outer skin of their society, but who, just for a moment, were kin to her.

She grinned. Percy grinned. Billy grinned. And then they started to laugh.

Dorothy let it go for almost a full minute, then sobered.

'That's enough, lads. Billy, do as Percy says. We must dry off and be presentable for prayers.'

Billy shambled away and Percy said with unusual wit, 'Don't reckon as 'ow God'll mind us like this, miss.'

She looked at him, dripping but mercifully clean.

'I reckon God will be mightily pleased,' she said.

Billy emerged with the roller towel and offered an end. They went quietly into school. The word 'fleas' or 'lice' never crossed their lips and Mr Milsom-Parker did not refer to the episode then or ever.

ELEVEN

1940

Dorothy did not come in until past midnight.

Holly, hungry and cold now that the sun had finally gone down, lay in bed listening for her mother and feeling alienated from her for the first time in her life. Those Canadians – the three Bobs – and Mabs and Charles Crawshay . . . they had made her feel like an interloper in her own home. If only Dad had arrived on that last train. If only they'd come in together and she could have presented him as her . . . her . . . discovery almost. She thought of Dad. She thought of the trains arriving from Birmingham and herself searching the steam for his familiar lanky body and dear long face. Sentimental tears were hot in her eyes as she saw herself running towards him. He would drop his kitbag and hold out his arms and swing her round and hug her with delight. He might then look at her and tell her how grown-up she looked. Later as they went over the bridge to the gate he would ask her if she'd been looking after Mum. And she would nod and tell him about their trips to Dymock and how they sat in the evenings cutting and salting the beans and how Mum was actually a fire-watcher! And they would both laugh indulgently.

Because she *had* kept Mum 'safe'. She had never joined the Guides or the choir or anything that would keep her in school past three-thirty. She had told the billeting officer that Aunt Lizzie and Winnie would be back soon so they had to keep the room free for them. She had talked Mum out of doing war work by saying she needed her. In fact, everything was exactly the same as when Dad left for Scotland last Christmas. Preserved. Just like the beans and the bottled plums.

And then she'd come home from that . . . that vigil at the station . . . to find the house full of foreigners. Other men in uniform. And Mum beautiful at the piano. One of the hot tears trickled down her cheek and she turned her head into the pillow to mop it up. She heard Mum's key in the door.

'Are you still awake, Hol?'

The hoarse whisper would have woken her anyway. She grunted assent and Mum clumped upstairs, tin hat, gas mask and all and stood in the doorway.

'Still no telegrams?'

'No.' Holly sat up feeling much better. Mum had been thinking as Holly had been thinking all the time.

'What the *hell* is he playing at?' Mum exploded, divesting herself of hat and gas mask with a furious sweep of her arm that sent them clattering onto the landing lino.

Holly was shocked and straightened her spine convulsively.

Mum laughed. 'Sorry, Hol. I'm all of a doo-dah. Mabs brought round some of her turnip wine from last winter. It was rather potent.'

Holly was even more shocked. Was Mum drunk? What had been going on with those . . . those . . . men?

Mum continued in her reassuring voice, 'He's stuck in a troop train somewhere right up north. Can't get to a phone or a post office. He'll turn up. Don't worry.'

Holly wondered if she was imagining her mother's speech was slightly slurred. She cleared her throat and forced herself to say something. Anything.

'Miss Joliffe thinks I should go in for the Higher.'

That threw Mum. She put up a hand and massaged her head and her hair flew around her head with static electricity. It was still pure gold and looked, in the dim light of the landing, like a halo.

Holly said, 'I know I've got to stay on till I'm sixteen—'

'You certainly have. Dad signed a paper to that effect,' Mum put in smartly enough.

'But I'd like to leave then. They want girls at Rotol.'

'Not my girl, they don't. No fear.'

'I want to do some war work!' Holly protested, her voice rising childishly.

'How do you think I'd feel then? Stuck here day after day while everyone else is doing something of national importance?'

'You're one of the village fire-watchers!'

'As if the Jerries are going to drop any incendiaries on the Green! We're in a safe area, Hol!'

'But – but—' For some reason the tears were starting to spurt again. Holly swallowed and said feebly, 'You're keeping the home fires burning!'

'Hah!' Mum said loudly.

'Well – you've said yourself – it's a full-time job making the rations go round and getting enough coal for next winter and digging for victory and making jam—'

'And seeing no-one all day! And feeling so bored you want to scream!'

'It's the same for Aunt Lizzie!'

'She's got Uncle Edward!'

'Well, Gran then.'

'Gran has never expected anything else from life except to keep the home fires burning! And anyway Gran is in her seventies! I'm thirty-five!' The words ended on a kind of wail of despair, the head dropped onto the chest and the hair hung down in glorious loose waves.

Holly was frightened. The world seemed to be tipping slightly. Mum wasn't Mum any more and Dad was heaven knew where and Gran was . . . old.

She said in a small voice, 'I think you're drunk!'

Dorothy straightened and stared.

'You think I'm what? I've had some turnip wine to get me through the evening and you think I'm drunk?'

Holly cowered. It was years since her mother had hit

her, but any corporal punishment was always meted out by her, never Dad.

And then, through the awful silence, they heard a car. They both stopped breathing. The car pulled up outside the cottage and the engine was switched off. The gate creaked and there were footsteps.

'It's Dad,' whispered Holly. She pushed herself out of bed. She and Mum tumbled down the stairs one behind the other. Mum unbolted the door and flung it wide. Sure enough it was Dad. In his arms was a weeping Kildie dressed in a strappy sunfrock and wearing no shoes or stockings. Behind them both was Marcus' sports car.

Jim had been in transit, as he put it, for nearly forty hours. A great deal of that time had been spent in the corridor of an unheated train, sitting on the floor practically doubled up. The train had been full of soldiers when it arrived at Prestwick; an Ulster regiment had boarded at Stranraer, still throwing up after the crossing from Belfast. The smell had been atrocious, the haul up to Glasgow interminable. Once there, they had been stabled for two hours until the line to Carlisle was cleared and somewhere between Carlisle and Preston they had been shunted into sidings twice to permit enormous trains of tanks to use the main line. At one place during the hours of darkness – he could not remember when – two women had appeared on the steep railway embankment and passed enamel jugs of tea up to them. No-one knew where they came from; the blackout revealed nothing. The women wore headscarves obviously binding in their steel curlers. They were wearing the latest siren suits, made popular by Churchill himself, and their lumpy silhouettes moved slowly up and down the train, reaching for empty cups, passing up the full jugs, saying incomprehensible things in a Gracie Fields dialect.

At ten o'clock the previous day, the train had pulled into Crewe and the men had been disgorged onto the platform. Jim had waited four hours to use the phone kiosk. When he got through, the line was so bad he suspected his message would never reach Dorothy. So he had phoned again.

Kildie had sounded so happy. So excited. He could imagine her greeting Marcus with the news that they must drive into Gloucester immediately and tell Dorothy that he was on his way. He wondered whether Holly might ride one of the bicycles up to the station so that he could get home quickly whatever time he arrived. Holly thought of things like that. He was willing to bet his King's shilling that she had been meeting trains ever since he sent the telegram to say he was coming home. Perhaps Dorothy had gone with her. But no, Dorothy would want to be getting a meal ready for him at home. He smiled as he replaced the receiver. It would be so good to see them all. He had missed them terribly and wondered how he would survive at the training school in Canada. His CO had said, 'You're one of the lucky ones, James. You're going to have a quiet war teaching the Canadians everything you know about the inside of the Sunderland.' It would have sounded crazily heroic to say he'd prefer to stay and take his chances here with the bombs. But it was true. Here there was always a chance he could get home and see Dorothy.

He was ready to get off the train as early as Churchdown and released the leather window strap as soon as the tall signal box at Tramway Junction came into sight. Nobody was on the platform. A couple of women porters ran alongside the brake van ready to take off mail. A few ghostly blue lights gleamed on the enamelled advertisements for Mazawattee Tea. He swung expertly with the door and ran alongside the train as it snorted to a stop. Then he pulled the window up again and slammed the door, automatically checking the handle.

No-one was there to take his pass and the booking office was shuttered for the night. He looked around the booking hall; no bikes. And there'd be no taxis either. He made a face. It would take the best part of another hour to walk out to the Green.

And then he saw Marcus' car and his face split into a grin. So Villiers wasn't such a bad chap after all. He must have been hanging about for ages with no idea when Jim's train might arrive.

He ran up to it and looked inside. Kildie, dressed in something very flimsy, was asleep across the two front seats. There was no sign of Marcus.

She started to weep as soon as she woke and simply could not stop. Jim, light-headed after the ordeal of the journey, dealt with it as best he could, but he had never forgotten Kildie's words on the railway platform last year and though he could not understand what she was saying now, his imagination painted a lurid picture which made him feel sick. However, there was nothing in his stomach except the Yorkshire tea, so he leaned against the car with her full weight on him and tried to hold the world still for both of them.

He said at last, 'Kildie, you must go back home. I will come with you, but you must—'

She tightened her grip on him and let out a small scream of protest.

'Of course you haven't *stolen* the car, Kildie!' Jim fixed his eyes on one of the dimmed street lights, aligned it to a silhouette of a building and held it in place by will power. 'The car is as much yours as it is—'

She babbled a denial and tried to tell him how much the car meant to Marcus. He nodded against the top of her head so that she would know he was listening, but still said, 'You are not a criminal, Kildie. Please stop crying and let us decide what to do. It's almost midnight and—'

'. . . come home with you . . .' He deciphered the words coming from his airforce-blue uniform. '. . . Dorothy . . .'

He thought of Dorothy with an explosion of relief. Of course. She would take this problem off his hands immediately and deal with it expertly. She would know what to do. He narrowed his eyes ferociously at the street lamp which threatened to slide sideways, and nodded with what he hoped was vigour.

'We'll go straight home then. Let go of my neck, Kildie. Give me the ignition key. Where is the handle?'

She released him but her sobs continued. He repeated the question sternly before the street lamp could hit the ground and she said, 'Self-starter.' He almost fell into the driver's seat.

The drive was a nightmare. He should have made for the Tewkesbury Road but he thought the country lanes would be easier for him to manage. They weren't. Twice he avoided a ditch by inches and Kildie screamed again and again so that he too began to see the whole thing as centred around the blasted car. As they negotiated the pump and chugged past the church at the Green, he could have sobbed with relief. And then, Kildie began to weep again and would not get out of the car. He reached inside and lugged her through the door and she fell in a heap at his feet. Somehow he hoisted her into his arms; she was heavier than she had been when he last lifted her. He staggered through the gate and up to the door. When it opened and Dorothy and Holly were framed in the blue light of the hall, he too could have wept.

And then Dorothy said in a high-pitched voice, 'So that's where you've been, is it? Why didn't you spend the night there?' And she closed the door very forcefully.

It was opened again almost immediately, whether in response to Kildie's sleep-shattering screams or at Holly's insistence, he did not know, but somehow they were all inside and Kildie had transferred her arms to Dorothy's shoulders and was saying, 'Why didn't you tell me he was unfaithful? Everyone knew except me, I suppose? Oh Dorothy – I thought I was the only one! Oh Dorothy . . .'

Jim met Dorothy's gaze above the tousled dark head. Dorothy's eyes were intensely blue, the pupils pinpricks in the half-light of the blacked-out hall. Just for a wonderful moment he thought they were going to narrow in a conspiratorial grin. Then Dorothy's voice, precise and schoolmarmish cut through Kildie's awful keening.

'You'd better sleep with me for tonight, dear. Jim can go in the little room. The bed's still aired from Lizzie and Winnie.' She half turned to Holly. 'Can you get your father a hot drink, Hol? We'll sort all this out in the morning.'

And she propelled Kildie's body just ahead of her up the stairs.

Jim said, 'D'you mean to tell me you've been meeting trains ever since you got my wire, Hol?'

'Only now and then. I kept thinking, This might be the one . . .'

'Oh, my love. How I wish it had been.'

Jim watched his lanky daughter as she reached down the cocoa tin and adjusted the gas under the kettle. He too imagined the scenario where he had stepped out of the train and she had resolved from the steam like a mirage coming to life. He wanted to weep. Badly.

She turned and smiled at him over one shoulder.

'I knew it would be today. I couldn't hang on too long after the party of course. But I knew you'd come.'

'Party?'

'Oh you don't know.' Her smile nearly split her face. 'Miss Joliffe gave us all a tea party at the Cadena because of the exam results. I got the School Cert all right. Distinctions in English and General Science, too.'

He knew he should jump up and hug her. The tears in his eyes starred her image. He croaked, 'General Science? I didn't realize—'

'Nor me. Nor Miss Jollybags!' She giggled. 'She was really surprised. But she thinks I ought to do Higher. I don't want to, Dad. I want to leave when I'm sixteen and do some war work.'

War work. Holly doing war work. And he would be in Canada unable to help with any decisions; unable to watch her going off to the factory with her hair in a turban.

He choked, 'Oh Hol . . . you'll grow up and I won't know about it.'

She stopped smiling. And then her face crumpled and she came close to him and put her arms around him and held his head to her flat chest.

'Oh Dad, don't cry . . .' But she was sobbing incoherently. 'Dad . . . Daddy . . . I love you. Don't cry.'

And he held her tightly and thought he'd never been with so many weeping women in his life before.

The non-appearance of Marcus was like a deafening silence. The car stayed outside the cottage, an object of great curiosity to everyone in the village, reminding the shattered family in the cottage of Marcus' existence, waiting for him just as they waited.

The anticlimax of it all was too much to bear. Dorothy, unwilling recipient of Kildie's confidences, began to wonder whether she and Jim were almost too wholesome in their sex life. Did other people behave as Kildie and Marcus behaved? How could she know? She watched Kildie's unconsciously provoking looks and gestures at Jim. He appeared not to notice them. But it still made her feel as if Kildie were some kind of time-bomb in the cottage. She tried to recall the Kildie of Dymock school-days; the Kildie she loved who was Jim's little sister. Only Kildie was really Jim's niece, not his sister. And incest was rife in Dymock anyway.

Dorothy woke up with a headache from the turnip wine; but two days later she still had the headache. Everyone seemed to think she could deal with this ridiculous situation.

'What are we going to do, Doll?' Jim asked as she struggled to prepare meals for two extra people without two extra ration books.

On the third day she said, 'We've got two options. Either we go back to see Marcus, or we go to see Gran.'

Kildie wailed aloud as she so often did, making them all jump nervously.

'I can't face Marcus ever again, Dorothy! You know that better than the others!' She cast a wild look around the kitchen table. Jim looked at the grain in the wood, Holly coloured.

'Then it's Gran,' Dorothy said briskly. 'We'll catch the three fifteen. Or we could cycle. It would do us good to cycle.'

Kildie wailed louder still.

'I can't possibly bike all that way!'

'Then we'll go on the train.' Dorothy tried to make her voice absolutely matter-of-fact. She wanted to scream at Kildie to clear off anywhere as long as she was not here.

Kildie must have picked up that thought and whimpered, 'Why can't we stay here, Dorothy? Marcus will come for the car sooner or later.'

'So you want to see Marcus?' Dorothy pursued logically and relentlessly.

Kildie put her hands to her face. 'I don't know. Jim—'

Dorothy snapped, 'Never mind Jim. Let's find out what you want to do, Kildie. Do you want to see Marcus or not?'

Kildie cowered. 'I don't know-ow-ow.'

'Because if you do, I rather think he will look for his car at Gran's rather than here. Most wives run home when they leave their husbands . . .' Dorothy was getting into her stride. 'And your home was at Dymock.'

Kildie sniffed back a sob and said, 'But when he doesn't see the car outside—'

'Then we'll take the blasted car!' Dorothy almost shouted. 'We'll eat this ghastly food – corned-beef hash it was called in Lord Woolton's food leaflet. Hah! I'd like to give him corned-beef hash!' She took a deep breath. 'And then we'll go. Jim can drive. You and Holly can manage in the dicky seat. We'll come back on the train.'

'But – the car—'

'You will stay at Gran's, with the car.' Dorothy was now talking very loudly and very slowly. 'Perhaps you should hide in the boot. Then he'll take you home with him!'

Kildie wailed anew. 'Oh Dorothy . . . don't be angry!'

Dorothy did not bother to tell her that she was not angry. It would have been such an obvious lie. The awful thing was she knew she was not only angry with Kildie; she was angry with Jim too. She was even angry with Holly who seemed to be accepting this ridiculous situation so easily.

Gran said, 'Well, this is a surprise. Holly, why don't you pop up to the Gatehouse and let Aunt Lizzie know you're here? And Doll, I want to show you the fern bed. It's done really well this hot summer.'

By the time Dorothy had said, 'Gran, please don't call me . . .' she was halfway down the garden, Holly was disappearing in the direction of the Grange and Jim and Kildie were left. Together. And alone.

Dorothy said, 'What are you trying to do, Gran? You have no idea what Kildie has told me. I simply do not trust her to be alone with any man – let alone Jim who she idolizes!'

'Don't be silly, Doll. They're like brother and sister, those two. And I think Kildie needs to discover that the only man she really wants now is Marcus Villiers.'

Dolly fetched up opposite the brick wall which was damp against all odds and sprouted the greenest of ferns in spite of the heatwave. She stared at them with loathing.

'I know that and you know that. Jim doesn't. He doesn't want her to go back. Ever.'

'Then he needs to find out the truth more than she does perhaps.' Gran stooped with difficulty and smoothed the cabbage leaves of a saxifrage over a stone. Dorothy stared at the gnarled fingers. Gran was a couple of years away from eighty years old. Was she still the wise woman Holly thought she was?

Gran straightened again with even more difficulty and

said, 'People will do what they want to do usually, Doll. So give them the opportunity. Let them get it out of their systems.'

'Like Sarah and Edward?' Dorothy asked boldly.

Gran did not answer.

Dorothy said, 'I don't want that to happen to Jim and Kildie. Sorry, Gran. I'm not a doormat like Lizzie.'

'I know that.'

'And I cannot be as objective as you are.'

Gran's grey eyes were hooded by her wrinkled lids. Dorothy wondered whether Jim's would do that as he got older. They were so alike.

'I ain't . . . what you said, Doll.'

'But you let people go their ways. That's being very objective.'

'Doesn't mean I like it. I just know it has to be.' She turned slightly so that she was facing the church spire. 'Don't think that Lizzie is always a doormat, Doll. Or that Sarah is always . . . wayward.'

Dorothy said quickly, 'Gran, I'm sorry. I did not mean to hurt you.'

Gran turned and she was smiling.

'You didn't hurt me, Doll! I know what my children are like. That is how I know that Marcus Villiers is the right man for Kildie.' Her smile faded. 'And I know Jim. He is my son. I know him to be faithful beyond death, Doll. Kildie might well make a fool of herself. But Jim will put her straight.' And then, almost as if she were touching wood, she said again, 'After all, they are practically brother and sister!'

Dorothy looked down at the saxifrage. She said in a low voice, 'I'm sorry, Gran. I don't trust Kildie. She expects too much of an uncle . . . or a brother.'

'So you want to go back to the house now? Before Kildie can show Jim just how foolish she can be?' Gran sighed audibly. 'Poor Doll. Come on then.'

She turned and started back up the garden path and Dorothy, feeling that somehow she had been tested and found wanting, followed behind and said irritably, 'I just wish you wouldn't call me Doll!'

Kildie watched Gran and Dorothy go down the garden and felt again the terrible sense of loss which underlaid the agony of hurt pride. She had thought Marcus worshipped – yes, worshipped – her alone; that there had never been anyone else for him; that she had appeared on his horizon and knocked him flat. That was the basis of their marriage. Marcus the dominant adorer; Kildie the adored one.

The sudden knowledge that she had not been the first by any means, had shocked her self-esteem into nothingness immediately. Then had followed the terrible wounded anger that had made her leave Hill House and steal Marcus' car and meet Jim. And since then had come the realization that she had to be adored – worshipped – by someone. Not Marcus. She hated Marcus. There must be something wrong with him if he was so certain she was not pregnant. But she hated him anyway. If he came looking for his car she wanted to tell him so. If Gran was there she would be able to scream at him . . . send him packing.

If Jim hadn't been coming home, she would doubtless have gone straight to Gran's as Dorothy had obviously thought was right in the circumstances. But Jim *had* been coming home. He had rescued her, comforted her, given her sanctuary in the face of Dorothy's disapproval. He could do something about this frightful emptiness if only Dorothy would let him.

He said, 'Come on, Kildie, I've put the kettle on. Get down those cups and saucers and let's have a cup of tea.'

She reached up unwillingly.

'They're dirty.' The bottoms of the cups were encrusted with sugar. 'Oh dear God, Jim. They're awful!'

He took the cups from her quickly and poured the warm water from the kettle over them in the sink. He knew his mother was not coping as she had done. What could anyone expect at her age?

'Say nothing,' he advised tersely. 'Get a clean tea towel from the dresser and dry them off.'

She did so, roused out of self-absorption by this new problem.

'Even this towel doesn't look that fresh. It could do with a good boil.'

'I don't suppose Gran can light the copper any more,' Jim lifted the beaded net from the milk jug and sniffed. It was all right. The marble slab in the pantry had kept the milk fresh. 'How often do you come down, Kildie?'

'We were all here. Not long ago.' She did not mention that she had left Marcus then too.

'Did you take any of her laundry back with you?'

'No. I thought Dorothy—'

'Dorothy comes on her bike, Kildie.'

'I didn't think of it. She's so independent, Jim. You know that.'

'Yes.' He smiled at her reassuringly, terrified she would start weeping again.

They carried the tea things into the living-room and this time it was Jim who looked through the window to see where Gran and Dorothy were. Gran was bending over touching a leaf. Dorothy's arms were akimbo, her shoulders hunched.

Behind him Kildie spoke stiltedly, like the small girl he still thought her.

'Jim, I'd like to say, now, while we're on our own . . . thank you for rescuing me.'

He did not turn. 'Don't be silly,' he said sternly.

She gasped a laugh and said, 'Oh it's true. I suppose Dorothy is right and I should have come here straight-away. But . . . well, that wouldn't have done. You were sent home at that time . . . just for me. I mean . . . it was meant . . . I needed you . . . you didn't turn me away or try to drive me home . . . you comforted me and . . . and—'

221

Gran was coming back down the garden path. Jim turned and said, 'It wasn't like that, Kildie. I didn't know what the devil was happening. I'd been in transit for—'

Her dark eyes were swimming again. He clamped her shoulders between his hands. 'Kildie, pull yourself together. We cannot put this sort of strain on Gran any more. She's getting too old to—'

'I don't want to put a strain on anyone. I can live here with Gran and help her. But it would be easier if you would admit – just admit . . . I wouldn't come between you and Doll. You know that. But there is something special between us, Jim—'

'We're like brother and sister, dammit all!' he snapped, holding her now because she had put all her weight on his hands. 'It's only natural that I should care about you and you should care about me—'

'Oh, it's more than that, Jim. We know it must not be, yet it is. I know it only too well. And you know it, only you're frightened to say so.' She sobbed. 'Jim, everything would be bearable for me if you would admit it. I have to know that you love me. I have to know that, Jim. Otherwise I might as well be dead.'

'Kildie, what are you saying? Don't even think like that – don't even—'

'Why? Because you couldn't live without me?' She fell against him. He knew she was going to kiss him as she had kissed him when she said goodbye last year. He had never forgotten that kiss. And then Gran came in very quickly from the kitchen and said, 'Not more waterworks, Kildie? Come on. What you need is a cup of tea. Doll, will you pour?'

Dorothy followed more slowly. Her face was deathly white as she came to the table where Kildie had collapsed on one of the chairs.

She said quietly, 'You'll be all right here with Gran, Kildie. Don't cry.'

And then Holly came in with a rush and stood there

222

like some tragedy queen and said in a loud voice, 'Charlie's gone! He's joined up! He's gone for ever!'

And Kildie began to cry all over again.

1924

'She held both their heads under the pump!' Kildie reported faithfully to Jim as soon as he arrived home. 'I told her that Billy Matson was shaking his fleas onto my head! And she went straight out of the classroom and—'

'But I thought you said she wasn't as big as them?' Jim tried to picture a frail city girl holding Billy and Percy by the ears and marching them around to the pump in the school playground.

'She's not! But she just did it!'

'How?'

'Don't know. John Weywood stood on the desk and could just see through the window but all he said was—'

'Yes, you said. She was holding their heads under the pump.' Jim stared at her, his own grey eyes as round as her dark ones. 'They'll kill her!'

Kildie started to hiccup on sobs. 'They will! I know they will!'

'Who will kill who?' Gran arrived from the back kitchen where she was making plum jam. Her hair, already iron grey, was straggling out of its bun and wisping around her narrow face which was bright red from the steam. She looked ready to kill anyone at the drop of a hat.

Jim forced a casual note into his voice. 'Only going on about the Matsons again, Ma.' He put his little case on the table. 'Where's Pa?'

'Where would he be at this hour?' Gran asked, opening the case and investigating his lunch-box. If there had been a crumb left she would have been cut to the quick.

'I looked into the office when I got off the train. No sign.'

She looked up sharply. 'Who gave right-away to the train then?'

'I did. Jack Bowie was on duty. We checked the door handles. Alf Warden was guard.'

She sighed exasperatedly. 'Honestly. Just because he knows he can trust Jack and Alf—'

'And me!'

'And you,' she repeated, with a glimmer of a smile. 'He's asleep somewhere. He'll have some cock-and-bull story for us about examining the line and he'll have been asleep all afternoon!' Her annoyance was superficial. She sounded indulgent. Even so, Kildie and Jim rushed to take up defensive positions.

'It's very hot, Gran.'

'There might be buckling up by the loop, Ma.'

'And my jam might be sticking on the bottom,' Gran said, 'so go out to the wash-house, get yourselves cleaned up and start laying the table. It's rabbit pie.'

Jim and Kildie did as bidden. It was a Michaelmas summer, as hot as it knew how. Yesterday the rabbit had been in a stew which today would have a pie crust on it.

'John Weywood has cold salmon,' Kildie observed as they went across the yard. 'Out of a tin, what's more.'

'Golly,' Jim came back enviously. Emmie would not allow food to enter her house in tins.

'I wish I hadn't said anything about the fleas,' Kildie mentioned. 'I hate that paraffin scrub Gran gives me. She tries to get it through to my brain!'

Jim laughed then sobered.

'Poor Miss Prosser.'

'And she did it for me!' Kildie mourned, holding her hands limp-wristed beneath the tap. 'I feel responsible!'

'Had we better walk along Middle Lane right now? Make sure she got home?' Jim asked, already thinking about his mother and what they would tell her and in any case what could he possibly do if they found Miss Prosser in a ditch.

'Mr Milsom-Parker took her home in his new car.'

Kildie raised her brows, surprised. 'He said he wanted to try it out on rough country roads. D'you suppose he was just being kind?'

Jim too was surprised. 'Can't imagine Millie doing anything halfway decent. But you never know. Anyway, that's a relief. No trouble tonight then.' He rinsed his own hands. 'And those two louts will never be early enough in the mornings to catch her.'

'So . . . Millie takes her home tomorrow and Friday . . . that will be this week finished.'

Jim gnawed his bottom lip.

'I'm on lates next week.'

They looked at each other. They were frightened.

It had never occurred to Dorothy that she might fail in her probationary year, she had never failed anything yet. She was used to people worshipping her too: her parents had always done so, the girls in her various schools, her fellow-students at College, even the lecturers. So she was not surprised by the devotion of her own junior class nor by the sudden adoration of Billy and Percy. The day of the dousing they were hanging about outside her class-room door determined to walk her down the long Middle Lane to Applecross Farm. When she was swept off in Millie's new car – something that had never happened before – their enslavement was complete. If she could win over Mr Milsom-Parker, she must be very special indeed. They trailed to their respective hovels, singing her praises in their harsh newly broken voices, already vying with each other for her favours.

'She put me under the water first,' Percy remembered, dotingly.

'Ah. But she got her fingers right into me 'air. No-one ever done that before. It was . . . nice.'

'Feels better, dunnit? Without the cra'lers.'

'Aye, it does that.'

The boys ruffled their silky locks experimentally, then laughed like corncrakes and, just as suddenly, sobered.

'I'd do anything for 'er,' Billy said, throwing caution to the winds.

Percy had to go one better. 'I'd die for 'er,' he said.

They spent the next two days trying to get to school early enough to open the gate for her, find the bell, fetch the coke, put out books . . . literally anything. There was no cause for Percy to die, but he sniffed very loudly and declared he thought he had a cold.

'Not that it were the water, miss,' he hastened to assure her.

'Probably accompanying your father on his nightly trips,' Dorothy said drily.

'Ah. Could be.' He grinned sheepishly, loving it that she knew all about his misdemeanours.

'Try going to bed early for a few nights, Percy,' she advised. 'See if you can be up to walk me to school on Monday morning.'

His face opened ecstatically. 'I'll be at Mrs Thrupp's at eight sharp!' he promised.

Billy said, 'An' I will!'

'I don't leave until eight fifteen, boys, as you very well know.' She looked at them and smiled and they nearly fainted. 'But I expect Mrs Thrupp will give you a drink of milk if you have to wait.'

They both abhorred milk but for her they would have supped poison.

'Coo, miss,' said Billy.

'Done,' said Percy as his father always said when he sold a brace of pigeons.

So it was that Jim, starting his week of 'lates', found himself looking at the two hulking youths when he walked down Middle Lane at ten to eight on Monday morning.

He was appalled. Kildie had woken him at seven with a cup of tea and lots of encouragement, otherwise he might have been tempted to forget his resolution of the week before.

'She was all right last week,' Kildie said earnestly. 'Millie is still taking her home at night and those two lollops are never early enough in the morning to catch her before she gets to the school gate. But I heard them saying they were going to be at Mrs Thrupp's by eight this morning. Honestly, Jim, it's true. I wouldn't wake you up early on your late turn if I didn't know for sure—'

'Right-oh.' He had had a day off yesterday and had gone fishing with his father. It had been past midnight when they crept up to bed. 'You don't have to keep on, Kildie. I'm awake now.'

'Drink this.' Kildie was anxiously domineering like her grandmother. 'And I'll bring you some more hot water for your shave.'

'Do I have to shave?' Jim felt certain it was a question of walking briskly down the lane and walking briskly back again. Billy and Percy were quite incapable of getting out of their beds until they had to and though the summer was still with them, the mornings were chill and everything pearled with dew. Neither lad cared for dampness.

'Of course you've got to shave! You're walking Miss Prosser to school!' Kildie was horrified. So was he.

'I thought I'd go ahead of her. Just in case . . .' he protested over the rim of his cup.

'They could slip between you and push her into a ditch before you'd know it,' she pointed out sensibly. 'Now hurry up, do. I'll empty the gosunder.'

'You'll do no such thing. And I'll come down for my shave. Now skedaddle!'

She obeyed, well satisfied, and he finished his tea and thought how damned awkward this was going to be. He'd not been introduced to Miss Prosser and here he was turning up on her doorstep to escort her down the road. Probably it was all a wild-goose chase anyway. He determined to stick to his first plan. He'd round the last bend of Middle Lane and watch the front door. When she came out he'd go ahead of her, like anyone from one of the cottages along the way. In fact, he'd take his case to make it all look more credible.

So to turn that last corner and see the Matson and Jenkins boys practically sitting on her front doorstep was dismaying to say the least. He hovered just out of sight, not knowing what to do. The damned cheek of those boys left him unprepared. He had thought they might lie in wait for the girl, throw stones, use catapults . . . but to accost her in broad daylight was beyond belief. They'd end up in the cells, of course. But meanwhile poor little Dorothy Prosser would suffer.

He peered around the hawthorn again. They seemed to be drinking something. Yes. They tipped back their heads and he saw they were drinking from the Applecross milk measures; two-gill canisters with long hooked handles for lowering into the churn. Thieves too, as well as rapists.

Jim was brought up short by that last word which he had so nearly whispered aloud. It was a word that was only ever whispered in Dymock. After all it so rarely happened. Local girls would become pregnant and whimper as their father whipped them that they had been forced. No-one believed them.

This was different.

Jim felt the metal corners of his case tap against his right calf and realized he was trembling. It was as if he had gone for a walk at dusk, expecting the small dangers of the countryside; marauding badgers, poachers' gin-traps, and instead had come right to the edge of the precipice which dropped into the quarry at Red Marley. He would have to do something. And Jim was not a man for decisions.

He peered again. The two hulkish louts had now apparently thrown their gill measures onto the doorstep and were doing a sort of jig to the garden gate. There they stopped and held on to each other, literally tittering with glee. It was horrible. Jim withdrew again and realized this time that in spite of the chilly dew he was sweating profusely.

When he heard her voice, something happened. She

must have come around from the back way because there were no doors slamming. He realized her presence by that clear ringing greeting.

'Good-morning, boys!'

It was her courage, her sheer effrontery, that stiffened his sinews. She had, after all, ample opportunity to turn and run. They'd never have caught her before Mrs Thrupp emerged with her rolling-pin held above that enormous bosom. But Miss Prosser did not run. She knew – must know – why Billy Matson and Percy Jenkins were waiting for her just outside the front gate, yet she called to them as if it were the most normal thing in the world.

'Good-morning, boys!'

There was no reply. He did not expect it. The two louts in question were practically inarticulate anyway. Jim's heart pumped blood around his body at an accelerated rate, and he emerged from the hawthorn with a war-cry that must have echoed in Kempley church, brandishing his metal-bound case like a ball and chain.

He was upon them before they knew what was happening. Indeed, they made no attempt to parry his swingeing blows, but cowered before him, bewildered by his yells and whoops, terrified by this sudden and unexpected apparition. As soon as they had regained a semblance of reality they took to their heels and by the time Jim had spun himself to a standstill they had cleared the ditch with a mighty leap, shoved their way through the hawthorn and were both disappearing across the wheat stubble under the impression that the gamekeeper had tracked them down at last.

Jim stood there, drooping from the shoulders, panting like a Jack Russell, unable to credit himself with such an unexpected victory.

Miss Prosser's voice said from behind him, 'Well, I really do not know who you are, but that was indeed a spectacle. Did you have a reason for it?'

He turned and looked at her and fell in love. He may well have fallen in love with her voice a moment before, or the picture painted by Kildie last week, or the idea of a damsel in distress; but he had not been conscious of anything before that moment except fear. Now he knew. This whole sequence of events had been set up to bring them together. Jim James and Dorothy Prosser.

He took one long last breath, expelled it and said, 'Miss Prosser.'

She was looking delightful that morning. She wore a navy linen skirt whose hem just covered her silken knees. The jacket above it was hip length, buttonless and boxy and the cream shantung blouse showed a square neckline revealing her lifted, determined chin and long smooth throat to perfection. Her hat was varnished straw, pushing her short golden hair into wings above her ears. Shoes and gloves were discreet beige. He wanted to fall at her feet.

She said coolly, 'I am indeed Miss Prosser. And you?'

'I? Me?' He was acting like a yokel; no better than Billy Matson. 'My name is James.'

The hauteur on her face melted somewhat.

'Walter James's son? From the Station House?'

'Yes.'

'And Kilda's brother?'

'Well, actually . . .' It was too difficult to explain about Sarah having Kildie and dumping her on his parents. 'Yes,' he said.

She began to smile. 'Kildie has been anxious on my behalf?'

'Yes.'

'I understand, I think.' A smile appeared in her blue eyes. How on earth could eyes be so blue? 'She has said to me once or twice that when her brother was on nights he would be only too pleased to escort me to and from school.'

'Yes.' He wondered whether the conversation would ever get past question and answer.

'So you are on nights?'

'No. Late turn.' He swallowed with a terrific pumping of his Adam's apple. 'I go to work on the one-fifteen and get back on the . . .' He simply could not remember when he got back home at night. He was drowning in her gaze . . . her beauty.

She turned away from him, giving him a moment's respite. But when she turned back it was worse than ever. He had to clamp his teeth together to prevent his jaw from dropping.

'Well,' she said briskly, 'it looks as if my other escorts have completely disappeared. So perhaps we had better set off.' She began to walk down the lane. 'I did think—' She twisted her head to talk to him and he caught a flashing glimpse of her clavicle beneath blouse and jacket. Gleaming waxily it looked at once vulnerable and indestructible. 'I did think Mrs Thrupp would hear the rumpus and come out to investigate. Obviously it wasn't as bad as I imagined.' She smiled suddenly. 'I thought you were a madman, escaped from Westbury workhouse. I was about to run as well. Then I noticed your case.'

'Case?' He took a very long stride to draw level with her.

'GWR stamped into the leather. And I put two and two together.'

'Oh, I see.' He was amazed at her quickness and perspicacity. No wonder she was a good teacher. Lucky, lucky Kildie. 'So you knew who I was right from the start?'

She didn't prevaricate as Lizzie and Sarah would have done.

'Of course. I'm not stupid enough to wait around to be knocked unconscious.' She glanced at him. 'Or worse.'

He blushed to the roots of his hair and she burst out laughing.

'I'm sorry, Mr James. I'm teasing you, am I not? And all that is missing is your white horse!'

'White horse?' He was at it again, repeating her words.

She stopped and looked at him, her eyes enormous and apparently innocent.

231

'You are my Sir Galahad, surely? Coming to my rescue? My knight in shining armour riding a white stallion?'

'You are teasing me again, Miss Prosser!'

She dimpled. 'So I am. So I am.' She turned her mouth down ruefully. 'You see, Mr James, it is good to have somebody to tease after so long. Do you know Mr Milsom-Parker?'

'I do indeed.'

'And you have obviously met Messrs Matson and Jenkins before today. So you see my plight.'

'Yes.' He counted four paces then said, 'I think you are very brave as well as beautiful.'

'And what of you? Tackling those two with only a small leather case.'

'Bound in brass.'

'Very well. Bound in brass.'

'I am not brave.'

'I beg to differ.' She glanced at him again. 'What did you think they were going to do to me?'

'I thought they might . . . harm you,' he said, as red as a gobbler once again.

She held his glance and they both stumbled slightly on the rough road, then leaned forward to hold each other up.

She could have told him the truth then and he would have been diminished so much that their friendship would probably have ended on the spot.

But she whispered, 'I know what you mean, Mr James. How can I ever thank you?'

He said hoarsely, 'By letting me walk you to school every morning this week.'

She tucked her hand into his arm and he felt her frailty and her strength.

'Done!' she cried, sealing Percy's bargain without a thought in his direction. 'And the week after that, when you are on nights, will you walk me home?'

'I thought Millie was taking you home in his new car?'

'He is. But I'll get rid of him that week.'

Jim had never been so happy. His mother would create at him getting up at three in the afternoon instead of the prescribed five o'clock. He did not care.

TWELVE

1940

Marcus Villiers drove his hired car carefully through the city, convinced the cumbersome gas bag lolloping on its roof would catch into lamp posts, telegraph wires . . . anything and everything. He hated the car with an intensity that surprised even himself. He was a man of deep and dark passions, but only when he dealt with inanimate objects did these passions rise to the surface and become obvious to himself.

It was a week since Kildie had left Hill House. He had not permitted himself to consider she might have left *him*. She had gone away for a time and that was all. His deep sense of loss was for his car. He had telephoned the police half-expecting there to have been a terrible accident. Kildie had driven with him by her side, never alone. And he had not been at all impressed by her performance. He did not think he would see the car again. And he grieved deeply.

It was good when he got hold of this Wolsley with its drunken gas bag. It released all his hatred, which was so much more positive than grief. The gas did not enable the car to go faster than thirty miles an hour and that made him angry to start with. It had been a hearse in the past and the big, black chassis made him furious. Its capacious leather seats could hold six people which was also ridiculous. The Morgan was designed for two people. It had two dicky seats, but it was intended for two people: Marcus and Kildie. He loathed the Wolsley because it would admit other people who would come between Marcus and Kildie. Nevertheless, when he left it and took the lift to his office, he felt another sense of loss. Without the Wolsley there was – for the moment – nothing specific to loathe, and the sense of desolation returned to fill the vacuum.

He walked along the carpeted hall at the top of the tall building past a long row of office doors – staff, accounts, buyers and stock – to his own large office which looked down the enormous stairwell of the store and took in the galleried floors: hats and haberdashery at ground level; ladies fashions first floor, followed by an austere gents outfitters; a wilderness of furniture and carpets on the third floor; the fourth floor shared by linens and restaurant. The orchestra had arrived and was setting up between the potted palms. He thought sourly that they looked ready for the Wolsley in its capacity as hearse. They were all ancient and so gaunt they may well have suffered from tuberculosis earlier. For the first time in his life he wondered why he was here, why he bothered with this enormous store that each day became more unwieldy and cumbersome like the gas bag on his hired car.

His secretary came in with the day's letters. He had never mixed business and pleasure, so Miss Ashe was in her late fifties with breasts at waist level and thick ankles. But she smelled good. He could not bear the smell of unwashed female.

'A reply from the Ministry, Mr Villiers. They will agree to your plan for a special dining-room for men in uniform.'

'What about extra rations?'

'A man from the Food Office will be here this afternoon to discuss that.'

'Good.'

He remembered belatedly it had been Kildie's idea. She had suggested that he ought to partition part of the 'Food Floor' as she called it, for servicemen only, and spread the extra food allowance over the whole restaurant. It had been one of those times when she said, 'Darling – please – let's just talk for once! We never really say anything to each other . . .' And when he had told her she was too beautiful to be interested in sordid business, she had come up with the idea so quickly he had realized she gave quite a lot of thought to the store.

The memory of that time sent a pang through his whole body which must have been all too obvious because Miss Ashe said, 'Are you all right, sir? Would you like a glass of water?'

They probably knew of course. The place was a hive of gossip. He hated them for knowing. He should hate Kildie; she had taken his car. Oh God . . . his car . . .

'No thank you, Miss Ashe. Are these the figures from the buyer? And these—'

'Stock, sir. Running low, of course. The clothing factory in Cheltenham has been requisitioned for army uniforms. Millinery still have the peaked hats . . . they are not going at present.'

'They will,' Marcus said. 'Women will be looking for fashions to emulate service uniforms and those hats are made on the same blocks as the officers' caps.'

'Yes, sir.' Miss Ashe went through the rest of her bundle without interest. She was efficient and she minded her own business, but she had no enthusiasm for Villiers' Department Store. It was how he liked things to be; too much interest threatened interference. Like Kildie's suggestion. Though that seemed to be turning out well. He shook his head fiercely. Kildie had taken his car . . .

After Miss Ashe's departure, Marcus spent a frustrating half-hour on the telephone. The managers of most of his regular wholesalers were in the Forces, and no-one seemed to know what was happening. During one of the interminable waits while somebody asked somebody else for information, his opaque black eyes sharpened suddenly. He had been staring unseeingly through the internal window at the masses of people moving like ants up and down the stairs. One of them, he now saw, was Jim James. He was not in uniform. The mouse-brown hair, lying flat across his scalp, was unmistakable. He turned and stared right into Marcus' office and though Marcus knew the windows were clouded from Jim's side, he nevertheless leaned back in his chair before replacing the telephone receiver.

Jim continued up the last flight of stairs to the fifth floor where the door marked 'Private, Staff Only' was even now being opened for him by Miss Ashe.

Jim James was home again and was coming to see Marcus Villiers.

Lizzie could not seem to get out of her bed. Edward told her why this was in no uncertain terms, but she could not quite believe him.

'I haven't gone to pieces, Teddy darling!' she wailed. 'Well, yes, I have, I suppose. But not because Charlie's joined up! He's been on about it ever since we moved into the Gatehouse. He was on about it before we split up, after Croydon—'

'We did not split up, Lizzie,' Edward said angrily. 'Not in that sense anyway.'

'Well, I didn't mean . . . Oh darling, don't be horrid to me.'

'I'm not being horrid . . .' He leaned over and kissed her because since they'd come back together things had been rather wonderful. 'I just want you to pull yourself together, sweetheart.'

'I can't, Teddy!' She mumbled against his face. 'Every time I sit up the room goes round.'

Edward moved to her ear which allowed them both to breathe. 'He's practically eighteen after all, sweetheart. He'd be called up sooner or later. And I suppose he thought rather than getting sucked into the mud here like me, he'd be better off—'

'Teddy, you're not being sucked into any mud—'

'I'm having to dig for victory alongside the gardeners! Dammit all, Liz, even revered Uncle joins in at times!'

'But that makes it better, don't you see? Everyone pulling together—'

'Yes. I know, baby.' He moved his mouth down her neck to her clavicle. 'And you're right, of course. As usual.' He was, in fact, enjoying the hard physical labour, the companionship, the sense of purpose. And Lizzie.

She said in a tight voice, 'Teddy, please don't. I feel too ill.'

He should have known better. He had the key to Lizzie's passions now. Strangely, she was very like Sarah in that any kind of 'messing about', as she so elegantly phrased it, put her off. If they were going to make love, they were going to make love, and the sooner the better. He began to undo his trousers.

'Teddy – no. I mean it. I'm sorry—'

He said, 'Oh darling, you know very well you enjoy it—'

'Teddy – oh darling – I think I'm going to be sick!'

And she was. And some of it went down his trousers. He could have murdered her. Instead, as he cleaned them both up he muttered, 'Bloody Charlie! I'll kill him when he's finished his square-bashing!'

But he thought perhaps the time had come for the doctor. And when the new young chap who had been turned down for the RAMC, so must be damned ill himself, said, 'It's too early to say definitely but I rather think Mrs Richardson is expecting a baby,' he knew a moment of such piercing joy that he loved everyone. Charlie, Winnie and especially Lizzie.

He knelt by the bed, holding her hand.

'I worship you. You have made me so happy—'

Lizzie stared at him. She had thought he might be horrified to be starting all over again. After all, Charlie was in the Army and Winnie was a gawky fifteen.

'You weren't like this over the other two,' she said.

He remembered that time. He had been running around after a girl in Kempley. He had barely registered that Lizzie was pregnant.

He almost wept with remorse. 'I know. But – somehow – this is like a gift. We thought we were past it – you've only wanted me before to make you a baby. This time—'

She turned bright red. 'Teddy! Stop it! Sometimes you are so coarse!'

'You know what I mean. This child is coming from our love. Not just our—' She put a hand across his mouth before he could utter one of his guttersnipe words. He held it there, kissing it, smiling, beginning to weep involuntarily.

She said wonderingly, 'I didn't know you could feel like this. I feel as if we're starting again, Teddy. I've always loved you. You know that. When you . . . you . . . strayed . . . I still loved you.'

'Oh darling . . . Lizzie, I'm sorry—'

'No. Don't be. Perhaps we had to be like we were – to arrive here.' She leaned down and kissed his forehead very chastely. 'It was because I thought I was losing you to Sarah . . . I knew then that I wanted you. Wanted you,' she repeated meaningfully.

'Lizzie, I'm sorry. I promise you that underneath it all, I loved you—'

She smiled. 'I was the only girl who held out. That was why you married me, Edward. We both know that.'

'I don't care – I don't care – I love you—'

She put her hand across his mouth again. 'Listen, dearest. You needed love. Desperately. You knew you were unwanted. That was why . . . you did . . . what you did. I've always known that.' She leaned down and kissed his forehead. 'Come to me now, Teddy. Come now.' She drew him to her.

He held back, gazing at her with his blue eyes wide.

'Darling, we mustn't. Not now you're pregnant. We might do something awful to the baby.' He struggled to his feet. 'I'm going to get you your lunch now. I'm going to look after you properly. And when Winnie gets back from Gran's, we'll tell her and we'll have a tea party. Up here in our bedroom.' He was like a young boy, again. He laughed. 'Darling, I'm going to be different from now on! I'm going to be a proper family man! I promise you!'

Lizzie looked at the door, closed carefully after him to avoid its usual squeak. She put her hands on her abdomen. It did not feel as if a child could possibly be there. It felt empty. She began to weep herself.

Jim said, 'I know I have no right to interfere—'

'Damned right you haven't,' Marcus came back smartly.

'But as Kildie's legal guardian was my father and I am her only male relative—'

'And don't let's forget that! Relative.'

Jim lost his thread and stared, and then the treacherous colour mounted his already rosy skin. He had refused to use the lifts to get up here, wanting to delay the inevitable awfulness of this interview, but now he wished he had saved his breath.

'Just what do you mean by that?' he asked, then wished he had not.

Marcus turned away contemptuously. 'We're alone, James! Can't you admit that you lust after your niece? I know bloody well she lusts after you!'

Jim kept his hands rigidly by his sides. Physically he was fitter than he'd been for years and he knew he could have knocked Villiers cold with one punch.

He said, 'How dare you talk about Kildie and me in those terms? How dare you foul our family love by dragging it down to your filthy level?'

'Hah!' Marcus kept his back turned. He wanted to cry and scream like a child. 'I suppose she's told you everything?'

'Of course not! She's talked to Dorothy, woman to woman.' Jim too turned away, unable to look at the man any longer. 'I knew what you were like that first time. The tea party at home. The way you mauled her—' He remembered what Kildie had said that day on the station platform and coloured again. He did not let himself think of that often. The way she had kissed him . . .

Marcus said, 'She wants that. She needs to know that

she belongs to me. Me alone. You have always come between us.'

Jim found some resolution from somewhere. The way Kildie behaved now – she was what Marcus Villiers had made her. He was destroying her innate innocence.

'You're talking rubbish, Villiers. She's left you and you're throwing stones at anyone! I've come to talk some sense about your marriage and I can't do that if you're going to keep accusing me of luring her away from you!' He watched a girl walking along the gallery below the fifth floor, sitting at one of the small basket tables, ordering a coffee. She had honey-coloured hair falling from beneath a black beret and cascading over her shoulders; she reminded him piercingly of Dorothy. She was as unattainable as Dorothy too. Dorothy who had said coldly last night, 'I'm not going to compete with Kildie, Jim! You had better sort all that sordid business out in the morning!'

Marcus was saying something about Jim James being the last person in the world to sort out anything to do with Kildie. Jim drew a breath and turned back into the room.

'Look. I know now what you think I am – you do not need to repeat it yet again. I certainly know what you are. But my wife tells me that Kildie is better off with you. And as it seems you do not actually hit her—'

'Oh I've done that, never fear!'

Jim held on to the back of the chair and stared at the sleek black head above the immaculate suit jacket.

He said quietly, 'You have actually hit Kildie? Physically hit her?'

Marcus too turned and met Jim's gaze. Both pairs of eyes were opaque and flint-hard.

'Only when I know she wants it,' Marcus said insolently.

Jim stopped thinking. He lunged forward, his right fist swinging up from below waist level, gaining momentum, until it hit Marcus' face at the side of his nose at perhaps twenty miles an hour.

The force of the blow sent the lighter man stumbling backwards to crash against the far wall, then to slide ignominiously to the floor. Blood poured from his nose. He put a hand to his eye.

Jim stood above him, breathing like a dragon.

'How do you like it, Villiers? I wouldn't have done it only I knew you wanted it! Christ Almighty, you've been begging for it ever since I came into this office, haven't you?' He leaned down and lugged the other man to his feet. 'It's no good talking to you, is it? You don't understand – you don't listen! You can give orders and that's about it!' Villiers flailed at him with a kind of despair and Jim leaned away from him and shoved him into the chair by the desk. The black eyes were watering profusely; already one of them was half-closed.

Jim leaned over him.

'Listen to me, Villiers. I came here – my wife persuaded me to come here – to try to mediate between you and Kildie. She – my wife – is under the impression that Kildie still cares for you. I rather doubt that myself. However, I was supposed to make some kind of arrangement for you and she to meet and talk.' Jim drew a breath. 'I've changed my mind, Villiers. I do not think you are fit to live with my niece. I am going to do my utmost to persuade her to leave you for good. Do you understand that?'

Marcus made a strangled sound and tried to stand up. Jim pushed him down.

'Do you understand?' he repeated rather more loudly.

Marcus nodded and snarled at the same time. Jim continued to look at him contemptuously for another five or six seconds. Then he released him and left.

1924

When Dorothy Prosser came to tea at Dymock's Station House, she had no real apprehension of how momentous was the occasion. She knew that Jim James had fallen for her in a big way. She was used to men falling for her, indeed, she wondered whether Mr Milsom-Parker might be on the same road; certainly Percy and Billy were in a state of adoration. But this time it was different. She had always remained totally in control of every man who had fallen for her. She was a basically kind girl and made quite certain that when someone fell for her they emerged all the better for it. But now she was not totally in control. She felt such a tenderness for Jim James, she wondered whether she too was falling in love. But the whole family were fascinating. Kildie was by far the most intelligent pupil in the school, besides being pretty to the point of beauty. Walter James had been to Oxford and had chosen the humble life of a country station master so there was more to him than met the eye. Sarah, one of the daughters, was, apparently, a widow and had a career on the stage, and that was why Kildie had been adopted by the grand-parents. Elizabeth, the other daughter, was married to Adrian Frost's son. Mrs James seemed the only 'ordinary' person in the whole family. She could not stop thinking about them. And probably it made her more sentient than usual because she knew exactly how Jim felt. He would be thinking of her constantly, while he ate, slept and worked. It would be as if he lived in a huge, multi-rainbowed bubble, where reflections of herself danced before him and shimmered at night. He would be happy, but he would also have a permanent nagging headache. She knew all this because it was the same for her, except that the reflections were not only of Jim James, but also of the whole family.

The headache was a warning. She was afraid it might become permanent if she went further. And yet . . . and yet . . . she could no more have refused the invitation to tea, than set fire to her classroom.

She told herself it was curiosity and that if something went wrong that would show her not to proceed further. Indeed to proceed further was counter to all her plans. Married teachers were not accepted in the county and she desperately wanted to finish her probationary year and do at least another five years before she left the profession. So she steeled her heart. But she still accepted Mrs James's invitation to tea on Sunday, 12 October.

Kildie was so excited she couldn't sit still in church that morning and had to be tapped very firmly several times by Gran. Jim sat through the service with a smile going from ear to ear even when the vicar promised hell and damnation to anyone with evil thoughts. Walter, glancing at his son, knew that this was it. He and Emmie had to like the new teacher because she had captured Jim's heart completely. And Emmie, also glancing sideways and noting the ridiculous grin on her son's face, hoped she would be able to mould this girl into a good housekeeper.

It did not bode well that Dorothy Prosser was not in church herself. But then, neither was Lizzie, though she had a good excuse what between little Charlie crawling under the pews last week and untying the shoe laces of anyone he passed, and the fact that Lizzie was almost certainly pregnant again and was suffering from morning sickness.

So Walter, Emmie and Kildie sat there praying everything would be 'all right', and Jim remained secure in his bubble in a state of ecstatic thraldom.

Dorothy arrived promptly at three o'clock, as instructed by Jim. She had dressed with great care; a plain organdie blouse in deference to the autumn sunshine, but a severe dark blue skirt covering her knees because it was Sunday and almost winter by the calendar. She did not even realize that the cut of both garments set them apart from anything Emmie and Lizzie had in their wardrobes. The blouse was cut like a man's shirt and even sported cuff-links. The skirt clung to Dorothy's narrow hips and then widened at the knee in a series of ridiculously short box pleats. She had bought them in Villiers' Gowns in Westgate Street, noted for their 'Parisian' styles.

Jim's smile widened still further at the sight of her – a white blouse and dark skirt were obviously the epitome of conservative taste – and he took her hat and gloves reverently to the chiffonier. Kildie made the introductions and by the time Dorothy had shaken hands with Emmie and Walter James, their daughter, Lizzie, her husband Edward Richardson and their small son Charlie, she was laughing and relaxed and certain that, as usual, people were liking her as much as she was liking them.

'Would you care to see the garden, Miss Prosser?' Kildie asked – as Gran invariably did to all visitors.

But – 'After tea, Kildie,' Gran said repressively. 'Miss Prosser has walked far enough already this afternoon.'

Dorothy smiled happily. 'Such a delightful walk. I plan to do many this winter. I should like to see some of the beauty spots. Lassington Oak. And Symonds Yat—'

Edward, one arm along the mantelpiece, grinned almost as widely as Jim. 'We could take you in the trap, couldn't we, Liz? How about next Sunday?'

'I'm afraid my condition—' Lizzie put her hand on her flat stomach, determined on getting some attention. Dorothy glanced at Jim who said nothing, so she made no further enquiry.

And Edward said immediately, 'The offer is still open, Miss Prosser. I'd be delighted to show you around the Forest.'

Lizzie gave him a furious look, but it was lost on Dorothy. She was still looking at Jim and just for a moment – which seemed like eternity to both of them – she was caught in his bubble. They stared at each other, both smiling. And then she said, 'We'll have to see, won't we, Jim?'

And he said, 'Yes. But we will go. Some time. I want to show you everything.'

And she said, 'Oh yes,' on a sigh. Because, of course, if they never went anywhere ever again, they would still see everything because love gave them universal vision.

Emmie glanced at Walter who very slowly closed one eye.

Charlie, restrained on Kildie's lap, suddenly realized

245

that this new lady was not paying him any attention and let out a howl. Kildie shushed him anxiously and Edward leaned forward about to haul him up by his collar, when Dorothy turned to him and said quietly, 'We will be quiet. Now!' It was her usual phrase for a group of squabbling children and was an automatic reflex. It worked instantaneously. Not only did Charlie close his mouth he also held out his arms to Dorothy and after a moment's bewildered hesitation – while she emerged fully from Jim's bubble – she took him on to her pristine knee and held him close. Although she had no family experience of small children, she was good at comforting her pupils and Charlie snuggled into her arm as if he was quite used to it and was soon grinning up at her.

Everyone applauded.

Except Lizzie and Emmie. Emmie smiled, glad that the girl had a maternal streak in her. Lizzie did not even smile.

After the hubbub had died down, it was time for tea.

'Cloth, Lizzie,' Emmie said. 'Then you can help me carry in. Teddy, take Charlie outside. Kildie, show Miss Prosser the bathroom.'

The bathroom was rarely used. It had been dusted for this occasion but the dusty dryness of the wash-basin told its own tale. Dorothy thanked Kildie and told her to go back down to help her grandmother. And then she closed and bolted the door.

Tea was laid in about five seconds. Edward returned from the privy with Charlie. Kildie and Jim were about to go out to the wash-house, when the air was split by terrible screams.

Just for a moment they were all frozen around the big dining table. The screams were coming from the bathroom and their imaginations leapt from one horrible disaster to another. Everyone shared a vision of Miss Prosser bleeding to death on the linoleum, but how this had come about varied considerably.

Jim was the first one up the stairs.

'Dorothy—' He had difficulty to shout above the

blood-curdling noise from behind the door. 'Dorothy – what is it? Open the door! Quickly!'

There was a sort of hiccuping pause, then the door started to rattle. It did not open. The screams redoubled themselves.

Jim was frantic. He pushed the others halfway back down the stairs and took a run at the door. It splintered and crashed open in Miss Prosser's face, casting her to the ground. Blood spurted from her nose. She did not stop screaming.

'Oh my God! Dorothy – speak to me – what is it?'

Jim knelt above her, propped her head, dabbed at her nose with the hem of her organdie blouse.

Emmie knelt the other side. 'Prop her against the lavvie,' she instructed. 'Now. Bridge of nose.' She pressed expertly and the bleeding was immediately staunched. A handkerchief was passed to her and she wetted it at the basin and dabbed expertly.

'You're all right, Miss Prosser. Just relax.'

'I've got to get out!' panted Dorothy. 'Please – please – let me get out!'

'We're all here, Dorothy,' Jim thought his heart would break at the terror in her face. 'Nothing can happen—'

She said in reverberating tones. 'Look in the bath.'

They all looked.

A very large, very black, very furry spider stood on the dusty cast-iron base, obviously shocked into immobility.

'A spider,' Emmie commented. 'Get a lot of them in the autumn.'

'Oh dear Lord!' Dorothy began to shudder. She could not stop. 'Oh my Lord! Please – please, Jim. Take me home.'

'But, Dorothy. The tea . . . if you have a cup of nice hot tea . . . it's just a spider, nothing to be frightened of—'

'Jim – Please—' The shuddering was like an ague, her teeth chattered loudly. Kildie began to weep.

Walter strode over the assembled bodies and put his hands beneath her armpits.

'Come along, child. We must get you out of here. Teddy, bring the trap around the front. Jim, you must go with Miss Prosser and stay with her until she is better.'

Kildie quavered, 'Is she going to die, Grandad? Oh Gran – is she going to die?'

Suddenly Charlie had had enough. Something had happened to his nice lady and he had no idea what it was and neither, it seemed, did anyone else. He opened his mouth as wide as it would go and began to scream.

Walter put his teacup into its saucer with unnecessary force. Especially as Emmie had resurrected his father's best set in honour of Miss Prosser.

He looked around at the depleted party and said, 'Look. There is no need to go on and on about it, Lizzie. The poor girl suffers from arachniphobia and simply has no control of herself when she sees a spider. It's not her fault. It's not our fault. Emmie, of course you have cleaned the bathroom. She knows that as well as we do. There was no criticism in her reaction. None at all. And if *you* are going to keep criticizing the girl, you will alienate Jim completely.'

Teddy, who had left Dorothy in Jim's arms at Applecross Farm, said stoutly, 'It's no more than your fear of . . . certain things, Lizzie. Everyone has their obsessions—'

'And we all know what yours is!' Lizzie said furiously, knowing only too well that Teddy was referring to her disgust of his love-making.

But Teddy chose to misinterpret that counter-accusation. He had a bad reputation with the local girls which he justified to himself because of Lizzie's coldness. But he knew that local opinion attributed his wandering ways to his parentage.

'If you are referring to my promiscuous father, look at your own family if you please, Lizzie!' He glanced meaningfully at Kildie who was still quietly weeping into her jelly. 'Your sister's reputation isn't snow-white, I believe!'

Emmie said swiftly, 'Kildie, love, will you fetch your old Gran a few of those late radishes. Lift up the lid of the frame very carefully and pull them gently like I've shown you.'

Kildie brightened. Gran rarely let anyone pick anything from her vegetable garden. She left the room importantly. Charlie, asleep on the sofa, stirred, opened an eye and rolled over.

Walter said, 'I forbid you to speak of my daughter like that in this house, Teddy. I've always liked you – we've got on well – but if you think you can insult me—'

Teddy was aghast. He had been getting at Lizzie and completely overlooked the fact that Sarah was also Walter's daughter.

'Look, I'm sorry. It's been such an afternoon—'

Emmie said, 'No harm done, Walter dear. And I believe – now that we're alone – Edward and Lizzie want to tell us something.'

Lizzie looked bewildered. 'You know about the new baby.'

Teddy said, 'I haven't actually mentioned—'

Emmie smiled thinly. 'No. I heard about it from your father. Apparently he is backing you financially.'

'He called here?'

'On his way home from his visit with you.'

Lizzie said querulously, 'What? What are you talking about? Adrian was only here for one night. Why did he call here?'

Emmie's smile filled out. 'He came to ask if he could dedicate his next book of poems to me.'

Walter glanced across the table and smiled too. 'What did you say?' he asked curiously.

'I told him, certainly not! And then he told me of your plans.'

'What plans?' Lizzie looked at Teddy, suddenly on the

verge of tears. 'I tell you everything and you never confide in me.'

'I was going to tell you tonight, old girl. Honestly. I know how fed up you are here – people gossiping – I thought a clean break . . . And this place was advertised in *Farmers' Weekly*. Huge acreage. Fruit and cattle. Horses too. Ideal farming country – a real bargain. So I wrote to Adrian and when he came down we talked it over. He thought it would be good for us to get away too. And he offered—'

'Where is this farm?' Lizzie asked, not knowing whether to be furious, intrigued, or just terrified at leaving her parents. Because she knew very well that if Teddy had made up his mind that was that.

'Suffolk,' he replied. He leaned forward enthusiastically. 'The nearest neighbours are over a mile away, Liz! Place surrounded by dykes. Completely private. Wonderful place for Charlie and the new baby. What do you say?'

She stared at him. He was so good-looking . . . clever like her father . . . he was wasted at the Dymock farm. It wasn't much bigger than a smallholding. And if the Suffolk place was that isolated, there could be none of his so-called flirtations.

'If it's what you want, darling—'

'It's what I want,' Teddy said.

Dorothy's remorse was almost worse than her shaking terror.

'Jim, I don't know what to say. The tea party and everything . . .'

'Darling girl. It's not your fault—'

'Of course it's my fault, Jim. How could I be such a fool? It's against my nature to lose control like that – I just hate myself!'

'Darling . . . dearest . . .' He had never used these terms before and adored the way they came off his tongue. 'Everybody understood. Once Pa explained about

arachniphobia, we knew it was something you couldn't
help—'

'But, darling Jim! Your mother – she'd got tea all ready
and I've taken you away as well as myself!' She wailed
aloud. 'Oh Jim! She'll never forgive me!'

'Darling, darling, darling . . .' Applecross was blessedly
empty for the afternoon and he had carried her to her
room and put her on her bed where her head was cradled
in his arm. With his free hand he stroked her hair away
from her hot face. 'My father will be explaining it – very
scientifically – right now, and my mother will understand
instantly. That's how it is with those two. They . . . they
. . . *listen* to each other.'

'That's important, Jim, isn't it?'

'They're the happiest people I know, my darling.'

She looked into his grey eyes. They were very close to
her blue ones. She whispered slowly, 'Apart from us, Jim.'

He held his breath, then very carefully lowered his
mouth on to hers. Her lips were as soft as gossamer. He
brushed them with his own.

'Oh Jim . . .' she whispered.

'Darling . . .' he whispered back and continued to touch
his lips to hers.

She wept uncharacteristically and said, 'I'm so sorry,
Jim . . .'

And he got onto the bed and held her body against his.
'It's all right . . . all right, my dearest dear. My darling
girl . . .'

Their love-making was clumsy and painful and afterwards all he could do was apologize. Dorothy felt she had
let him down all over again. She rolled onto one elbow
and smoothed his face, kissing him repeatedly until they
were both aroused again. This time it was much better
and they lay quietly, side by side, exhausted emotionally
and physically.

He whispered, 'What about Mrs Thrupp?'

'They've gone to see her sister.'

He said, 'Oh darling . . . I'll always adore spiders.'

She breathed a laugh. 'It's only happened once before since I was an adult. At college there was one crawling across the Principal's desk during a lecture.'

He too laughed. 'My dear Lord. Not really . . .'

'Really.' She kissed him, already familiar with the shape of his mouth, the taste of him. 'Oh darling. You really are my rescuer, aren't you?'

'When shall we get married, Doll? Soon? Let it be very, very soon.'

'Oh sweetheart, don't call me Doll. I can't marry you for ages yet. You know that. Married teachers are not—'

'But we have to get married, Doll!' He raised his head, shocked. 'We have to get married. Now.'

She laughed with an intimate tenderness that melted him completely.

'Don't be silly, dearest.'

And soon they made love again.

THIRTEEN

1940

When the row started – before it started really – Holly left the house and walked down the garden to the double row of beans. It was a glorious morning and Mum had managed to get some ham off coupons so they were going to have a salad for lunch. Holly had found the old picnic table at the back of the shed and set it up on the lawn and Mum had washed the lettuce and wrapped it in a tea towel on the clothes line to drain.

'As soon as Dad gets back from town,' she said, scrubbing radishes at the sink, 'we'll dish up the potatoes and sprinkle on this parsley and they can cool while we have your punch.'

Holly had made a concoction of blackcurrant jam and fresh greengages and it had been standing on the cold slab in the pantry overnight. Ever since they'd left Kildie at Gran's they had all been working at making Dad's embarkation leave really special. And, as Mum had said at breakfast time, 'Once you've seen Marcus Villiers, you'll be able to forget the whole sordid business.'

Holly had not been tempted to ask questions. It had been obvious from Kildie's highly emotional state, that something dreadful had happened at Hill House. And though they had left the whole problem with Gran, Aunt Lizzie's letter which arrived with the first post had not been reassuring.

'. . . I can't do much as I am feeling so ill myself. And Kildie will not stop crying. Unless you want poor Ma to be ill herself, I think you should try to talk some sense into Marcus. After all, he is her husband . . .'

Mum had looked at Dad and said, 'She's right, Jim. If he's not going to go out to Dymock and fetch her back like he did last time, then perhaps he's feeling guilty. Perhaps he needs a bit of reassurance. We've only heard Kildie's side, when all's said and done.'

Holly knew how Mum felt; she wasn't really unsympathetic. She simply wanted everything sorted out quickly so that Dad could go to Canada with a quiet mind.

And when Dad left for Gloucester, pedalling across the Green just as he'd always done, Holly too felt a sense of relief. Once Kildie was back with her husband, Holly herself could go and stay with Gran and be there for when Charlie finished his square-bashing and came home for his first leave.

So the two of them started to get the picnic ready. It was like a party. They changed into fresh cotton frocks and Mum looked out a big sun hat. She put it on and danced around the grass. 'We're celebrating, Hol!' she carolled, her golden hair flying.

'What are we celebrating?' Holly loved it when her mother 'went mad'.

'We're celebrating a return to the *status quo*!'

Dorothy stumbled against one of the garden chairs and clutched it and Holly called, 'here he is – here's Dad!'

And soon after that, as she carried the parsley potatoes to the table she heard Mum say very loudly, 'You what? You hit him? You brawled like a couple of dogs after a bitch . . . ?' And she put the potatoes down and walked towards the flowering beans.

Marcus managed to get himself into his swivel chair. He leaned on the desk and staunched his nosebleed as best he could and thought of how he could punish Jim James. And after a while he knew.

He stood up with some difficulty and examined his face in the glass on the wall. His right eye was almost shut and his nose was spreading to meet it. There was no disguising the fact that he was hurt. Well, that could be used to his advantage. But first he had to get out of the building without arousing any curiosity.

He opened the door and looked into the passage. No-one was about. He closed the door again and spent some time fitting his hat at a rakish angle so that it cast a shadow over the right side of his face. Every movement hurt. Every pain stiffened his resolution. Jim James did not really want him to take Kildie back. So he would take her back. And he would flaunt her in front of that stupid great oaf . . . flaunt her in front of everyone . . . even the blasted Food Inspector. Even Miss Ashe.

He took the service lift and whipped through the stock room looking neither left nor right. Everyone knew better than to look up at his passing anyway; they kept their heads down and made a show of working even when there was no stock to check or move.

Outside, the gas bag on the Wolsley heaved gently in the summer breeze. He got into the car and sat for a moment, breathing deeply. His eyes were watering again. He took out his bloody handkerchief and mopped ineffectually. He hated the James family with a passion that made his fingers shake. But he wanted Kildie. And he wanted his car. But he had to have Kildie.

He drove with infuriating sedateness along the Tewkesbury Road, turned off for the Green and parked the car at least a quarter of a mile from the cottage in the woods where he and Kildie had cavorted on their occasional visits to see Dorothy and Jim. He looked sourly around him as he started to walk towards the hamlet. Gran James would know which of these leaves to pick to ease his swollen face. The old girl was probably a witch anyway. Yet he had never had any opposition from her. Only her blasted son.

He emerged from the woods just in time to see Jim get off his bike at the gate of the cottage. Holly ran out to meet him. There was no sign of the Morgan.

Marcus cursed but he was glad. Kildie must be at Dymock and Gran would be much easier to deal with than

Jim. Though he had wanted to woo Kildie back in front of them all.

The drive back into Gloucester and along the Severn bank to Dymock seemed endless. His eyes watered again and he knew he was blubbing like any damned schoolboy. Blubbing for his car. Blubbing for his wife. Blubbing.

He saw the car long before he reached the junction of Middle Lane. Mrs Ball was standing by it propping her large frame against the bonnet. Gran James was . . . she was actually . . . dusting it! He pulled the Wolsley into the side of the road with a jerk. The old girl was dusting his Morgan; keeping it spotless. For him?

He switched off and got out of the car with care. His back was hurting now. He was, in fact, hurting all over. He had wanted to see Kildie alone before he had to face Gran, but the two women could be out there all morning and pretty soon he would have to lie down.

He pulled his hat down fiercely and walked forward towards the junction. Beyond the row of cottages an engine whistle screamed and Gran turned automatically to watch the smoke mark its sporadic course to the station and then halt. He heard her say, 'Midday from Ross. Two minutes late. That'll be the woman porter at Newent. Takes her too long to load the mail.'

Mrs Ball came back, 'How you do remember them all, Mrs James, I don't know.'

Gran said briskly, 'Measured my life by the trains, so I did. Got to have something to mark time passing.'

It sounded arid, empty. According to Kildie the old girl had had a high old time with her husband in days gone by. Now she was left with the trains. Like him with his car.

He shuddered. It wasn't enough. He had to have Kildie. Kildie waiting for him, living for him. Kildie, voluptuous and warm yet eternally schoolgirlish and naïve. If he had to take her back by force and lock her in her room, he would do it.

Gran heard his arrival and turned as if expecting him. Then she saw his face and her eyes widened.

She said immediately, 'Did our Jim do that?'

'Yes.' There was no point in prevaricating. He had to save his strength for Kildie now.

'Is he all right?'

'Yes.' Blast it, Jim James was fine. Marcus could have ground his teeth if they had not been hurting so much. He said, 'Where is she?'

Gran hesitated. 'You en't going to hurt her?'

'No. I'm taking her home where she belongs.'

Gran took a breath and let it go slowly.

'Ah. Well. You're right. She don't belong here no more, that's for sure. But she won't want to come. An' if you lay a finger on her—'

Marcus allowed himself a delightful split-second vision of himself beating Kildie; ripping her knickers down and forcing her over his knee and thrashing her bottom until it was fiery red.

'Don't be absurd, Gran. I'm not going to touch her!'

'All right. She's upstairs in my room. She's sleeping with me. Hasn't got up yet.'

That was his Kildie: lazy, unable to use her time properly. Waiting for something to happen, someone to organize her.

He went through the gate, around to the back, glanced at the ferns with loathing, and strode through the kitchen, living-room and then up the stairs.

Mrs Ball, round-eyed and scared said, 'Oh Mrs James . . . I'm that sorry . . .'

Gran gave a concluding flick of her duster and said with aplomb, 'Not at all, Mrs Ball,' and went back into the garden.

After a terrified glance at the silhouette in the doorway, Kildie hid her head in her arms and sobbed words at him hysterically.

'I didn't hurt it! It's quite safe out there—'

'Why did you leave? You had no right to leave. You are my wife!'

257

'I couldn't stay! Not after what you said – everyone knew except me, of course! Laughing at me behind their hands – hateful, hateful—'

He went to the bed and gripped her arm furiously.

'What the hell are you talking about? Of course no-one knows I can't have children! Do you think that's the sort of information I bandy around the town?'

She whimpered with pain. 'Not that – I don't believe that – I'm sure I'm . . .' Her voice crescendoed into a scream as he yanked her arm behind her back. She twisted furiously. 'Leave me alone, Marcus! I loved you – and all the time – all the time – you were with other women!' She wept again. 'How could you? How could you go from me to—'

He yanked her round to face him. She saw his face and gasped and was still.

He said, 'For God's sake, Kildie! It wasn't like that! In the past – well, you know my reputation! That's why your blasted uncle didn't want me to marry you in the first place! I've never let you think I was lily-white! But since I married you . . . Kildie, there's not been another woman since I married you. You're everything to me. I'm thinking about you all day, waiting to get home to you, waiting to . . .' He looked down at her face. It was almost as swollen as his; her hair was tangled and matted, her nightdress pulled off one shoulder. He sobbed.

She whispered, 'What has happened? Marcus – you've been fighting.'

He dropped his voice too. 'Jim came to the office. He said I was never to see you again. He threatened me. When I insisted I had to see you, he hit me. He kept hitting me, Kildie. Even when I was on the floor.' He was almost convinced that was what had happened. His whisper softened. 'Darling, nothing would keep me away from you. If he'd kicked me nearly to death I would have crawled here.'

'But Jim never . . . he doesn't fight.'

'He's been trained, Kildie. Trained to kill.'

'Oh my God, Marcus . . .'

'I didn't know where you were. When he told me to keep away from Dymock I knew you were here.'

'Marcus, your poor face. Your poor face . . .'

'You are everything to me, Kildie. Can't you see that? You are my mother and my child. I want to be the father you never had. I want to be your child too. I want us to be all-in-all to one another, Kildie.'

'Oh my darling. My baby. Oh my sweet boy . . .' She held on to him while he made love to her and knew that he was her destiny. But as the ecstasy subsided, she lay, staring at the ceiling and knowing that Jim had nearly killed for her.

She smiled and turned her face to kiss the swollen eye and nose.

'My dearest boy, I love you. Oh I do love you.'

Holly fought against resurrecting Blanche. She was fifteen and fifteen-year-olds did not have imaginary friends even when they were gilded with the term *alter ego*. But though she burrowed her way into the tunnel of beans and put her hands over her ears, she could still hear Mum's furious voice and could imagine only too well Dad's expression of dismay and utter confusion.

And then it went quiet. Very quiet. Mum had gone upstairs. Dad had followed her. Holly said aloud, 'Oh . . . all *right* then!' And there was Blanche sitting opposite her, looking as scruffy and matter-of-fact as ever.

Holly said glumly, 'Dad went to see Marcus Villiers. Something happened and he hit Marcus Villiers, Mum is livid.'

Blanche said the very thing that Mum should have said when Dad arrived back from Gloucester.

'Well, listen, Holly, if your Dad hit Marcus Villiers, did Marcus Villiers hit back? I mean, is your Dad *hurt*?'

Holly said miserably, 'I don't know. All I know is Dad went to try to persuade Marcus to take Kildie back. But now he has told Marcus never to go near Kildie ever again!'

'Well . . . from what you've said, that doesn't sound a bad idea.'

'I'm not sure.' Holly was getting more unhappy by the second. 'I know Kildie ran away from him and kept crying and everything, but . . . but she sort of wanted him to turn up and take her home. I think.'

Blanche sat back. 'I don't get it,' she said flatly.

'Neither do I,' Holly agreed.

'It's one of those grown-up things. Say one thing, mean another,' Blanche concluded with some disgust. 'Like your Aunt Sarah saying she loves Kildie but not ever wanting them to live together.'

Holly was silent. She still had wonderful daydreams where she and Aunt Sarah were 'doing the town' and meeting up with Charlie. Aunt Sarah had held her by the shoulders all those years ago at Kildie's wedding and said, 'I think I'm in love with you, Holly James!' But what did that mean exactly? Charlie thought he was in love with Kildie. And what did that mean?

She said, 'It's too difficult. And Dad is going to Canada for the duration. I don't think I can bear it.'

And then Dad's voice said from above her head. 'Of course you can bear it! And so can I! Think of how wonderful it will be when we meet up at the end of the War and tell each other everything that has happened!'

Of course Blanche had gone – if she had been there at all – and Dad thought Holly was simply talking to herself. She crawled out of the wigwam of bean sticks and stood up, grinning sheepishly. Dad put his arm around her sun-strapped shoulders and hugged her hard. 'It *is* difficult,' he agreed, ruffling her hair. 'But it could be much worse, Hollyhock. I can send you food parcels from Canada—'

She nodded against his shirt and said, 'And you'll be safe.'

Strangely enough that did not seem to comfort him. He gave a short and unamused laugh.

'Yes. I'll be safe. As usual,' he said.

260

Mum called in a thin falsetto, 'Punch is served, lady and gentleman. If you could take your seats for the first course—'

They both laughed very quickly and went up the garden path to the lawn and the garden table. Dad tried to encircle Mum with his free arm but she was busy dusting the plates with a tea towel and flicked him away.

They all pretended they were happy. If Blanche had been there she might have made one of her usual rude wartime comments, like, 'Put a sock in it!'

But Blanche was not there.

1924

By that Christmas of 1924, Dorothy was fairly certain she was pregnant. As she and Jim had made love at every practical opportunity since the tea party in October, this was hardly surprising. Perhaps she was not surprised; she was certainly shocked. For the first time in her life she was trapped. The fact that she would have to marry Jim James made her slightly less keen on the idea. And the main repercussion of marriage – giving up her career before her probationary year was done – was galling.

She went home to tell her parents that she was engaged as early as Bonfire Night. Already she suspected 'the worst' and she knew her mother would be devastated if she guessed that Dorothy had anticipated the marriage bed. An engagement of at least six weeks was necessary to make the marriage 'suitable'.

Her father had been an elderly fifty-two when she was born and at seventy-three behaved like a centenarian. Her mother's life revolved around his routine but she was delighted by Dorothy's news.

'A railway clerk? My dear girl, how suitable. A good, salaried position – and here in Gloucester? Then we can meet him soon, I hope.'

'Certainly, darling.' Dorothy smiled ruefully. 'He is so suitable. I know you will like him.'

It was a shame that Jim's eminent suitability somehow diminished his image for Dorothy. She tried to see him again as her knight in shining armour.

Ellen Prosser said, 'Let me see your ring, dear girl.'

'Ring?' Dorothy was above such minutae as rings. 'Ah. We are going to choose it together, Mummy.'

'As a Christmas present.' Such practical common sense pleased Mrs Prosser more than ever. She smiled. 'You know, dear, I thought you would choose either an earl or a dustman as a husband! You cannot conceive of the sheer relief to hear—'

'That I have settled for mediocrity?'

'For a good, solid young man—'

'His father is practically an aristocrat!' Dorothy declared defiantly.

'And has he an occupation?'

Dorothy breathed out slowly. 'He is the station master. At Dymock.'

'Your father will be delighted. He has always been interested in railways. Indeed, it was the sale of his railway shares that enabled you to go to college.'

Dorothy could have wept. 'And where did that land me?' She forced herself to laugh happily. 'Practically working on the railway!'

Ellen Prosser hugged the slender shoulders, suddenly understanding.

'Darling, one can so rarely have one's cake and eat it as well! But who knows? You may well find that in the future all schools will be only too pleased to employ married teachers. And meanwhile . . .' She looked at the nodding figure of George Prosser on the other side of the fireplace. 'Meanwhile, my dear, I can only assure you that a good marriage is priced above rubies.'

Dorothy was emboldened to ask, 'Can you still say that, Mummy?'

'Yes, indeed. It has always been good to have a

comrade-in-arms. But now . . . we savour the fruits of victory together.'

Dorothy laughed again, sincerely this time.

'Mummy, you should have been a poet. Or a philosopher. Apparently, there is a poet in Jim's family.'

'Perhaps I shall meet him. At your wedding?'

Dorothy took the hand from her shoulder and held it tightly.

'Now, look, Mummy. We are not going to have a wedding. Jim is much too shy and the whole thing is expensive and ridiculous. We shall slip off together one morning—'

'Darling – surely you will tell Daddy and me?'

'I doubt it. Neither of us can bear claptrap and that is what a church wedding is, Mummy.'

'We could plan a small affair. When you come home at Christmas—'

'Darling, I have been asked to stay at the Station House for Christmas. It will be the last one there for Jim's sister and her little family. And as I rather disgraced myself on their last visit—'

'Disgraced yourself?'

Dorothy told her about the spider and made it sound hilariously funny. Ellen Prosser laughed a great deal and started to cough rather worryingly.

Jim shared none of her forebodings.

'We'll get married before Christmas! Tell them Christmas morning!'

His face almost compensated for being trapped. His grey eyes shone and as they walked down Middle Lane he kept doing little skips and hops. He was like a schoolboy.

She said, 'Hold your horses, Jim! They'll know something is up if we do it like that!'

He laughed. 'Oh Doll! Of course they won't guess. They'll know! Who cares? We'll get a flat in Gloucester and be as snug as two bugs in one rug!'

'Jim. If you don't mind, I'd prefer not to be the gossip

of Dymock. We'll announce our engagement at Christmas if you like. And get married in January some time. That way I can work out my term's notice and stay on until Easter. It's better than nothing.'

'Won't that be a strain, my dearest Doll? When will the child—'

'I don't *know*, Jim, for goodness' sake! I started feeling horribly sick two weeks ago—'

'Don't be cross, Doll. Dearest, darling Doll. My lovely lady-love. My angel. My—'

'Jim. Be sensible . . .' But she was laughing because when he swung her round and kissed her nose and eyes beneath the brim of her cloche, it made her feel cherished and wonderful and she hardly noticed the awful, perpetual nausea.

He put her down very gently. 'So it's only just started.' He did some quick mental arithmetic. 'We've got time to do it as you wish.' He kissed her more tenderly. 'We'll go into town on Saturday and buy the ring.'

'And see the registrar. And find a flat,' she added.

'No need for a flat, sweetheart. Not yet. If you're going to be going to school every morning, we'll live at home.'

She looked at him, big-eyed. 'With your mother?'

He laughed. 'Well, she won't be moving out!' He sobered. 'Doll, she thinks the absolute world of you. I promise.'

'But she'll know.'

'About the baby? Yes . . .' He was going to tell her that his mother probably knew already, then thought better of it. 'Everyone will know. Eventually. But they – she – will be even happier about that. Promise.'

It wasn't the way Dorothy had visualized starting married life. She tried to weigh the pros and cons objectively. Finish her term at school and live at the Station House. Take a flat in Gloucester and have nothing to do all day.

'All right,' she said slowly. 'If you think she really won't mind—'

'She'll be like a cat with two tails!'

Dorothy smiled because Mrs James was not unlike a long, lean cat.

The snow came on Boxing Day. Dorothy would have dearly loved to go outside and make a snowman but Kildie had a cold and was 'confined to barracks' as Walter put it. Dorothy's job seemed to be to play Snap or Snakes and Ladders and make up stories about small girls called Kildie who got lost in woods or snow or deserts. Jim had the day off but there were plenty of trains running and he was out before dawn helping his father to thaw out the points to the slip road and grease the levers on each of the ground frames. The signal-box was steamed up, what with the Aladdin stove going full blast and the kettle steaming for tea, and she was allowed up there while Kildie slept to wipe up the condensation and receive congratulations from the signalman on duty who seemed to think Jim had snapped her up from Mr Milsom-Parker!

When they climbed carefully down the slippery steps, she asked Jim what the signalman had meant.

'Mr Milsom-Parker, of all people! And anyway, he's married!'

Jim said, 'I don't think that has made much difference in the past.' He pulled down his mouth. 'It could be why none of our student teachers has stayed past her probationary year. Millie and the Matsons combined are a bit much.'

Dorothy was about to put him wise about the Matsons – and, indeed, Millie – but thought better of it. It was necessary for Jim to believe in himself in order that she should too.

She said gloomily, 'And the very person who would have stayed isn't going to!'

'Oh darling – darling Doll—' He went into his usual ecstasies and she said, not quite for the first time, 'Jim. Dear. I wish you wouldn't call me Doll. It sounds practically bawdy!'

It was the wrong adjective. He laughed uproariously and kept murmuring, 'Doll, Doll, dearest Doll,' as he hugged her over the slippery track and onto the platform. And there, waiting for them, was Walter with two visitors.

'Jim! Dorothy!' Walter was beaming happily. 'Well met – very well met indeed! You remember my father's friend, Edwards? Here he is, come to wish us a good Christmas! And with him is the Assistant Manager!'

Walter had never made excuses for his position in life; and he was burstingly proud of his family. Now he had Dorothy to add to it.

'May I present my son and his future wife, Miss Dorothy Prosser. They became engaged yesterday – Christmas Day. Dorothy, here is the man responsible for me being the station master at Dymock! And this is Sir Archibald McKinnon, the—'

'My dear – delighted. Absolutely—' Both men had eyes only for Dorothy. Her golden hair and blue eyes captivated them, her obvious intelligence and spirit were impressive.

Mr Edwards, pigeon plump, wrapped in an enormous grey greatcoat, delighted with everything he found down here in the country, pumped her hand and then Jim's.

'Congratulations, my boy. Came to the school last September? Didn't waste much time, did you? Did you, eh?'

Sir Archie, known throughout the Great Western system as a hard drinker and one of the boys, risked a kiss on the girl's cold cheek.

'Welcome to the Great Western, my dear. God's Wonderful Railway, don't you know. You're one of an enormous family now and we look after one another. Rest assured. You're one of us. I can tell that immediately.'

Dorothy looked into the rheumy eyes and felt again she was being trapped. And yet they were all so kind. Sir Archie took her back into the house, his arm around her shoulders. Emmie had laid out the cold poultry and pickles by the dozen and there was the St Stephen's pudding bubbling in its pot and a jug of cream. Kildie had brightened up and was sitting prettily holding a new doll and ready to be patronized as much as anyone wished. Nobody minded – or noticed – but herself. Emmie, who was one of the most independent souls alive, smiled rather grimly and concentrated on looking after everyone's needs. Both men called her Emmie, as if she were a servant instead of the mistress of the house. Dorothy smiled too and determined to allow herself to be drawn into this self-congratulatory circle. She thought she had succeeded; until later in the afternoon.

'Well, James, we've had a good day. A good day indeed.' Sir Archie smiled fleetingly up at Emmie, still on her feet. 'And a good dinner into the bargain. Didn't expect that, did we, Edwards?'

Mr Edwards sunk his head into his plump chest and looked smug. He had boasted of the James's table, told Archie the tale of the unlikely marriage. The man had come to satisfy his curiosity and had been rewarded. All credit to L. J. Edwards.

'Now, before it gets quite dark, I want one thing more.' Sir Archie looked around confidently. He was doing them all the honour of doing him a favour. 'I want to do the run on the ganger's trolley.' His expression became roguish. 'Inspect the line, don't you know!'

Walter glanced at Mr Edwards. This small secret could only have come from him.

He admitted it with a guffaw. 'Don't look like that, my boy! Of course I've told Archie about our expeditions on the velocipede! No harm done – no harm done at all!'

'Breaking every rule in the book!' Sir Archie reminded them all, but still with a grin. 'And I intend to break them too! So how about it, James?'

'Well, sir . . . the five o'clock from Ledbury will be coming in—'

'God boy! I'm talking of now. Three-thirty! And back for tea! Eh, Emmie? Hey?' He slapped Emmie's backside but she was so cushioned with petticoats it was like the wind flapping a sail. 'We boys will go and have our fun. And you'll get some tea for us. Hey?'

'Certainly, sir,' Emmie caught Dorothy's eye and looked away quickly.

'Come on then! The boy can help pump us up, James.'

Jim was actually grinning. Dorothy tried to kick him under the table and must have caught Sir Archie's heel because his grin came round to her.

'You can come and watch, little lady. Switch the points for us, eh? And what about Kilda. St Kilda here?'

'I did it before. I'll show you, Miss Prosser!' Kildie was suddenly better. She avoided her grandmother's eye and ran for coats and scarves. Emmie said in a low voice, 'Once you've done the points, bring her back in, Miss Prosser. It's too cold for her with that chest—'

'We're not going,' Dorothy reassured her. 'We're staying to help with the tea.'

'Someone will have to go.' Emmie looked at her. 'You do it. I'm all right. You do it.'

Dorothy had the strangest feeling that Emmie was asking her to do more than change points. She trudged outside and down to the ground frame which controlled the siding. It was bitterly cold. If it hadn't been for the snow it would already be dark.

'What happens . . .' Kildie's breath condensed in the cold and she breathed inside her scarf to warm her throat. 'They take the trolley up the slope – they need the points for the main line, see. Then when they get to the top of the bank, they freewheel down and we change the points to run them into the siding.' She looked up regretfully at her adored teacher. 'It's such fun, Miss Prosser. We'll go another day. You go so fast and it's like tobogganing only smoother and safer – oh I wish we were going.'

It took Dorothy's full strength to move the icy points and as the trolley went slowly past she did not get so much as a thank-you for her efforts. It was as if she had lost Jim to some mysterious male-orientated world. He and Walter see-sawed the handle back and forth between them, the older men sitting sedately on the ganger's bench. It was obviously extremely hard work. The wheels of the trolley slipped on the rails and the gradient was steep. 'Tally-ho!' shouted Sir Archie into the still, iron-cold air. 'Wagons roll!' in the best tradition of the popular Wild West shows.

'They're like elderly children,' Dorothy said scornfully.

'Don't you like Sir Archie, Miss Prosser?'

'He's – he's a stereotype,' Dorothy said.

'What's a steer – what-you-said?'

'A very obvious person.'

'Oh.' Kildie stared after the trolley, already disappearing into the dusk. 'Well . . . I suppose we can put the points back for the siding now and go indoors. It's ever so cold, isn't it?'

'Yes.' Dorothy tugged the lever across to the slip road and dusted the snow from her gloves. 'Come on, Kildie. Let's go and get on with some women's work!'

Emmie was working full-stretch, clearing away the last meal, laying up for the next. It made Dorothy angry and somehow hurt.

She said, 'Please, Mrs James. Sit down. Let me.'

Emmie said, 'No. It – it's expected of me.' She smiled suddenly. 'There is something you could do. Unless you've already done it?'

Dorothy stared, uncomprehending.

Emmie said, 'I'll never forget the first time I worked the points for the boys to joyride. I got it wrong and they went on down the main line!'

Dorothy stared again.

Emmie said, 'It took them ages to work the trolley back up the gradient.' She jerked her head at the window. 'You did it all right, did you?'

Dorothy said, 'Do you think I should check?'

'Well, if you're not sure . . .' Emmie was already on her way back to the kitchen, apparently dismissing the whole subject.

Dorothy slipped outside and went back to the ground frame. The points were set correctly for the siding. She gripped the lever, one hand above the other as Jim had shown her, and pulled them across for the main line. And then she went indoors.

A toasting fork lay in the grate. Dorothy picked it up and fitted a slice of bread on to its prongs. Was this, after all, what Emmie had wanted her to do? Toast bread? Not change points at all? Dorothy was beginning to feel rather odd. What had she done and why had she done it? Was she making a point for Emmie? Or herself? Or all women? Or was she simply reacting against Sir Archie's assumption that she actually *wanted* to be part of 'God's Wonderful Railway'?

Emmie bustled in followed by Kildie carrying a kettle.

'We'll watch them go by first of all, shall we?' She stacked bread on the fender. 'We'll have to go into the front room.'

Dorothy allowed herself to be herded into the icy parlour. They all stared through the Nottingham lace. The siding was to the left. The main line much more plainly seen through the station canopy.

Dorothy felt distinctly sick. It must be the baby. Or the awful intense cold. Or her conscience.

She said, 'I wonder . . . did I set the points correctly? Perhaps I had better—'

'They were fine, Miss Prosser!' Kildie flashed her a smile. 'I checked them!'

Dorothy turned as if to go out, but Emmie put a hand on her shoulder.

'Come round this side. You can just see them coasting down the bank . . . ah, here they come!'

It was too late. They all watched as the velocipede came hurtling down the main line from Newent and began to slow to take the level siding and come to a halt at the buffers. And then, of course, it did not do that. Gaining speed again, it jolted slightly past the points and ran through the station to the accompaniment of shouts of alarm from its passengers. Walter looked wildly sideways and waved his arms in a meaningless semaphore at the

Station House. Jim tried to seize the free-wheeling handle and control the accelerating trolley. It was too strong for him, his arms pounded back and forth like a puppet's. The two middle-aged men on the bench clutched the edge of their seat with one hand, their hats with another and shouted with dismay.

The three women were silent, watching the trolley disappear towards Ledbury.

Kildie looked round, one apprehensive hand covering her mouth.

Dorothy said, 'What will happen? Oh my God – the train – there will be a terrible crash—'

Emmie said very calmly, 'It's not due for another hour. What will happen is that they will have to manhandle the trolley back.' She smiled slightly, 'Probably all four of them will need to do it. The incline is quite steep.'

And then Kildie's giggles burst from the palm of her hand. And incredibly, Emmie was laughing too.

Sir Archie was red to bursting point. He gasped, 'Remind me never to give you a job as a signalwoman, my dear! Could have been nasty – very nasty indeed.'

Walter said, 'It shows why the Rules and Regulations were written in the first place, does it not, Sir Archie?'

Mr Edwards puffed and pouted and did a lot of back slapping. 'Now come along, everyone. No harm done. And we've had some much-needed exercise! Looks as if these good ladies have prepared a tea which we shall be able to do justice—'

Jim whispered, 'Don't worry, sweetheart. We all understand.'

And Dorothy knew that she had made a terrible mistake. She had not struck blows for herself or womankind or indeed Emmie who ran around faster than ever waiting on Mr Edwards and Sir Archie. Yet Dorothy could have sworn Emmie had instigated the whole thing.

FOURTEEN

1940

That winter of 1940 was as hard as any of them had imagined. By the time the coal merchants had supplied the city, there was very little left for the outlying villages and Holly and Dorothy lit their fire in the evenings only and used wood they had picked up in the nearby bluebell wood.

The first snow fell on the second of December and Holly wobbled home on her bike, skidding in the tracks left by the latest convoy from the Camp at Innsworth, the air hurting her nasal passages, making her eyes sting and her head ache.

She was late because Miss Joliffe had asked her to help clear away the apparatus from their latest experiment, and the shaded light on her handlebars threw shadows on the snow and made her wobble more than ever.

Miss Joliffe had said, 'I suppose you're like the others, Holly. Immediately you are sixteen you'll be wanting to leave school.'

Many of Holly's friends had left already and were working in the newly opened RAF Records Office, or even in the many munition factories around the city.

Holly said, 'I don't know, Miss Joliffe.'

'That means yes,' Miss Joliffe said with resignation. 'Hitler has got a lot to answer for.'

'Yes, Miss Joliffe.'

'Put those pipettes in their holders, child. And then you'd better leave the rest to me. It's a very dark night.'

'Yes, Miss Joliffe.'

And it was. She had not even got the energy to summon

Blanche. And the prospects at home weren't much better either. Mum would not light the fire until Holly actually entered the house, so it would be ages before the living-room was warm. And they'd eaten their eggs and cheese rations so it would be toast with blackcurrant jam. Nice enough, especially for Holly who had had stew and dumplings at school, but Mum was looking thinner each day and toast with jam was not the best food value, whatever Lord Woolton said.

She rounded the bend which led to the Green, looked up for a second to check on Mum's blackout and fell off her bike. The snow was packed hard already and her right knee and thigh met it with a jarring bump that was frightening. She lay still, panting sobs, certain she had broken something. It was almost a disappointment when she moved cautiously away from the bike, to discover everything worked. She stood up, pulled the bike up with her, thumped it angrily just to show it who was really master, and began to limp exaggeratedly towards home. If only Mum had the fire lit. If only she could meet her with outstretched arms, see to the bike, take her in by the fire and fetch hot water and cotton wool and ointment and lint and bandage up the stinging knee while Holly sipped tea . . .

The door was flung wide and Mum was indeed there.

'Darling! I wondered where on earth you'd got to! D'you know it's almost six o'clock? We've been waiting for you! Two of the Bobs have come to supper and we thought we'd have a hand of cards and we need you to be a fourth!'

She did indeed take the handlebars of the bike, but only to shove it against the tangled mass of old man's beard under the window. Then she led the way inside where the fire was burning halfway up the chimney, the table was covered by a dark green cloth and pulled very close to the grate, and the cards were laid out ready. The two Bobs stood up with much scraping of chairs and wide white grins. They had unbuttoned their tunics and their blue

273

shirts were immaculate. They wore belts which emphasized their waists. They wanted to know how everything was with her. She told them about Miss Joliffe and the pipettes. They said, 'Gee.' She nodded.

'Contract, darling!' Mum trilled. 'Remember we played it round at Mabs' in the summer? Come and sit here as close as you can get to the flames, poor love! It's so cold!'

Holly said austerely, 'Should you have lit the fire yet, Mum? There won't be enough wood to last all evening.'

'The Bobs came with a sack of logs, Holly – wasn't that marvellous? They couldn't have brought us anything better, could they? Though actually, they also brought a tin of spam and some real coffee! So I've made some sandwiches and we'll have coffee in their honour!'

Holly thought of coffee and her mouth watered. She was warm for the first time that day. Spam sandwiches and coffee.

One of the Bobs said, 'My little sister is about your age, Holly. She's at Junior High. I've told her about you. She wants to travel to Edmonton in the summer and meet with your Dad.'

'Wouldn't that be just great?' the other Bob enthused. 'Hands across the ocean. All that kind of thing.'

'Yes, it would.' Holly smiled. Mum dealt the cards and she picked up her hand. She had the ace and king of spades. Her smile widened. After all, the Bobs came from where Dad had gone. No need to look on them as interlopers.

They spent Christmas at Gran's. The snow had gone and the earth was like an overloaded sponge. Only the sprouts and ferns seemed happy in the pouring rain. Gran went from kitchen to living-room, from living-room to kitchen holding the furniture. For the very first time Holly reprimanded her.

'You're always telling me to keep my shoulders back, Gran. But you're going right over!'

Gran smiled at her tall granddaughter who had Walter's long legs and her own grey eyes.

'Too late for me now, our Holly,' she said with her usual grim humour.

Holly said apprehensively, 'You feel . . . OK, Gran?'

'Don't pick up what them Canadians say, girl!' Gran's smile straightened out. 'OK. What does that mean, OK?'

'Sorry, Gran. Do you feel all right?'

'I'm not going to die just yet, if that's what you mean, girl.' Gran edged her knuckles along the table and picked up the teapot. 'Let's go and top this up. There's plenty of life left in these tealeaves.'

'I'll do it, Gran. And I didn't mean . . . what you said.'

'You did. But you won't have to think about me dying for a long time yet, our Holly.' Suddenly Gran looked tired. 'Ninety. That's what I said. I'd 'ang on here till I was ninety.'

Holly had heard this before. It was a promise Gran had made to Grandad a very long time ago. Just two years ago the reminder of the promise would have made her weep. Now she took the teapot and made for the kitchen without a word and with dry eyes. These days all her capacity for anxiety was taken up by Dad being in Canada, Charlie having disappeared from the face of the earth, and the three Bobs making Mum look young and beautiful again.

After Christmas dinner of boiling fowl, globe artichokes, sprout tops and potatoes, they went over to see Lizzie, Edward and Winnie. The Richardsons had been up to the Grange for their lunch, so the Gatehouse was unnaturally tidy and odourless. Lizzie was arranged on the sofa with a cushion to support the bulk that was the new baby and Winnie was still dressed in her siren suit which was practically *de rigueur* with the Squire. She greeted Holly with a kind of gloomy passion and immediately took her upstairs.

'If I don't change out of this hairy chastity belt, I'll go

275

simply ber . . . serk!' she announced, leading the way up the winding staircase energetically.

Holly grinned. She understood now that Winnie had to talk like that. It did not really mean she was about to lure Alf Matson into Red Marley churchyard. Winnie had told her the old story about Aunt Sarah and Red Marley churchyard back in the summer. Strangely enough it had made Kildie's plight more heart-rending than ever and Aunt Sarah's attraction stronger then before. Holly was frightened sometimes at her own dark thoughts.

Winnie tore at the buttons and shed the suit onto the floor.

'I hate Winston Churchill,' she continued, going through the clothes that were piled on her unmade bed. 'I thought I'd got rid of sharing his bloody name when I left school but would you believe it, even Uncle Charles called me 'Winston' at lunch-time!'

Holly said comfortingly, 'He doesn't make jokes, Win, I bet he used your proper name and you thought it sounded like Winston.'

Winnie looked up from a flowered blouse she had obviously made herself. 'Listen, Holly.' She spoke slowly and clearly. 'Winston. Winsome. Notice the "t" sound in the first name?'

Holly laughed. 'Oh, Win. For goodness' sake. Never mind that. Tell me what it's like not going to school. Tell me what you've been doing since I saw you last summer. How is your mother?' She licked her top lip which was suddenly sticking to her teeth. 'Any news of Charlie?'

'It's awful being at home, I can tell you that.' Winnie took off her vest and revealed a brassière. Holly goggled. 'Dad says my duty is to look after Ma, and it's no joke – I can certainly tell you that. Fetch this, carry that . . . God Almighty, I thought I was going to have to cook the bloody Christmas dinner! Thank Christ for the Squire and his lady – God bless 'em!' She pulled an imaginary forelock, then slipped on the blouse. 'What do you think? Ma looked out the pattern. I adapted it a bit.'

276

She had adapted it with a series of tucks beneath the bustline.

Holly said obediently, 'You look marvellous. But you can't look after your mother all day. What else do you do?'

Winnie shot her a look. 'That would be telling. And you're still too young to understand.' She fended off a pillow and giggled. 'Uncle Charles has let the old servants' quarters to bombed-out families from London.'

'I know. Gran said. Two sisters and their children. Four boys. She said the Squire thought he might get free labour next summer.' She too giggled.

Winnie nodded. 'They're . . . desperate. Absolutely desperate. That's why the brassière. It's a bit of protection.'

Holly absorbed the implications of this statement and did not take it seriously but she still felt a funny quiver at the tops of her legs.

'They're only kids!' she scoffed. 'Gran said twelve years old!'

Winnie smiled, unperturbed. 'The youngest is twelve. The oldest is fifteen.'

'Well, if I'm too young at fifteen—'

'I'm educating them, Hol.' Winnie buttoned the waistband of a very tight skirt and smoothed herself provocatively. 'This is my war work. I've failed miserably with you. But I'm doing all right with Eric.'

'Eric?'

'Eric Battersby!' Winnie slid her bare feet into court shoes. 'Eric Battersby is crazy about me. Rhymes, see?'

'Oh shut up, Win,' Holly said, unexpectedly irritated. 'Last summer it was that cinema manager in Croydon. Old enough to be your father. This winter it's someone young enough to be your baby brother—'

'I thought you were going to leave it at baby for a minute,' Winnie said. 'That would be a scream, wouldn't it?'

Holly said, 'What do you mean?'

'Well . . . it's obvious. If I had a baby. You know. A *baby*. If Eric gave me a baby.' Winnie flopped impatiently onto the bed. 'Oh surely you know about that, Hol?'

'Of course I do. But . . . well, it wouldn't be much of a scream.'

Winnie looked at the tiny black iron grate set halfway up the chimney wall. It was full of sooty newspaper. She said dreamily, 'You should see the fuss Dad makes of Ma. Stroking her stomach all the time. Making sure she's warm enough. Lifting her feet up on the sofa and bringing her books from the library at the Grange . . .'

'Yes, but . . . that's different.'

Winnie focused her eyes with difficulty. 'Different? Ma's told me about Aunt Sarah, Hol. They pampered her just the same.'

'Grandad was alive then. Grandad was . . . different.'

'I know.' Winnie's interest sharpened. 'He was, wasn't he? Maybe he liked illegitimate children, or something. He didn't mind Ma marrying Pa. And – and – sometimes I think Aunt Sarah and Ma . . .' her voice trailed off.

Holly frowned. 'What? What?'

'Nothing. I'll tell you when you're older. And wiser.' She laughed. 'And there's no news of Charlie, cousin dear. Don't think I don't know that if you had the chance you'd love Charlie to give you a baby!'

Holly flushed dark red and leapt from the bed.

'How can you talk like that, Win? You're horrible – swearing and talking about educating those poor evacuees – it's all horrible!'

'And you enjoy hearing about it, so don't come the pious innocent with me, Holly James! Your dad had to marry your ma because she was expecting you! Otherwise he'd have gone off with Kildie – we all know that—'

She stopped speaking on a scream because Holly's hand connected with her face.

The Villiers had very bad hangovers on Christmas Day that year. They had thrown a party to end all parties on

Christmas Eve; it continued until four in the morning and only finished then because the RAF transport had to be back at Brize Norton by six and it was delivering people from all around the city and the Cotswolds before it reached its destination.

Marcus had opened his dining-room for the Forces at the end of November. It had been a dignified but enjoyable occasion and Kildie had cut the ceremonial tape which guarded the door. Already it was seen as rather an exclusive Officers' Club. Personnel were permitted to take their female relatives, so it became a rendezvous. Kildie thought it was terribly romantic. Marcus was more realistic.

'It's a high-class knocking shop,' he said, piloting her along the office corridor with one hand on the back of her neck. 'Why do you think we go there so often?'

She laughed very loudly as they pushed past the lift boy. 'Marcus. Darling. You are absolutely incorrigible!' It was a word she had learned soon after their wonderful reconciliation last summer. It seemed to make some of Marcus' actions acceptable. He simply could not help himself. He was incorrigible.

He kissed her now, in front of the lift boy, pushing her into a corner of the tiny box, still holding her throat. She knew it was just his little-boy way of showing off.

He did offer his arm as they went through the stock room to the staff car-park and into the car, but no-one dared look up from their work anyway.

'At least we don't have to cultivate any of those awful RAF types any more,' he said, starting the car with a roar. 'The dining-room is in full swing now with or without their influence.'

'Oh, darling boy . . .' She leaned her head on his shoulder.

He mouthed her forehead. 'I know why they all put in a good word for us with the Min of Food. It was your doing, my love. Nothing to do with me.'

'Well . . . I'm one of your many assets, aren't I?' she

279

said, smiling round at him as he reversed like a rocket.

He grinned back. 'Don't I know it.'

'Then why not go on using your assets?' She cuddled against him. 'Let's give a party, darling. Something to make the whole of the area look up and take notice. We could persuade Group Captain Donaldson to come so that he could pick up the Mastersons—'

Marcus snorted. 'You don't honestly think the Mastersons would come to a party thrown by us, do you?'

'Oh I certainly do. You underrate yourself, Daddy. You are one of the most powerful men in the area and they know it.' She trailed a gloved finger down his arm. 'Petrol. Meat coupons. Beautiful clothes. Lovely, lovely booze . . .'

'I suppose we could see what happened.'

'We could, couldn't we? Can't you just imagine the family gossip?'

He just wished Jim was home. He might even have invited him and watched him squirm.

He said, 'All right, Mummy. We'll do it.'

He didn't often call her Mummy, though she referred to him as Daddy especially when they made love. She smiled and cuddled closer.

The party was a wonderful success, but the next day was very different. He looked at the wreck of the kitchen. Mrs . . . was not coming until after Boxing Day.

'Do you mean to tell me,' he asked savagely, 'that after I've supplied every damned thing under the sun to wine and dine those . . . those . . . drones . . . there is not an aspirin in the house?'

She whimpered, 'Don't shout, Daddy, please! Baby's head is going to fall off and roll under the sofa if Daddy shouts one more time.'

'Is there an aspirin or isn't there?'

'I think there's some bicarb. At the back of the sideboard. Somewhere.' Kildie closed her eyes. But he continued to storm around the lounge, picking up ashtrays and making noises at the various messes on the carpet, so that at last she said, 'Daddy, darling, Mummy is going to have to go to beddy-byes. No lunch or anything. Just rest.'

She got up and trailed upstairs and was rather relieved when he did not follow, though it showed the true extent of his mood. He yelled after her, 'Do you realize it's bloody Christmas Day!' and she made a little murmuring sound of surprise and assent and fell onto her bed. The house was gloriously warm; Marcus had had an enormous Ideal boiler installed in the kitchen that burned anything, and the radiator next to the bed was almost red-hot. She closed her eyes and thought compassionately of the cottage in Dymock. And then, quite suddenly was awake and terribly homesick. She knew it was still the drink. Maudlin. That's what she was. But as Marcus had just reminded her, it was Christmas Day, and Gran would have wrung the neck of some unfortunate hen, plucked and dressed it expertly, and be basting it even now. And Dorothy and Holly would be arriving and piling railway coal on the fire in the living-room, and though it might be chilly everywhere else in the house, the living-room and kitchen would be like two steam rooms and Holly would make them all sing 'Jingle Bells' in spite of the incessant rain. Kildie lay on her back and thought of the time Dorothy had messed about with the points at Dymock station in the snow and ice. She smiled, then sobbed and turned into the pillow and smelled beer. She was out of bed and at the top of the stairs in an instant.

'Marcus!' She was furious. 'Marcus – come here this minute!' And when he appeared, surprised and dishevelled beneath her, she ranted like a fishwife about someone sleeping in their bed.

'Well, what did you expect me to do?' he asked, angry himself but also plaintive. 'It was a bloody Squadron Leader with someone else's wife! If I'd made a scene the party would have been a complete fiasco—'

'It's disgusting! Absolutely disgusting!' Kildie turned

and went back into the bedroom and tore the bed to pieces. She found sheets and remade it with difficulty. She was not accustomed to much domesticity. In her handkerchief drawer were several lavender bags made by Holly. She threw them all between the clean linen, then went into the bathroom and ran a twelve-inch bath which was practically illegal in wartime, and soaked and simmered until she calmed down. She dried herself perfunctorily and finished off with a cloud of talcum then went back into the bedroom and found her oyster satin nightdress and matching négligé. She smiled at her reflection. It was three o'clock and she felt better. Marcus was in for a treat.

She trailed downstairs, deliberately languid, passing the trail of linen, bath towels and soiled clothing without noticing them. Downstairs she went from room to room looking for Marcus, but she knew almost immediately that he had gone out. By the time she reached the kitchen she was furious. Where the hell had he got to on Christmas afternoon? It was pouring with rain and almost dark, she had not heard the car leave the garage and he was no walker. She opened the back door and peered across the terrace and into the valley. Far below a light winked momentarily before blackout curtains could be drawn. The Woolpack. They were breaking every licencing law in the book. And Marcus had probably bribed them to do it.

She slammed the door and stood there fulminating. She could take the car and go to Gran's. She had a jolly good mind to do just that and then pretend to Marcus that she had been going for help because he was missing. But he might not stand for it a second time. And Jim was in Canada. She felt a sudden terrible yearning for Jim. If only he could see her dressed like this, smelling of gardenia-scented talcum, with her hair about her shoulders. He would be scared at first . . . dear, cautious Jim. And then she would reassure him and gradually, very, very gradually, she might persuade him that it was all right.

The front doorbell chimed. It sounded like Big Ben,

and at first she thought the radiogram must still be switched on in the lounge. But it went again, much too quickly for Big Ben, and she knew that Marcus had forgotten his key.

She smiled again. He had not gone to the Woolpack after all. Perhaps he had been merely tinkering with the car and locked himself out. She almost ran down the hall and pulled the door wide, prepared to throw herself into his arms however wet he was. But the man who was standing there was not Marcus at all. He wore khaki and big boots and he held his forage cap in his hands like a polite schoolboy.

It was Charlie Richardson.

1925

Dorothy had hoped for an invisible wedding. She thought it would have to take place during Jim's early turn; she planned to catch the three forty-five in to Gloucester and meet him at the Register Office in St John's Lane just as the gas lights were being lit above the little bookshops. She pictured the scene vividly, rather like a play with footlights and outer darkness. Jim would accost two passers-by for witnesses and afterwards they would go down to Regent Street and have tea with her parents before telling them what had just happened. Then they would go back to Dymock and tell the Jameses. There would be astonishment, amusement, and, of course, plenty of quiet rejoicing. And it would be, most definitely, one in the eye for Emmie.

It still did not occur to Dorothy that Emmie might not like her, but she sensed a certain rivalry and a kind of withdrawn disapproval. Emmie did not mind being treated like a servant by Walter's superiors. All right; she had apparently started life in service. Yet she had a dignity and an authority all her own. She was a curious mixture. Dorothy found herself respecting Emmie at times, impatient with her at others, very wary of her most of the time. She was ashamed and embarrassed that Emmie had witnessed her complete disintegration over the spider. And she was certain that Emmie had encouraged her to reset those blasted railway points.

She longed to be able to say out of the blue, 'No, actually we did not go shopping. We got married.'

But, of course, Emmie guessed it was going to happen because Jim's mounting excitement was so obvious. She said nothing, apparently did nothing. But when Jim and Dorothy arrived at Regent Street at six o'clock on 31 January 1925, the house was dark and empty. They caught the six-thirty by the skin of their teeth, Jim carried her from the rail car to the front door of the Station House, and there were her parents; Lizzie, Edward and Charlie who had still not left for Suffolk; even Sarah and Kildie dressed in identical outfits and holding up a banner which read, 'Good luck for the Rest of Your Lives.'

Dorothy told herself she was being mean-spirited about the whole thing and kissed Emmie resolutely on her dried-apple cheek. Jim was shouting with laughter and pumping his father's hand while Edward clapped him on the shoulder and Sarah and Kildie jumped up and down and shrieked. Lizzie sat by the fire, one hand on her abdomen, tears in her eyes. They were leaving the next week and she was already homesick.

Her father got on very well with both Walter and Jim and Ellen was so delighted with the whole idea – the match itself, the surprise wedding and tea party – all she could do was clasp her hands and say to anyone and everyone, 'This is like a fairy tale! A real fairy tale!' Dorothy was amazed how well they fitted in. To her, Dymock had been a different world with its poachers and fleas and strangely plump, butter-fed children. The Station House itself had been a curiosity: Dorothy was used to a quiet, elderly atmosphere at home and she rather enjoyed the comings and goings of family and villagers at the busy Station

House. Even so, when she had seen Emmie wring a chicken's neck for the first time, there had still been the sense of living on the fringe of civilization.

But her father recognized Walter's culture instantly and they spoke, not only of railways but of communication networks generally. George Prosser had been present at the opening of the Suez and the Manchester Ship canals. He maintained their economy and reliability above the railways.

Walter turned down his mouth. 'I agree with you, sir, up to a point. The economics of the Suez are indisputable. But in a small country such as ours, the railways have the edge. Speed alone—'

'Speed!' scoffed George Prosser. 'Why the necessity for speed all the time? A barge can take as much coal as a twenty-wagon train and speed surely does not enter into it.'

'Perhaps not, but people . . . speed could save a life.'

'And take another.'

Walter nodded judiciously. 'What have you to say about the aeroplane, Mr Prosser?'

Ellen unclasped her hands and flung them pleadingly across the table. 'Please, Mr James! We shall be here for the rest of the month if you ask my dear George about aeroplanes! Talk to him of . . . of . . . fishing. Or philately. Or—'

'Fishing?' Walter's eyes lit up. 'Would you care to join me one weekend for a fishing trip, Mr Prosser?'

Under cover of this new enthusiasm, Jim's hand reached beneath the table and found Dorothy's waiting.

'I cannot believe it,' he whispered. 'Are you as happy as I am, dearest?'

Of course she was happy. But she was not excited like Jim. Rather she felt a quiet relief that the deception would soon be over. In another month she could make her announcement; in three months the spring term would be over and they could move to Gloucester. And then . . . it wouldn't matter.

Ellen said, 'Dearest girl, I think I should pay a call. Will you show me the bathroom?'

Dorothy smiled gratefully. She needed to 'pay a call' also, and the thought of the cavernous bathroom was still a nervous prospect.

Kildie said, 'Mother, when are you going back to London? Will you stay a long time? A week? A month?'

Sarah, gorgeous in a turquoise wool twin set with a treble row of pearls lying on her high breast, laughed and kissed her daughter's dark head.

'Darling, how can I? Gran and Grandad have one room, you have another, and Jim and Dorothy the third.'

'You could sleep with me, Mummy. Like tonight.'

'Oh dear! Just the thought of those two next door to us makes me green with envy!'

'Why, Mummy? Don't you like Miss Prosser?'

Sarah laughed lightly and pulled Kildie's plaits beneath her chin so that the small dark face was framed in hair.

'Sweet little Kildie. I forget how young you are. Of course I adore your Miss Prosser! Who is now Mrs James!'

'Mrs James . . .' Kildie caught Sarah's hand and held it against her face. 'Mummy, if you can't stay in Dymock, please can I come and live with you? Please, Mummy. Please.'

Sarah removed her hand fairly quickly and gave her light laugh again. 'Oh sweetie – you are funny, aren't you? You know that your home is with Gran and Grandad. What on earth would they do if you left them?'

'They wouldn't like it. But – but, Mum – they would understand!' Kildie loved Gran and Grandad, was secure and happy with them. But she worshipped her mother.

Sarah moved her chair slightly. 'Darling, you know how much I adore you. But I've got to earn a living—'

'I'd help you, Mum—'

Sarah laughed again. 'I'm sure you would, sweetie! Maybe later . . .' A hand touched her thigh and she turned her head for an instant and smiled at Edward Richardson.

'Now, Mum! Please—'

The hand slid upward and Sarah said sharply, 'I've said no, Kildie. Don't pester!' She softened her voice. 'Now, go and talk to Charlie and your Aunt Lizzie for five minutes and give me some peace!' And she turned in her chair and said, 'Darling, you haven't changed one bit, have you? And my poor sister the size of a house!'

He pretended outraged surprise and she tipped back her head to laugh again and expose her beautiful throat.

'I'm leaving next week, you know, Sarah,' he said, his hand still moving on her thigh. 'Off to the far-distant Fens! I don't suppose you'll ever see me again!'

She shook her head at him. 'You're a hopeless case, Edward Richardson! Poor Lizzie must have an awful time!'

'Listen, Sarah,' his voice was urgent, 'she thinks it should only happen when babies are required! Honestly! Stop laughing – I'm telling you the absolute truth!'

She put a hand over her mouth. 'I believe you, darling. But does that mean you've slept together just twice?'

'Not much more!' He sounded like an aggrieved schoolboy. 'And, after all, it must be in my blood, Sarah.'

Sarah stopped laughing and looked across the table at her mother, already in her sixties.

She said slowly, 'Well, it shouldn't be in mine, darling. So I haven't got a solitary excuse.'

'You're just bad, Sarah.' He spoke half jokingly but she was stupidly hurt.

'I'm not bad at all, Edward Richardson! I've always known they didn't love Lizzie and me like they loved Jim! So when . . .' her voice trailed away as she remembered.

'When what? Come on, confession is good for the soul!'

'There was a vicar. Friend of Pa's. Years ago – I was about six or something. And then Hope Chapel's uncle—'

'Hope Chapel?'

'You must remember her – no, you were probably away at school – anyway they kept you pretty well hidden until you were about twenty. She was the choir mistress. And

287

her uncle ran a sort of concert party. She took me along and . . . well . . . that's how I came by Kildie.'

'Am I supposed to burst into tears?'

She pulled away from his hand. 'You've spent a lot of your time looking for affection. So have I. That's all I'm saying.'

'With the likes of Alf Matson? In Red Marley church-yard?'

She looked straight into his eyes. 'Yes. With the likes of him. And Edward Richardson. What's the difference?'

He smiled. 'I'll show you. I'm going up to the bath-room. Join me when you can.'

'Dorothy is up there.'

'Oh God. I'd better hurry in case there are spiders.'

He left the table and Sarah turned back to Kildie. But Kildie was gone with Charlie, and Lizzie was staring into the fire with a face as long as a yard of pump water.

Walter came up behind Emmie in the kitchen and put his arms around her waist.

'You didn't mind too much? About them nipping off to get married on the quiet?'

'Best all round in the circumstances,' she replied, carving more ham and assiduously avoiding watching the kettle so that it would surely boil quickly.

'You think—'

'Of course. Remember the day of the spider?'

'Am I likely to forget?' He snuggled his nose into the back of her neck. 'Mrs Know-it-all.'

'You don't have to be a know-it-all to put two and two together when it's right under your nose.' She smiled as the kettle began to sing. 'Let's make some more tea, Walter. And rest assured I don't mind that they tried to keep their wedding secret any more than I mind that they've been forced to keep the baby secret!'

He released her, laughing.

'You mind. With one half of you you mind very much

that Jim has to get married to Dorothy Prosser whether he wants to or not.'

She poured water into the teapot and said equably, 'He wants to. That I am sure about.'

'So that makes it all right?' He was not entirely certain. And more than anything he wanted Emmie to be happy about Jim. About all the children, but especially about Jim.

She put the teapot on the table next to the ham and then looked at him. 'What worries me is that Dorothy has to marry Jim,' she said quietly.

He smiled into her eyes. 'Darling Em, you had to marry me. Did you mind too much?'

Her brows shot into her hair. 'I didn't have to—'

He put his arms around her and held her not at all sedately.

'Tell me the truth now. Did you really have much choice? Was there one chance in a million that you would turn me down?'

She leaned into him and let him kiss her.

'You are a very unusual woman, Esme James,' he whispered into her ear. 'Neither Jim nor Dorothy will ever know how unusual. Unless you let me tell them.'

'Never.'

He had known that would be the answer and he kissed her and then held her again.

'I wish . . .' He brushed his cheek against her tight grey hair. 'I just wish we could help Jim. Like we helped Lizzie and Edward. And Sarah too.'

She leaned back and stared at him, surprised.

'How can you say that? We have given Jim a gift far beyond money, Walter. We have given him a happy nature. He was born because of our happiness. And has been reared in the exact centre of our happiness. That is our legacy to Jim. *And* he doesn't have to wait for it till after we're dead!'

Her last words took away any sentimentality and they were both laughing when Jim came into the kitchen.

'Look at you two!' He was delighted with every small thing that had happened during the day, and this was yet another.

'My good Lord! Both in their sixties and acting as if they were lovesick children!' He sobered and stared at them as if he had never seen them before. 'Ma . . . Pa . . . if my marriage is anything like yours, I can't go wrong, can I?'

Walter shook his head. 'You cannot, son.'

But his mother reached for the teapot and made clicking noises with her teeth.

'Standing about while people are panting for another cup of tea! Carry this ham, our Jim.' She looked at him. 'And remember, a good marriage has to be earned, my boy!'

And she marched past him into the crowded living-room.

Dorothy said, 'Mummy, you'll have to go now if you're going to get the seven fifty. Are you sure you can manage Daddy on your own?'

'I got him here, my dear! I'll get him home again!'

Ellen Prosser was still beaming. 'This has been a wonderful day, Dorothy. I am so happy for you.'

'Dearest Mummy. I've always been a worry to you. Now you've handed me over to Jim!'

'What nonsense you talk!'

'Remember the rag-and-bone man's horse?'

'Oh Dorothy . . .' They went down the dark stairwell, laughing, and Dorothy rifled through the hall stand for coats and gloves while Ellen returned to the party to collect her husband.

Edward Richardson appeared from the parlour.

'I was waiting for the bathroom,' he said, smiling his attractive smile. 'Any more spiders?'

Dorothy smiled back. Edward was another Dymock enigma. She could not help but be intrigued by him.

'Nary a one,' she said. 'Won't anyone ever forget the day of the spider?'

'Not likely. Especially you and Jim, I imagine!'

She opened her eyes wide, wondering if Jim had said anything. Then she relaxed; after all, they were married now.

He registered everything and said slowly, 'You're pregnant. I should have guessed, I suppose.' He smiled again. 'Don't look like that, Dorothy. Jim is a lucky chap. Bloody lucky!' He leaned forward, 'Let me kiss the bride, then I must leave you quickly!'

The kiss was experimental. She should have withdrawn immediately but she was confused and embarrassed. The living-room door opened and Sarah came into the darkness of the passage. Dorothy sprang back.

Sarah said in an amused voice, 'Sorry. I was going upstairs to the bathroom.'

'So was I.' Edward did not look at all put out. 'After you, Sarah. I think I'll nip outside for a breath of fresh air.'

'Yes. Why don't you?' said Sarah. And went on up the stairs.

Jim blew out the candle and tucked the bedclothes around them both.

'Are you warm enough, my darling?' he asked tenderly.

'Yes. Are you?'

'I am. I am.'

They were already used to each other and moulded their bodies together for sleep.

'There will be a thick frost by morning,' he murmured contentedly.

'The windows will be all iced flowers,' she murmured back. 'Mmmm . . .' she sighed. 'Jim, I am so happy. And so thankful.'

'I am too.'

She smiled into the pillow. It was going to be all right after all. There had been admiration in Edward

Richardson's voice when he discovered she was pregnant. Suddenly she was proud of what they had done; the child that was theirs, within her. There would be others. They would have a big family and she would be a matriarch like Emmie James. And Jim would be gentle and wise and clever. Like Walter.

FIFTEEN

1940

Holly heard Gran get up long before it was light. She lay next to Mum and listened to each tiny sound from next door and knew exactly what Gran was doing. Two and a half years ago she would have been sleeping with Gran, getting up with Gran, going early to feed the hens and collect the eggs, fishing kindling out of the side oven of the grate and making newspaper knots to start the fire. Everything was different now. Dad was not here to sleep with Mum. And Gran no longer roamed the countryside with her little kitchen knife at the ready and an eye open for mushrooms.

Holly sighed deeply and Mum said, 'Wossamar? Cuddle up and go to sleep, darling.'

But Holly could not curl up against Mum's spine as she would have done yesterday. Not since Winnie had told her . . . what Winnie had told her.

Of course Winnie exaggerated so much she was practically a liar. But what if she wasn't in this particular case? Of course Dad had to look after Kildie. They were practically brother and sister. Of course he had to champion her when Marcus was so horrid . . . of course. But Mum hadn't thought of course. Mum had been definitely ratty about the whole thing. Still was. She and Holly had gone to see Dad off at the station, and she had hugged him almost frantically. But Holly had known. And later Mum had sighed and said, 'Trust your Dad to be spending the War in a land of plenty.' And then she had added almost to herself, 'At least it gets him right away from Kildie and her sordid little marriage.'

The stairs creaked and then the living-room door was very carefully shut. The next minute a dreadful grinding sound came from the fireplace wall.

'Oh God . . .' Mum groaned and turned onto her back. 'Gran's riddling the blasted ashes already! Couldn't she have left that till dawn at least?'

Holly said very levelly, 'She's had the kettle on all night. She needs a flame just to bring it to the boil.'

Mum groaned again, turned towards Holly and was asleep.

It simply wasn't fair. She had so much on her mind . . . or she should have . . . and here she was sleeping like a baby. Holly turned and looked at her. She had not cut her hair for two years and it fanned across the pillow as if she'd arranged it there carefully. Her skin was better than Holly's, not a pimple or blemish anywhere, and her dark golden lashes were long and curly. Holly ran her hand through her own short brown mop and thought of the spot which was threatening to distort her nose at any moment. And Mum was . . . how old was she? She must be thirty-five. Halfway through her life. And Holly herself was fifteen. Fifteen.

Holly started to do some very basic sums, hampered by the fact that though she knew her parents had wedding anniversaries, she was not at all sure how many they'd had.

But she was almost sure.

When the light around the blackout curtain began to pale, she edged out of bed with enormous care and gathered up her clothes. Gran had told both of them to bring their clothes down and dress by the fire. Holly decided to obey her.

The living-room was empty but the fire crept up the sooty chimney and there was a pot of tea under the cosy. Holly dressed quickly and peered through the window. Gran's back was visible beneath the veranda as she bent down to feel around the nesting boxes. Holly watched her unsmilingly. Gran's occasional animosity towards Mum could be explained if . . .

Holly went back to the table and poured herself some tea, looked at its orange colour, then decided she could not face Gran nor Mum for a while and went back into the hall. She gathered up mackintosh and umbrella and let herself quietly out of the front.

The rain had given way to a tangible mist; there was no sign of sky, daylight was oozing in imperceptibly. Mrs Ball drew her curtains in her bedroom and for an instant an orange glow leapt out, then she switched off the light hurriedly. Holly slid sideways past the junction with Middle Lane, towards the churchyard. She wanted to walk along the ridge that overlooked the Leadon; to look down on the church and Grandad's grave and then over towards the Grange. She tried to block all thoughts of the hated Winnie out of her head. She would never speak to her again, that was certain. And as for those dreadful Battersby boys up in the attics at the big house . . . Someone should warn them about Winnie. Blanche would tell her to go and do it herself. But that was Blanche.

Holly leaned against the stone angel that guarded the Richardsons' family tomb and turned her back on Dymock to stare along the line of hedge that bordered the road. She said aloud, 'If only you were a year older!' It was Blanche speaking, though nowadays Blanche tended to stand behind her where she couldn't be seen.

Holly herself said, 'Why?'

'Then you could go. Leave home. Join up.'

'At sixteen?'

'Lie about your age like Charlie did.'

'Charlie was almost eighteen.'

'Well, that's what you'll have to do eventually. If your Mum's . . . like that . . . and your Dad is in love with his own sister, you'll have to skedaddle, my girl. No nonsense.'

Holly loved it when Blanche spoke in that commonsensical voice. She said, 'The whole thing – the whole thing – it makes me feel sick!' But she turned her head slightly and smiled so that Blanche would see and

295

know that her words had given comfort.

And as she turned, so the roar of engine cut through the blanketed silence and from the direction of Newent a glow-worm light proclaimed a fast-approaching car.

It was so unusual to see a car now, that Holly's attention was riveted. She watched the glow come closer and stop about half a mile from the station. Then there was a great deal of shouting and slamming. The car reversed into a field and shot off towards Newent again. And a lone figure stood in the middle of the road and watched it go. The car was Marcus Villiers' Morgan.

Holly scrambled down the ridge and padded silently through the wet grass on the river bank towards the hedge. When she got there the man – it was definitely a man – appeared to be picking things up from the road. She peered over the hedge. The man was naked save for vest and knee-length underpants. He was retrieving articles of clothing which were strewn all over the road and piling them onto a kitbag out of the general wetness. He rammed a khaki forage cap on his head, placed a boot on top of the kitbag, picked up a pair of trousers and began to fight his way into them. He was swearing fluently. Holly would have known the voice anywhere. It was Charlie's.

By the time he was dressed it was as light as it would be all day.

He said, 'I thought I'd go to Gran's first and dry out a bit. Rather a shock for Ma and Pa when I turn up anyway. They don't want to think I've been in a fight.'

Holly said in her tight, withdrawn voice, '*Did* Marcus hit you, Charlie?'

Charlie laughed. 'He would have done. Kildie stopped him. I thought he might have a go at me in the car. Or when he threw me out of the car. His revenge was to make me shiver all the way and then chuck my clothes up and down the road.' He laughed, actually laughed. 'That's the sort of man he is.'

For the first time ever, Holly felt some sympathy for

Marcus Villiers. She said, 'He wanted to make you look ridiculous. That was the only way he could . . . bear it.'

But Charlie evidently did not care. He was almost chortling with suppressed excitement.

'It was all . . . meant, Hol. What do they call it? Predestined. That's what it was. Predestined.'

Holly walked just ahead of him. She wanted to put her hands over her ears.

'I mean, I was hoping for a lift to Dymock. Obviously. I wanted to get home for Christmas dinner with Dad and Gran and everyone.'

Holly wondered whether he knew about the baby.

'And then this Corp drew up in a ruddy great truck towing a Messerschmitt, would you believe!' Holly made a sound and quickened her pace. He thought she hadn't understood. 'You know – one of the Jerry fighters. Came down on Windermere so it was practically intact. He had to tow it to Brize Norton, passing the gates of Hill House itself!' He let out a great gusty laugh. 'Well, I thought good old Marcus probably wouldn't mind giving me a couple of brandies and driving me down to Dymock in time for tea! So I took the lift – duly grateful – rang Kildie's bloody awful bell—' surely he hadn't sworn quite so much before '—and there she was in a satin nightie. Three in the bloody afternoon, Christmas Day, and she was ready for bed!' He laughed again, so much so he had to stop in the middle of the road and double over. Holly stopped walking. She thought she might be sick. He did not even notice her obvious distaste. He was so full of himself, so triumphant.

After quite a while he straightened and huffed and puffed delightedly before tramping on.

'Course . . . good ol' Marcus had bribed the landlord of the Woolpack to open up for him. So he was out of the way. Did I tell you that already?'

'Yes,' Holly said.

'If I'd had my wits about me – or if Kildie had had any herself – we could have been downstairs with the kettle

boiling for tea. But we both went to sleep!' He laughed
again. 'Exhausted! Marcus fell asleep downstairs. Totters
upstairs about three o'clock this morning! And there we
were!'

'So you said,' Holly responded faintly.

'You can imagine the rest! Kildie tried denying it at first.
Then she said it didn't matter between cousins, especially
as I was just a boy!' He guffawed. 'She's the tops, Hol.
An absolute trump! I wish you could have heard her.'

Holly tramped on. They passed the junction to Middle
Lane. She wanted to break into a run and hurl herself on
Gran's black bodice.

He stopped at the gate and suddenly was serious. Very
serious.

'This is all between you and me, Hol. Not a word to
anyone else, mind. Can I trust you?'

'Yes,' Holly said.

'I know that, really. You were the one person in the
world I could tell. I could trust. I'm so happy, Hol. You
wouldn't understand what I'm talking about. But—'

'I do understand, actually,' Holly said quickly. 'I do.
Really.'

'I've loved her since I was a kid. There's no-one else in
the world for me.'

There was a pause. Holly said, 'What will you do? After
the War? I mean . . . Marcus . . .'

'She doesn't care two straws for him, Holly. It's me.'

'But . . . she says that. She always goes back to him.'

'Listen. I'll tell you one more thing. But this is really
deathly secret. Will you swear never to tell?'

'I don't think you should even tell—'

'Swear, Holly!' he commanded.

'All right. I swear.

His voice dropped to a whisper. 'She's going to have
my baby. She's pregnant, Holly. I made her pregnant!'

She started back and the gate swung with her.

'You can't know that, Charlie! it's impossible.'

He swung her back so that she was pressed against him

298

through the wooden pickets. He smelled of Kildie. And it was horrible.

'She said to me that I must give her a baby. She said that. So I did.' He shook her gently. 'Don't you see, Hol? He'll throw her out anyway. But even if he doesn't, she'll come to me. It will be my child. He won't stand a chance!'

She got off the gate and turned towards the door.

'Yes. I see,' she said politely and went around the back to where the ferns dripped and Gran was lighting the copper for the pudding cloths.

'Look who's here, Gran,' she called gaily. 'The prodigal son himself!'

Dorothy heard her and came running out in her dressing-gown. The two women hugged him and exclaimed at his dampness and drew him in to the fire. Holly made another pot of tea and put an egg on to boil. After all he had gone through he must be weak.

Dorothy blamed herself for what happened at the Gatehouse two hours later. She said she should have gone ahead and warned Lizzie and Edward that Charlie had appeared. Or sent Holly. But Charlie wanted his homecoming to be a surprise and he jollied them along and hugged Gran and tried to dance Holly around the table until she pulled violently away and crashed into the chiffonier sending the Christmas cards flying.

Dorothy held onto the table-cloth before that was dragged off and laughed protestingly.

'What have they done to you at that training camp, Charlie Richardson? You used to be such a nice quiet boy!'

And he hugged her too and said mock-seriously, 'And now I'm a big rowdy man!'

Dorothy shook her head at him.

'Oh all right. You can give them a surprise then. But please let us go in first. Your father is anxious – overanxious – about your mother. We don't want to put his back up.'

Charlie couldn't imagine that. 'Dad? Anxious about Ma? Come off it, Aunt Doll!'

Holly did not come with them that morning, she said she felt sick.

'It was them nuts,' Gran said with satisfaction. 'What did I tell you about them nuts?'

'You said I'd turn into a squirrel, actually,' Holly came back with most unusual sarcasm. 'So I'll sit by the fire and hibernate, if nobody minds!'

Dorothy said, 'Are you sure, darling? Would you like me to stay with you?'

'No,' Holly said quickly. 'I want to read your present to me.' Dorothy had given her the latest Dornford Yates.

'All right, darling. We won't be long. We'll just deliver Charlie.' Dorothy knew Holly had had a row with Winnie the day before. It was not really surprising. Winnie had inherited her father's gift of the gab. She barely knew the difference between fact and fiction.

So they left Holly to her book and tramped down Middle Lane towards Applecross and Mrs Thrupp and then cut over a field to the imposing carriageway and the Gatehouse. It wasn't really a short cut but Gran hated walking along roads when she could use the old field paths.

It was ten o'clock. Edward had gone to check on the milking sheds which were being checked in the New Year by the food inspector. Lizzie was still in bed. Winnie was in a very ancient dressing-gown making tea in the tiny kitchen. She did not immediately see Charlie.

'Oh hello.' She looked up unenthusiastically from the soggy wooden draining-board. 'We didn't think you'd come over today. Where's Holly?'

Dorothy said, 'She's not feeling too good.' She held Winnie's gaze meaningfully and the girl actually flushed. What on earth could she have said to Hol? Dorothy stood aside. 'We've brought you a surprise.'

Winnie peered into the dark hall, saw the khaki and still did not realize who was there.

'Hello, our Win,' Charlie said, grinning from ear to ear.

And Winnie screamed. She flung herself onto her brother and kept screaming. And Lizzie, woken from a doze after a terrible night of discomfort, scrambled out of bed, rushed along the landing and fell down the stairs.

1925

Although Sarah kept in sporadic touch with her family, she had not set eyes on Edward Richardson again until Jim's wedding day. She liked to make what she called flying visits; play the fairy godmother for Kildie, leave a solid silver christening mug for Charlie, a dinner service for her mother, a new rod for her father. She bought extravagant outfits for Kildie, silk ties for Jim. She spoke of her 'patron' but refused to name him. She sang in night-clubs, occasionally in a variety show. Bertie had been killed in 1918 and to her amazement had left his flat to her. She was quite famous for her small parties. The Fairchilds came often; Miss Crombie-Smythe – Alicia – was a good friend. Sarah sold the flat and moved into a house in Pimlico. Francis Passmore-Williams introduced her to his friends: businessmen, men of the cloth, government officials. She 'looked after' them. She called herself a consort, drove them around, invited them to her parties. Sometimes Francis had to warn her against being loud. It was fashionable in the Twenties to be heard; but not to be loud. He called this her education. At first she had been glad of this education. It meant she could sleep with men and never become pregnant. It meant she knew how to tackle the array of cutlery at dinner parties, when to scorn Dadaism and when to praise it, and especially how to listen. Later she was less appreciative of Francis' efforts. She hated him calling her loud. When she told him that Jim was getting secretly married and she was going to be the surprise guest at the wedding, he groaned. 'You'll come back shouting your head off and I'll have to start all over again!'

She said furiously, 'I thought you liked me going to Dymock to do your spying for you! Won't you want to know whether my parents are still sleeping together now they're in their sixties?'

He replied smoothly, 'Yes, I would like to know that. I think you should try to discover just how long they have been in this state of married bliss too.'

'Why on earth do you want to know that?'

'Oh, *I* already know. I think it would be good for you to know also, my wild gypsy girl!'

She knew he was being horrid; she could always tell. She knew so much about him yet understood nothing. Part of his undoubted attraction was his mystery. And his mastery of everything. And there was his money, of course. Sometimes, when she was very low she knew that he was just a glorified pimp and she was his prostitute. Yet – yet – it was more than that. At times they liked each other.

She said now, 'Why don't you simply tell me, Francis? Whatever it is you want me to discover – why don't you simply tell me?'

He took on his pedantic role, knowing it drove her mad.

'It is in the pursuit of knowledge that one matures. The actual acquisition of it brings an end to that process.'

'Supposing I never find out, whatever it is?'

'If it goes on too long, I might tell you.' He smiled indulgently.

She said cheekily, 'Well don't leave it too long – you might die!'

Surprisingly that hit home. He said, 'I am almost ten years younger than your father, my dear! What *will* be disappointing is if he dies suddenly!'

Just the thought of Walter's death made her feel physically sick. She raised her voice to a definite shout and said, 'Why don't you just bugger off, Francis?'

Even so, it was quite a shock when he did and she missed

him seeing her off at Paddington and fetching her magazines and chocolate for the journey.

Perhaps that was why it was such a pleasure to see Edward Richardson. It amused them both that while the Prossers were being seen off on the station and Lizzie was doing the washing-up with Kildie downstairs, they were on the marital bed long before Dorothy and Jim. Edward took the precaution of tucking a chair under the door handle and, of course, knowing each other as they did they were very quick indeed.

Edward said afterwards, 'My God, Sarah, you haven't changed!'

'Neither have you, my lad. I know what you were up to with Dolly Prosser just now in the hall!'

He laughed and kissed her appreciatively. 'And you didn't mind! You're a good girl . . . in many ways!'

They both laughed in gasping whispers. Sarah wished they had more time; she would have liked to tell him many things.

He said, 'So you were in France. I never got further than the War Office. Only joined up because I thought I might see you!'

'Liar! But then, so am I. I never went to France, darling. I did my bit in London.'

He groaned. 'I could have seen you every damned day!'

'It wouldn't have been fair to Lizzie. I was determined not to let that arrangement continue, Teddy dear.'

'That's rich! What are you doing now, pray!'

'I didn't intend this, I can assure you. When you put your hand on my thigh I was about to brush it away—'

'And then you had second thoughts!'

'Lizzie is expecting again. So I supposed you were . . . all right.'

'Yes. And we're going to the Fens. Fresh start.'

She rested on one elbow and looked at him. He was very good-looking.

She said, 'I'm glad. Lizzie is so good.'

'I know. I wish she weren't.'

Again they had to stifle their laughter. And then they began to dress.

Pulling on a long silk stocking, Sarah said, 'Darling, have you heard of someone called Francis Passmore-Williams?'

'No. Should I know him?'

'He's a businessman. Very behind the scenes. I think – I'm sure – he knew my parents. Before they were married.'

Edward buttoned his jacket and settled his tie inside his waistcoat.

'Then why don't you ask them?'

It seemed so obvious. Sarah fastened her suspender and said thoughtfully, 'Because I think that is what Francis would like me to do.'

She had said teasingly to Kildie that the thought of Dorothy and Jim in the next bedroom made her green with envy. But as she snuggled next to Kildie that night, she felt something worse than envy. It was her own isolation; the peculiar vacuum that her life had become; she felt a knife of unhappiness cutting deep into her soul. She lay next to a child who was beautiful, intelligent and charming; her child; the child she had given away. In the next bedroom was her much-loved brother, only two years younger than herself, yet always treated as the baby of the family until Kildie's arrival. She had pushed him out of her life by her own behaviour and although he had kissed her warmly and been delighted to see her at his wedding, she sensed a caution in his manner that did not extend to Lizzie. He respected Lizzie. He did not respect Sarah.

She drew in a deep breath at the pain of it. Thoughtlessly she had betrayed Kildie, Jim and her own sister. And by doing so she had also betrayed her parents. Betrayal was what brought this isolation; she wondered if Judas had known it too.

Somewhere in the small hours she slid out of bed and crept barefoot down the stairs. It was bitterly cold. She dared not riddle the ashes from the banked-up fire. She took her father's uniform greatcoat from the hall and huddled into it, then she went into the kitchen and lit the gas stove. She was holding cupped hands over the blue flame when her father came in.

'Sarah! What on earth are you doing down here at this hour? Can't you sleep?'

She was so pleased to see him she almost wept.

'No. Too excited, I expect. Are you the same?'

'Oh, I shall sleep. But your mother and I always have a cup of tea . . . at this time.'

He reached across her for the kettle and put it on the gas. She realized belatedly what he meant. Ma and Pa had been making love! At their ages! Well, she had the information Francis wanted. If she chose to give it to him.

Her father said, 'Are you really all right, Sarah? Honestly?'

'Of course,' she replied robustly. 'My own house, my own car, lots of engagements . . . it's what I always wanted, Pa.'

'Yes.' He went to the kitchen window and stared out at the sky. It was a brilliant frosty night. 'Sarah, we know how you get these things. We might live in the country but we still know the way of the world. I . . . I'm afraid I've failed in my duty to you, my dear. Perhaps now is the time to say I'm sorry.'

She was shocked. 'Pa! Nothing of the sort! You did your duty and I rebelled.' She hugged his arm. 'I'm glad you know – glad you told me – I hated the thought that I was lying to you and Ma.'

He held her hand against his side with his elbow.

'You have always been frank, I'll say that for you.' He laughed wryly. 'Sometimes a little too frank for us!' He looked down at her. 'I'd like you to know that if – if – you ever need us, this is still your home. It might drive you mad with boredom, but it's here!'

She was speechless with gratitude. She had not been isolated after all.

305

He turned and made the tea, put on a padded tea cosy and reached down some cups.

She said wonderingly, 'Pa, since . . . that time . . . you know . . . before Kildie . . .'

'I know.'

'You have been so understanding. I don't deserve it. No other father—'

'It was your mother. She is the one. She never condemns. And besides . . . there are things you cannot know, Sarah. Things that happened a long time ago. I should have understood right from the beginning.'

She poured milk and spooned sugar. This was it. This was what Passmore-Williams wanted to know. She felt as if she stood on the brink of the precipice. She remembered her dream when her mother had saved her from unknown horrors.

'Tell me, Pa.'

He hesitated. She knew that words were trembling on his lips. Part of him wanted to tell her.

Then he said, 'I cannot. I promised your mother I would not speak of it.'

She could have screamed. She wanted to tell him that she needed to know this dark secret so that she could protect him from Passmore-Williams. But that would hurt him . . . maybe that was what would hurt him most of all.

She said, 'Let me carry the tray. Can you take your coat off my shoulders?'

He followed her through the living-room into the hall and hung his coat on the hook.

He said, 'Sarah . . . I would like you to know that your mother and I have been sublimely happy. Always. Right from the beginning.'

She turned and looked at him. The brilliant moon was shining through the transom above the front door. She could see his face, open now, sensitive and fine.

'I know that, Pa. I've always known that,' she whispered.

From above them came a sound; it was Jim and

Dorothy. She smiled at her father, no longer feeling a trace of envy or embarrassment.

He smiled back. 'They're both so young,' he breathed. 'Jim especially.' His smile turned to a conspiratorial grin. 'He was practically a honeymoon child, you know!'

She giggled too and turned to continue up the stairs. It was only as she slipped back into bed that she realized what he had said. Jim, a honeymoon baby. And she and Lizzie were two years older than Jim.

She was not shocked to learn that she and Lizzie were illegitimate. It explained some things. Especially her father's words all those years ago when he had seemed to think her escapades were his responsibility. But she was still very puzzled. How on earth could Francis use her illegitimacy to hurt her parents? It just did not make sense.

SIXTEEN

1941

On 1 May 1941 Holly planted two rows of beans in the garden at the Green. She felt she was just about keeping the flag flying; but it was a tattered banner, bloodied, very besmirched. Her letters to Dad were stilted, she felt separated from Mum and riven from Kildie by Charlie. She had had no communication with Winnie since that awful Christmas afternoon. The only person who had not somehow betrayed her was Gran.

It was Gran who had said the previous weekend, 'It's time to put in your beans, our Hol. You can do that next week.'

Holly had looked up drearily from an old copy of the *Citizen* and said, 'Don't you want me here any more, Gran?'

'Not every weekend I don't. I want you to keep an eye on things at home as well as here.'

'Mum's all right. Aunty Mabs is always round. Or . . . her other bridge friends.' She could not be disloyal enough to tell Gran that the three Bobs were there whenever they weren't flying their Lancaster.

'That's because you're over here!' Gran looked un-usually cross. 'Surely you can see that, our Hol? You used to have a bit of sense. Somewhere.'

'But . . . I thought you needed me!' Holly bleated, feeling as though her one foundation was trembling in the general earthquake.

Gran softened. 'Well . . . that I do, my girl. That I do.' She grinned gummily. 'You and Winnie between you been good to me. Seeing to the hens, keeping the washing down—'

Holly had to be honest. 'Mum does that when I take it back.' She shook her head. 'Gran, you've forgotten your teeth again.'

'I know that!' Gran was instantly aggressive. 'Can't abide the damned things in my mouth all the time. If you don't like it you can lump it!'

Holly grinned herself. 'I don't mind it.' She hesitated. 'Is Winnie . . . all right, Gran?'

Gran looked through the window. April had been typical that year; the last shower had washed the fern bed and the green fronds were glinting in the sunshine.

She said, 'Better than you and me could have dreamed, Holly. Your Aunt Lizzie can't be bothered to dress most days and Edward . . . well, Edward has found what he wants to do at last. But it means he's not in the house often. And when he is . . .' She let her words die away.

Holly, interested in the situation at the Gatehouse in spite of her abhorrence of Winnie, said tentatively, 'But he was so good when Aunt Lizzie was expecting the baby.'

'Well. You've hit the nail on the head, girl. She ain't expecting the baby no more.'

Holly said nothing. Ever since Christmas she had thought a great deal about women having babies. Poor Aunt Lizzie who was no longer having hers, Winnie who was so terribly tempted to have one, and . . . Kildie. She wondered – nearly all the time – whether Kildie was now expecting a baby. What would Marcus do then?

'One thing,' Gran went on, obviously glad now to have the opportunity to talk about it. 'They do hear from Charlie now and then. He's still with that there General Wavell. In Egypt, they are. Beaten right back. After taking all those Eye-talian prisoners—'

'We've got some of them at the camp in Innsworth,' Holly mentioned. 'They seem really glad to be there.' She was going to relay some gossip from the three Bobs, but decided against it.

'I shouldn't wonder.' Gran looked away from the window and began to stand up from the table laboriously. Holly said, 'Gran – let me – what is it?' but Gran waved her away and reached for a jam jar on the chiffonier. 'Here are your beans. You didn't keep any last year, I s'ppose?'

'No.' Holly was suddenly ashamed. She hadn't done anything in the garden except pick the winter greens.

Gran said, 'Put your sticks in first. Then two beans either side of each stick.'

'I know. I always helped Dad. And last year . . .' Last year seemed an age away. Mum had planted the beans last year. It had been before the arrival of the Bobs. Mum had had time for all kinds of things.

'And whatever eggs you find today I want you to take back home with you.' Gran lifted the cushion on her chair and fished out some newspapers. 'Wrap each one carefully. Last time your Ma was here I didn't like the look of her. Too thin.'

'She's OK.'

'Don't use that word!' Gran came back sharply. 'She doesn't eat enough. Prob'ly gives you her rations!'

Holly was silent. She wanted to blurt out that they had a tin of spam every week besides chocolate and chewing-gum.

'I've got plenty,' Gran said. 'And there's food to waste over at the Gatehouse. And Winnie's not a bad little cook.'

Holly could not imagine it.

Gran said defensively, 'She brings me some of that fatless sponge cake. If you put a lot of jam on it, it's quite nice.'

'Oh.' Holly knew she should admire Winnie for taking over the housekeeping at the Gatehouse. She herself hardly entered the kitchen at home; Mum eked out the rations in a way that could not brook interference. She felt inadequate and resentful of Winnie all over again. She longed to ask about the Battersbys, especially Eric.

Gran said, 'Go and get them eggs, our Hol. Wrap 'em

up and put these beans in the bag with them and get off home.'

'I thought I'd stay till this afternoon, Gran,' Holly protested.

'Then you thought wrong, my girl.'

Gran edged her way around the table and went into the kitchen, her lips folded firmly around her gums.

Setting the bean sticks seemed to conjure Blanche into existence however hard Holly fought against it. She said angrily, 'I shouldn't need you any more! Talking to you makes me feel even more useless than usual.'

Blanche said, 'Oh for goodness' sake, shut up! You're leaning against that bean stick and pushing it right over. Snap out of it, girl!'

Holly righted the stick and gave up. 'Gran thinks Winnie is pulling her weight far more than me.' She spoke without preliminaries. Blanche did not need preliminaries. 'And she's right. I mean, it's not Mum's fault if I'm practically a bastard—'

'Language, Holly!'

'Well, they called William the Conqueror, William the Bastard. It's OK to say that.'

'And Gran doesn't like you saying OK either.'

'Oh, dammit all.' Holly leaned wearily against the last bean stick, pushing it askew again. 'I don't know what to think or say any more. I ought not to hate Mum, but I do. Almost as if it's her fault that Dad loves Kildie—'

'You don't know that your dad loves Kildie. And Kildie certainly can't love him if she . . . did that . . . with Charlie Richardson!'

'Kildie . . . I can't understand Kildie either. And she used to pray for ages. On her knees by the window, talking to Grandad and to God—'

'Tommyrot!'

'Yes. Well . . . At the time I thought that's what she was doing.'

Blanche said, suddenly thoughtful, 'What I'd like to

311

know is what Winnie meant about her mother and Aunt Sarah. Why don't you ask your mother about that, Holly?'

'I couldn't ask Mum about them! She hasn't got patience with either of them! She thinks Aunt Lizzie needs a good talking to!'

'It might bridge the gap, though,' Blanche went on, still thoughtfully. 'Something you could talk about. Properly.'

'Oh we've got plenty to talk about! Chemistry. Physics, Eng. Lit. Whether I'm going to get a State Scholarship!'

'Yes, but this would be different. More . . . well, intimate without being *personally* intimate. If you know what I mean.'

Holly, crouched again and put the last two beans into the earth with her long forefinger. The earth felt suitably soft and moist. There had been another shower yesterday on the last day of April. Holly could understand Uncle Edward's sudden fascination with ploughing up the land and cultivating it. At Christmas he had laughed and told them, 'I always loved muck, didn't I, Lizzie?' And Aunt Lizzie had laughed indulgently. That had been before they lost their baby.

She became conscious of someone near at hand and looked up, startled. The youngest Bob, the one with the sister who was going to visit Dad, was standing, smiling at her.

'I talk to myself all the time,' he said in his curious accent.

She was furious.

'I was talking to my *alter ego* actually,' she said haughtily. 'You wouldn't understand.'

'Of course I understand. Has yours got a name?'

She regretted her confidence and bent down to pick up Gran's jam jar.

He said, 'Mine is called Oscar. I think you need an unusual name. You don't want to get confused with people you might know. Or someone else might know.'

She knew no-one called Blanche, that was certain.

He moved closer and surveyed the row of sticks.

'Kind of a ritual, I guess?' he asked.

She felt stifled by his proximity. She could smell him. A mixture of cigarettes, petrol, brylcreem. Very, very male smells.

'We always plant the beans on May the first,' she replied in a withdrawn voice.

'Uh-huh.' He stood there, unmoving, just looking at the sticks. She clenched her hands. The earth in her fingers became mud and squelched around in her palms.

He said, 'Strange to think that whatever happens to us, these beans will grow and be ready for picking in three or four months.'

'Yes,' she said, stifled by the heat. How could it be hot?

'Life goes on, doesn't it?'

'Yes,' she whispered.

'I find that cruel. It kinda ploughs us under and goes on . . . remorselessly.'

She forced herself to breathe normally. She wanted to put her arms around him and wail but just the thought of doing that made her feel faint.

'Yes.'

He said abruptly, 'Your Mom asked me to tell you . . . Bob Lavery and Bob Winter. They were killed yesterday. The Lanc was shot down. Caught fire. No-one got out.'

Holly was rigid. Her legs, planted a little apart, seemed welded to the stone flags of the path. Two of the three Bobs were dead. She had not wanted them. And now they were dead.

He said, 'I was here, talking to your mother. Playing cards. Mabel came over. We played gin rummy.'

Holly managed to move the muscles of her throat and swallow.

'I should have been there. I caught my finger in the door of the mess. Bandaged. Couldn't use the machine-gun. I'm the tail gunner you know. Couldn't use the— ' He made a sound like a sob. 'I shoulda bin there. A squashed finger – Christ – a squashed finger—'

She knew he was crying. She squeezed her eyes shut.

He groped for her hand. 'Holly, I'm sorry. You're just a kid.' He took her balled-up fist and held it in both of his. He said, 'You shouldn't have to hear this. But . . . Christ, it's happened!'

She knew how he felt. Isolated. Left out. She opened her hand slowly and he stared down at the mud and then, very carefully, began to move the index finger of his free hand along the lines of her palm.

'What's here for you, little Holly? Life? Love?' He gripped her hand hard suddenly. 'Oh God, Holly, What-ever it is, let it be for those two as well! Oh Christ – they can't have kids or plant themselves a bean row, or eat another steak . . . Live for them Holly!'

She began to cry, her body shaking with the sobs she'd held in till then. And he looked into her face and said, 'I'm sorry, so sorry . . . oh Holly . . . I'm so sorry . . .'

Marcus Villiers glanced through the doorway of the special dining-room for servicemen and saw Kildie 'doing the rounds' as she called it. In spite of the fine day she wore a silver fox fur over one shoulder. Her peaked hat, very military, was pulled well down and slightly sideways. Her crêpe de Chine dress clung to three definitively plump rolls of flesh, one around her bust, one at her waist and one around her hips. They were not unattractive. He was certain they were nothing whatsoever to do with pregnancy.

He smiled grimly and went onto the staircase and the office floor. He had not spoken to her since that morning after Christmas when he had found Charlie Richardson in bed with her. She found it the hardest punishment in the world and tried to provoke some of their more interesting and noisy rows several times a day. Just once she had crept into the guest bedroom and slipped into bed beside him. He had turned his back on her and ignored her weeping pleas. She had not done that again.

Now, after four months, he was certain she was not

pregnant and had made up his mind to forgive her. He had worked out a scenario not unlike the one that had taken place in Gran's bedroom last summer. Now he needed the right time and the right place. The poor girl was doing her best to please him; she had put in her usual twice-weekly appearance at the store and had even taken over some of the cooking. He took great pleasure in totally ignoring her at work, and in pushing away any food she prepared. He was discovering many ways to bring Kildie to heel. But they were not as satisfying as the old ones.

He told Miss Ashe he was going home early and took the lift to the ground floor. The Wolsley was parked next to his Morgan. Kildie had driven it home from Dymock after their reconciliation and had kept it ever since. As he drove through Cheltenham he thought that the car suited the Kildie of today. With her extra weight and a certain sedateness she was not the wild girl who had stormed off that night and stolen his precious Morgan.

He parked at one side of the garage; Kildie hated parking cars, she would be flustered when she came in. That was good. Her sedateness also held an element of self-possession which was quite unlike the old Kildie. His scenario did not allow for any self-possession. He let himself in through the back door where Mrs Davis was just switching on the oven.

'Fish pie, Mr Villiers,' she said. 'New potatoes in the saucepan. Is you happy with yesterday's gooseberry fool?'

'Certainly.' He disliked the woman as much as Kildie did, but neither of them could do without her. He knew she relished recounting all his domestic dramas in the Woolpack. He had caught her at it once and enjoyed threatening her with a slander suit.

He went past her into the hall to put his coat and hat away. He was tidy by nature. A yellow envelope lay on the door mat. He picked it up quickly. It was a telegram from Edward Richardson.

'Regret tell you Charlie dead stop phone later stop Edward stop'

He crumpled the flimsy paper and stuck it in his pocket.

'Have you cleaned the hall today, Mrs Davis?' he called into the kitchen.

She appeared, struggling into her coat.

'Not my day for the 'all, sir,' she said self-righteously. 'Thursday's 'all. Saturday's kitchen.'

'Very well.' So she had not seen the telegram. He took out his wallet and extracted a crisp pound note. 'We'll see you on Monday as usual.'

'Thank you, sir!' She was suddenly all over him. 'I'll starch your collars like you said, sir. Better 'n the Chinese laundry, I'll be bound.'

'Thank you, Mrs Davis.' He opened the door for her and shut it quickly. Then he stood pondering until he heard Kildie's car lumber onto the drive. Charlie's death was a great personal relief. But he was sensitive enough to know that it could have no part in his scenario.

Kildie was even more aware than Marcus that she had changed. It was not only sleeping with Charlie at Christmas: that had been wonderful, making her feel important for the first time in her life. But it was followed by a stream of letters from him, sent to Gran's and saved for her weekly visit there. Such letters. She had not imagined such letters, not in her wildest dreams. They were madly erotic, but they were also adulatory; they were frank to the point of being coarse, but they were also sensitive and fine and they told her in no uncertain way that she had made another human being happier than any human could expect.

'If I die tomorrow,' he wrote in March, 'you must know that I die completely happy and fulfilled. You are my whole being and I have been one with you. When our baby is born perhaps it will be me! I felt as if I could crawl right inside you and nestle in your womb for nine months . . .'

Gran said, 'You've gone as red as a turkey-cock, our Kildie! What's that boy been saying to you now?'

'Teasing me, Gran. You know how he always loved to tease me.'

'He's in love with you, Kildie. Besotted with you, he is. You'll have to let him down lightly after the War.'

She wanted to tell Gran that she was carrying Charlie's baby and that after the War they would live together in perfect happiness. But she did not. Gran might not understand.

Meanwhile, Marcus' silence suited her very well. She tried to argue with him; once she even tried to patch things up by going to his bed. It would have been useful to announce her pregnancy soon after one of their violent love-makings. But she wasn't sorry when he turned a cold shoulder. She had no idea what he would do when he knew about the baby. He would throw her out, she supposed. It did not worry her unduly. She would live with Gran. Meanwhile she got on with things as best she could, doing her 'duty' at the store, trying to cook a few meals, writing interminable letters to Charlie, wrapped in a cocoon of happiness. She ate for two: black market milk and cream and butter and lots of steaks because she knew that dairy foods and red meat were excellent nourishment for babies. She was proud of her big stomach though she disguised it with her long fox fur when she went to the restaurant. Nobody seemed to realize she was pregnant. When Group Captain Donaldson had followed her into the lift, her extra curves had seemed to drive him right round the bend. He had kissed her as he often did when they were alone, and then pressed his hands into her buttocks quite painfully.

She had gasped and said, 'Really, Nigel darling! You're getting carried away!'

'I shall be soon! You're driving me crazy, Kilda. Absolutely crazy.'

She smiled as she pushed him gently back. 'You must control yourself, my dear. I'm very much a married woman.' And she planned how she would tell Charlie about this. Since you left, my darling cousin, nobody has touched me . . . though Nigel Donaldson has tried several times . . .'

Marcus' car had gone. She drove the Wolsley out of the town and along the Staverton Road. It was when she reached the foot of Leckhampton Hill that she realized she had a pain. It was a deep, dark pain. Low in her abdomen. She did not like it.

She swung the Wolsley into the small garage space, her mind completely on getting to the bathroom. Marcus was in the sun room, lying in one of the steamer chairs, two drinks on the small table by his side. Although he never spoke to her, she sensed his dark gaze on her and said, 'Marcus . . . sorry, darling . . . have to go to the lavatory . . .' The pain was not bad exactly, but persistent. It reminded her of something. What had she eaten?

He reached out a long arm and caught the tail of her fur; the cord immediately cut into her throat.

'Wait. I want you.'

It was so long since they'd had this kind of exchange that she got it completely wrong.

'What for? Can't it wait? I need—'

He pulled her onto his knee. She was heavier than he remembered and he gasped.

She gasped too with surprise. 'Marcus? What has happened?'

He managed to say throatily, 'Daddy needs Mummy.'

She propped herself on an elbow and looked into his face, sufficiently surprised to have forgotten the pain.

'But I thought . . . I thought you would never forgive me!'

He had not reckoned on such frankness, such fearless frankness. But perhaps it was better that way. He snaked his free hand between the buttons of her dress and underneath her brassière.

'Oh Kildie . . . What we mean to each other has so little to do with forgiveness or guilt or anything. It's just there. The whole time.'

She felt her usual melting thrill at his touch. After all, there was no point in making an enemy of him. Perhaps even now she might pass the baby off as his. She leaned down and kissed him.

'Daddy . . .' she whispered.

'Baby . . .' he whispered back. 'It's all right now. I had to be sure . . . quite sure . . .'

'Sure?' They were on the floor and he was having his usual way with her so that she hardly heard what he was saying.

'Sure that great oaf of a country bumpkin hadn't made you pregnant. I couldn't have forgiven that . . .' He kissed her.

She said nothing, but part of her mind stayed amazingly clear.

He spoke in short gasps. 'Just a kid, after all . . . could almost have been your son . . . like you said . . . bit of consolation before going to war . . .' He panted a laugh. 'I cooled his ardour, I can tell you. Dymock is a cold hole at the best of times. But without any clothes . . .'

Charlie had written to tell her what had happened. He hadn't cared. He said he had still been warm from her arms.

Marcus said no more for a long time, then as he lay on top of her breathing deeply, he delivered the *coup de grâce*.

'I can be generous, baby. After all the little runt is your cousin. When I found the telegram I knew I had to help you through this. Console you. But he deserved what he got, baby. Coming here and getting you into bed before you could turn round—'

'What telegram?' Kildie asked very clearly.

'It was here when I got home. From Edward Richardson. He took after Edward Richardson. Like father like son. Anything in skirts—'

'What did the telegram say?' Kildie asked.

'Charlie Richardson is dead. Edward is going to telephone tonight. I've taken the receiver off the hook.'

She lay there beneath him, not moving. After all, it did not matter whether Edward phoned or not. If Charlie was dead, Charlie was dead. She would think about it much

319

later. Or perhaps she wouldn't think about it at all in case it damaged the baby. She still had the baby. Charlie's baby.

She whispered, 'Daddy . . . I must go to the lavatory.'

'All right, Mummy.' He levered himself off her and even reached down to help her up. 'You're taking the news well, Mummy. Are you all right?' He looked into her eyes and then quite suddenly held her half-clothed body to his and kissed her. 'Daddy will look after you, baby. Daddy will always be here to look after you. Don't worry.'

It was amazing how comforting his words were. She almost wept then, leaning on him, yielding herself up to him again to be cherished and adored. But the pain was suddenly back.

She went upstairs, pulling on the banister like Gran did these days. And as she sat on the toilet, she knew that the pain was indeed very familiar. It was what Dorothy called menstrual discomfort.

She bowed her head over her knees and wept.

1925

It was during the Easter after Jim's and Dorothy's wedding that Sarah received a card from Francis Passmore-Williams inviting her to sing at one of his little gatherings.

These took place in the smoking-room of his house and she was nearly always the unofficial hostess. Halfway through the evening she invariably sat at the piano in response to Francis', 'Why don't you sing for us, my dear?' She enjoyed these functions; they were vaguely political and usually ended with Francis arranging to send clothing to India or medicines to Africa. Sometimes she dallied with the idea of him being an old softie at heart. Certainly he behaved like a philanthropist. But she knew he was not. Not really.

This time she almost turned down the invitation. She had kept a certain distance between herself and Francis since returning from Jim's wedding. She never told him that she had discovered that both she and Lizzie were illegitimate; she had certainly not informed him that her parents still made love regularly. She could manage without Francis Passmore-Williams now; the introductions he had given her over the years were quite enough to keep her in her neat little house in Lupus Street.

She fingered the small square of pasteboard thoughtfully, imagining with pleasure his annoyance if she did, in fact, decline the invitation. But then she shrugged. There was no way he could harm her or her family; and she was rather bored with the long wet spring. Also the food at these parties was always good, the company very flattering and in a strange way she was missing Francis. She was like a moth with a flame; much better off without it, yet oddly attracted. She could be honest with him, brutally honest at times. And although it was part of the mystery, it was also a relief that he never tried to get her into bed.

His greeting was delighted. He came into the hall when he heard her voice, helped her with her coat before his man servant could do a thing, pecked her cheek.

'My dear, I'm so glad. It seems such a long time since we had a proper party.' He put his mouth close to her ear. 'Do your best, Sarah. I'm playing for big stakes tonight!'

She knew what that meant. If she made a good impression on one of the gentlemen present, she would be expected to woo him insistently while he and Francis did their business – whatever that was.

He led her in with aplomb. The room was a haze of cigar smoke. No other women were there. About half a dozen familiar faces emerged from the smoke. There was one man she did not recognize. He wore a turban stuck with jewels.

'Most of you remember Miss James,' he introduced her. 'Maharaja, you have not had the pleasure. Sarah, my dear, this is a personal friend. Incognito, of course. From India. I think you might have a great deal in common.'

She registered the dark lascivious eyes, the full,

blood-red lips, and wondered what they could possibly have in common. Unless it were a love of jewels; and he certainly had a great deal of those. However, as he was obviously some kind of prince, she curtseyed as Francis had taught her and kept her eyes lowered after that initial look.

'Will you give us a song, Sarah? How about "The Roses of Sharon"?'

Francis made a big thing of leading her to the piano, drawing out the stool, settling some sheet music on the rack and adjusting the candles in their sconces. He enjoyed ceremony for its own sake but also because it made an impression. The Maharaja smiled appreciatively and continued to smile as she ran her hands over the keys and began to sing.

Afterwards, Francis took her hand and leaned over it to murmur to her under cover of the spattering of applause.

'He's taken the bait, my dear. Can you reel him in for me, d'you think?'

It was quite exciting to be involved in something so . . . so international. She sat by the Maharaja at supper and inclined her head when he made three statements in broken English.

'The food . . . tested.'

'I believe so,' she replied, wondering what on earth he could mean.

'Dark girl. Good.'

'Oh. How marvellous.' She hoped she was interpreting that one correctly. She dimpled and let her leg touch his.

'Not young.'

She removed her knee. 'Twenty-six, actually.' Dammit all, that was not, definitely not, old!

At the end of the evening when Francis was settling her coat over her shoulders, he said, 'Perhaps you would permit Miss James to show you some of the sights of London, sir?' He looked as jovial as a character from a novel. 'Memories to take back with you to your ancient country.'

There was more of this. The Maharaja nodded frequently; he appeared to understand more English than he spoke. Finally an appointment was made. Sarah would take a taxi to his hotel and they would proceed from there to the Tower.

Francis took her aside. 'After that, it is up to you. If I can secure a contract with this chappie, the whole sub-continent will be my oyster.'

She said, 'I cannot see that a few bales of cloth can be so important. But I'll do my best.'

He looked at her. 'Sarah, I am involved in important transactions. Only important transactions.'

She returned the look. 'Does that mean I am an important transaction, Francis? I thought perhaps you had filed me away.'

He smiled. 'I had not realized how much you were missed until you arrived this evening.' He patted her hand. 'Did you enjoy your visit home?'

'Yes. I've almost forgotten it.'

'Did you find out anything interesting?'

'My parents are still making love.' The words were out before she could stop them. She bit her lip and glanced at his face. Nothing happened. His lack of reaction goaded her further. 'And I also discovered that my sister and I were born before they were married.'

He started to laugh. She could have hit him.

'It did not bother me one iota, Francis,' she said tartly.

He said, 'You are so hard, Sarah. It would not bother you. D'you think it might bother your father?'

'No. My mother perhaps—'

'Esme. Ridiculous name for a servant. I am not interested in Esme's reactions, Sarah.' He leaned forward, suddenly serious. 'If you can bring the Maharaja to me, neatly parcelled, I will make you an offer you cannot refuse.'

She stared at him. Was he going to offer marriage? Just how rich was he? How long would he live? And what was in it for him?

She said, 'That might be interesting, Francis. Or again,

it might not. But I envisage no particular difficulty with the Maharaja.'

'Good girl.'

It was an intriguing challenge, and helped her to forget that she had told Francis the very things she had wanted never to say. It was as if he was seducing her into betraying her family. She knew that if she thought about it much she would begin hating herself again and then the feeling of isolation would be back.

So she put her heart and soul into looking after the Maharaja. She even wondered, as they looked at the Crown jewels and he turned away unimpressed, whether she might go to India with him and live in a golden palace by a silver lake.

But it was obvious from the outset that he would never take her back with him. The way he clicked his fingers at her when she did not understand his broken English and sat back in her modern chairs waiting for her to bring him tea made her feel like a servant as well as a whore. She saw him every day for a week and at the end of that time she loathed him. When he came to say goodbye he held out his hand for her to kiss.

'Mees Sarra.' He smiled indulgently. 'I have Mees Sarra *and* the guns, yes? That is good.'

She smiled mechanically and went to open the door for him. Then she put a pale green swagger coat over her skirt and jacket and walked down Lupus Street to Francis' house on the river.

His man servant told her that Mr Passmore-Williams was out, but she knew better. She swept past him into the hall and went straight upstairs to the large sitting-room with its view of the plane trees around the river gardens. The man servant was on her heels.

'Tell him I'm here,' she said, and she put her gloves on a low table.

Francis joined her about five minutes later. His greying hair was ruffled and he wore a dressing-gown. She glanced pointedly at her watch.

He said, 'I came as quickly as I could. What's happened, Sarah? Is he all right?'

'Perfectly. The deal is done. He is buying . . . what you are selling.'

'Excellent! Excellent, my dear! Well done. You need not have come here immediately. I knew you were seeing him this afternoon so I was not expecting you. Perhaps a little supper tonight? Just the two of us?'

She stared at him. 'What's going on, Francis? If I am involved in any gun-running I would like to know about it!'

He frowned, then spread his hand, palms up and changed the frown to a smile. He came to sit opposite her. The dressing-gown fell open. His legs were bare and very hairy. She realized suddenly he was entertaining a woman. Unexpectedly she felt a thrill of pure jealousy. She had assumed he was celibate and in a strange way that made him hers.

'Sarah. Dear Sarah. There is not the slightest need for you to worry about anything! Surely you trust me after all this time? I have looked after you now, Sarah, for—'

'Almost ten years! I know!' she said impatiently. 'But although my morals might not be the usual sort, I have my own code, Francis. I have never been involved in anything like this before. I don't like it.'

He said sharply, 'You have not heard my offer yet, Sarah. I promised you a cut in this and I meant it.'

A cut? She had thought he was going to propose marriage. She felt a fool.

He said, 'Sarah, I have to leave you now—'

She interrupted furiously. He was not going to leave her sitting here for another woman!

'You are selling guns to the Indians. Is it to promote another mutiny?'

He laughed. 'My dear girl, that all happened back in the last century! The Indians are now represented in their own parliament—'

'But they still have not got home rule.' She stared at

him. 'You know that man – cannot remember his name – he will not brook violence.'

'Mahatma Gandhi.'

'Francis, if you are sending guns to one of the country's princelings, they can be for one reason only: violence.'

'Perhaps they are for tiger shooting, child. I do not concern myself with that side of things. I must go now—'

'But you have involved me! I am now concerned with whatever it is! You did not give me any choice in the matter!'

He lost his temper quite suddenly. 'Look here, Sarah. You are no longer sixteen. You are no longer sweet. You are extremely fortunate that the Maharaja was interested in you. Luckily he enjoys voluptuous women. It is not easy for me these days to find you the kind of consorts—'

She got up, gathering bag and gloves as she did so. 'Why don't you get back to your bedroom, Francis? Doubtless there is someone there who is sweet sixteen and is not particularly voluptuous—'

She stopped speaking as the door opened. A boy of ten or twelve stood there, dressed only in underpants, shivering slightly; he had obviously been weeping, his eyes were red and his face streaked.

He said, 'Can I go home now, mister?'

Francis stood up and left the room abruptly, carrying the boy with him. Sarah also left the room and then the house. She sat for a long time in the cocktail bar of an adjacent hotel. It explained so much. In a way it was a consolation; Francis' sexual habits were of little interest to her. But the child looked so scrawny, so utterly miserable. And she remembered that Passmore-Williams had seen Jim at Brimscombe back in 1915. Jim must have been thirteen or fourteen at the time. Big grey eyes and brown hair over his forehead. Jim had never passed on any message to her from Passmore-Williams. He had never spoken his name.

She did nothing about it. She hardly knew what to do. She continued to see her regular men friends and to give small and intimate parties but for the time being she turned down Francis' invitations and saw nothing of him for the rest of that summer. There were rumours that he was unwell; that he had gone to Nice, then Cannes. She told herself it was good riddance.

So it was a surprise when just before Christmas of 1925 he arrived at one of her soirées. He carried his hat and left his scarf around his neck; the maid followed him into the drawing-room, but he waved her back. Sarah was sitting at the piano as usual.

Caught off guard like that she was almost glad to see him. But she was also shocked. He was definitely thinner than when she had seen him last and his hair was almost white. She worked out that he must be fifty-three. He looked ten years older.

'How charming you look, Sarah! I had not realized how much I was missing you.' He picked up her hand from the piano keys and touched his lips to it. She smiled a welcome in spite of herself.

He looked around at the other men. 'Pleasant to see you, sir. And you too, Arnold. Oh and Sidney too . . . I hope you will continue to forgather like this when I am gone.'

Sarah raised her brows at him, then looked around at the others. They stared down at the piano. She said, 'I understood you had been travelling, Francis. Where are you going now?'

'That would be telling, my dear. The object of the exercise is to disappear.' He smiled. 'I had to come and say goodbye however. And I am delighted to find so many of our mutual friends are here also.'

'I don't understand,' she frowned. 'Why must you disappear?' She remembered the Maharaja and his guns. 'Ah . . . I see.'

'I'm sure you do, Sarah. I have always likened you to your mother, have I not? But you are most definitely your father's daughter. A streak of the pious, I think.'

She became still.

327

He looked around again. 'Well, I'm sure you gentlemen are pleased to know of Miss James's . . . er . . . piety. It is best to remember it, always.'

He turned to Sarah. 'Play me out, Sarah. How about that rag? "Harlem Rag", was it? I should have known then that you were cleverer than you looked!'

She began to ask him what had happened, and then shrugged. Defiantly she put her hands on the piano keys and began to thump out the ragtime melody that was now so popular everywhere.

After he had gone, the other three men were not slow in taking their leave. She saw them out herself and turned to her maid, still bewildered.

'There's more to this than meets the eye, Sadie. Something has happened.'

'It's that kid they found,' Sadie said darkly. 'You know, the one in the river. My gentleman friend said as how he'd heard the Police interviewed Mr Passmore-Williams. He went off to France or somewhere. But they was waiting for him when he came back. He's had to pay a lot of money to get out of it.'

'Get out of what, Sadie?' But Sarah knew with a dry mouth, just what.

'They suspect him, miss. He's one of them queerohs. Only he's more queer than most and he likes boys. And this were one of his boys.'

'He wouldn't – no, he wouldn't—'

'Well, someone told on him. And before they could interview the kid, he turns up dead!'

'Oh Sadie.'

'Yes, miss. You're better off without him, I reckon.'

Sarah knew that was true in one way. But Francis had let it be known that he thought she was the informer. She knew her 'friends' would be friendly no more.

She was right. No-one came to her next soirée. And life changed dramatically for her. Three years later she sold her house and moved into a flat in Bayswater. Her parents had retired and bought a cottage close to the station which had a room for her. She wrote privately to her father to see if there was any work locally.

'I am dallying with the idea of becoming respectable!' she wrote with lots of underlining and exclamation marks. 'If I sell up here I might have enough for a small dress shop. What do you think?'

He wrote back that he would keep his eyes open. But nothing came up and eighteen months later he died.

The really frightful thing was that her mother had not been told of her move and the letter telling her what had happened went to Lupus Street.

She used a great deal of money to hire a taxi to drive her to Dymock immediately and arrived too late for the funeral service. The mourners were gathered around the open grave. Her mother stood very erect and as Sarah began to tear across the grass towards her, her mother drew off her wedding ring and threw it onto the coffin.

Sarah had spent the morning in a state of grief which bordered on despair. This was the final straw. With a cry of agony she cast herself into the grave.

SEVENTEEN

1941

It was September and the leaves in the bluebell woods were turning all shades of gold. Rain had fallen the night before and the footpaths through the beech trees and silver birches were muddy, but where the trees gave way to huge mounds of blackberry bushes the coarse grass was dry and there were plenty of molehills for seating.

Bob, Dorothy and Holly had just finished a picnic and were all in various poses of repletion, eyes half closed, staring up at the gently moving treetops. They had spent a great deal of time together that summer and had reached the stage in their relationship where they no longer had to think what to say.

Dorothy murmured thoughtfully, 'I think we must have picked at least six pounds of blackberries. Mabs has given me some of her bee sugar, so I should be able to add some apples and make about twenty pounds of bramble jelly.'

'Bee sugar?' queried Bob.

'She keeps bees. If it's a bad year for nectar, you're allocated so much bee sugar.'

'Was it a bad year?' Bob asked, knowing the answer.

'Officially, yes. Unofficially, no.'

Holly said, 'So Aunty Mabs lied in other words.'

'Don't be censorious, Hol.' Dorothy grinned across the molehill they had used as a table. 'If you feel strongly about it you need not have any bramble jelly!'

'Aw . . . shucks!' said Holly and was deeply glad when Bob laughed uproariously. Her mission this summer had been to make Bob laugh again. She had found a deep satisfaction in thinking of Bob before everything else. It had enabled her to come to terms with Charlie's death and to do something positive about it. She had visited Winnie and Kildie. She had expected histrionics from both and had been surprised by their withdrawn composure. Kildie especially had changed; she was busy in a way she had never been before. Marcus had noticed it too because he had teased her about trying to lose weight. Winnie was quite the opposite; her wide stare and slow cautious movements reminded Holly of a frightened animal. Gran said, 'She needs someone to love. We all need someone to love.'

Holly wondered if Gran knew about Eric Battersby, or whether the Battersbys were in the big house any more.

But Gran was right because in loving Bob, Holly herself found salvation. And it was after Gran said those words that Holly knew she loved Bob.

She said now, 'Listen, you two. See that big leaf on the beech tree to the left of the path? Right at the top. Fluttering like mad?'

Mum said, 'The one with the mascara around the edges?'

Bob said, 'And the big dopey smile?'

'That's the one,' Holly agreed solemnly. 'Now, I am conducting an experiment. Sort of metaphysical. Based on the united will-power of a group of people. I want to write it up for Miss Jollybags next term, so please pay attention.'

'Yes, ma'am,' said Bob.

'I hope old Jollybags appreciates this,' Mum said.

'She will. I want us all to concentrate on bringing that leaf down at the count of ten. Look at it. Will it to drop off the tree when it hears that magic three-letter word. Now . . . one, two, three . . .' Mum started to laugh and Bob reached out with his napkin and flicked her. Holly counted on. When she reached eight the breeze strengthened and the leaf waved down at them, hanging on to its twig by a mere thread. 'Nine-and-a-half,' Holly intoned. 'Cheat!' Mum yelled. 'Nine and three-quarters,'

Holly continued inexorably just as the leaf fluttered down. 'Ten!' she yelled hurriedly.

And, just as she had hoped, Bob rolled on to his face, laughing helplessly.

He had helped her pick the beans last weekend and asked her how the plums were going. Holly and half the Lower Sixth were picking plums in the orchards around Wainlodes Hill as their war effort.

'OK,' she said. 'We're allowed to eat as many as we can. The idea is to sicken us of them. None of us is sick of them yet.'

'You're starved of sugar, that's what it is,' he said. 'I wish I could get some more chocolate—'

'You get us enough of everything as it is, Bob,' she put in quickly. 'It's just that the plums are really good this year.'

He put a handful of beans in the enamel bowl between them. 'What about school next week, Hol? Are you going?'

'I don't know. I ought to be doing something a bit more important than school.'

He stopped picking and watched her through the twisting leaves. She felt his eyes on her and coloured.

'Now that Mum has been sent to the Records Office, she's never here—'

'She's home soon after six, Hol. Be fair.'

'But I would be too if I went to the aircraft factory. Or something.'

'Yes. But, if you get home by four as usual, you will be able to light the fire and do your homework so that you have the evening together.'

'Yes, but—'

'And the assembly line at the factory is awful boring, Hol.'

'You've been talking to Mum!' she accused.

'I don't need to! I hear you two arguing the hind legs off several donkeys!' He reached through the vines and took her arm so that she was forced to stop picking. 'Hol, please stay on at school. For me.'

She swallowed and stood very still. If the impenetrable wall of stick beans had not been there she might have leaned her head on his shoulder then. But it was, so she did not.

'Will you, Hol? Please? I just hate the thought of you chucking it all away. Going into one of those huge workshops where you'll hear . . . everything. I don't reckon your father would like you to do that either.'

Holly closed her eyes and let herself think only of his fingers on her upper arm. When the silence became unbearable, she said simply, 'All right.'

He tugged her arm twice, companionably, and said just as simply, 'Thanks, Holly.'

She went to stay with Gran for half-term. Mum did not like her to be at the cottage all day on her own and anyway Gran had not seen much of any of them through the summer.

She was still anxious about Mum.

'They don't have no right sending her out to work whether she's fit for it or not!' she grumbled, picking the curly green tops and stripping them off into her big colander there and then.

'She likes it, Gran. It's not very exciting work, of course, but she meets other people—'

'All them airforce people, I s'ppose,' Gran put in.

'Other women, like herself, Gran.' Holly thought of the two Bobs who had been killed on the first day of May. She had been so foolishly jealous of them even in death when Mum had mourned them for so long. It was good to think that she was with about fifty other women now.

Gran said, 'She went so thin. At that service your Aunt Lizzie had for Charlie, I thought she looked ready to drop.'

'Well . . . that was an awful time.'

Gran straightened with difficulty and looked at her

granddaughter. 'I thought it would be worse for you, my girl. You always had a leaning to your cousin.'

Holly felt almost guilty. She wanted to tell Gran that in a way she had lost Charlie last Christmas. She wanted to tell Gran . . . something.

She bowed her head as she picked randomly among the tall greens.

'I think . . . you won't laugh, will you? I think I might be – sort of – in love. With someone.'

'Well, don't make that an excuse for picking the sprouts before we've had any frost on 'em!' Gran snapped. 'Come on, we've got enough greens here for our dinner. And there's enough chicken too.' She stumped down the garden path without a glance at the ferns. Holly followed, feeling as if she'd been caught in a naughty deed.

Gran went into the kitchen and put the colander under the tap which she then turned on full force. She picked up her little kitchen knife and tackled the potatoes waiting in a bowl.

'I'll do those, Gran,' Holly said nervously.

'No, you won't. You peel them so thick there's precious little spud left!' She glanced sideways. 'Wash them greens and put them in the pot. And mind there's no snails left in! How them French can possibly eat snails beats me!'

Holly rinsed carefully, leaf by leaf. She could have told Gran about escargots, but she probably knew anyway.

Gran said, 'So it was off with the old and on with the new, was it? All I can say is, poor Charlie!'

'Yes.' Holly thought of Charlie, so amazingly in love with Kildie; had he really thought Kildie was pregnant and that their child would live on for him? She swallowed.

'Well, he got what he wanted before he went, I suppose,' Gran said on a sharp sigh as she put the potato saucepan onto the gas stove. 'Poor beggar.'

'Oh Gran,' Holly said.

'You knew all about it, my girl. You were the first to see him that morning. St Stephen's day, weren't it?'

'Yes, Gran.'

'You were fifteen then. And now you're sixteen and in love with someone else. Surprising what a few months can do.'

Holly sobbed. 'Almost a year, Gran!'

'May was when we heard.'

'But don't you see . . . my heart was broken – I *thought* my heart was broken on St Stephen's day!'

Gran turned, surprised by the tears.

'You don't think I'm blaming you, do you? I'm glad – I'm that thankful, my girl – that the good Lord sent you someone.' Suddenly Gran did something most unusual. She took Holly in her arms and cradled her against one black-clad shoulder.

'But, listen to me, child, you're not Kildie James. You're Holly James. And there's a world of difference. Kildie can find consolation – like her ma before her – without any difficulty at all. You got to go deeper, Holly. You got to go real deep. And long. And hard. But when you find it, my girl, it will stay with you. Just remember that. Always. It will stay with you.' Gran turned and went back to the potatoes as abruptly as she had left them. 'Even after death.'

'Oh Gran!' Holly wailed. 'I've never forgotten . . . never . . . so long ago, but I've never forgotten.'

'And what haven't you never forgotten, Holly?' Gran asked as if indulging a small child.

'That day I saw you – Mum said you'd slipped and fallen on Grandad's grave. But I knew really. All the time. You were holding him, weren't you? You were holding Grandad to you!'

Gran leaned down to lower the gas under the bubbling saucepan. She said, 'Are those greens ready, my girl? Let's put them in with the spuds. Save on the gas.' She stuffed the springy curly greens into the boiling water and crammed on the lid. Then she said quietly, 'It were something Adrian Frost taught me, our Hol. That was your Uncle Edward's father. A crazy man, but wise too. I'll tell you. No-one else, mind.'

335

'Oh Gran.'

'I'm no good at explaining, Holly. But what he said was you got to train your thoughts – your head – through your body. Your Grandad is alive in me. An' . . . an' I've got to *know* that. My body has got to know it.' She paused and sighed deeply. 'All I can tell you, Hol, is that when I lie by your grandad out there—' she jerked her head to the window, '—then it's easier for me to know we're still together.'

There was a long silence. Gran lifted the saucepan lid and jabbed at its contents. Holly wept very quietly.

They went for a walk. Down Middle Lane to visit Mrs Thrupp at Applecross, and then across the fields to a big loop in the little river Leadon. A watery sunshine made it seem like spring instead of autumn. Holly skimmed some flat stones like Grandad had showed her years before and Gran laughed and said, 'Five hops! That's better than your Dad, our Hol!' Holly laughed too and wondered whether this was going to be her thing in life: to make people laugh. First Bob, now Gran. Maybe she would write a proper letter to Dad tonight; not one of the stilted things she'd been writing since Winnie told her . . . what Winnie had told her. Tell him about this afternoon and how Gran was pleased because she could skim stones across the Leadon. She tried to take Gran's arm, but was shaken off summarily. Even so, she felt very uplifted. Everything was somehow so wonderfully, yet sadly, beautiful.

'If I en't going fast enough for you, my girl, run on ahead!' Gran said. 'I can't get up that bank. You go on. Look at the view over the gate and then slide back down. I know that's what you want to do!'

Holly laughed herself, her euphoric melancholy disappearing in an instant. The bank reared up at this point towards the Dean Forest; there was a five-barred gate in the hedge at the top. If you ran hard enough the impetus would take you to the gate where you could cling on, then turn and slide back down on the wet grass sitting on your heels. She and Winnie and Charlie had done it when they had visited Gran in the old days.

'Go on!' urged Gran. 'You're not too old to be a child, my girl!'

Holly walked back a few paces to measure her distance and then ran at it. She had forgotten how hard it was and yesterday's rain had made the grass unusually muddy. In fact, some other idiots had done this quite recently and churned up the surface. She dug in the toes of her school shoes and pumped her legs madly. Just as she thought she must slide ignominiously back, she managed to make a grab for the bottom bar of the gate and hang grimly on. Below her Gran cackled a kind of cheer. She pulled herself up, put her arms akimbo on the top of the gate and concentrated on breathing.

The effort was worth the making. It was as if the whole of the ancient royal forest was spread below her, although, in fact, she knew this to be only a small corner of it. She remembered Dad telling her that Dean has supplied most of the oak for the Navy in Nelson's time and she looked at the enormous trees sitting among the undergrowth of fern and saplings like solid granite sculptures and wished that this war could be like that one. How simple things were when you read about them years later in books. This happened and that happened and the million tiny incidents that made the mountain of an event were lost, or smoothed out in some way. Blanche's voice spoke in her ear with some exasperation, 'Well, you're not going to cry about *that*, are you? All you do lately is cry!' And she smiled a watery smile and said, 'I've only been crying with happiness, Blanche Cooke!' And they both giggled and at the sound there was a squeak of alarm from the hedgerow further along and a head emerged from the ferns. It was Winnie.

Holly too squeaked and then said, 'Oh, it's you,' and Winnie said, 'Oh, it's you,' and then they both grinned sheepishly and Winnie emerged fully and came towards her.

She had changed; there was no doubt about that. From the few things Gran had said, and from discussions with Mum about the whole situation at the Gatehouse, Holly had assumed that Winnie had been press-ganged into becoming a kind of drudge. Certainly she looked somewhat bedraggled as she shook the dried bracken from her skirt and scraped her shoes on the grass to clean off the mud, but no more bedraggled than Holly herself, whose coat front was liberally daubed with mud. The difference lay in the fact that Winnie was wearing the kind of clothes she had only 'dressed up' in before. She had no coat or cardigan and her blouse was the very latest fashion, it had an elasticated neckline that could either cling coyly around the throat or be stretched right off the shoulder. At present it was indeed so far off the shoulder that it was obvious Winnie wore neither vest nor brassière. Her skin was blotched and the lipstick, put on much too thickly, was smudged. Even so, she carried her skimpy costume with a certain daring aplomb.

'Well. Fancy seeing you up here,' Winnie opened, standing six feet away, hands on hips, staring brazenly at Holly.

'I'm with Gran. For the week. Half-term,' Holly came back, biting back the obvious questions for the more general, 'How are you?'

'Fine. Marvellous. You should come over. You might cheer up poor old Ma.'

'But Gran says she won't let anyone in the house.'

'Oh, you're different. Gran's trying to protect you, as per usual.'

'From what?'

Winnie mimicked, 'From what – from what? From real life. From real misery. You know, little things like that.'

'Win – I'm sorry I hit you. It was just—'

'I know why you hit me. I know why you haven't been over since. I know *everything*!'

'I'm sorry,' Holly repeated miserably, thinking now of the baby and Charlie's death and how she had cut herself off from it all so conveniently and turned to Bob.

'Don't be. Real life is great fun at times.' Winnie dropped her voice. 'Guess who is back there in the ferns?'

Holly said even more unhappily, 'Eric Battersby, I suppose.'

Winnie crowed with delight. 'You haven't forgotten him then? And my plan for educating him?'

Holly leaned over the gate earnestly. 'Listen, Winnie. You must be careful. We're doing all that stuff at school and you could have a baby so easily—' She stopped because Winnie was laughing helplessly.

'Oh Hol. You don't change do you? Look at you – school gabardine, sensible shoes, lisle stockings – and navy blue knickers I bet!' She calmed down and came a little nearer. 'And all your education is happening at school. Oh Hol. Let me give you a lesson. What do you think these are?' She pointed to one of the red marks just above the elastic of her blouse. 'They're love bites, Hol. And why do you think my lipstick is all over the place and there are leaves in my hair?'

Holly said, 'Shut up, Winnie. You always have to spoil everything with that horrible talk.'

'Sometimes education is horrible, cousin dear. You don't like the thought of your dad wanting to give Kildie love bites, do you? But he does. He might have already done so—'

'Like Charlie?' Holly said loudly. 'Like Charlie did?'

Winnie was cut off in mid-stream, her mouth still open.

Holly said bitterly, 'Is that something you actually did not know, Winnie? That Charlie had been with Kildie all Christmas afternoon and night? That they wanted a baby? That they tried to have a baby? And they evidently failed? Is that a bit of education you missed, Winnie?'

She did not wait to see what reaction she had provoked. She turned, squatted on her heels and pushed off. When she reached Gran again she was filthy with mud.

Gran said resignedly, 'We shall be the rest of the week cleaning up your clothes, young lady!'

Holly wondered if ever she could clear up her mind. And then she remembered Bob and smiled and hugged Gran's arm and Gran said, 'Don't get near me, Holly James! This is a clean coat. Or was when we left the cottage!'

Holly said, 'Oh Gran. I do love you!'

1930

It was two weeks after Walter James's funeral and at last Emmie was alone with him. The children had been removed from the Grange and taken to their homes; Kildie was back at the bank, Sarah had gone . . . wherever she went. Jim was on late turn so he would not be popping in this afternoon as he had done last week when he was on early turn. Until Kildie came home at six, she had eight precious hours.

She crouched by the raised mound of earth under which Walter's dear body lay in its coffin. She was calm now, though she knew that later she would be racked with the terrible sobbing of despair that overcame her when she had time to think what had happened. She had used the outside lavatory under the veranda often since that terrible day, the seventh of November. The wide wooden seat supported her grief and through the open door she could see the fern bed beginning to sprout along the perpetually weeping wall. She thought of the keening women of Israel and understood their need for ritualized and noisy grief. She could not give way to such a luxury. She knew the family were frightened to leave her alone; there was always someone within call. She thought that probably the iron roof of the veranda would reverberate to her private sobbing, but that could not be helped. They must put up with that.

She looked all around her now. The churchyard was deserted and nobody would be coming to do flowers or polish brasses in the church today. She knelt down by

Walter's grave, bowed her head at the sudden intensity of pain and let herself think of him.

Twenty-nine years they had had. It was not long enough but it was more than she deserved. It had been a marriage of convenience for him; in a way she had taken advantage of that. There had been other women – in Hereford certainly, probably hundreds of them in London where he was living – who would have been far more suitable candidates. But she had dangled this vision before his eyes; a small station with a free house, responsibilities easily shelved or shared, time to read, time to fish, time to simply be. She had known instinctively it was what he needed; she had known that the idea of pastoral bliss would take hold easily and quickly. She had also known that none of the women he might wish to share it with him, would consider being the wife of a country station master. The woman he really adored was dead. He needed to get away, start again on a completely different tack.

She said aloud, 'I got you on the rebound, Walter. And then, when you was all at sea after losing your Pa, I . . .' She grinned tremulously. 'I seduced you, din't I? A big raw-boned country woman I was; prac'lly forty. And I seduced *you* who was a gentleman and a scholar and in love with someone else.'

Tears filled her eyes as she recalled the hot night she had gone to his room. She knew she should not think of such things now. Walter's spirit had left his physical body; he was not here under this earth, he was in heaven with his father and his beautiful dead mother.

She blinked hard on tears and whispered fiercely, 'But your body was what I knew, Walter. It was what I loved. I didn't understand your mind, even when you talked to me. I loved your round face and your brown hair and the veins on your hands and your toes and shoulders and . . .' She was weeping freely now and put a gloved hand over her shaking mouth to stop the words and the sobs.

And a voice said above her, 'Emmie. I came as soon as

341

I heard. I'm sorry. So sorry. He was too young – hardly any retirement—'

She leapt to her feet and turned angrily towards the voice. It was Adrian Frost. Huge in a caped overcoat and bowler hat he stood mountainously by her side holding out his arms.

Her anger melted. She cast herself into them.

It was the first time she had allowed herself to be comforted. Mr Edwards had patted her shoulder and she had held herself tensely until he finished. Kildie had wept into her nightgown when they went to bed; Dorothy and Jim had held her between them. But she had remained dry-eyed and strong in the presence of everyone. She had to be. For Walter's sake she had to continue to hold them all up, their heads just above the waters of life.

And now this man, who had come out of the blue to help Walter set up a marriage for Lizzie and Edward, who had given so generously of his money that he now had none left . . . this man was the one who could offer her comfort.

He said above her gasping apologies, 'Of course I couldn't hear you. But I have eyes. I recognized your grief.' He tightened his hold and after a while said, 'There is no-one within hearing distance anyway. Scream, woman. Scream, for God's sake. Be angry that he has gone. Be angry with him for leaving you.'

She lifted her head slightly, her nose and throat were choked with tears and mucus but she gasped, 'Not with him – never with him.'

'Then with God. Just scream.'

She could not scream. She gave a gasping shout of protest then she rested her head on his damp-smelling coat and let her breath go in long drawn-out groans of despair. He measured his breathing to hers. It was as if he too was wailing her grief, taking some of it from her in the sharing.

When at last it died, he whispered, 'You have to take

him inside yourself now. He must live in you. Do you understand?'

Now that the storm of wailing was over, she felt coldly miserable. She shook her head hopelessly.

He said, 'Yes, you do. You took him inside you every time you made love. And I think that was often.'

Her responding groan was different now; it came from her abdomen and lower. She whispered, 'Sinful bodies . . .'

He quoted, ' "Sinful bodies, made clean by his body." ' He laughed gently. 'I am no Christian, Emmie. But that is what the good book says. And you will take Walter inside your body without sin and he will remain there for ever.'

'How?' She lifted her head and wailed the question in despair. 'How can I do that? He's dead! He's in there – dead—' She turned her head to the mound of earth.

He said, 'You must *know* it, Emmie. You must simply . . . know it.'

She nodded, still hopeless. ' 'Slike the Reverend said. Faith. That's all it is, faith.'

'Call it what you like. It has to be certain.' He held her off slightly and then nodded. 'Come, lie down. On top of him. Lie on top of Walter.'

She shrank away, appalled.

He shook her, gently, insistently. 'You have to do something so that your body knows and understands. Let's leave the mind for a moment. You have put your body on Walter's body often, Emmie. Do it now. Come.'

'It – it's muddy—'

He laughed, actually laughed. Then he released her and unbuttoned his huge greatcoat and swung it over the raw earth.

'Lie down, Emmie.'

She stared at him, amazed and incredulous. But after a while she knelt on the hem of the coat and then with a sudden cry she pitched forward, feeling the shape of the

343

mound under the tweed, holding it to her, herself to it, straining to feel Walter's body far beneath her.

Above her prone body, Adrian Frost, pastoral poet and man of passion, watched and wept.

Later he sat her by the fire in the living-room and went into the kitchen alone to make them some lunch. She pushed a poker into the banked-up ash and revealed the volcano beneath and then stared into it wondering what had happened down there in the churchyard, whether she had brought back some kind of comfort or whether it had all been a surrender to histrionics.

When he brought in raw onions and cheese and a huge pot of tea she said, 'How did you know I always have a raw onion for my dinner?'

He said, 'I did not know. They were there. I like them.'

She smiled unwillingly. 'I thought you must be . . . a bit odd like that.'

'Psychic? No, Emmie, the only comforts I can offer are these—' he held out his arms, '—and now this. Eat, my dear. The body affects the mind. Keep it fed. Keep it warm. It will heal you, Emmie. Your strong body will heal your shocked mind.'

Tears – treacherously easy now – welled again. 'I wish my body weren't so strong, Mr Frost. I wish I could've died with Walter.'

'Like the Indian women. Suttee.' He told her of the fiery funeral pyres. She nodded.

'You could not do that, Emmie. They need you.' He jerked a head at a family snap, framed on the chiffonier.

She followed his gaze.

'No. They do not. There is Kildie, of course. But Jim would take her. They are like brother and sister. He would take her.'

'Would that be . . . quite wise?' he asked tentatively.

She looked at him sharply and tried to brush the question aside.

'Whatever do you mean? She adores Doll. Doll was her

344

schoolteacher before she was . . . and Holly. She and Holly are real close friends.'

'Of course. And yet I think Kildie is better here with you.'

Still she blustered. 'An old woman and an empty house?'

Adrian Frost said, 'You know what I mean, Emmie. I have eyes and a brain, and I have visited this house every time I have come to see my son. Kildie is very like her mother. And she thinks too much of Jim. Better to keep them apart.'

Her grey eyes flashed and then were still. He leaned forward and cut her onion into slices. The sharp smell filled the room. Outside, the November day was dark and damp.

She began to tell him about her family. He listened, unsurprised. The molten mass of the fire suddenly burst into flame and licked up the chimney. He nodded, then nodded again.

When she had finished he said, 'Now eat.' She obeyed him and he said, 'I will make some enquiries. In London. About Lizzie and Sarah.'

She munched, enjoying food for the first time since November the seventh.

'What sort of enquiries? Why?' she asked through her bread.

He shrugged. 'I'm not sure what kind of enquiries. As to why . . . because I don't really believe what you have told me.'

Her eyes flashed. 'I have told you what Walter told me. Walter would not have lied to me.'

'Not knowingly. Of course not. Perhaps Walter was . . . duped.'

She resumed eating, then said, 'Don't. Don't do anything. There's no need now. Walter is dead.'

'But you're not. And neither is he while you are alive.'

'I – we – don't want to know,' she said definitely.

He smiled. 'What don't you want to know, Emmie?'

She banged her bread back onto her plate. 'Anything!' she said angrily. 'Anything about the past. 'Tis water under the bridge, Mr Frost!'

He waited while she calmed down, then again while she finished her food. Then he said, 'You see, Emmie . . . sometimes it is important for people to know about the water under the bridge. I do think that in this case it is important that *you* should know – and then you can make up your mind whether the family should also know. Do you understand that?'

'Of course I understand it!' she flashed. 'I don't agree with it, but I understand it!'

He said humbly, 'I apologize. I did not mean to imply you were stupid.' He looked up at her and smiled slightly. 'Sometimes, Emmie, I think there is nothing in the world you do not understand.'

She stared at him for a long moment, then took a deep breath.

'Do you really think you could find out the truth for sure?'

'I do not know. Parish records . . . maybe. But I could try.'

She turned to put coal on the fire. When she replaced the tongs in the grate he was already donning his filthy coat. She tutted and fetched a clothes brush but the mud was still wet and would not be removed.

He said, 'Stop fussing, woman. I am a poet and expected to look like a scarecrow!' He pecked her forehead. 'Goodbye, Emmie. I don't think I'll see you again. I am glad I have known you.'

She did not question this. As she went to the door she said, 'You and Walter . . . you talk to me as if I'm like you. Clever. You talk to me as if I am equal.'

'Then we should not. Because you are superior to both of us.' He stood in the porch and looked down Middle Lane. 'You think Walter married you for expediency and then loved you for your strong good body. That is not so, Emmie. He loved *you* – all of you. Your whole self. Just as you loved him.'

He turned without another word and made for the station. And she closed the door, leaned against it, and smiled.

Kildie opened the back door as she had done since Walter died, tentatively, fearfully.

'Gran? Are you all right?'

Emmie turned from the gas stove, the teapot in her hand.

'I am, Kildie. Come in quickly and close the door on this dreadful night.'

But still Kildie hovered.

'Gran, I've brought a friend with me. Someone from the bank. I wondered . . . I hoped you wouldn't mind.'

Emmie said, 'Then go round to the front like you should when there's guests, Kildie. Bring her in proper like. The door is on the latch. You can put your brollies in the stand and go through to the living-room. We'll have boiled eggs.'

'It's not a her, Gran. It's a chap. A nice chap. He plays the piano.'

Emmie, already planning on more bread and butter and the cake left over from the funeral, said sharply and automatically, 'You're only fifteen, Kildie!'

'Oh this is nothing serious, Gran!' Kildie glanced over her shoulder and a snort of laughter came from behind her. 'He's only fifteen too. But he's ever such good company.'

'And he's there all the time, is he?' Emmie said drily and pulled on the door handle. 'Come on then, my lad! Skulking about in the garden on a damp night like this! Get in by the fire and behave yourself!'

Kildie laughed aloud with relief. She had not been able to face Gran on her own again; the total misery of the cottage without Walter was impossible to bear.

'His name is Bill Masters, Gran. Bill, this is my Gran.'

Emmie made sure her hands were full so that there was no question of over-formality. She shoved them ahead of her into the bright, gas-lit living-room. The table was only half covered by a cloth; she and Kildie always sat by the fire with their tea. Kildie fluffed it out properly and Emmie set down the tray.

Bill Masters looked older than his years, and obviously thought Kildie was the bee's knees. Everything was the bee's knees as far as Bill Masters was concerned.

'I say, this is a jolly decent piano,' he said when they ventured into the icy front parlour where it sat in solitary state draped with an Indian shawl. 'It's the regular bee's knees here, isn't it?'

And then, when he left for the eight forty-five, 'It's been a tophole evening, Mrs James. I think you,' he swallowed and blurted nervously, 'I think you're the absolute bee's knees!'

She let Kildie walk with him to the station and she smiled again as she closed the door. Kildie and Bill Masters. After all, Sarah had been Kildie's age when she'd got herself into trouble and Kildie was Sarah's daughter. Kildie and Bill Masters . . . whatever had or had not happened all those years ago, if Kildie made a match with Bill Masters, there would be no need to worry about Kildie and Jim.

She walked back into the warm living-room and riddled ash through the coals ready to bank the fire for another night.

'Water under the bridge,' she said aloud. 'Just water under the bridge!'

EIGHTEEN

1941

It was during that autumn and winter that Kildie began to write regularly to Jim in Edmonton. Until then her letters had been few and far between. She was conscious that she had returned to Marcus that summer of 1940 against Jim's wishes. In spite of that the whole situation had filled her with a kind of triumph; as if she had won both men. But what with Dorothy's attitude and everything, it had been difficult to know what kind of voice she should adopt in her letters and for a long time they tended to consist of the sort of messages she associated with seaside postcards. 'Dearest Jim, the weather has been simply awful today and Mrs Davis is like a witch. But wish you were here!' She had sent off an ornate Christmas card with silver letters announcing 'A Happy Christmas to a Wonderful Brother'

And then Charlie had arrived. And the following May he had died. And there was no baby.

She kept her grief right inside, in quite a small compartment. It was so small that sometimes she forgot it was there. She would lie in Marcus' arms – because their reconciliation had been everything he hoped – and groan aloud with pleasure and then, when sanity prevailed again, she would lie there idly planning the next day's menu and wondering whether she could grow a crop of artichokes. She seemed to have inherited Emmie's green fingers and had chopped up part of the lawn to plant some winter greens. It was another way of pushing her grief into that small compartment.

Marcus had been appalled.

'You're not to do heavy work like that, baby!' he said, holding her muddy fingers in his hands, more horrified than she was by the state of her nails. 'You could injure yourself. You know how delicate you are.'

'Oh darling daddy!' She kissed him lingeringly. 'Digging for victory! That's all I'm doing!'

'My God! You're at the store twice a week, you've got this place to keep going – the cooking, the cleaning and now the blasted garden! I thought I paid Stan Davis to do that?'

'Sweetheart. You pay *Mrs* D. to do the cleaning. *You* do the cooking and the shopping. *Mr* D. mows the grass and does the borders. Can't I have the teeniest little vegetable plot?'

It was not strictly true – any of it – any more. She did most of the cooking now and had relieved Mrs Davis of the vacuum cleaner altogether. But Marcus still did the shopping.

However, with dire warnings from Mrs Davis of imminent back trouble, her Stan dug out the side lawn completely and Kildie planted potatoes and artichokes. She picked her own greens for Christmas and after the American navy was bombed at Pearl Harbour and entered the War, she proposed a special American evening in the store, the whole place to be decked out with stars and stripes.

She had something to tell Jim then.

'My dear, it was a good Christmas in spite of the War. Do you think I am awful to think that? But I have never done a Christmas dinner before and to cook my own greens and roast my own artichokes was quite an experience! Dorothy and Holly are looking very well. Holly made some crackers that really went bang. Gran brought a chicken with her. I wanted Edward and Lizzie and Winnie to come, but apparently Lizzie won't go outside the house and won't let anyone in now except Gran. Dear old Gran is doing too much, of course, but is not looking too bad. I worked out that she must be almost

350

seventy-nine now, Jim. Approaching her eightieth year. That sounds properly old, doesn't it?'

She had already written to him telling him about Charlie. It had come to her suddenly that she could not bear this thing alone, and Jim was the only person who would not condemn her. Had he not fought for her with his fists? He would understand that she had not done anything really wrong. She had hurt no-one, only herself.

'It is so difficult to describe what it was like, Jim. You have spoken of our family bond. Perhaps it was that. I opened the door, feeling alone and not very well, and there he was. My family. He represented all of you at that moment. I knew he had always had a soft spot for me. Even when we were children he used to show off in front of me. Did you ever notice? That time in the fens? And before then, at Grandad's funeral, it was his idea to watch from the top of the churchyard. There were lots of times, Jim. There was always something special between us. I expect you have heard the story from Gran, or maybe Dorothy. But I can only tell you that it seemed the most natural thing in the world. I loved him, Jim. I will always love him. So much of what I do now, I do because of him – for him. I hope you will not think less of me because of this, my dear.'

The letter that came back was all that she could have hoped for.

'Kildie, I had heard nothing about this from anyone, but am honoured that you have chosen to tell me what happened between you and Charlie. It is obvious this was no frivolous affair, my dear. That boy loved you although he was eight years younger than you. Age makes little difference, Kildie. You are very young for your years; Charlie was evidently mature for his. As you say, you hurt no-one . . .'

She thought of Marcus and knew that he had been hurt; she thought of Holly who had so obviously known and must have been hurt because she loved Charlie herself. And then she thought of Charlie. Mature for his years?

351

Quite the opposite. He had been just an overgrown schoolboy revelling in his newest acquisition. Those letters of his! Would it have lasted? Could it have lasted? Supposing she had been pregnant and had gone to Gran and waited for him to come home from the War. Could they have lived together in penury?

She put her hands over her face. She still loved him, but, oh God, she was glad now that there had been no baby.

She wrote to Jim: 'Your letter has been such a consolation. I cannot begin to tell you how much I needed to confess to you what had happened and receive your absolution. I have been trying to think what I could do as a kind of penance. For dear Charlie. Something that would please him and you too. And I am going to visit – force myself – on poor Lizzie and see if I can help her. You are so right, dear Jim, about the family. They mean everything to me too. In fact, Jim, I sometimes wonder whether I am only capable of love within the family. First you, then Charlie.'

This time he wrote back about his life in Canada. About the intense cold already that winter. About the fascination of maintaining the huge aircraft and then test flying them over the Great Lakes themselves. Of the kindness and generosity of the local people. Of a visit from Miss Cecilia Larkay whose brother, Robert, had been a guest at the cottage on the Green . . . He said no more of the family.

Much to her surprise, Holly enjoyed Christmas at Hill House. She had not wanted to go one bit because Bob had Christmas Day off and they would miss seeing him. But somehow Bob got himself invited and even borrowed a car so that they could go when they wished and leave when they'd had enough. They picked up Gran and her chicken, plucked and drawn but with its head still dangling from the newspaper coat it wore.

It was good to see Kildie somehow returned to the girl they had all known, the fat all gone, the smile back in place even if it was now more cautious and controlled. She had organized the meal down to the last forcemeat ball, and they sat down at three o'clock and pulled Holly's specially made crackers – with some help from Miss Joliffe's laboratory. Marcus got the motto that said, 'He who laughs last, laughs longest.' And he put Kildie's knuckles to his lips and said, 'Well, that's true in my case.'

They were a little lost in the big chairs and very big rooms of the house. Gran kept looking over her shoulder as if she thought someone was creeping up on her over the thick pile of the carpet. Dorothy reacted to so much space as she had done years before in the fens and danced across to the french windows with her arms outstretched. Kildie switched on the radiogram and held out a hand to Marcus. Bob danced with Dorothy and then with Holly. It was so perfect Holly thought she might weep.

Bob was perfectly at ease. He 'saw to' the drinks at the large cocktail cabinet against the wall, fetched ice from the refrigerator in the kitchen. Dorothy and Holly exchanged glances; it was obvious this was his kind of lifestyle at home.

Kildie said, 'I understand from Jim's last letter that your sister has visited him, Bob?'

Holly watched Dorothy become suddenly alert. Bob said easily, 'I haven't heard from home myself for a coupla weeks, Mrs Villiers. But Cecy promised she'd go see him and she's a girl who keeps her promises.'

'Oh she's kept this one. Miss Cecilia Larkay. That's right, isn't it?'

'Sure is.' Bob was beaming.

Dorothy said, 'What other news, Kildie? I didn't think any post was getting through what with Christmas and everything.'

'That was all, I think.' Kildie sounded vague and she did not offer to show the letter around.

Gran grunted. 'Well, now them yankee-doodle-dandies or whatever they call themselves have joined in, it'll all be over soon and Jim back home.'

Marcus said, 'Kildie's got this great idea for the store. A sort of dress show based on America.'

'We need to get hold of some of their uniforms. Can't you just imagine those dear little sailor hats they wear? And I thought I might get Lizzie to make me an evening dress from the Stars and Stripes.'

'Lizzie?' Gran said.

'It might be just the thing to bring her back to life, Gran,' Kildie said firmly.

Gran sucked her gums for half a minute while Marcus began to put obstacles in the way. Then she said, 'Why don't you take our Holly? Lizzie might not let you in. But if Holly has gone to see Winnie it will be different.'

Holly said quickly, 'She lets you in every day, Gran. So if you go with Kildie—'

Gran tucked her sharp chin into the top of her black blouse.

'Thought the idea was to give me a day off?' she said.

Nobody had mentioned giving Gran a day off, but nobody was going to remind her of that either.

Kildie said, 'It would please Jim so much. To know we were going to try to cheer poor Lizzie up. The James girls to the rescue!'

Everyone laughed, even Dorothy.

It was arranged that Kildie should drive down in the Wolsley, pick Holly up from the Green and they would continue together to Dymock. A Saturday in January was fixed; but Kildie changed that twice for various reasons and it was the first day in February when they set off.

Dorothy had already left for work, pedalling slowly down the lane, bent against the rain, her body and half her bicycle muffled in one of the latest cycling capes. It was a genuine February fill-dyke.

Kildie shook out her umbrella and came in, shivering melodramatically.

'Isn't it absolutely beastly, darling? Sorry I'm late. Of course Marcus can't use the Morgan when it's wet –

the hood is unreliable. So I had to go into the stores first.'

'Have you got the material?' Holly asked, pulling the brim down on her school velour so that the rain would drip away from her neck.

'Yes. And a pattern. And pins and tacking thread . . . I'm not going to give her a reason for saying no.'

'If she's too ill to do it, that will have to be that.'

Holly was dreading seeing Winnie again. The fact that they had changed the arrangements so often would not have pleased Winnie any more than it had Holly. She would want to get it over too. Holly wondered whether she could possibly dread the day as much as Holly did.

Kildie said, 'What about bringing wellingtons? You're sure to want to go outside with Winnie however wet it is.'

'Holes in both. I mended them with cycle patches last night but the patches will lift if I get them wet.'

'Oh my God – what are wellingtons for except to get wet!' Kildie opened the door and struggled with her umbrella again. 'Marcus will get you some new ones, don't worry. What size are you?'

Holly hated admitting to her big feet. 'Sevens,' she mumbled as she slammed the front door and turned the key and put it on the ledge of the porch. 'And you can't get wellies without a permit.'

Kildie opened the car door for her. 'Marcus can,' she said, grinning. 'Matter of fact Marcus can get anything, do most things.' She used the self-starter. 'Except dissuade me from seeing my family. He did his best – the first time he said that Dymock was too depressing for me. The second, it was not good for you. And this time, of course, he needed the Wolsley. He didn't think I could get ready in time to go to work with him.' She chuckled. 'I wouldn't have bothered any more, except that I know it would please your father.' She drove to the Tewkesbury Road and turned left. 'Sometimes I feel closer to Jim now than I did when he was at home.'

Holly said nothing. Dad and Kildie . . . Kildie and Dad. Was it possible? Of course not.

They went first to Gran's to make sure everything was all right.

'Thank the good Lord you came this time,' Gran was looking distinctly harassed; even her hat was askew. 'They'm in a fine old tissle over there. That family – the Battersbys – up and left a week ago. Took half the silver with them. Squire's taking it out on Edward, for some reason. So Edward's taking it out on our Lizzie and Win. You'll 'ear them a-crying and carrying on before you get out of the car!'

Holly would have postponed the visit yet again had it been up to her, but Kildie had cast herself in the role of saviour and was not to be diverted a third time. They drove through the imposing gateway and swung around behind the tall, crenellated house. The rain swept across the banks of rhododendron and the birches thrashed in a sudden wind.

'Looks like a haunted house!' Kildie quipped, holding down her skirt as she opened her door. 'My God. No wonder poor Lizzie's going into a decline stuck here!'

Holly held her velour hard onto her head and thought of Winnie, also stuck here with no hope of escape.

The inside of the Gatehouse was at least dry, but offered very little comfort when compared with the cottage on the Green let alone Hill House. Lizzie was still in bed; Winnie was doing vegetables at the sink. She looked so different from the Winnie of last half-term. Gone was the make-up; the perm had grown out into rat's tails, she wore a jumper and skirt of awful antiquity.

'Hello.' She allowed her cheek to be kissed by Kildie and, after a terrible moment of indecision on both sides, by Holly too. But that seemed to soften her. 'It . . . it's nice to see you.' She rolled down the sleeves of her jumper and picked up the kettle. 'Shall I make some tea?'

'That would be nice.' Kildie, surprisingly, picked up the

knife. I'll finish the sprouts. Then I can take a cup of tea to your mother.'

Winnie said gloomily, 'I told her you were coming. She said she didn't want to see you.'

'We can't always have what we want,' Kildie said, undaunted. 'There's some biscuits in that bag, Winnie. Put them on a plate, there's a dear. You can look at the material if you like.'

Winnie unwrapped it carefully and shook it out. It was dark blue artificial silk with stars on one side of the length, stripes the other.

'Can you see the difficulty?' Kildie went on. 'I think the bodice should display the stars and the skirt the stripes.'

Winnie stared at the dress length for a long time.

'Gosh,' she said at last.

'It is attractive, isn't it? What do you think, Hol?'

'Yes,' Holly nodded. She was not in the least interested. She was thinking of Bob who had told her tightly the evening before that he would be going on another raid quite soon. She wondered if they were waiting to be scrambled even now. She thought, Please God, let him be all right.

Winnie said, 'Actually, Kildie, if Ma won't help, I think I could cut something out for you. On the cross. So that it swathed over one shoulder maybe. And the stripes would be diagonal then too and sort of drape over the hips . . .'

Kildie looked over her shoulder. 'Winnie! That sounds brilliant. Could you do it really?'

'Well, Ma used to help me alter my clothes. And I've been making things for ages now. I made one of those new blouses with the elastic in the top.' She folded the material carefully and laid it on the table then looked at Holly. 'You saw it, didn't you, Holly?'

Holly nodded.

Kildie was full of admiration. 'Well I never. You've inherited a lot from your mother. I didn't realize.'

Winnie laid a tray carefully. 'The only snag is . . .' She

poured the tea. 'I would need . . . I mean, I should have to keep doing fittings, Kildie.'

'Well, I could pop down whenever—'

'No, I mean, I should need to be with you. Stay with you.' Winnie looked up from the teapot. 'I couldn't work here anyway. Meals to get and Dad always late . . . you know.'

Kildie said slowly, 'I see.' She sipped her tea. 'What about your mother, Winnie? Could you leave her? How would they manage?'

'If I wasn't here, they'd have to manage, wouldn't they?' Winnie asked belligerently.

Kildie sipped again. 'That's true. That is perfectly true. I'm not sure what Marcus would say . . . he's a very private person as you know.'

'Ma says you can twist him around your little finger,' Winnie said, smiling as beguilingly as she knew how.

Kildie laughed. 'I suppose I can,' she agreed. 'Anyway, let's see what your mother says first. The purpose of the exercise is to snap her out of this awful depression she's in.'

'Well if I wasn't here, she'd soon snap out of it!' Winnie said unbeguilingly.

'Yes. Well . . . we'll see.'

Kildie poured more tea and put some biscuits on another plate. 'I'll just take these up. You two have a nice chat.' She glanced at Holly meaningfully over the top of Winnie's lank locks. 'Tell Winnie all about Bob Larkay, Hol. Such a coincidence that his sister is visiting Jim.'

But Winnie was not interested in anything Holly might have to say. She crammed another biscuit into her mouth and spoke through it.

'I've got to get away, Hol. If Kildie won't take me, can I come to you?'

Holly was too surprised to respond immediately as she should have done.

Winnie said bitterly, 'This is your chance to punish me, Hol. And you're going to, aren't you? Just cos I've

shocked you – made you see yourself properly as a
stuck-up, pious hypocrite – you're going to say,' here she
began to mimic Holly's voice, 'I'm so terribly sorry,
Winsome dear, but just at the moment what with my
studies and Mamma's work at the RAF Records Offices,
it's not frightfully convenient—' She stopped abruptly and
said, 'Holly, if Kildie won't take me, please let me come
to you. Please.'

'Yes. Of course. All right. But you've done so well here.
I don't understand. I thought you were enjoying being
your own boss and . . . things.'

'Well, the things have gone. Didn't you know? They
decamped in the middle of the night. Can you believe it!
Took Uncle Squire's silver too. I'm glad – not glad they've
gone but glad they took his precious stuff! Serve him
right. I wish this was Russia.'

'Oh Winnie.' Holly thought suddenly of how it would
be if Bob went. 'Oh I'm sorry. You really loved Eric
Battersby, didn't you?'

'Loved him? *Loved* him? I don't love anyone, Hol!
Don't intend to either. If you love someone they either
die or leave you!' She ate another biscuit, munching
furiously. 'Eric . . . Eric made life worth living. That's all.'

Holly watched her doubtfully. She knew she loved Bob.
And he made life worth living. What was the difference?

Winnie took a slurp of tea and swallowed what was in
her mouth. She put the cup down and then looked at
Holly.

'You might as well know. Then you can crow. Feel
superior. Like you always do.' She picked up the cup and
drained it. 'I'm expecting, Hol. Expecting the patter of
little feet. It probably happened that day you caught us
up in the forest. I'm three months gone. Got over the
sickness now and can't seem to get enough to eat.' She
took three biscuits and put them in her skirt pocket.
'When you told me about Charlie and Kildie, I thought
– Good luck to him! He did what he wanted before he
died! It didn't work properly cos there's something wrong

359

with Kildie. Nothing wrong with our Charlie! Nothing wrong with me either. And I've wanted a baby – I've wanted a baby for as long as I can remember! So I went back to Eric and let him go the whole way. I expect he knew then they were going back to London.' She sighed sharply, resignedly. Then she looked at Holly. 'Ma will have the screaming habdabs if I tell her now. Probably end up in the loony-bin. So I thought if I came and stayed with you or Kildie, someone else could break the news. Later.'

'Oh . . . Winnie! Oh, you poor, poor thing! Oh Winnie, I'm so dreadfully sorry—' She stopped speaking in the face of Winnie's obvious contempt. 'Don't you – I mean – don't you mind?'

'Don't be a fool. I just told you. It's what I want. Can't you remember what I said a year ago? Everybody looks after you when you're pregnant. Once he's got used to the idea, Dad will love it. And Ma – I can persuade her it's the baby she lost. And Gran – well, Gran's used to it, isn't she? What with Ma and Aunt Sarah and Kildie . . .' She giggled, 'You, of course—'

Holly felt herself reddening. She said, 'But the baby will be illegitimate—'

Winnie did not care. 'Ma and Pa will adopt it I expect. Like Gran and Grandad adopted Kildie. History repeating itself and all that.'

'What do you mean about Lizzie and Sarah?'

Winnie smiled at her. 'You never guessed then? Work it out. Your Dad was born a year after Gran and Grandad were married. I went through the chiffonier and found Gran's marriage lines and Uncle Jim's birth certificate. No certificates for Ma and Sarah. But they are two years older than Uncle Jim.' She started to giggle again. 'Poor old Gran. She had to get married. Just like your ma.'

The colour drained from Holly's face, down into her neck. She wanted to say something cruel to Winnie. Such as, 'You don't have to perpetuate the custom!' or 'Pity you can't get married, isn't it?' But, of course, she could

not say or do anything against Winnie now because of her
. . . her . . . condition.

Uncle Edward came in for lunch at twelve-thirty. He
pecked Kildie's cheek appreciatively but was not surprised
by her lack of success with Lizzie.

'I called in a specialist chappie. He reckons women go
like this sometimes after babies. Especially at Lizzie's age.
If only there could be another . . . but she's past it now.'

'Surely there's something we can do, Edward?' Kildie
tackled her rissole without enthusiasm. 'We can't just let
her moulder away down here.'

'Hardly moulder, my dear,' Edward said. 'She's got
Winnie, Gran and me all waiting on her hand, foot and
finger. Once the summer comes we'll get her outside
again. We'll manage, don't worry.'

'The thing is, Teddy dear, Winnie has said she will help
me with this American frock. She wants to come and stay.
I'll have to consult Marcus, of course, but how would you
manage here?'

Edward looked sharply at his daughter. She looked up
and spoke whiningly.

'It's all very well, Dad, but I need a break. A real break.
Hol has invited me back there for a couple of weeks and
if Kildie can have me, then I'll go to her for a week or
two – till this show thing is over – and perhaps by then
Ma will have been forced to get out of bed and do
something!'

Edward said, 'I see your point, Winnie. Just at the
present time with your uncle in a state about those
wretched evacuees – he's inclined to think you were a bad
influence on them, Win – it might be as well if you
were away.' He held up his hand at Winnie's vociferous
gratitude. 'But I am not at all sure how your mother will
take it. In the house on her own all day.' He helped himself
to the last of the potatoes and sprouts. 'Look, you go with
Holly. I'll keep an eye on your mother. If we can't manage,
I'll come and fetch you. Will that do?'

'Oh Dad . . . thanks.'

Holly wondered what Mum would make of the un-expected visitor, and knew she must remind Winnie to bring her ration book. And there was Bob. It would be difficult to have time alone with Bob what with Mum and now Winnie.

The rain let up as they piled Winnie's case into the car. Edward said, 'Go and say goodbye to your mother, Win. Tell her you're going to Holly's for a few days. Don't mention Kildie.'

Winnie disappeared and when she returned she looked sick. They drove to the main road and passed the place where Charlie had leapt around collecting his clothes over a year ago.

Kildie said, 'What is it, Winnie? You're crying.'

Holly looked at her in surprise. Winnie was indeed crying.

'Ma said . . . ' She hiccupped on a sob. 'She said, "First the baby, then Charlie. Now you. I wonder when your father will leave me?" '

'Oh my God,' Kildie exclaimed. 'Oh, Winnie. D'you want to go back?'

'No. I've got to get away!' Winnie said fiercely.

'Well, listen, you two. I have to pick up Marcus at six and it's gone five now. Can I just throw you out at the Green. Dorothy won't be home yet. You can let yourselves in and get the fire going, can't you?'

'Of course.' Holly was thankful. There would be enough fuss without Kildie's explanations. She lugged Winnie's case and Winnie brought all the bags containing books and shoes and knitting. They let themselves in and Holly knew immediately her mother was back; she could smell the soot heating up in the living-room chimney.

'Mum! I'm home. Got a visitor!'

The two girls went to the open door of the living-room. The sofa was drawn up to the fire. Bob was peering over its back, obviously startled by their sudden arrival. He seemed to be stripped to the waist. Mum struggled from a lying position. Her shoulders were bare.

She said, 'We didn't expect you for another hour at least. Where's Kildie?'

Holly said nothing. Winnie, just behind her, said brightly, 'Sorry to interrupt. Kildie just dropped us. She has to meet Marcus. Holly invited me to stay. Is that all right?'

'Of course!' Dorothy sounded absolutely normal. She looked at Holly whose face was the colour of the National loaf. 'Bob is just going, Hol. He is working tonight.'

Still Holly said nothing.

Winnie giggled. 'So he is,' she said.

Dorothy's expression hardened.

'Take your stuff upstairs then, girls. Then you can help me get the tea.'

The awful – the appalling – thing was, Bob left the house without saying goodbye. When the girls came down, Dorothy was in the kitchen, fully dressed, the sofa was pushed back against the wall and the table brought forward.

They heard two days later that Robert Larkay was dead.

1931

During the August after Walter's death, they went to Suffolk to stay with Lizzie, Edward and the children. Gran and Kildie caught the train into Gloucester, where Jim, Dorothy and Holly were waiting with their cases. They caught the nine-fifteen to Paddington, crossed to Liverpool Street and took the two-thirty to Cambridge.

The journey fascinated Holly. She was six years old. Her straight brown hair parted in the middle and bobbed with a fringe, framed a round face, dominated by enormous grey eyes and a long curly mouth. She had all Jim's features and was as shy as he was, yet she was unmistakably

Dorothy's daughter too. The way she turned her head when someone spoke to her; her enormous interest in the people around her; the graceful way she walked and moved her hands – in fact, all her mannerisms – were like visual echoes of her mother.

But her love of train travel came from Jim. She enjoyed being on Gloucester station, and the trip to Dymock was a never-ending delight. But this one, which would probably take the best part of the day, made her feel like Dr Livingstone or Mr Stanley. Jim took her on his knee and pointed out the various signal boxes. When the train stopped inexplicably, he would let the window down and try to discover why.

'Distant signal at Off,' he would say over his shoulder. It was like a faintly familiar war cry. 'Distant signal at Off.' She said it to herself when she went to the lavatory at the end of the corridor. She went three times and held on to the flush so that she could see the rails flashing by the opened flap on the bottom of the pan. She called it down into the furious echo which came from the wheels. 'Distant signal at Off!' They agreed with her and yelled something back.

Dorothy had made salmon sandwiches as a treat for Dad. He loved tinned salmon better than anything. Gran did not approve of tinned food and had brought bread and cheese in a clean tea towel. Kildie looked apologetically at her as she took one of Dorothy's sandwiches.

'We used to just *long* for tinned salmon when we were young, didn't we, Jim?'

'I knew that,' Gran said, munching grimly on her crust. 'It was the Weywoods. They lived on tinned stuff. John Weywood died young.'

Dorothy could not resist saying, 'Like Percy Jenkins then.'

Gran looked up darkly. 'Ah,' was all she said.

Jim put in quickly, 'We're almost at Reading. Let's wait till we stop, then we can pour some tea from the Thermos.'

They'd tried to do it when they were roaring through Didcot and it had spilled everywhere. That was why the salmon was so welcome. It was moist compared with the bread and cheese.

If the trip to London was exciting, it was nothing compared with the underground. Holly stood on Jim's feet and they joined the escalator in tandem. A porter lumped their luggage down expertly and Gran used the ordinary stairs and stumped alongside them as if she were seventeen instead of seventy.

Then came the fens. Holly had never seen so much sky. It was a glorious day with a steady breeze which made the corn bend and ripple like the sea and sent the little clouds scudding across the huge arc above them as if trying to keep pace with the train. And at Cambridge, there was Uncle Edward with Charlie and Winnie up beside him in the most wonderful trap pulled by two horses. Holly loved everything about it. She held out her arms as they bowled along between the dykes, half hoping that she would take flight like the birds. Winnie said, 'What you doing, Holly?' But Charlie knew. He smiled at her across the bouncing trap, then held out his arms too. Gran said, 'Don't swing them arms around like that, Holly! If they catch in anything they'll be ripped out their sockets!'

But there were no hedges; nothing to catch the flailing arms. Charlie yelled, 'Kildie, look at me! I'm going to fly right out of this trap any minute! Look at me!'

Kildie laughed and Gran said, 'Don't encourage them, Kildie!' And Dorothy, sitting up by Edward and Jim, suddenly threw back her head and cooeed to the sky. Uncle Edward and Jim laughed too and everyone laughed except Winnie and Gran, and Gran said, 'You're all drunk!' And pulled down her mouth to stop herself from joining in.

Aunt Lizzie was very pleased to see them. She was all pink and pretty with her hair fraying out of its bun around her face and her dark eyes bright and lively. Quite different from the Aunt Lizzie at Grandad's funeral. It was a huge farmhouse with outhouses all around the yard. Holly, used to the tiny compactness of the cottages at the Green and Dymock, wanted to explore everything at once. But Aunt Lizzie had spent most of the day baking bread, scones and cakes, and had laid a huge spread for them on the big kitchen table. Everything was big in Suffolk; the sky, the enormous fields of swaying wheat, the dykes, the farmhouses, even the cattle and horses. The bedroom she was to share with Gran and Kildie had four beds in it, two enormous wardrobes, a chest of drawers the size of a bus and a marble washstand like one of the tombs in Kempley churchyard. And there was still space for Kildie to teach her how to do the foxtrot.

Holly leaned out of the window to watch the sun land on the edge of the earth at eight o'clock that first night. Far away she could see a windmill and perhaps a house huddled by its side. The fields around the farmhouse were for the cattle and horses. They were feeding very close to the edges of the dykes where the grass was greenest. Gran told her that cows and horses never hurt you and she believed her. But they were very large none the less.

Kildie came behind her and hugged her convulsively.

'Isn't it fun? D'you know, sweetheart, this is the first time I've felt Gran was enjoying herself since – you know.'

Holly nodded beneath Kildie's chin.

'Come on. Let me show you the quarter turn!' Kildie whirled her into the middle of the room. The wide old floorboards were ideal for slithering around in imitation of Fred Astaire. Kildie showed her how Bill Masters danced, elbows right out, cheek to cheek.

'I love Bill Masters,' Holly confided to her as they collapsed onto one of the beds.

'Yes. He's not bad, is he?' Kildie said, very off-hand. 'He's going to get a little three-piece band together this winter. See if we can get a few engagements. Professionally, you understand.'

Holly was round-eyed. She understood.

'What will you do,' she asked, awestruck.

'Sing. Bill says I could look like Hedy Lamarr if I curled my hair up and wore black.' Kildie giggled, suddenly selfconscious.

'You're more beautiful than Hedy Lamarr,' Holly maintained stoutly. She knew that Hedy Lamarr was a highly attractive film star, but she had never seen her and could not envisage anyone being prettier than Kildie.

Later that night, when Kildie dropped to her knees at the window, Holly whispered, 'Kildie?'

'Hol! I thought you were asleep!'

'I stayed awake purposely. Kildie can I come and say my prayers with you?'

'Of course. Come on.' Kildie held out an arm and Holly flew to it and knelt within its circle. They were silent for a long time. Then Kildie said, 'Why did you want to say prayers with me, Hol?'

'You're always so long. I thought . . . perhaps . . . God talked back to you,' Holly whispered.

Kildie's arm tightened. 'Oh Hol. I wish he did. Gran says he does, but in your heart.'

There was another spell of silence. Then Kildie said, 'We'd better get into bed now, darling. If Gran comes up and finds you out of bed there will be trouble.'

Holly got under the sheets and lay very still. And after a while Kildie got up again and went to kneel by the window. Holly wished – oh how she wished – that Kildie would tell her how to pray properly.

The days drifted by in a haze of sunny air, big meals, Uncle Edward teaching Kildie how to ride, Winnie telling Holly how boring life was on the fens, Charlie showing her his den which was tucked under one of the river banks rather like Ratty's in *The Wind in the Willows*. Holly thought it was splendid. Charlie was nine years old and oscillated between being very grown-up and wanting to talk to Kildie all the time, and 'acting like a silly great kid' as Aunt Lizzie put it scathingly.

'So long as we don't get our clothes muddy, it doesn't

matter what we do,' he told Holly. 'So we'll take our clothes off before we get in the den.'

Holly was shocked. 'Gran wouldn't like that,' she said. Gran always insisted Holly kept her vest on when they slept together.

'Don't be daft!' Charlie scoffed. 'Water rats don't have clothes on, do they? And if we're going to be Mr and Mrs Water Rat—'

But Holly kept her locknit knickers on and washed them out before she put her other clothes back on. She was thankful when Charlie followed suit. That was what was wonderful about Charlie; he knew how she felt without her having to find difficult words to tell him. They both waited to catch their deaths from wearing perpetually damp under wear, and when they didn't some of Gran's credibility was diminished.

In the afternoons when the farm work was done for a few hours, they went for walks or took very slow drives in one of the farm wagons pulled by a massive shire. Gran made a collection of water plants and kept them in jam jars in the big bedroom. They had a day in Cambridge and punted on the river. Jim bought Dorothy a hair band that kept her short golden bob behind her ears. Lizzie said petulantly to Edward, 'You never buy me anything now! I suppose you've got what you want!' And Edward said, 'Not at all, Mrs Ball!' And they all laughed except Gran and Aunt Lizzie. And, strangely enough, Uncle Edward.

It was on the road from Cambridge to Ely that they saw the billboard proclaiming the flying circus.

'We must go!' Dorothy pronounced excitedly. 'The very thought of flying – defying gravity – becoming a bird—'

'Such nonsense,' Gran grumbled. 'If God had meant us to fly—'

Charlie jumped up and down. 'Oh yes – yes! They loop the loop and people walk on the wings and perform death-defying acts!'

Kildie laughed. She knew that Charlie said nearly everything for her personal entertainment and thought he was being extravagant again. But he wasn't. 'You'd like to go, Uncle Jim, wouldn't you?' he begged, knowing better than to ask his own parents.

Jim still had memories of the Flip-Flap at the Three Counties Show. He said cautiously, 'Your father is in charge, Charlie.'

Edward glanced sideways at Dorothy's laughing face, then down at Kildie, and said masterfully, 'Of course we must go! It'll be the other side of the river beyond the Cathedral!'

So the big old shire clumped his way across a field to where, on the flat lands, half a dozen pilots from the War had assembled their frail machines.

The sky was not as clear as usual and the canny folk of the fens saw no point in paying good money to watch something that could be seen from their own gardens for nothing. The Richardsons and the Jameses were the only spectators.

One of the airmen, short, sandy-haired, came across apologetically.

'Sorry, folks. Your ticket money wouldn't pay for our petrol.'

The children chorused their disappointment. Jim looked relieved, Lizzie smug.

Edward said, 'Look here, old man. How about a joyride? The nippers have been looking forward to seeing you go up but a joyride would satisfy them. Our money would cover the fuel for one plane, wouldn't it?'

There was a deathly hush. Then the man shrugged. 'I suppose it would. Yes. All right, why not? A fiver a time. Who's going to be the first one?'

A babble broke out. Charlie wanted to be first. Gran, Jim and Lizzie were horrified at the whole idea. Edward was rather foxed by the price. He had exactly half a crown in his pocket.

Dorothy jumped out of the wagon.

369

'Listen. I'm fairly certain my nephew and I are the only ones who are really keen. Couldn't you take us both?'

'Sorry, madam, as you see, two cockpits only.'

Dorothy smiled at him; her special smile, the one Jim always called dazzling.

'Charlie would sit on my lap. And, you see, we could not really afford a tenner. So we'd have to toss up for it.'

'Well . . .' The pilot looked back helplesly for some help.

Edward said, 'What about me?'

'Oh sorry, Edward . . .' Dorothy was mortified. 'I thought – I mean – it's quite expensive—'

Edward said, 'Look. I'll take Winnie—'

'No!' shouted Winnie.

'All right then, I'll take Holly, and Dorothy can take Charlie. That's a tenner. You might as well make a tenner, old man, as nothing!'

Such logic was beyond argument. But Holly held tightly on to her father's hand and in the end did not go. Edward borrowed the money from Jim and settled himself behind his pilot. The rest of them watched tensely as the leather helmets were strapped on and the goggles adjusted. Charlie could barely sit still for sheer excitement.

The planes bounced ignominiously as they started the take-off. Rabbits scurried from beneath the undercarriages and they almost reached the river bank before they quite suddenly rose into the air. Everyone cheered, even the other two pilots. 'You never quite get used to it,' one of them said to Jim who was looking sick and ill.

Gran said grimly, 'Why would you? It's against nature. That's what it is, against nature.'

But Dorothy and Charlie thought quite the opposite.

'It was like being part of the universe,' Dorothy said.

Charlie said to Holly, 'You should have gone with Dad, Hol. Then you'd have been a bird too!'

Edward had little to say. He climbed into the wagon and flapped the reins. 'Home, James!' he said as he always did. But without conviction.

He enjoyed Kildie's riding lessons better than she did
herself. On their final day he settled her feet in the stirrups
and patted her calves not very gently.

'You've got good legs, young lady. Like your mother's.'
Kildie flushed and said nothing.

Edward grinned. 'Like that, is it? Well, never mind.
Now. Can you grip with your knees? Go on, push your
knees into the horse like I'm always telling you. Let go
the pommel, for God's sake. Use your knees – sit back –
chest out – be proud of it – go on. Now, I'm not going
to use the leading rein today. I want you to walk around
the yard. Then trot. All right?'

Kildie let the horse walk around the farmyard once,
then twice. She was not a natural horsewoman and longed
to hang onto the pommel. Aunt Lizzie came out of
the kitchen and clapped and Bessie snorted and Kildie
screamed.

'Go on in, Lizzie!' Edward said angrily. He grabbed
the bridle and looked up. 'Calm down, woman! Bessie
was simply answering your aunt, that's all.'

He had called her 'woman'. She was sixteen now
and Bill Masters was her sweetheart in a way, but
no-one in the family thought of her as a woman. And
anyway, Uncle Edward was . . . not exactly special . . .
but certainly different. She knew her mother flirted
with him quite outrageously, but then, Ma flirted with
everyone.

She swallowed and said, 'I'm sorry, Uncle Edward. It's
such a long way to the ground.'

'It is. But I'm going to show you how to get there
without hurting yourself, so don't worry. And you can
drop the uncle when I'm teaching you to ride.'

'Very well . . . Edward.'

She saw that under the brim of his hat he was smiling.
She felt a little surge of power.

* * *

Dorothy said, 'This is strange countryside, isn't it? The boundaries are into the ground instead of above it, it just looks like an – an expanse.'

For once she and Jim and Holly were by themselves. Kildie was having a riding lesson – though the poor girl would never enjoy horses. Like Dorothy, she was afraid of them. Gran was helping Lizzie with the weekly baking and Charlie and Winnie had gone on the annual Sunday School treat to Cromer.

Dorothy put an arm around Holly. 'You like it, darling, don't you?'

Holly nodded vigorously.

Jim said humorously, 'What about that Cooke girl?'

Holly said nothing and Dorothy put in quickly, 'Don't laugh about Blanche, Jim. She is very necessary.' She hugged Holly. 'Have you invited Blanche to come along, darling?'

Holly looked up adoringly and shook her head.

Dorothy murmured, 'You see, Jimbo, there is no need for Blanche when things are going really well.'

'Yes, Professor Jung,' Jim said and halted their progress to kiss Dorothy soundly. Holly held out her arms. 'Up!' she commanded, and they lifted her between them and kissed her too.

Dorothy said, 'I do believe your knickers are damp, Hol!'

Holly shook her head firmly. 'I haven't been Mrs Ratty today,' she said. 'They're dried. Right off.'

'Mrs Ratty?' queried Dorothy, suddenly anxious. 'Do you mean you've been in the water?'

'Just to wash my knickers.' Holly put an arm around each parent and drew their heads together. 'More kisses,' she said. They complied but Dorothy was not to be deflected. 'Darling, if I'd known you were anywhere near those dykes – they're terribly dangerous!'

Jim said comfortably, 'Tell us about it, Hol. You pretended to be Mrs Ratty and got muddy, did you?'

Holly beamed at them both. 'Charlie has got his den

in the bank. Just like in *The Wind in the Willows*. It's a big hole. We can both get inside it.'

'Oh my dear Lord!' Dorothy said.

'We're not naughty, Mummy.' Holly was aware of trouble ahead. 'Charlie wears his pants and I wear my knickers. Always.'

'So your knickers have been wet. Always,' Dorothy concluded tremulously.

Jim said, 'Darling, stop worrying. Charlie is very sensible—'

'For a nine-year-old. I agree. He is also very daring.'

'Because he came up with you in that Sopwith?' Jim reminded her gently.

'You didn't want us to go? You didn't say anything!'

Holly slid to the ground between them. She hated it when they were angry with each other.

'Of course not. It would have been unreasonable to spoil your fun.'

Dorothy was furious because, as usual, Jim was putting her in the wrong.

'You're always so *reasonable*!' she accused him. 'I suppose you think it was reasonable for our only child to risk drowning in the blasted dyke!'

Holly wandered away. Encircling the farm there was, in fact, a hedge with a gate in it. She climbed the gate. The field was full of horses. Gran had told her horses were friendly so she walked towards them.

Jim said, 'Of course not! Any more than you do!'

'Then you tell her not to do it again! Don't always leave me to be the strict disciplinarian!'

'What's the point? We go home tomorrow. Charlie is out for today. There will be no more opportunities for playing near the dyke! Next time we come to see Lizzie, Charlie will be too old to play at *Wind in the Willows*.'

'Taking the easy way again, Jim!'

'Doll – that's not fair!'

'Don't call me Doll.' But she knew he was right. She was not always fair to Jim and she did not know why.

Unless it was because they could not seem to have another child and he did not mind and she did.

From the barn came a sudden shrieking sound. It was unmistakably Lizzie.

Jim and Dorothy looked at each other, knowing instantly what had happened.

'Oh my God!' Jim rarely took the Lord's name in vain. 'It's that damned Edward. With Kildie!'

Dorothy said, 'I'll go. Don't worry, I'll smooth it out.'

But Jim wanted her to be proud of him. He said, 'No, Doll, let me. She's my niece and he's my rotten brother-in-law!'

He took to his heels, vaulted the gate, passed the startled Holly at a gallop, jumped the opposite gate and disappeared into the barn. At the same time the biggest horse, startled by the running man, began to advance towards Holly.

Dorothy was at the gate. She might be terrified herself of horses, but she was far more terrified for Holly.

'Stand still, darling,' she commanded, her voice much too calm. 'I'm coming. Just wait for Mummy there.'

She swung herself over the gate and began to walk briskly towards Holly. The horse stood still, lowered his head, pawed the ground, snorted.

Dorothy took Holly's hand.

'Right, Hol. We'll go and see what all the fuss is about, shall we?' She started to walk, almost saunter, towards the opposite gate. The other horses seemed fidgety now. She realized that there were a couple of colts among them. The big horse was probably the stallion. She remembered the bath and the spider and controlled herself with difficulty.

The shouting in the barn stopped quite suddenly and Edward emerged, marching self-righteously for the house.

'Edward!' Dorothy tried to make her voice lilting but it shook up a scale like a choirboy's at puberty.

Edward turned, stopped and ran for the gate.

'Dorothy, what the hell? For God's sake, woman! Run! Run as fast as you can!'

As he spoke Dorothy heard hooves pounding the soft turf. She threw a terrified glance over one shoulder and saw the horse coming towards them. She scooped Holly up and over her shoulder and took to her heels. How she kept ahead of the horse she never knew but when she was still six feet from the gate she hurled Holly from her with all her might then fell flat on her face. Edward lifted his arms, plucked the child from the air, set her on her feet, leapt the gate and stood over Dorothy waving his arms and shouting like a maniac.

The stallion reared, it's front legs pawing the air, its mane lifting with the breeze. It crashed down a few feet from Edward who addressed it furiously.

'Get back and stay back! D'you hear me? No-one's going to hurt your mares! Do as I say!'

The horse snorted again but did not retreat. Edward said in a low voice, 'Crawl towards the gate, Dolly. Slowly and steadily. Pull yourself up and stand by the gate ready to get over quickly.'

Dorothy did not raise herself. Using her elbows she dragged herself along, hoping she was invisible to those mad, staring eyes so far above her.

Edward said more quietly, 'Calm down, boy. Everything is all right. We're going now.'

He turned and marched for the gate. The horse reared. He yelled, 'Over, Dolly! Go on over!' And he took two more steps and leapt himself. Jim was waiting. He gathered them both to him. Gran was holding Holly. Kildie and Lizzie stood by, apparently petrified by fear.

Edward and Dorothy were heroes. Nobody ever referred to what Lizzie had discovered in the barn. Kildie herself was bewildered by her aunt's shrieks and Jim's precipitate arrival. Uncle Edward – Edward – had been removing a hayseed from her eye. But whatever had really happened was all forgotten in the joyous rescue.

They left early the next morning. Holly wept when Charlie whispered, 'Farewell, Mrs Ratty. Farewell for ever.'

She knew he was right. There would be no more games in the dykes for either of them.

NINETEEN

1942

It was Miss Joliffe who arranged for her to start her nursing training.

'I know you're not going to stay on at school,' she mourned, staring into a retort as if it were a crystal ball. 'And I accept what you say, that you have to get away from home. The aircraft factory is therefore no good – I am very thankful to say. I think nursing might suit you very well, Holly.'

'Nursing?' It had never occurred to Holly. 'But the Infirmary is still only half an hour from home!'

Miss Joliffe glanced up momentarily. The girl had told her so little. She knew that a cousin on the father's side had been killed in Africa last year; now Holly had told her someone else, very close to the family, had been shot down over Germany on 2 February. But there was more to it than that. It was as if the child had suffered a betrayal. It must be calf love. The bane of all teachers.

Miss Joliffe quoted reluctantly, 'Remember, Holly, it is better to have loved and lost than . . .' She caught a glimpse of the girl's face and went on hurriedly, 'They are taking student nurses at St Jude's in North London at Easter. You will be almost seventeen and they are desperate for staff. The matron was at university with me. I think I might arrange it. You would probably live in the nurses' home—'

'Miss Joliffe – could you? Would you? I would be eternally grateful!'

Miss Joliffe almost smiled; the child had always been inclined to theatricality and could still turn a dramatic phrase, so she had not been completely destroyed by whatever had happened.

She said, 'You have a definite scientific leaning, Holly. I think the theoretical side of nursing will appeal to you. But at first it is no more than a skivvy's job. Menial is hardly the word. And the discipline is still very rigid. Florence Nightingale and so forth.'

'But that would be ideal, Miss Joliffe.' Holly wanted to surrender herself to something, give her mind and body over to another agency to use and control.

'Leave it with me then.' Miss Joliffe turned up the Bunsen burner and the liquid in the retort began to evaporate. She risked taking her eyes off it again for a second. 'And remember, human beings are never ever perfect, Holly. The trick is to accept them as they are.' She went back to the experiment which a girl in the Upper Fourth had ruined this afternoon. 'I should know,' she added gloomily.

If Winnie had not still been at the cottage it would have been impossible. She could not have left Mum completely alone and would have succumbed to the first fusillade of objections. But Mum herself knew how Holly felt; she never actually forbade the project though she put all the obstacles she could in the way.

'You won't be seventeen by Easter anyway,' she said, her white face intensifying the dark blue of her eyes.

'Nobody will know that – and they won't care if they do!' Holly stared out of the window stiff with the defiance with which she had armoured herself against the awfulness of what had happened.

She added more reasonably, 'The intake is at Easter. If I don't go then, it will be September.'

'That's not long, Hol. The summer at home . . .' Mum was pleading with her.

'You've got Win. She could do with a bit of specialist attention!'

Mum said drily, almost in her old way, 'Thanks!'

Holly said, 'Miss Jollybags thinks it's a good idea. She says it will continue my education.'

'Yes. Well I agree with her that it's better than the aircraft factory. But it's so far from home. What would Dad say?'

Holly said even more quietly, 'I'll ask Kildie to write to him and tell him.'

Mum said no more.

Winnie was as coarsely frank as ever.

'I know why you're going. You can't take it, can you? That your mum was cuddling up to that Canadian airman! For God's sake, Hol! Where's the harm in that? He was frightened, poor bugger! She was comforting him—'

'Shut up, Winnie!' Holly wanted to hit her again. But that had not helped before. As Blanche had said at the time, 'Hurt you more than it did her, didn't it?'

'Why can't you talk about it? Christ Almighty, anyone 'ud think it was your ma pregnant instead of me!'

Holly could have groaned aloud at that. She said, 'You don't know what you're talking about, do you? Have you forgotten Bob was killed that night? Am I allowed to grieve about that?'

'Yes. All right. But that's not why you're running away.'

'I am *not* running away! I am going to do some war work at long last!'

'And leaving me stuck here!'

Holly opened her eyes, surprised. 'I thought you wanted to stay here? I thought you preferred it here to Hill House? You said—'

'Yes. Yes. Yes. I do.' Winnie went to the window of the bedroom and stared down the garden. 'It's just that . . . dammit all, I shall miss you, you stupid cow!'

For the first time since the day in February, Holly was able to see outside her own head and into someone else's.

She said, 'Oh Win . . . I'm sorry. I have to do this.'

'I know.' Winnie turned and flashed her a smile. She was changing shape almost daily now and she rested her abdomen on Holly's window-ledge and patted it. 'Don't worry, I like your ma. A lot. I'll keep an eye on her. And I'll let her keep an eye on me too!' She giggled. 'Not that I'm easily overlooked now, am I?' She perched herself on the ledge. 'Now, I need some instructions. Where do I find wood for the fire? And how do I persuade your ma that I am quite capable in the kitchen? And why can't I go fire-watching with Aunty Mabs?'

Holly felt suddenly guilty. It had never occurred to her to take her mother's turn at fire-watching; and she had no idea how to persuade her to share the kitchen.

She said lamely, 'I'll show you the bluebell woods. There's plenty of firing there. And perhaps you'll be more successful with the coalman than Mum is.'

She looked around her room which was so blessedly familiar.

'Win . . . if I stick this and I'm not here on May the first, will you plant a row of beans? Gran will have saved some from last year. She'll tell you—'

'Christ Almighty, d'you think I've never planted bloody beans before?'

Holly looked at her cousin and thought that she was going to be much better at coping with life at the Green than Holly had been.

St Jude's was twenty minutes from Oxford Circus by underground. Mum, who had been to London perhaps three times in her life, stared at the serried ranks of bunks with horror.

'Holly, you shouldn't be coming here at all. This is a danger zone, darling! What am I thinking of letting you put yourself at such risk—'

'Mum, don't start that again! Once I've done my preliminary year, I can go somewhere else! But there's really nowhere that isn't a danger zone—'

'I'll have a word with the matron. See if there is a nice

380

convalescent home somewhere in . . . in the Cotswolds perhaps—'

'Don't you dare! And – Mum, I don't want you to come in with me! Seriously! I've got to stand on my own two feet!' Holly had pangs of homesickness already. She knew that if Mum came through those tall iron gates with her that would be the end.

There had been no interview; Miss Joliffe had arranged it all over the telephone and this was the first time Holly had seen the place. It looked grim beyond words, but Mum obviously thought it looked safe too – in the way that prisons were safe. She compromised swiftly.

'Listen, I'll have lunch over there. At the station café. If you need me . . . otherwise I'll get back to Paddington for the four-fifteen.' She aimed a kiss at Holly's cheek and turned to go into the café. 'I cannot believe this is happening,' she said in farewell.

The sheer unreality of it all took Holly past the porter and to the back of the enormous grey stone building to the nurses' home. As far as she could see Kilburn consisted of one main road going somewhere else probably just as depressing. The hospital was right on that road and though the traffic was minimal, she was soon to discover that convoys regularly used it throughout the night. The building itself looked like a cross between a very big school and an orphanage, both from the mid-Victorian era. The windows were meant to let in light and not to provide views; they were all close to the ceilings and arched as if pointing to heaven.

The home was slightly better. It was red brick with ordinary sash windows, criss-crossed with anti-shatter tape. Inside the door was a lobby with an umbrella stand full of umbrellas and . . . hockey sticks! And inside again was a long corridor, its bleakness broken by small clusters of pictures. Holly put her case down and walked the length of the corridor. All the pictures were of flowers; Miss Joliffe had told her that Matron – Miss Margaret Oglethorpe – was an amateur botanist.

At the end of the corridor was a kitchen, to the right a door leading into an enormous dining-room. And there, above the oil-cloth-covered tables was a noticeboard with a list of names on it. It was a relief to see 'Holly James' in big black capitals with a room number by its side. She had started to wonder if they'd forgotten; even if she were really here at all.

A small girl came out of the kitchen and looked enquiringly at her.

'I'm new,' Holly explained nervously. 'I see my room is number twenty-one. Should I find it and get settled in?'

'I'll show you.' The girl went off down the corridor at a pace that was nearly running. She took the stairs two at a time. 'I'm catering,' she said over her shoulder. 'Molly Preston. Live down the road in the council flats. Got your uniform and cap?'

Holly's case was getting heavier by the second. 'Yes,' she panted.

'They'll show you how to make it up. You won't see a soul till off-duty. Have a nap. Or something.'

She disappeared and left Holly to feel the full effect of homesickness and to look at her watch constantly to check whether Mum would still be at the station café.

But the room was not that bad. It had a chest of drawers which evidently doubled as a desk, a wardrobe and an iron bedstead. The lino was highly polished and everything smelled strongly of disinfectant. She put her things away and that seemed to burn any possible bridges back to the 4.15 from Paddington. Then she made up her bed with the sheets and blankets on top of the wardrobe. And then she looked at her watch. Mum would be on her way home.

It got much better when two more probationers turned up just as she had and were conducted upstairs by Molly Preston, still rushing, still talking in truncated sentences. But she did pause long enough to tap on Holly's door and introduce them all.

'Rose Martin. Gladys . . . what did you say?'

'Story,' whispered the taller of the two in a Welsh accent.

'Right. Martin and Story.' And she was gone.

The three girls drifted into their separate rooms, but when the day staff came off-duty and the home filled with a surge of noise, a Staff Nurse collected them and took them to her room to show them how to make up their caps. Luckily, she used Holly's for her example: Holly knew she could never have done it for herself. Then they were taken down to supper.

The dining-room, so empty and cavernous before, seemed full of jostling white doves, Holly was quite sure there would not be a place for all of them. However, when Sister tapped with her knife for grace, everyone was standing behind a chair – there was even one for her – and once the meal began it was broken only by requests for sugar and bread. Holly had not eaten since that morning, which seemed years ago. She wolfed her two sausages with the best of them and filled up with bread and margarine and rice pudding.

The convoys started to roll past the hospital at midnight and Holly gave up trying to 'think nice thoughts' and succumbed to homesickness. At last she got up and looked around the blackout to see searchlights criss-crossing the sky. At four o'clock she let herself weep. 'Bob . . . oh Bob,' she sobbed into the hard pillows. She must have fallen asleep then because the next thing she knew someone had flung open her door, yelled, 'Six o'clock, Nurse!' and closed it again with an enormous crash.

Breakfast was bacon. Just one small piece but with as much bread and margarine as could be eaten in the twenty minutes allocated to the meal. Holly was glad when her name was read out with Rose Martin's. They were both sent to the men's surgical in charge of Staff Nurse Davidson who had shown them how to make their caps.

They ran up so many stairs and along so many corridors, Holly knew she would never find her way back to the home. But Rose was slightly more confident. 'I think I came along here when I had my interview last Christmas,' she whispered. 'Anyway, all we've got to do is to stick to the others.' There were three others besides the Staff Nurse: the sister who was called Adams, Nurse Lewyn and Nurse Morgan. Six of them to deal with forty patients. They whipped through some double doors and hovered outside Sister's office while the change-over was made. Davidson immediately took off her cloak and bustled down the ward saying good-morning here and there, checking charts and thermometers as she went.

'Take off your cuffs, you two,' she called back. 'Roll up your sleeves. Martin, you go with Morgan. James, you come with me. We've got all these beds to make.'

Staff Nurse Davidson looked like a man in disguise, but the patients seemed to like her.

'Watch my stump, Davy' . . . 'Just rub my back, can you, old girl?' . . . 'Been longing to see you, Davy.' She introduced Holly. 'Nurse James. She'll soon learn the ropes, especially if you help her.' But Holly felt she was drowning in a rough sea. She was told to get diabetic specimens and gastric feeds and had no idea what they were. When it came to cutting bread and butter and sweeping up, she was not much better. Mum had always done everything.

They broke for elevenses which was called lunch and she discovered she was hungry enough to face the left-over bread and a big bowl of dripping.

'My mam says to eat as much as you can.' Rose could not have weighed more than seven stone but she had an appetite like a horse. 'She did nursing in the last war and she says you need all the energy you can get.'

That was true. Holly had no more time to be homesick until she fell into bed that night. And then it was compounded by exhaustion and a complete lack of confidence. She could have howled aloud except that she had distinctly heard the girl next door using what Gran called a gosunder. The walls must be thin.

*　　*　　*

Winnie walked in the woods every day and took back as much kindling as she could manage. It might be Easter but it was bitterly cold out of the sun. She took great pleasure in making the house warm and welcoming for Aunt Dolly when she got home each evening. The exclamations of appreciation made everything worthwhile. She'd never had so much as a thank-you for keeping things going at home; certainly Gran had told her several times that she was a good girl but her mother barely spoke and her father took her completely for granted. She hoped viciously that they were missing her now.

She thought infrequently of Eric. He had made life worth living for a while, and she had enjoyed exciting him and then letting him down with a bump. Once he'd got what he wanted last autumn, she'd lost interest and he had pestered till he was just plain boring.

She wondered about her parents. After that dreadful day when she had seen Aunt Sarah and Dad down on the river bank, they seemed to have got on so well together. It was as if Ma suddenly surrendered herself to Dad, instead of fighting him all the time. But since the miscarriage, things had gone from bad to worse.

Winnie bent down with a grunt to pick up a dead branch that would keep the fire in most of the evening and thought how strange the whole thing of men and women was. Angry and aggressive, yet loving too. None of it made any sense. Holly probably had the right idea with her high-minded dreams of knights in armour. Except that she'd probably never find anyone good enough for her.

She lumbered up to the gate and opened it with difficulty. The coal dray was delivering to the vicarage. There were two one-hundred-weight sacks still on the flat-bed of the wagon. The horse had his head in his nosebag. Surely the vicar wasn't entitled to all the bags.

She dropped the wood behind the hedge and hurried across the Green as fast as she could and caught the man just before he shouldered the next sack.

'Ah Mr . . .' She smiled winningly and held her coat hard over the outline of the baby. 'I am so delighted to see you!'

'The name is Porter, miss. What can I do for you?'

'Mr Porter.' Winnie released her coat and held out her hand. He hesitated then wiped his on his trousers and took hers. The customers did not usually shake hands. Winnie's smile widened further. 'I'm staying with my aunt. She said you might be calling this week and I am so glad I did not miss you. I'll go and unlock the coalhouse, shall I?'

'Sorry, miss. Nothing for the cottages this week.'

Winnie opened her eyes wide. 'But, Mr Porter – it's so cold!'

'Allocations for the cottages ran out last delivery, miss. Only six-bedroomed 'ouses gets an April delivery.'

'But now I've arrived surely things are different? My baby is due in two months. I shall need to keep a fire in for the delivery!' Winnie forced a tear from somewhere.

He said, 'Miss, I'm that sorry. If it was left to me—'

'But you've still got two bags on the wagon, Mr Porter. Couldn't we have just one?'

'Well . . .'

'I know I'm a nuisance. But I'm sure the rector – being a good Christian – would be only too pleased . . . Would you like me to have a word with him?'

'He's out, miss. They're both out.'

Winnie glanced at the smoking chimney. 'And leaving a fire to burn . . . my goodness.' She smiled. 'But then, the gentry don't know what it is to economize, do they?'

In the end he let her have both sacks of coal. She relocked the coal house and shook his hand again.

'You are so kind, Mr Porter. Perhaps when you come next week you could stop for a cup of tea? I've got a very good recipe for a fatless sponge . . .'

'Good of you, miss.' The vicar's wife had never so much as offered him a glass of water. And she never tipped him either. Winnie's sixpence would buy him a glass of beer that evening. He settled his leather jerkin more comfortably and smiled back at her. After all, it was the likes of her they was fighting the war for, wasn't it?

Winnie waited until the horse clumped out of sight before returning to the gateway and retrieving her wood. She built an enormous fire, laid the table and lit the gas beneath a stew of scrag-end of mutton.

Dorothy was tickled pink when she got home.

'Winnie, you are an *enfant terrible*!' she said with an exaggerated French accent. 'I hope you didn't have to vamp old Porter to get just two hundredweight of coal?'

'Would you disapprove?' Winnie said cheekily, dishing up the stew.

'Only if the front of your maternity smock was ruined with coal dust!' Dorothy came back and they both laughed.

Kildie smoothed the artificial silk over her hips. 'Winnie, it's perfect. My God, you're better than Lizzie.' She looked at herself in Dorothy's long mirror. 'It – it's so professional!'

Winnie struggled from her knees with some difficulty and sat on the edge of the bed.

'It's 'cos of your figure,' she said enviously. 'Anything would look good on you, Kildie.'

'No, it wouldn't. It's this draping . . . it's very flattering. You should do this all the time. For a living, I mean.'

'Dress-making.' Winnie made a face. 'Sounds bloody exciting.'

'Winnie, your language! And I didn't mean dress-making in that way. I meant designing. Working for a proper firm . . . Lordie, Win, you could work for us!' She stared at the girl, suddenly taken with the idea. 'No, really, Win! I'm not saying it just to be kind or anything! Darling, we could have our own designs! Exclusive – that sort of thing!'

'Marcus wouldn't stand for it.'

'What d'you mean? It was you who said I could wrap him round my little finger.'

'No, that's what Ma said.'

Kildie looked at the girl and felt a pang. She had come to Hill House for a week but then had wanted to return with Holly.

'Win . . . did he say anything when you were with us?'

'No, of course not. But he wants you to himself.'

Kildie was amazed at Winnie's sentience. She understood . . . men.

'My dear, I'm so sorry—'

'Don't be daft!' Winnie sounded robust enough. 'I wanted to be with Holly. I've always . . . well, you know. We're almost the same age and everything.'

'And now she's gone,' Kildie observed.

'Yes, but Aunt Dorothy needs me.' She saw Kildie's expression and said, 'She really does. Not to replace Hol or anything. There's things that have happened . . . she needs me.'

'All right.' Kildie turned back to the mirror. 'But I want you both to come to the American evening. And after the baby is born, Win, think about my suggestion. Funnily enough, Marcus listens to what I say about the store. And I rather think the idea of our own personal designer might appeal to him.'

'OK,' Winnie said without much enthusiasm. How on earth she could take a job when she had a child to care for she did not know. She did not want to think of the future. She could not stay at the cottage with Dorothy for ever. The thought of the Gatehouse gave her the shivers.

Kildie said, 'Help me out of this, darling, and we'll have a cup of tea. You are a clever girl, you know. I've brought some black-market chops for your meal – put those on low. I'll just stay till Dorothy gets home, then I must get back.'

Kildie was more observant these days and it did not escape her notice that the cottage was warmer and more welcoming than it had been since Dorothy started at the

Records Offices. And when Dorothy arrived home, Kildie also noticed how well aunt and niece managed together.

Kildie said laughingly, 'I don't think I've ever seen you sit down for so long before, Dorothy!'

'Winnie spoils me,' Dorothy acknowledged. 'I really don't know what I should do without her, to be honest.'

'She came at the right time. Filled the gap that Holly left.' Kildie tried not to notice Dorothy's expression and added quickly, 'Any news from Holly?'

'She's settling in slowly. She likes anatomy.' Dorothy looked up helplessly. 'I don't really know. She doesn't say anything important.'

Kildie drove home slowly in the Wolsley. It was almost a year since Jim had gone to Canada and Dorothy was not the same person. Her old drive had gone. She was being worn away somehow.

The Morgan was awkwardly parked in the garage so that Kildie had difficulty in getting the Wolsley inside. But she didn't care so long as he was there. She went in to him and fell into his arms, weeping.

'Kildie – darling girl – what has happened?' he asked, alarmed. He was used to her more even temperament these days.

She sobbed, 'Oh Marcus, I am so lucky to have you! So lucky!'

And he held her close and called her 'Daddy's baby' and wished Jim James would stay in Canada for the rest of his life.

1940

By the time the letter came from Francis in the August of 1940, Sarah was becoming desperate. She had sold all the presents she had been given in the halcyon 'Francis days' as she called them now. Her father's funeral and Kildie's wedding had both incurred enormous expenditure. When Edward and Lizzie had moved from the

Fens to Croydon, Sarah had assumed that Edward would look after her just as her gentlemen friends of the past had done. But Edward never had a bean and it was something of a relief when Lizzie decided that the raids were excuse enough to move back to Dymock. Edward told Sarah that in fact he was going to stay at Gran's with Charlie, while Lizzie and Winnie were going to Dorothy's house outside Gloucester. She quizzed him about engineering a convenient separation. But Edward, oddly enough, would have none of it.

'You know very well I've always been faithful to Lizzie in my own way,' he said austerely. Which made Sarah laugh so much she almost cried. She too imagined that she had kept faith with her sister. Keeping infidelity in the family seemed a kind of loyalty. While Edward was with Sarah he couldn't be with any other women.

She missed Edward terribly but after his protestation she could not really believe he would leave Lizzie and move in with her. She was lonely and extremely hard up. She too toyed with the idea of returning home on the pretext of looking after her mother. The prospect was not pleasing. She remembered only too well that no tinned food entered Emmie's house and all the vegetables had earth around them.

Then came the letter. It had been forwarded from the Lupus Street address. It was dated January 1940. It was from Francis; he was in America.

My dear Sarah. I think it is time I forgave you. Your betrayal did me no harm after all. I have had a most interesting decade here; our American cousins are so practical and very amenable to my business methods. However, my dear, I have missed you. You are probably one of the few women I find interesting. Indeed bearable. I need a secretary, an assistant. I need someone I can trust and I take it that having exacted your revenge on me, you can be trusted once again. If so, send a cable, my dear. I will arrange for you to join me as soon as you wish.

390

One word about the secret you discovered. I would point out, that I was the injured party. I gather you betrayed me because you were so angry. But why was your anger directed against me, Sarah? Because you knew my patronage was – at least in part – due to my intense jealousy of your father, Walter James? If I had wanted the ultimate revenge, Sarah, I could have simply ruined you. But you see, I loved your mother – the only woman I ever loved – the woman who could have saved me from my other self – so I looked after you. I hoped you would become dependent on me and we could come to some arrangement. I still have dreams of arriving at Dymock with you on my arm. How your father would have hated that!

However, with your father's death, that is over. I do not know what he must have told you when you went to stay at Dymock, probably it was his wife, the servant woman, who poisoned you against me. All I can tell you is that your father and I both loved your mother – she was a wild wanton just like you – she played us one against the other and when she discovered my other self she went to your father and eventually died when she bore him twin girls. I never forgave him for taking her from me and I certainly never forgave him for killing her.

A simple enough story, Sarah. And I dare say at this distance it seems foolish to you. In a way I hope so. But I expect you would like to know more about your mother, and I am the only person in the world who can tell you.

I would like to see you, I would like to get you out of Britain before it is overrun with Nazis, I would like us to be companions.

          Yours, Francis.

Sarah was a long time absorbing the contents of this letter. She had to deal with the shock which was akin to hearing of a sudden death. Then came the disbelief: Francis was lying. He had always been devious, twelve years of living in the States had made him more so. But when she reread the letter it was obvious Francis thought she had learned the full truth back in 1925.

She hardly ever cried but suddenly tears began to ooze insidiously down her face. She stood up and walked around the flat, noticing – not for the first time – the significance of various things she had never sold. After her father's funeral she had begged his uniform greatcoat; the one she had worn that night they made tea together in the icy kitchen at Dymock Station House. It hung on one of a row of angular hooks, as if the owner were still there.

Sarah buried her face in it and then pushed it away almost angrily and went into her bedroom. There on the ring stand was Emmie's wedding ring. After Kildie's wedding her mother had given her the wedding ring which Sarah herself had rescued from Walter's grave.

'I b'lieve it belonged to your grandmother,' Emmie had said. 'Keep it, Sarah. Your sister has got her own wedding ring.'

Sarah had protested but Emmie had been adamant.

'Some day it might be important to you, that ring.'

And it always had been, but never more so than now. At least she knew who her father was!

She put the ring on her left hand with a kind of defiance and went back to the letter. And gradually she began to rearrange everything that had happened over the years and to look at it from a different angle. And it made such good sense she knew that Francis was not lying. Her mother had always been so . . . so . . . objective. While her father had been practically devastated by her disgraceful performance with Alf Matson all those years ago, Emmie had been cool. Even when they had both thought her lost at the Three Counties Show, Emmie had stood aside and held Jim in her arms. And not because she was basically a fair woman, but because . . . because she did not care!

Suddenly the fact that her mother was not her mother, made Sarah double over with physical pain. The sense of loss was as sharp as when Walter died. Yes . . . that was it

. . . her mother had died and her father's servant girl remained.

She whipped up her anger as a kind of defence. They had all been duped. Or had they? Did Jim know that he was the only true child of the marriage? But Lizzie did not know – Edward would have let that slip a long time ago. And Kildie did not know. And, until now, Sarah had not known. She forced herself to imagine Emmie smiling sardonically at her well-kept secret. How amusing it must have been at times! Twin girls, by-blows from Walter's affair with someone terribly beautiful and . . . and vivacious, and . . . Sarah searched for a word that could make her real mother utterly superior to Emmie. Dynamic.

So there had been a bargain. Walter's conscience was such that he would never have let his daughters go to foster parents. He had said, 'I'll marry you if you will look after my children.' And of course Esme Dart, servant, had jumped at it.

But how had Jim been born? And so soon?

Sarah leaned over her knees yet again; Jim was her half-brother. She had always thought they were from the same mould completely. She had let herself pretend that Holly was half hers. She had set out to woo the child . . . had half succeeded. She wept for this second, smaller loss.

She waited a week, reading Francis' letter several times a day. A letter came from Edward: Lizzie and Winnie were still at the Green with Dorothy and Holly. He had a feeling that she would not come back to him. His uncle had so far refused him any accommodation. His life was in ruins.

Sarah went to Dymock. She felt heavy with all the secrets of the past and sitting on the train from Paddington she almost held her head in her hands to take the weight of it. She and Lizzie were orphans. Worse than orphans because they had thought they had a mother! She groaned and muttered, 'God. I cannot bear this!'

'Are you all right, dear?' said the woman opposite.

'Yes. Sorry – yes. Tired, that's all.'

'It's that blessed Luft Woffy. I know how you feel. Night after night. I said to my sister, I said, we got to get out somehow.'

'Yes.' Of course Ma wouldn't know about that, though Edward and Lizzie might have enlightened her. Sarah bit her lip. She had no 'Ma'. The servant woman who had married her father as part of a bargain was nothing to do with her. Although . . . she was Jim's mother. That was certain.

By the time she got out of the Ledbury train at Dymock station, Sarah felt sick and ill. She walked past the Station House – another loss – and stood at the gate of the cottage steeling herself to greet Emmie as normally as possible. She was determined to hold her cards close to her chest until she had talked to Edward. She was longing to see Edward.

Charlie emerged from the hen run holding a basket with four eggs in it. He stared at her, not recognizing her in her pre-war suit and hat. She assumed her prodigal daughter role without any difficulty at all.

'Charlie! It's your Aunt Sarah! Come here – aren't you tall – give me a hug! Oh I just love young men in their shirtsleeves!' She flirted with him effortlessly but thought from his slightly withdrawn response that he 'knew about' Aunt Sarah. If Edward had said something she would personally kill him!

It was something of a shock to find Kildie in the cottage looking white and strained after a row with her husband. Sarah hugged her too and sat with her at the table for a long time so as to avoid any physical contact with Emmie.

It was another shock to watch Charlie mooning about after Kildie like a love-sick calf, even though it accounted for his lack of response to his Aunt Sarah. There were at least eight years between them, and Kildie was a married woman. Sarah bit her lip. Kildie was, after all, her daughter. Charlie was Edward's son. She wanted to weep again. The sins of the fathers visited upon . . . how many generations? She would have to talk to Kildie; tell her not

394

to throw away a rich husband for the sake of a . . . Not
that Kildie was in the slightest bit interested in her young
cousin. Of course not.

Sarah began to feel extremely odd. She said abruptly, 'I
think I need some fresh air. I'm going to walk down by
the Leadon. Where Pa used to fish.'

She did not glance in Edward's direction. But when he
joined her there, she was so glad she wept again, drawing
him into the bushes and stifling his words about Lizzie
with frantic little kisses.

'Sarah – darling Sarah – I really don't want to—' But
he did not struggle as she eased his jacket from his
shoulders. 'Lizzie must have guessed. That's why she has
gone to Dorothy's—'

'Lizzie has never guessed. And Lizzie is not here now.'
She drew him to her. 'I've missed you so much. London
is so big and empty. And something really dreadful has
happened—'

However, afterwards, she did not tell him about Francis'
letter. She felt strangely at odds with him. She watched
him button his waistcoat and teased him unkindly about
staying in Dymock with Emmie, implying he was frightened of the bombing. And then when Lizzie appeared,
out of the blue, wielding her handbag, screaming like a
fishwife, she was somehow inveigled into his plans to go
'back to the land' thereby getting a free house and
exemption from the Forces!

She should have despised him, instead she drew on her
acceptance of the real – which had probably turned
into cynicism years ago – and went with them to see
Edward's ghastly uncle and aunt and do her stuff. It was
a minor triumph when it worked. And somehow it was a
just punishment for the young Richardson family: an
ignominious return to Edward's illegitimate roots, taking
old Matson's job and mouldering down in this ghastly
hole. She almost laughed at Edward's excitement when
Lizzie gave him the glad eye. He did not even realize that
he had little Sarah to thank for that!

And then, quite suddenly, they were all gone. Kildie's adorable, masterful husband came and reclaimed her – how lucky she was, and she did not even know it!

Then Dorothy and Holly caught the train back to Gloucester with their bicycles and some carefully wrapped eggs and a huge hunk of cheese. Then Edward and Lizzie took the children to look at the Gatehouse. And Emmie and Sarah were alone.

Emmie took a bowl of potatoes and her small sharp knife and went outside to sit under the veranda. Sarah stood at the kitchen window watching her for a long time as she scraped the young potatoes rhythmically. She tried to hate her: her grandfather's servant who had been the only available female willing to take on two bastard girls. Esme Dart. That had been her name. What a catch for Esme Dart to become Emmie James.

But her father had told her how happy they had been. She remembered him talking very seriously that night in 1925 as if he had known that one day she would have to face this.

She went through the kitchen, into the garden and sat down by Emmie.

'Well?' The grey eyes, so like Jim's, glanced sideways for a moment. 'You managed to talk the Squire into giving them the Gatehouse?'

Sarah shrugged. 'I don't know. Perhaps.' She said scornfully, 'Men are such fools.'

Emmie looked up, suddenly alert, then said slowly, 'Women too, Sarah.'

Sarah kept her eyes on the fern garden. 'Not you, though. You – you've always known which side your bread was buttered on.'

There was a very long pause. Sarah had forgotten how good Emmie was at waiting and she burst out at last, 'Why didn't you tell us? Why did you let us think we were all a normal family? Did it amuse you to know that my . . . wild ways . . . were nothing to do with you?'

396

Emmie made a sound; a long sigh as if all the air in her body was released. Then she put the saucepan of clean white potatoes on the bench by her side and looked at Sarah properly.

'You know why I didn't tell you, Sarah. There are a hundred reasons why your father and I brought you up as a normal family. Mainly it was because that was how he wanted it.' She glinted an unexpected smile. 'And – finally – we *were* a normal family!'

Suddenly, unexpectedly, Sarah began to cry. She was furious with herself for blubbing yet again, and when Emmie put a hand on her shoulder she shook it away immediately.

'All these years . . . living a lie . . . making me feel guilty for being like I am . . . and knowing that I couldn't help it! I was taking after my mother! You had no right . . . no right—'

Emmie sat there, her head bowed as if blows were being rained upon it. Once she had started, words poured from Sarah. '. . . understand now why you gave him back his ring when he died . . . the bargain was over, wasn't it? You had to get rid of it somehow, so you gave it to me! Why didn't you tell us then? Lizzie still thinks . . . she'll die of shame . . . Kildie – no grandmother—'

Emmie said in a low voice, 'Have you told Lizzie?'

'I haven't had the chance yet. Arriving in the midst of all this . . . like Paddington platform with the evacuees trying to get out—'

'I beg you . . .' Emmie's voice was so low Sarah did not hear it for some time. 'I beg you, Sarah. On my bended knees—'

'What? What are you talking about? Lizzie has a right to know!'

'If you tell Lizzie she won't be able to keep it to herself.' Emmie looked up at last. Her bones seemed to have shrunk so that the skin of her face hung loosely in a million wrinkles. It was greyer than her eyes. 'Sarah, don't take my grandchildren from me!'

Sarah was speechless for several seconds. Then she exploded.

'You want to go on living a lie? You are so monumentally selfish you cannot give up what you got by trickery? They are *not* your grandchildren! Holly is your only grandchild and she has always been your favourite—'

'That is not true, Sarah!' Emmie's voice gained strength. 'I have seen more of Holly than Winnie and Charlie, that is all. And . . . Sarah . . . whatever you say, I am not only thinking of myself. Winnie and Charlie and Kildie . . . they need me. You are the independent one of the family, Sarah, but the others . . . they need an anchor. I have to be that anchor!'

Sarah stared again. She wanted to scream that she needed an anchor as much as anyone. Did her mother – did Esme Dart – really think she was so independent? Had she painted such a rosy picture that they really imagined her living a life of luxury in London?

After a while she turned her gaze down the garden to the fern bed.

Emmie whispered, 'Sarah, this has hurt you terribly. But it need not hurt the others.'

Sarah hiccupped childishly on the remnants of a sob. She said, 'You'll be telling me next it is what Pa would want.'

'Water under the bridge,' Emmie murmured.

'I prefer to think of it as dirt under the carpet.'

Emmie flinched but said nothing.

Sarah made up her mind suddenly, 'I am going to America.'

Emmie blanched. 'To America? We're in the middle of a war, Sarah—'

'That's why. I can't stand the shortages – no decent clothes – the raids—' Sarah thought of Francis. He was her anchor. She needed him. Without him, life had gone steadily down hill. 'I'm going for the duration at least,' she said, suddenly positive again, suddenly in control. 'I've been offered a job out there.'

Emmie was silent, looking at the profile that was already losing its definition.

At last she looked away. 'Sarah . . . does this mean you have decided to keep it to yourself?'

'Yes.' Sarah turned her dark eyes on the woman she had always thought to be her mother. 'I can see your point.'

Emmie said, 'Sarah – thank you – thank you, my dear—'

'Oh for God's sake! Don't thank me! But I shall keep in touch with Lizzie. If they are in difficulties . . . well, I shall expect you to help them.'

'Of course. You don't have to threaten me, Sarah.' Emmie sat up very straight on the bench. 'I love you all. You must surely know that?'

'You got rid of me quickly enough!'

'You wanted to go.'

Sarah drooped. 'Yes.' She wondered where this was leading. Emmie had not always been objective, sometimes she had championed Sarah. And Edward had always told her that it was Emmie who had summoned Adrian Frost and made it possible for him to marry Lizzie. And it was her father, after all, who had kept the secret.

She said defeatedly, 'Anyway, you're right. It doesn't matter any more.' She stood up. 'It really doesn't matter, does it?'

Emmie did not answer. She said instead, 'How did you find out?'

'Someone told me. Someone who had loved my mother.'

Emmie asked no more.

TWENTY

1942

Miss Joliffe had prophesied that Holly would enjoy the theory of nursing, and she was right. Sister Tutor – known as Toots – had the effect of sending everyone else to sleep. But Holly was delighted to find that anatomy and chemistry and human biology all fitted in with what she had done back home at school. It was like making discoveries for herself, and she recalled Miss Joliffe's smug expression when an experiment worked out exactly as forecast, and knew just how she had felt. Her diagrams of the pancreas and digestive system were works of art; she poked around her ear to discover the external auditory meatus and was fascinated by evidence of a tubercle on one of the specimen bones handed around.

Luckily her burgeoning friendship with Rose Martin prevented her from becoming a complete prig and the other girls tended to cultivate her company for help with their papers. Holly was too shy to revel in this spurious popularity, but for the first time she discovered she was enjoying the company of her peers. She had made vague plans that after her first year she would probably leave and return home to Mum with all that frightful business with Bob forgotten. Now she thought she might sit the 'Preliminary' and see how she got on. The course for becoming state registered lasted three years. It was like looking up at the stars: a long way off and unattainable. But just now and then she dallied with the idea of wearing frills and medals and actually being proficient in dressing wounds and hoisting the leg pulleys for the fractured femurs.

Gradually, very gradually, she was learning to be practical. She could pull the curtains around a bed without becoming hopelessly entangled in them. She could go for the dressings trolley and actually get it inside the curtains without exposing the patient to the avid gaze of the ward. She could make tea, cocoa and Bovril practically at the same time and was now learning about plaster bandages. She was still constantly told off, but then so were all the other nurses. The old-fashioned scorn for any kind of praise still held good in the nursing profession. Crackly aprons, starched cuffs and well-made caps were the first priority; a patient's comfort came at the end of quite a long list.

In July she went on night duty. For the first week she hated it; her body clock refused to adjust and she found herself falling asleep literally standing up at about four o'clock every morning. At five when they began to get the patients up, she recovered sufficiently to make sleep very difficult for the rest of the day.

But the interesting thing about night duty was that there were times when she was alone in the ward. Holly James, seventeen, hopeless and helpless, was responsible for forty sick people. Sometimes it was only for ten minutes, other times for almost an hour while the senior nurse fell asleep on the lavatory. Holly never sat at the desk during these periods. She would walk slowly up and down the ward, using her torch to check on the seriously ill, going up to the wakeful ones when they whispered, 'Any chance of tea, Nurse?' whispering back, 'As soon as Senior comes back – not long – got the kettle on low.' It made her feel like a real nurse.

One night she put her shaded torch carefully onto the face of an old man who was not expected to last the night. He had been brought in two days ago having fallen down his stairs. He had stayed in his tiny hall for almost a week before the neighbours had realized anything was wrong. He was suffering from multiple fractures and had not regained consciousness.

Holly checked his pulse nervously. There were deaths all the time in the men's surgical, but she had never been alone when it happened.

The pulse pressed infinitesimally against her fingers and she breathed a sigh of relief. She was about to move away when a thread of sound came from the bed. She moved her torch to the wizened face; his eyes were open.

'Mr Partridge?' She leaned down. 'Don't worry, everything is all right. You are in hospital. I am a nurse.' She picked up the flaccid fingers and held them gently. His hand reminded her of Gran's; almost worn down with work.

Someone to her left asked for tea.

'In a moment.' She pressed the fingers. 'I'm going to put the kettle on, Mr Partridge.'

She shone the torch with her free hand, the dull old eyes were fixed on the blackness of her face. She thought they seemed to be pleading with her.

'Do you want me to stay?' she whispered.

There came a tiny movement of the head.

'All right. I won't go.'

The Senior nurse was furious when she came back.

'You're in charge of the whole ward, not just one bed!'

Holly knew better than to point out it was the man in the bed who claimed her attention. She went to put on the kettle as promised but she returned throughout that night to take Mr Partridge's hand and tell him she was there.

He died just before the day staff arrived. She was glad. She had not wanted anyone else to be with him. He had made contact with her in the middle of the night; she felt they had been special.

She told Rose about it later when their day off coincided.

Rose said acutely, 'That's what makes it all worthwhile, I suppose. I mean that's the picture you have of a nurse, isn't it? Sitting with someone, giving them comfort at the end.'

'I don't know whether I did any of that,' Holly replied, the euphoria of her experience long gone. 'It was . . .' She almost sobbed. 'Oh, Rose, it was almost as if he was my Gran!'

Rose said, 'Holly, why don't you go home and see your family? When you get a weekend you could easily do it.'

'I will soon. I didn't think I could, but perhaps this autumn . . .'

But then Winnie's baby was born.

There was no question of Winnie going into hospital. Dorothy went with her to the local doctor every month and each time she came away with a clean bill of health. By the time the midwife realized it was a case for a Caesarean, Winnie had been in labour for forty-eight hours and was very weak. She could not be moved.

Dorothy was frantic. She said furiously to old Dr Marks who had dealt briskly with all their ailments, 'You must operate immediately! My God, she's going to die!'

He was used to setting broken joints, writing prescriptions, removing splinters; it was probably forty years since he had seen the inside of an operating theatre.

He said, 'She will be all right, Mrs James. Please do not distress yourself—'

'Then what about the child?' Dorothy wanted to hit him, shock him into action. 'You know yourself that child is starved of oxygen after all this time! For God's sake, man—'

'I shall need help, Mrs James. Mr Carridine at the Infirmary could give advice.'

Dorothy had the front door open at his words. 'I'll go over to the Rectory and telephone. Carridine . . . yes, I've heard of him.'

Dr Marks went upstairs again and told the midwife to get ready for an operation. He needed a proper sterilizer; gloves, a mask . . . he began to wash up. After all, there was a war on.

Dorothy used all her old authority and Mr Carridine arrived only an hour later in a small Austin that used little petrol but could hardly contain his bulk. Winnie was blessedly anaesthetized, sheets dripping with disinfectant were hung around the bed, the incision was made and the baby delivered. It was a boy. The midwife cleared his throat and pounded his back unmercifully.

Mr Carridine said quietly, 'Give up, Nurse. Let nature have its way for once.'

He continued to affix sutures. At the end of it all when he was doing his own swabbing, there was a faint cry. They all looked round at the bundle in the prepared cot. A fist moved spasmodically and the cry came again.

Winnie said, 'Listen, Aunt Doll.' She was the only one Dorothy allowed to use the truncated version of her name. 'Send for Hol. She'll get compassionate sure as eggs are eggs. You can't cope with this on your own and if Ma won't bloody well move herself—'

'Language, Win.'

'And Marcus isn't going to let Kildie come down for longer than two or three hours at a time, it's ridiculous.'

Dorothy peered into the cot. 'How's Chas? Incredible how he sleeps in the day, isn't it?'

They had named the baby Charles without a second thought, but they couldn't bring themselves to call him Charlie. He became Chas during the first week.

Winnie groaned. 'If only he'd just have two or three hours in the night, it wouldn't be so bad.'

Dorothy had not been in to the Records Office for three weeks. She had Chas in with her from midnight until six in the morning and slept off and on through the day.

'He'll soon settle down, Winnie,' she said without conviction. 'After all, the poor darling had a horrid start to life.'

'But meanwhile, Aunt Doll – please send for Hol.'

Winnie looked so woebegone Dorothy decided to write

to Holly then and there. Besides, she wanted to see her daughter very badly indeed. It was four months since she had left for St Jude's. Winnie sat there watching her aunt as she wielded the fountain pen given to her last Christmas by Bob Larkay and thought how lucky Holly was to have a mother who cared. Winnie's voluminous nightie had been sent by Mrs Davis together with three romper suits and some kid booties. When Winnie had spent the difficult week at Hill House back in February, Mrs Davis had taken an instant shine to her and confided lugubriously that her own daughter had lost three babies. Winnie had no doubt where the gifts came from, but she did not mind. It seemed fitting somehow because the doctors had not expected poor Chas to live at first. Lizzie had sent nothing; not even a letter or a card. Edward had visited twice but had been too harassed to stay longer than an hour. 'The Gatehouse is like a bomb-site,' he grumbled, obviously holding Winnie at least partially responsible. 'The other day she managed to put my collar studs in the coal scuttle. Can you understand that, Win? I mean, why the coal scuttle?'

Winnie said wearily, 'She puts bits of rubbish in with the coal. To burn . . . She must have thought—'

'She's mad. I told her I could get her certified tomorrow if I wasn't so soft.'

'You mean, if you weren't frightened of Gran,' Winnie said.

'And *she's* not what she was. We had a rice pudding yesterday and you could have broken your teeth on the rice. Practically uncooked.' He looked across the bed pathetically. 'When are you coming home, Win?'

Winnie sighed. 'Soon, I suppose. When I'm well and Chas has settled down.'

'And that's another thing. You won't like me saying this but I have to. It will just upset your ma – more than ever – if there's a baby in the house. And it occurred to me – Kildie can't have kids, can she? Why don't you ask her to have the baby for a couple of years? Till your ma gets right again.'

Kildie's fascination with Chas had not escaped Winnie's notice. She said violently, 'No! He's mine!'

'All right. All right. Women folk!' Edward stood up. 'I'll have to go, kitten. Come back as soon as you can with or without the baby.' He paused by the door. 'By the way, Win, those two Battersby women were arrested in Stepney – the house was full of Uncle Squire's stuff. They didn't even have the gumption to find a new address – police found them in their old house!'

'Oh,' Winnie looked at him.

'Don't get upset, kitten. Your ghastly Eric – or whatever the name was – he's enlisted. He won't be behind bars for a bit.'

'Oh,' Winnie said again.

Afterwards she was surprised at how little she cared. She thought that perhaps having discovered what men were like she wasn't very keen any more. Whereas the thought that Holly was coming home was like a beacon of light.

In the event the beacon turned out to be more like a whirlwind. Holly bathed Chas, powdered him, greased his bottom, dressed him and told him he was going to be a good boy. Amazingly he slept through that night. The next day she started on the house and cleaned it from top to bottom. It was as if she could not stop; or indeed she was frightened to stop. The situation at the cottage seemed to her bizarre. She had been away just four months and in that time Mum and Winnie had become . . . settled. It was as if they'd lived together all their lives. They listened to the wireless and Mum must have picked up news from working in the Records Office, but it seemed to Holly they could hardly see beyond the village pump. They had second-hand news of Gran and their only contact with the outside world was Kildie. Kildie was a regular visitor and though she came to see Winnie, she and Mum seemed to get along all right. And that was due to Winnie too. When Kildie popped in to say hello to Holly she positively raved about Winnie and the wonderful dress she had made for the Villiers' Gala American evening. She brought them some butter and a leg of lamb and some sugar. When Holly said the black market was strangling the country, she said blithely, 'Darling Hol, you'll never change, will you? If it puts your mind at rest, this is not black market. It came from the new Forces' dining-room at the store. And if they deserve it, so do we!'

Such logic escaped Holly. She picked some mint and made mint sauce to go with the lamb and thoroughly enjoyed it, black market or not. Winnie had planted the beans as promised and they were at the top of the sticks and in full bloom. Holly sat among them and wondered about talking to Blanche, but in the end there was nothing to say. Blanche would know instantly that she was jealous.

The weather became very hot during the two weeks she was home and every afternoon she put Chas in his second-hand pram and took him for a walk. He was not a handsome baby; Aunty Mabs, accompanying her one day, expressed doubts about him.

'He was two and a half days being born,' she said glumly. 'I wouldn't be surprised if he was backward. See what you can find out at your hospital, Holly.'

'I've still to go on Maternity,' Holly said and felt a surge of anticipation. 'And when we've done our Prelims, we can apply to other places. The Red Cross badly need nurses for their hospitals.'

'Yes. Well . . .' Aunty Mabs looked at her doubtfully. 'Don't forget your Mum, will you, dear? When Winnie goes home she's going to feel very lonely.'

Holly wished for a moment she had Sister Adams' acerbic tongue and could suggest that Mum might find a few more Canadians for bridge.

She leaned down and drew a thin sheet over Chas' bare shoulders. The sun was very hot.

'Perhaps Winnie will stay on,' she said instead.

When Chas was three months old, Winnie went home.

'We've stock-piled the coal. There must be over a ton in the coal house. And try and force yourself to eat the canteen dinners. You don't want to be cooking every evening. And try to come to Dymock at weekends.' Winnie tucked the baby into his cradle. The pram was folded down and stood by the gate with her case. Kildie was coming to take her back to the Gatehouse.

She looked up at Dorothy. 'I shall miss you like bloody hell,' she said.

'Oh Win. Language.' Dorothy was almost weeping. 'I shall be fine. I'm so tired at night all I want to do is sleep. And when spring comes perhaps the War will be over.'

'Yeh,' Winnie said. 'I don't want to go, Aunt Doll. I've never had someone to myself before. It's been . . . nice.'

'I know. You'll come again. Don't worry.'

The Wolsley appeared from the lane and began to round the Green.

Winnie said, 'What will you do? Right now when I've gone?'

'I'll write to Jim. A nice long letter.'

'Give him my love.'

Winnie grabbed her aunt by the shoulders and pecked her quickly then picked up Chas' cradle and lugged it through the front door. Kildie hurried up the path and took it from her.

'Come to Kildie then . . . little lovie . . .' She smiled above his head. 'He knows me. Did you see that? He smiled!'

Winnie rolled her eyes heavenward. Kildie went on, 'I've had a most interesting letter from Jim, Dorothy! The Larkays are taking him to Niagara Falls! Isn't that exciting?'

Dorothy smiled and nodded.

Later when the house was empty and terribly quiet, she

sat at the table with Bob's fountain pen in her hand and tried to write to Jim. But somehow there was never anything much to say.

Winnie stayed six months at the Gatehouse. Every afternoon she wheeled Chas down Middle Lane to visit Gran and they sat in the garden together and watched him lie on his blanket and kick and then begin to crawl. It was the only time she had anything to do with her son. Lizzie might be too ill to wash-up, cook or clean, but she was not too ill to cuddle Chas, give him his feeds, rock him to sleep and sit up with him during the night.

Mrs Ball, together with most of the villagers, cut Winnie dead if she saw her in the village. The pair from the Grange never visited her. Yet the first time Lizzie set foot outside the Gatehouse for eighteen months – wheeling the pram – people materialized from nowhere and told her how well she looked and what a bonny grandson she had.

Winnie said, 'Gran, I don't think I can stick it. I don't know what to do.'

'People will get used to it, our Winnie. Take no notice.'

'It's not just that. Dad is literally up to his elbows in muck – he was out all last night with one of the cows. Ma drifts around cuddling Chas like someone in a trance all day. I don't know how you've put up with it, Gran! Going there day after day, doing all the washing and everything. She . . . she's utterly selfish!'

'She's my daughter, our Win. Remember what you're saying, if you please.'

Winnie gave Gran a quick look. 'Oh yes. I forgot. I suppose . . . yes. Sorry, Gran.'

Gran shook her head. 'But there again, you'm my granddaughter.' She hesitated. 'Win, I'm going to say something. Sit down, child. Drink your tea.'

Winnie did so, wondering whether Gran was going to confess about her own illegitimate babies. But no such thing.

'I know you wanted this baby, Win . . . someone of your very own. Now you've got 'im. You tell me your Ma looks after 'im – dotes on 'im – most of the time. You don't do nothing about it, our Win. Why is that?'

Win raised her brows. 'Well, she doesn't do anything else, Gran. It's the one thing she will do, look after Chas. What's wrong with that? I'd be an idiot if I tried to stop her!'

'You'd be an idiot perhaps. But a natural idiot. It won't be long before Chas turns to your ma instead of you.'

'He does that already . . .' Winnie stopped speaking. 'You mean I'm losing him?'

'I mean you're letting him go, Win. The only time you have him to yourself is when you bring him here. He sleeps in your ma's room – she gives him his food—'

'Are you saying I'm an unnatural mother, Gran?'

Gran shrugged. 'I don't really know what a natural mother is, our Win. Only that you might be happier not being a mother.'

Win frowned. 'You're beating about the bush, Gran. It's not like you.'

Gran smiled. 'No. I was thinking of Sarah and Kildie. Sarah couldn't have borne to stop at home to look after Kildie.'

'But you and Grandad – you were so much better for Kildie. And anyway, are you saying I'm like Sarah?'

'No. I'm saying that you've learned something hard, but real, in the past few months. You've learned about having a baby. You tell me you'll never have another one—'

'You can say that again!'

'And perhaps you are now learning that looking after a child is not what you want.'

Winnie stared hard at Gran's leathery old face. At last she said, 'Kildie's been talking to you.'

'She says you could have a job any time at the store. A good job.'

There was a pause then Winnie shook her head. 'I

couldn't leave Chas with Ma and Pa. They're hopeless.'

Gran sighed sharply. 'Nobody is hopeless, Win. *They're* certainly not hopeless. It would be the making of them. Your ma would have to organize herself again – she was a good organizer, have you forgotten? And your pa would have to stop hanging about up at the Grange and come home early of evenings. He'd do it. He wanted his own baby and this one could fill its place.' She leaned forward. 'Don't you see, Win? Chas would be the making of them.'

Another very long pause. Winnie said slowly, 'Talk about history repeating itself . . .'

'Well it has to really, doesn't it?' Gran said reasonably. 'There's only so many things that can happen so they've got to happen again and again.'

Winnie thought of Gran having her twins before her wedding day, of Sarah having Kildie, and now she herself having Chas.

She said glumly, 'Oh . . . bloody hell!'

Gran did not reprimand her.

1940

Francis had 'ensconced himself' as he put it, in the burgeoning town of Miami in Florida. He could have lived anywhere, but this state was being opened up rapidly and because of its ideal climate was attracting the elderly at an enormous rate.

'They've got money and a determination to spend it before they die,' Francis said. 'This was the first hotel I bought. All the suites are like this one. In fact, it's a service flat with the addition of tennis courts, swimming-pool, et cetera, et cetera, et cetera.'

Sarah sensed an awkwardness in his manner to her which had not been there before. There was no longer a feeling that he was using her. He might even *want* her to stay with him.

She said conversationally, fighting exhaustion, 'And it's warm like this all the year round?'

They were sitting on an enclosed veranda which was like a clear blister on the face of the two-storey building. Outside the veranda, the white-jacketed waiters were going the rounds of the pool with drinks. It reminded her of the early Twenties; the time just after the first war, when she had been so young, so determined to enjoy herself. Now she was forty-one and an exile; she had no parents, no real background any more. And somehow by coming out here she was betraying her father yet again.

Francis smiled without any of the old sardonic condescension.

'Absolutely. There are storms, of course. Even hurricanes. That is why the building is low. But the warmth – the sun – is always there.'

She was so tired she felt ill but the sun was like balm on her pinched skin. The voyage across had been fraught with terror. The ship had been full of women and children looking for a safe haven in America; all frightened, all feeling this ghastly sense of cowardice in the face of danger. There had been a convoy of boats surrounding them, but at one point they had all melted into the surrounding fog and the captain had ordered the engines to be cut and requested that they all maintain silence in case U-boat radio operators were listening for them. Sarah had tried to breathe quietly and had heard her heart knocking urgently against her ribcage.

And then, even on shore, there had been the long train journey south to this raw new place of water and islands and orange trees and blessed warmth. Only Francis was familiar. Only Francis understood her. She prayed he would ask her to marry him. It was nothing to do with sex; both of them would be well aware of that. She needed identity; she needed status.

She said, simply, 'It's good to see you, Francis.'

He nodded. 'It's good to see you too, my dear. You've

lost weight. But it suits you. Has it been awful – rationing, bombing, all that?'

'Of course. But it was finding out about my mother – about my father's wife. That's what was awful.'

His brows shot up. 'You didn't know? I thought – when you went home for your brother's wedding – I thought you must have discovered it then?'

She shook her head. 'No. I told you what I discovered then. My illegitimacy. And . . .' Walter had told her something else, what was it? She remembered. 'And that my father was very happy with . . . with—' Suddenly tears welled up in her eyes. She wanted, quite desperately, for Emmie to be her mother.

Francis said, 'I've ordered tea. And some bread and butter. It will sustain you until dinner.'

Her tears dried instantly. 'Real butter?'

He smiled. 'You haven't changed, Sarah.'

'Neither have you. You won me over with food that very first time.'

They both laughed, looked at each other, looked away.

He said, 'I expected too much of you, Sarah. You were still so young.'

She flared instantly, 'I did not betray you to the police or anyone else, Francis! I could have done. I knew you'd seen Jim at Brimscombe when he was thirteen. I was terrified you might have . . . hurt . . . him in some way. But Jim is – was – so steady. I knew nothing could have happened. Otherwise . . . yes, I think I would have betrayed you then.'

There was a long silence. She took a deep breath and stood up to look out of the window. At home all this expanse of glass would have been criss-crossed with anti-shatter tape. It restricted vision. Here, the world seemed free and wide.

He said at last, 'I believe you, Sarah. I think . . . there would be no point in you lying about it. And you do not lie to me.'

She thought back. 'No. I have never lied to you, Francis.

Sometimes I have wanted to keep things from you. But I haven't been able to do that either.' She turned her head and smiled fleetingly. 'You are one of the few men – perhaps the only man – person – with whom I can feel completely . . . myself.' She thought of Emmie. She had always been herself with Emmie. But then she had thought Emmie was her mother. She stared through the clear glass again. An elderly woman emerged from one of the hammock chairs, walked to the edge of the pool and dived in. She must have been at least seventy. The same age as Emmie when Walter died. But so different . . . so different.

Behind her, Francis spoke weightily.

'I did not kill that child, Sarah. I fed him, gave him money . . . I did not kill him.'

She took another breath. To breathe properly, deeply, was a pleasure.

'I know. I knew at the time. You are a great many things, Francis, but you are not a murderer.'

She heard his sigh and was pleased that her belief meant something to him.

There was another silence. Then he said, 'It seems I owe you an apology, my dear. After my visit to you that evening, I dare say a lot of your support was . . . withdrawn.' He cleared his throat. 'That was what I intended. I thought you were responsible for linking my name with the dead boy. That was my revenge. I was not proud of it at the time. I very much regret it now.'

She turned instantly, smiling reassurance.

'That is handsome of you, Francis. But . . . well, it wasn't that bad. I survived. I think I'll always survive.' She came and sat opposite him again. 'Why did you invite me to come here? If you still thought of me as an informer, I cannot imagine why you would wish to see me again. After all, you have managed very nicely for over fourteen years.'

'Fourteen years.' He looked past her head. 'What a

waste of time.' He smiled suddenly. 'I always enjoyed your company, Sarah.'

She waited. Now he would say it.

'And I need you as much as I did in the old days.' He leaned back in his chair. 'Do you still play the piano?'

'Yes.'

'There is a baby grand in the foyer here.'

'Francis, if you expect me to vamp your clients, you had better think again. I am over forty, my dear!'

'I need you to oil the wheels, Sarah. I am too English. I heard one of my managers call me a pompous idiot and I do not doubt there is some truth there.' His smile widened. 'Nobody will ever call you a pompous idiot!'

'Better not!' she returned sharply.

He laughed. 'If you will represent me, Sarah, you can travel. Look at new places for me. Order furniture . . . work out colour schemes . . . deal with the staff.'

She stared at him. 'What will you do?'

There was another silence. He lifted his shoulders slightly. 'The doctor says I could go on for ever, if I watch my diet and rest during the day.' He shook his head irritably. 'I have a stomach ulcer, that is all. After all, I am over sixty!'

She offered no sympathy. She was still waiting.

He said in the same irritable tone. 'Well?'

She looked out at the swimming-pool. The woman was emerging, water pouring from her well-preserved body. She wore a cap covered in thin rubber roses. Sarah was suddenly glad that Emmie would never wear such a thing.

'You want me to take on your work, your responsibilities, with the addition of a little amateur nursing?' she asked, still not looking at him.

'I suppose that is exactly what I want. Except that I would still be signing everything, paying the bills. So you would be relieved of those responsibilities.' His voice returned to how she remembered it: thin, clipped, cynical.

She turned back to him, stared right at him.

'What would I get out of it?' she asked directly.

His face relaxed enough to let in slight surprise.

'A very pleasant life – the kind I imagine would suit you excellently. Power. You have never had real power, Sarah. It is . . . satisfying. You would also have a great deal of freedom.' He injected some quizzicality into his gaze. 'I take it you still enjoy male company? You would have the opportunity – the money, the time – to choose your own.'

'Just as you do?'

His eyebrows twitched. Then he inclined his head. 'As I do,' he agreed.

She knew then that he was not going to ask her to marry him. Was it because it had not occurred to him? Or that he feared a rejection?

She said as briskly as her exhaustion would allow, 'My status in all this . . . might it be convenient to be your wife?'

Comprehension dawned very obviously in his dark eyes. And he smiled. Then he said quite gently, 'I don't think so. Do you?' She did not reply and he leaned forward. 'You will be my personal assistant, my dear. I think clients, employees, business associates will find that rather intriguing. Whereas a wife – especially a wife who wears the trousers – no, that would not do. I'm sure you understand that.'

She understood only too well. He might pay her a huge salary and become an understanding companion. But legally she would always be his employee.

She leaned away from him.

'I understand, Francis.'

'And you agree?'

'Of course.' She stood up injecting her last ounce of energy into the movement. 'And now I think I'll go and look at this baby grand! And then . . . bed!'

It was good to see the knowing look in his eyes change to one of admiration.

'Ah, Sarah. You never change, do you? A great little trouper!'

She smiled. 'The show must go on, Francis!' she said. And believed it herself.

TWENTY-ONE

1943

When Winnie went back to the Green to stay with Dorothy, Gran went with her. It was such an unprecedented move that it set the family by the ears. Lizzie wheeled Chas to the Grange to use the telephone and rang Kildie. Kildie went down to see what was happening.

Gran was adamant that she had done the right thing.

'If I'd have stayed home, Lizzie would have been sending for me at the first hurdle,' she said. 'And I reckon if Winnie's going to be at the store and Dorothy is working all day, I'm needed here.'

Dorothy was not quite sure how she felt about the whole thing. The winter without Winnie had been awful. It was as if she came face to face with herself and did not like what she saw. She had lost Jim, then the three Bobs and then Holly. In one way it was quite marvellous to have Winnie back again. But Gran had always been something of an unknown quantity. And she had never slept at the Green.

She said cautiously, 'I dare say Lizzie would have leaned on you, Gran. But don't feel you have to stay here to look after this place.'

Winnie just said, 'Good move, Gran,' and went to fetch a sketchbook full of designs she'd done through the awful winter months at the Gatehouse.

Kildie made sounds of non-committal. She felt herself being gently but surely pushed into some kind of a corner. It was obvious that Winnie was going to take her up on the rash offer she had made ages ago of a job at Villiers'. And it was more than likely that Gran's presence was partly due to that; Gran seemed to think she had some influence with Marcus. But Kildie had never mentioned the idea to Marcus. And what with the country having been at war almost four years now and the restrictions tightening all the time, he tended to turn down any new ideas. She sighed deeply. The family seemed to think her life was a bed of roses; little did they know.

After a week, Gran had organized herself into life with Dorothy and Winnie. The Green might be much nearer Gloucester than Dymock was, but in many ways it was similar. Just across the lane from the village pump was the five-barred gate leading to the woods, and Gran went there every morning during that summer of 1943. She never came home empty-handed. Wood was broken or chopped and stacked neatly at the side of the coal-house. In the clearings on the other side of the trees, she found mushrooms and wild strawberries. She threatened to lay rabbit traps when an 'r' was in the month again. Dorothy was secretly appalled but told herself Gran would have gone back home before then.

Gran did the laundry in Dorothy's gas boiler without enthusiasm. 'What's the point of using gas when you could have a copper in your coal house and keep it going with rubbish?' she asked. But the sheets and pillowcases were just as white as they would have been in Dymock. She used starch liberally. Winnie teased her about it. 'If any of those old fuddy-duddies at Villiers' wanted to give me a quick cuddle, they'd have a job – my blouse is better than a chastity belt when you've been at it with the starch!'

In the afternoons she did the garden. In the evenings she mended.

And meanwhile the situation at Dymock was improving all the time. The first time Winnie went to see Chas, she brought back glowing reports.

'I think Ma is going to be all right. Chas certainly is.' She grinned. 'Poor old Dad has still got a lot to learn!'

'Let him get on with it then,' advised Gran.

Marcus said he would take Winnie on a month's trial.

'Not long enough.' Kildie kissed his cheek. 'Listen, Daddy. Let her produce half a dozen dresses. Just six. Exclusives. Give her a corner of the ladies floor and see what she can do with them.'

'Baby, that would be fine if it weren't for the blasted War. But no-one's interested in exclusive dresses any more.'

Kildie sat back and looked at him in astonishment. 'Are you serious, Daddy darling? Women are not interested in model clothes because there aren't any!' She cuddled up again. 'Listen. There's a little cubby-hole off the stock room – sewing-machine, cutting-table already there – I think it was for alterations before the War. Let's put her in there – pay her the same as Miss Ashe – yes, darling, the same if not more – and see what happens. You know we can afford it. And, apart from her salary, what have we got to lose?'

'Nothing I suppose,' he grumbled. 'But I don't want you thinking I can take on all your family!'

'Who else is there? Holly? She'll get married, Daddy.'

'I was thinking of your grandmother.'

Kildie widened her eyes. 'I thought you liked Gran?'

'I admire the old girl. And she's been fair, especially to me. I'd fork out for a nursing home – anything like that – but I don't want her here, Kildie. I'll tell you that now.'

Kildie felt a physical pang; she had always pictured Gran in Hill House one day. Maybe with a trained nurse. Certainly with lots of shawls and grapes and things. She was almost jealous of her going to stay with Dorothy now.

She said, 'She's been more than a mother to me, Daddy. You know that.'

'I do, and if it weren't for her, I don't think we'd be together now.' Marcus put a hand on her neck and drew her face to his as he had done so often in the past. Claiming her exclusively.

She said breathlessly, 'Does that mean she could come here?'

'It means I want you all to myself. Always.'

She said no more, closing her eyes and giving herself over to him as she always did. After all, Jim would be home by the time Gran needed any care. Jim would expect Gran to go to Kildie; it was surely an unspoken agreement with them. And Jim had mastered Marcus once before.

Winnie found a bedsitting room in Gloucester.

'Aunt Doll, I hate to leave you, but it's such a curse cycling into Gloucester all the time. And when it's raining this winter it will be just awful.'

'Don't I know it!' Dorothy agreed. It took her nearly an hour against a head wind to get to the Records Office in Eastern Avenue.

'Listen, why don't you move too? Go on, Aunt Doll! I'll look for a proper flat and we can share the rent—'

'Winnie, I'm so sorry. But I have to stay here.'

Winnie rolled her eyes. 'Oh God. For Uncle Jim and Holly. Of course.'

'Language, Win.'

Winnie had made her six frocks for the shop and six more. They were labelled 'Winsome' and had sold the day they were put on display, coupons or no coupons. She knew that Marcus would take on more staff if she asked him; but at present she too wanted to keep it small.

She moved in July when Mussolini was deposed. Dorothy and Gran were alone.

Gran said, 'You got to learn to drive a car, Doll.'

'A *car*?' Dorothy forgot to beg Gran not to call her Doll. 'What on earth do I want with a car!'

Gran had evidently done a great deal of thinking while she was gardening. She poured more tea and said, 'I shall go home for the winter. I don't like the thought of you getting on that bike and cycling to work every day in all winds and weathers!'

Dorothy was touched in spite of a certain irritation. Gran must surely have heard of petrol rationing.

'You'll have to get one with a gas bag,' Gran chuntered on. 'I expect Marcus will see to all that. I'll have a word with him.'

'You'll have a word with Marcus?'

Gran looked defensive. 'He's got a soft spot for me. I polished his precious Morgan once.' She sipped judiciously. 'And another thing, Doll. You ought to get your name down on some list somewhere. Go into the Shire Hall one day and see what they say.'

Dorothy was completely lost now.

Gran explained patiently. 'They must have a list somewhere of teachers they can call on. Illness and things. If you had a car you could go anywhere in the County.' She stirred vigorously although there was no sugar to go in her tea. 'Kildie always said you was a really good teacher.' She sipped again and looked satisfied. 'An' it would have pleased your ma.'

Holly at eighteen was as long and lean as ever, but had schooled her movements so that she could control her flying arms and legs into neat and economical movements. She had 'done' all the wards at St Jude's and was now back to men's surgical as Senior Night Nurse.

Rose had said to her, 'You volunteered for it, didn't you? How can you bear being on night duty in the middle of summer?'

And Holly replied, 'It's when the real nursing happens.'

She meant it. As she did the rounds at midnight, torch shaded, footfalls hushed as much as possible on the linoleum, it occurred to her that night duty encapsulated all that she had hoped for from nursing. The feeling of being 'commandeered' which irked so many of the girls, was a boon to her. When she had started she had wanted to place herself in front of someone and say, 'Put me to some good use – I can't do it myself.' And the Matron of St Jude's, Margaret Oglethorpe, had done just that.

She was no longer out of touch with home; she corresponded with all of them at fairly regular intervals. But she could school her mind away from them with ease. Here was Corporal Edwards who had got in the way of a gun carriage; here was someone her own age who had volunteered for parachute training and had broken both his legs at his first training jump.

The new houseman came in – quietly. She could hear him talking to the probationer, a girl called Millie Milton. He would be told there were no problems, nothing to chart, and he would leave. She came to the last bed, whispered that tea would be round soon, and worked her way back up the ward on the other side.

'Ah, Nurse.'

He hadn't gone. He stood there, stethoscope round his neck, white coat unbuttoned. He was tall, dark and if not exactly handsome, quite good-looking. She knew Mollie Milton had a terrible crush on him.

'Good-evening, Mr Jenkins.'

'Anything I can do?'

'I don't think so.' She sensed his disappointment. He had not been at St Jude's long enough to be thankful for an easy night. 'Well . . . she relented. 'There is a patient down here . . .' She led the way to Sergeant Wall on the end who could not sleep. 'A certain amount of discomfort after a shoulder wound . . .'

He leaned over the man, examining his dressings by the light of his torch.

'All right, Sergeant?' he whispered. 'Not too tight?'

'Jest right, Doc. I keep giving it a sniff. It's not going green.'

'I should hope not, Sergeant!' Mr Jenkins breathed a laugh and looked up into the darkness at Holly. 'Perhaps a nice cup of tea, Nurse?' He turned back. 'I'll give you a couple of pills. You'll sleep like a log and doze most of tomorrow, and when I come to see you in the night, you'll be raring to go!'

Holly made the tea and thought that she liked Mr

Jenkins. Some of the housemen barely spoke to the patients and talked about the beds instead of the people in them – just like Sister had.

She propped Sergeant Wall up while he drank the tea, then settled him back on the pillows.

'I wouldn't mind a cup myself, Nurse,' said Mr Jenkins. Holly gave her torch to Mollie and went into the kitchen. The sudden blaze of light made her blink.

He said slowly, 'Nurse James . . . It's not an unusual name. But there's a touch of Dean Forest in your voice. Have you any family in a small place just outside Gloucester . . . Dymock?'

She was surprised. 'My grandfather was station master there. Do you know it?'

'From a distance. Through my grandparents. Like you, I suppose.' He took his tea and sipped appreciatively. 'My grandfather was a bit of a character. He was a poacher actually. I never called him Grandfather. He was always known as Old Man Jenkins.'

She almost dropped her tea.

'Was your father Percy Jenkins? No, he couldn't be. He died when he was still a lad.'

'Percy was my uncle. My father's baby brother. He got pneumonia.'

Holly started to laugh. 'I'm sorry . . . how very unfeeling of me. But you see, my mother taught your Uncle Percy in Dymock school. And once she washed his hair under the pump in the playground. It was the following year when he got pneumonia, but people always associate his illness with being put under the pump by my mother!'

He laughed too, showing horsy square teeth.

'I've heard that one. Good Lord, your mother must be Dorothy Prosser!'

'Yes!' Holly was amazed. 'This is such a coincidence! I can hardly believe it!'

He put down his tea and held out an enormous hand.

'I'm very pleased – delighted – to meet you, Miss James!'

'And . . . and I you!' Holly said, pumping the hand vigorously and thinking it was rather large for a surgeon but could probably tickle trout or catch rabbits with ease.

1945

After the D Day landings, nurses were drafted to two new hospitals on the South Coast which received the wounded from France. Holly, Rose and Nurse Davidson were not moved until after VE Day. Holly was disappointed but as Tom said to her, the wounded men were going to need nursing for many years to come. 'The fact that the War is over makes it worse for them. After the euphoria of winning dies away they will need a lot of care. Their morale will be very low.'

He carried their cases and saw them off at Waterloo.

'I shall miss you, Holly,' he said through the open window of their corridor train. 'If there's any chance of joining you in Sussex, I shall do so.'

It was the first time Holly had had a friend who was a man. Charlie had been a friend at first, but then, like Bob, he had somehow acquired an aura of masculine mystery when she had fallen in love. Tom Jenkins was different. He had taken Holly to the cinema fairly regularly for the last year, but he never argued when she paid for herself. They had the same interest in the hospital, similar goals too. Tom wanted to get a practice and become a reliable family doctor. Holly was now State Registered. After the War she wanted to go on the district somewhere. Maybe back home, maybe not.

The West Sussex General was slightly more relaxed than St Jude's. There were no women patients and the men organized the wards to suit themselves. They teased their nurses unmercifully, but mostly they co-operated too. The recalcitrant ones stood out like sore thumbs. Holly was assigned to a ward of ten beds all with wounds of the upper torso. In many cases this meant shoulder wounds

425

and the men were able to move around the ward freely and go on to the balcony to smoke. But three of them had scar tissue on the lung and during the comparative silence of the night the darkness was split by their hacking coughs.

Just one had facial damage from a bomb blast. When Holly arrived his head was completely covered with dressings. He had had skin grafts to his jaw and an operation on his eyes.

'He's in a bad way.' One of the Tommies had been trying to spoon in some broth between the bandages and the man had struck him away.

Holly looked at his chart and read the relevant notes before the name. As she hung the clipboard back in place she only just stifled a gasp.

The man was Bill Masters. Kildie's first boyfriend, from the bank.

She nursed him assiduously, never telling him who she was in case he reacted against her. His jaw was wired almost shut and he was frightened of choking on his food so refused almost everything. Holly kept his broth simmering on the gas and gave him four spoonfuls every hour. She propped him high in the bed and as she gave him the food so she talked to him in a low voice, telling him where his bed was positioned, what he would see from it when they took the bandages from his eyes. Anything to take his mind off the fact that he was taking food.

'The man with the Yorkshire accent is Wilfrid. And next to you is a fighter pilot – he's from London. His name is Mike.' She stood up. 'I'm going to get you some jelly.' He shook his head. She said, 'Please. Just two teaspoons. I won't badger you to take more.'

He made no more signs of protest so she fetched the jelly and gave him some.

At the end of her second week at the West Sussex, he was taken to theatre again and his bandages removed under anaesthetic. He came round very slowly, moving his head from side to side on the pillow and groaning with the pain in his jaw.

She was not there when he opened his eyes but the night nurse greeted her with the news the next morning.

'James – he can see! Bill Masters – he can see! Not a great deal at present, but he can distinguish shapes and colours. I think he's goin' to be all right!'

Holly smiled. 'I'm glad.'

She made a point of leaving him till almost the last when she did her rounds but she could see him across the ward and knew that he was terribly disfigured. The grafts were livid against the rest of his face and made his blond hair look dark. She was used to seeing such sights, but this was Bill Masters who had been fair and handsome and who had loved Kildie.

When she reached his bedside she said gently, 'Can you see me? Just nod if I'm visible.' He nodded. 'Clearly?' He made a very small negative motion with his head. She took his hand. 'You will. By the end of the week you will recognize me.'

He said something. She bent lower to catch the words. His jaw was too rigidly set to allow proper enunciation but she knew what he said. He recognized her already; by her walk, the feel of her hands, her smell. She called one of the nurses to help her make his bed. He was going to be all right. She could have waltzed down the ward with sheer joy.

It was just a week later when the wires were taken from his jaw. He stared up at her when she came near, but said nothing.

She smiled. 'Still no idle chat, Bill? You have never even asked me my name.'

He returned her smile experimentally, then opened and closed his mouth twice.

Then he said, 'Patient and nurse relationships. Supposed to be quite false. I've started to think I can't live without you. Better not to know your name.'

She laughed. 'I think you can allow yourself to feel a

427

special friendship in our case, Bill. I'm Holly James. You taught me to dance.'

He was dumbfounded and said nothing. But his eyes were on her the whole of that morning and she was terribly conscious of them.

Before she went off duty he said, 'I can see it is you now. It's taken me all day to rejig my memory of you. You've got the same legs and arms. But you've changed your hair completely!'

'You should not be able to see my hair under my cap,' she told him. 'But yes, my arms and legs are still difficult to manage!'

He tried to laugh and hurt his face. She said quickly, 'I'll laugh for you in future!' and he held his lips together and made a sound like a horse snickering.

She looked at him and felt a rush of love for him. Her grey eyes told him as much – and more that she hardly knew as yet.

'You haven't changed,' she said.

Afterwards she thought how cruel those words must have sounded when, three weeks later, he went to the bathroom for the first time and saw the extent of his injuries.

But for those three weeks, they let themselves fall in love. Nothing was said, everything was known. They could not stop looking at each other. As soon as she was off duty she would change and come back to the ward to play draughts with him or just to talk about those days when he had played the piano at the Cadena and Kildie had sung her haunting little songs. They talked properly about Kildie, and Holly understood her a little better. Bill spoke almost casually of her 'innate sexuality' and the constant running battle of their friendship.

'She needed that Villiers chap. He was going to tell her what to do and how to do it every minute of every day. I couldn't have faced that.'

Holly said wonderingly, 'That's how it was. Until Charlie.'

'Cousin Charlie?'

She had forgotten he went often to Gran's and knew all her family.

'Charlie had a crush on her always. And he got a lift back from his first posting and went to see her – and . . . well, Marcus caught them and almost threw her out.' Suddenly she started to laugh. 'Instead, he forced Charlie into his car – it was an open one and the middle of winter and Charlie was in his underwear – and drove him to Dymock and left him stranded in the road! I saw everything! I'd gone for a walk and was just on the other side of the hedge when it happened!'

Bill made the snickering sound. Then he said, 'Is this the first time it has struck you as funny?'

'Yes! How did you know?'

'Because you sound so surprised yourself that it *is* funny!' He touched the back of her red, nurse's hand. 'Well done, Holly.'

She smiled. 'Thank you, Bill.'

'And how did it change Kildie – all this racing around the countryside?'

Holly said thoughtfully, 'Well, it's just something indefinable. As if she has kept a little corner of herself apart from Marcus. Just for Charlie.'

'You say that because it is what you have done.'

She smiled ruefully. 'I suppose so.'

He said, 'Tell me.'

So she told him about her own childhood love for Charlie. And then, after Charlie's death, her silent adoration of Bob.

She said in a low voice, 'Both times I thought my heart was broken for ever.' She tried to laugh. 'I suppose I'm like Kildie. After all, we have the same blood!'

But Bill moved his head from side to side. 'Kildie takes. You give.'

She looked at his bruised eyes and felt her own fill with tears.

He said urgently, 'Holly, don't. Love is never wasted.

It is something learned and developed. Remember that.'

After he had seen his face he was very quiet and complained of being 'utterly tired'. She said she would come back as usual that evening but he said, 'Not tonight, Hol. Leave me on my own. It's been a bit of a shock and I need to get used to it.'

When she came on duty the next morning he was dead. It was a heart attack.

Mr Conway, who had done his operations, came to see her himself.

'It could have happened at any time. We shall never know just why it happened last night.' He looked at the serious young face beneath the cap. All nurses tended to look the same to him, but he suddenly saw this one as a girl first and nurse after.

He said brusquely, 'I'll tell you one thing, Nurse. Every time I saw him he seemed happier than the time before! Maybe he couldn't go any further than that.'

She thanked him and went on with her work. She was not very surprised. Every man she had loved had died. She must make sure she never loved again.

It was Rose who said, 'Why don't you take some leave, Holly?'

'I'm better working,' Holly replied briefly.

'You should go home. Just for a weekend perhaps.'

'Why? My mother is teaching now. She doesn't really need anyone.'

Rose sighed with exasperation. 'But you do!'

Holly said nothing. She had thought of going to see Gran but Gran was well into her eighties now. It wasn't really on.

Rose tried another tack. 'Listen. Surely there's someone at home who should know about Bill Masters? If he was a friend of the family then they ought to hear about him. After all, he was a hero, Holly!'

Holly stared at her unseeingly. Then she shook her head as if clearing it and became alert.

'Yes, he was, wasn't he? Maybe Kildie . . . yes, Kildie ought to know about it.' She gave her usual tight smile. 'Thanks, Rose. I'll telephone her. I'll go to Hill House for the weekend and talk to Kildie.'

TWENTY-TWO

1945

Kildie hugged her niece with unalloyed delight. Some-times it seemed to her that Gran and Holly and Jim were the only people in the world she could rely on. She had adored Dorothy, and Dorothy had somehow turned against her; Marcus was . . . Marcus. Charlie had been killed and his parents were hopeless anyway. And Winnie . . . Winnie was tough and reliable in many ways, but there was a lot of Kildie's own selfishness in Winnie; if their interests ever clashed Kildie knew she could not trust Winnie. When Holly had telephoned from Sussex and asked if she could come for the weekend, Kildie had felt a lift of sheer happiness. The weather had not been good since VJ Day on 14 August, and the feeling of anticlimax was everywhere. Then, suddenly, the drizzle stopped and a gentle autumnal sun dried everything and made mists in the mornings and even-ings. Kildie looked at the wonderful view from Hill House and said aloud, 'Season of mists and mellow fruitfulness,' and Mrs Davis called from the kitchen, 'Them apricots you put in the glass house might ripen now, eh?'

Kildie ignored that and said quietly, 'And why is she coming here, I wonder? A row with her mother? Is that why she hardly ever goes home?'

She took the Wolsley to the station and got a platform ticket so that she could grab Holly as soon as the train pulled in. But in the hordes that got off she could not spot a nurse's uniform anywhere. And then a very tall, serious girl, brown hair pulled back under a beret, gathered skirt flaring from a tight-waisted jacket, touched her arm.

'Kildie! Don't you recognize me?'

Kildie shrieked and enfolded her immediately.

'I was looking for the uniform – silly me!' She held Holly from her and looked her up and down. 'I do believe you're still growing.' Holly groaned and Kildie shook her head. 'No, you look marvellous. Like one of those girls Winnie's always sketching.' She took Holly's very small bag. 'Come on. I've got the car outside. My God, you haven't got much in here!'

'I'm only staying one night. Pyjamas and a toothbrush.'

'You're not going down to the Green?'

'Well, Mum will be at school.'

They clambered into the commodious interior of the car. Kildie forebore to mention that schools did not open at weekends. Holly concluded, 'Anyway, I wanted to see you.'

Kildie could have flushed with pleasure except that she rarely flushed these days. She started the car with difficulty, the plugs needed cleaning. They trundled down George Street.

'D'you want to go shopping or anything?'

'Oh no. Straight to Hill House.'

Kildie flashed a sideways look; Holly sounded almost urgent. A thought occurred to Kildie – was the girl pregnant? Frightened to tell Dorothy yet able to tell her cousin who was more like a sister.

Following that thought she said, 'You know, darling, we're both only children. I suppose we look on each other as sisters.'

Holly looked out of the window. The plane trees were blotched yellow and brown; soon the gutters would be full of their leaves. Winter was coming again. It always did.

She nodded briefly, wishing now that she had not come, wondering again about Kildie and Dad. Dad and Kildie.

She said firmly, 'Gran is our link of course. Gran holds us all together. How is she?'

433

'You heard about her having that turn? Lizzie thinks it was a little stroke. She collapsed over Grandad's grave. It was lucky really, she could have fallen in front of a car or anything.'

Holly thought back. 'I don't think so,' she said.

They pulled up on the gravel sweep and went in through the conservatory. Kildie called to Mrs Davis to put the kettle on and led Holly up to the guest room.

'How is work?' she asked tentatively, opening the window and pushing the curtains right back. Wonderful not to have the thick old blackout curtains any more.

But Holly evidently did not want to confess anything just yet.

'All right.' She tipped her bag out on the satin bedspread. Her pyjamas had seen better days. 'I'm moving back to St Jude's.'

'But you've not been at the new place a year! I thought you loved the work in Sussex?'

'I do. But I know so many people at St Jude's.' She flashed a sudden smile. 'Did I never tell you about Tom Jenkins? Such an amazing coincidence! Percy's nephew! He'd heard about Mum– she's gone down in their family annals apparently!' Kildie looked knowing and Holly added quickly, 'He's a good friend. Easy to talk to.'

'I see. How nice.'

'Yes.'

They went downstairs and drank tea and then Kildie showed her around the garden. That was something they had in common.

Holly said, 'You haven't taken down the beans. Are you still picking?'

'No. That is something Mr Davis will do. Marcus hates to see me doing anything heavy.'

'Are you allowed to pick these blackberries?' Holly asked.

'Oh yes, of course! I'll get a basin.'

They were still picking when Marcus arrived home. He

was genuinely pleased to see Holly; he knew she would have to go back to Sussex tomorrow and posed no threat to the Hill House exclusiveness. He relaxed sufficiently to suggest they went to the Woolpack after supper and then to go by himself when they declined.

It was then, as the autumn darkness enclosed the house and they sat in the drawing-room gloriously unconcerned about the light spilling from the windows into the valley, that Holly explained why she had come.

'I'm not sure how it will affect you now, Kildie.' She sat in her chair with an air of resignation that did not fit on a girl of twenty years old. 'But I had to tell you face to face.' She looked up. 'Sit down, why don't you?'

Kildie said, 'I'm ready to put my arms around you, darling. That's why I'm hovering.'

Holly smiled slightly. 'I think I have the role of comforter this time.' She took a breath. 'No easy way of saying this. Bill Masters was in my ward.' Kildie gave a cry of surprise and then, suddenly, sat down. Holly went on quietly and slowly as if she needed to comprehend her own words. 'He was shot down over France during the D Day landings and had had a whole year of operations. His sight had gone and they were working on that. And the skin grafts . . . plastic surgery takes so long. The strain on the heart is pretty bad. They managed to give him back some sight. And he was able to walk. So he went to the bathroom and saw his face in the mirror. We don't know if it was that. Anyway he died that night.'

She stopped speaking and stared down at her gathered skirt. Kildie said, 'God . . . how awful. It would have been better if he'd died immediately.'

Holly's head dropped lower. There was a silence. Kildie wondered whether she ought to be upset about this. Bill Masters and she had been friends for so long. She began to remember the little 'combo' Bill had organized and the way he had pumped the piano pedal when he was playing. She remembered his blond curls and his roguish grin.

She started to cry.

Jim was one of the last to leave the training base at Edmonton. He had made friends; he had watched Cecy Larkay grow from a schoolgirl to a young woman just as Holly must have grown. He had gone to the Larkay home to see photographs of Cecy in her graduation cap and gown; then in a dark grey suit and white blouse starting business school in Toronto. He had also seen pictures of Bob in his school uniform. He had heard about the other two Canadian Bobs who had flown with him. He knew the sense of guilt Bob Larkay must have felt when he had remained alive after their death. Perhaps there had been a kind of relief when the shell exploded in the Lancaster and Bob knew that they had all 'bought it'.

He was looking forward to going home; life in Edmonton was good but he knew he could never leave England, over half of his being had been there the whole of the time. There was also an unwillingness to go. These people accepted him for what he was; he did not know whether he was strong enough to take up the burdens of family life again. Kildie said she was 'living' for his return. What fresh problems would she bring him? Dorothy, on the other hand, appeared to have made a good life for herself; she was teaching English at Newent and driving a little Austin car Marcus had had converted for her. He could do nothing for Dorothy; perhaps he could do something for Kildie.

And his mother, what of her? Though she had not said so, probably had not even thought so, he knew from her brief letters that Lizzie and Edward would surely have parted company if it hadn't been for her. She had looked after their house as well as her own. And now she would want some help. He was surprised Kildie had not insisted on taking her up to Hill House, if only for an extended holiday. Neither Kildie nor Lizzie seemed to realize Gran was eighty-two; as for Sarah, she did not seem interested in any of them. Not that she ever had been of course.

He had to report back to Prestwick. He had a sheaf of

papers six inches thick on modifications and suggestions for the continuing use of the old flying boats. Then he would go through the demobilization process and eventually leave the Airforce in two or three weeks' time. But before then he wanted to get off the train at Gloucester and go to see Dorothy. He loved Dorothy; he saw now that his love had not always been uppermost in his dealings with her. And five years was a long time for both of them. Things would have happened for her; people would have happened; maybe Bob Larkay; maybe someone else. She was beautiful and intelligent. But he must make sure she knew that nothing mattered to him except . . . Dorothy. If she still wanted their marriage to work, that would be enough. And – after all that – he simply wanted to see Dorothy.

Nobody was expecting him so nobody met him. Even so, as he got out of the third-class coach in a cloud of steam from the heating pipes, he remembered his dream of being met by Holly running towards him in her navy school gabardine, shouting, 'Dad – oh Dad!' He crossed the bridge and showed his ticket and went into the booking hall, heart in mouth. Supposing history repeated itself and Kildie was outside in Marcus' Morgan? But there was no-one there and he shouldered his kitbag and went for the Tewkesbury bus and felt strangely out of place. George Street bustled with people – it was market day, mid-afternoon – and in spite of the War and Jim James's absence, life had obviously gone on.

The bus took the corner occupied by Villiers' and lurched down London Road into Northgate Street. Everything looked unbearably shabby, no real maintenance had been done for six years now. Shop fronts were peeling and the road was full of pot holes. A banner across the front of the Catholic Church proclaimed the autumn fair in aid of the Displaced Persons. That's what he was, a displaced person.

He walked from the Tewkesbury Road to the Green. The trees were turning, though the orange and gold leaves were pale compared with the glories of the Canadian fall. A couple of children were playing around the pump catching the drips and hurling them at each other. He did not recognize them. Doll and he had moved into the cottage on the Green in 1926 and no-one new had moved in by the time he left in 1940. Perhaps these were the evacuees he heard so much about.

He expected to see the bikes propped against the old man's beard underneath the front-room window, but the cottage stood stolidly in its garden plot, unbelievably tiny, unbelievably neat. A new padlock hung on the coal-house door and beyond that was a neat stack of upturned flower pots and some loose bean sticks. Someone was putting the garden to bed for the winter. Perhaps Holly had been home on leave.

He dumped his kitbag and took out his keys, choosing the one for the back door with a kind of cautious anticipation. It stuck halfway as it always had done, then grated open. He went inside. The kitchen was clean but had an eroded look from six years of scrubbing and no replacement lino or wall paint. He went on through into the living-room. The fire was laid in the grate, paper, kindling and pine cones. The table was pulled close to it and a note left on the dark green plush cloth.

It read, 'Aunt Doll. Thought you were supposed to have Monday afternoons off? Have made myself some toast and tea, hope you don't mind. Had to come and tell you, have got a big order for Winsomes from Mayhew's. They've got branches all over the country! Aren't I lucky? Chas is coming to stay with me at the weekend and I'm going to kit him out with school uniform whatever Ma says. I know he's not very bright, but he's such a darling. Once he goes to school, he'll pick up. Ma mollycoddles him. Did you know Hol was at Kildie's at the weekend? I don't know what it was about. Marcus said Kildie spent most of the time crying. She does a lot of that, doesn't she? Love from your really tough niece, Win.'

Jim stared at the note for some time after reading it.

He knew that Winnie had been with Dorothy when her baby was born; he knew that they must have forged a bond during that time. Even so, this note was a surprise. Winnie had a key and came and went fairly often it seemed. She called her aunt 'Doll' and wanted to share good news with her as soon as it happened. But the real news was that Holly had gone to Hill House and it seemed doubtful that Dorothy had known about it.

Jim shook his head as if clearing it and knelt by the grate to light the fire. The fir cones spluttered and burned with little blue flames. He went into the kitchen and filled the kettle. The milk jug, complete with its beaded fly cover, stood on the stone shelf in the larder. There was bread in the crock and a curious mixture of margarine in a big basin. In the meat safe were two sausages and six eggs. He took them into the kitchen and began to make one of Dorothy's specialities, toad-in-the-hole. The strangeness of everything began to melt into a conscious familiarity. His hands opened the cutlery drawer and there was the egg whisk where it had always been and the sharp kitchen knife. In the cupboard above the sink were basins and bowls. He lit the gas in the oven while he beat the eggs into submission. The kettle whistled gently and he made some tea and took it into the living-room.

Dorothy drove home slowly. It was ridiculous to live so far away from the school where she was now on the permanent staff, but she loved the drive. It gave her time to look at the world and the weather and see what was happening to the trees. Autumn had a special feeling for her; it was then that Jim had come whirling out of the hedgerow brandishing his steel-tipped case and yelling like a banshee.

She smiled at the thought and then stopped smiling. Jim should be at Prestwick now and in a week or two he would be home for good. She wondered just how they would manage. So much had happened. So much water under so many bridges.

And then she wondered about Holly. She was due for a leave quite soon; Dorothy hoped that she would time it to coincide with her father's homecoming. Surely they could now forget all about that business with Bob Larkay. He had been just a boy and so desperately in love. She had kept him at arm's length until that day; then, when he came to tell her he was to fly again, she had known somehow that he would not come back.

She sighed and changed down to negotiate a bend. And there, coming towards her was the Wolsley with Kildie behind the wheel. Dorothy used her horn and waved, but Kildie was sitting forward over the wheel with eyes most definitely front. Dorothy frowned. Kildie was going to see Gran, which was fine. She hardly ever went to Dymock these days because she said that seeing Gran deteriorate upset her. So she would be going for her own sake, not Gran's. Dorothy tutted exasperatedly. Another row with Marcus. Why couldn't she keep them to herself?

She calmed herself deliberately and noted May Hill on her left with its ninety-nine trees perched on the rounded summit like a ridiculous little hat. And then the undulating Malverns. And here was her turning for the village. It would be good to get home; it was her afternoon off but there had been a netball match and no-one else to referee . . .

She let herself in at the front door, dumped her school work on the bottom stair and went into the living-room. The display of fir cones in the grate was burning merrily, topped with some of her precious coal ration for the winter; the table was laid with tea things, plates, knives and forks. It must be Holly. She went into the kitchen and smelled the sausages, so she glanced into the pantry. Both sausages and all the eggs were gone. What was Holly thinking of? She went to the open back door to call her. And there was Jim. He was in shirtsleeves, the pale Air Force blue twill deepening his tan. He was stacking the bean sticks in neat bundles behind the shed. He looked up and saw her, dropped the last bundle all anyhow and just stood there, his face open, waiting.

She felt her own face contort and wrench itself painfully to control her aching throat. And then she was running, just as Jim had run to her all that time ago, and her voice, a high croak, burst out involuntarily, 'Jim – my Jim!'

He held her hard against her uncontrollable shaking, wrapping his arms around her, feeling strength and certainty surge through his own body. As she turned her face into his neck, sobbing helplessly, he said into her ear, 'It's all right, my darling. My dear, dear girl. It's all right.'

And he thought with a shock of surprise: it really was all right. He could cope. With them all. Because Dorothy needed him.

Kildie longed to see Jim. He could help her over this. He had been around when Bill and she were together. He knew how it would affect her; he understood. She thought she could hang on until he got back from Prestwick. A week, two at the most, and she would be able to ring him up and say in a high, trembling voice, 'Darling Jim, welcome home. Something really rather frightful has happened. Could you come up here straight-away?' In a way Bill would be doing her a last favour because even Dorothy would understand that she needed Jim's support over something so personal.

But there was no news of Jim and by the first week in October, Kildie was desperate. Once she started crying she could not stop and though usually Marcus could console her, this time he was impatient.

'For God's sake turn off the waterworks, Kildie! You haven't seen the man since the War! And anyway, he didn't mean that much to you. You threw him over the minute I arrived on the scene!'

She sobbed harder than ever. 'You just came along and took me from him! I had no choice in the matter!'

She hoped he would take her now, claim her as he so often did, make her forget Bill Masters and his poor blind face.

But all he said was, 'Pull yourself together, Kildie.

You've always done exactly what you wanted. And you know it!'

She stormed out of the house and flung herself into his car, hoping that would provoke some explosion of passion. But Marcus had had a difficult day at the office and was anticipating Jim's imminent return without any joy whatsoever. He hoped that this business with Bill Masters could somehow be turned against Kildie. He watched her drive off down the hill and just hoped she would not damage the car.

She went to Gran's. Gran had been fond of Bill and her usual stoicism was definitely dented by Kildie's hysterical arrival.

'There, my girl. Sit down and sob it out of your system,' she advised, pushing the kettle into the coals on top of the range with one hand, patting Kildie's dark head with the other. 'Poor Bill. He were always so full of life and fun, weren't he? I remember the first time you brought him here back in thirty-one. Adrian Frost had been with me all day. It was as if he made me see straight again.'

Kildie had no wish to listen to Gran reminiscing when her heart was breaking about Bill.

'Marcus has no sympathy,' she hiccupped. 'He doesn't understand that Bill was special to me. Just as I was special to Bill.' She scratched her leg through the nylon stocking and felt a dewdrop gather on the end of her nose. 'Marcus is so cruel, Gran,' she said, fumbling for her handkerchief. 'I always keep it to myself because I know it would upset you. But I have to tell someone. Marcus is . . . is . . . like an animal sometimes.'

'Well, dear,' Gran said comfortably, 'animals are natural. He could do much worse than—'

'I mean *bestial*!' Kildie almost shouted, scratching her leg again. And then she let out a loud scream.

'Whatever is it, Kildie?' Gran exclaimed. 'If you get hysterical you know what I shall do!'

Gran's cure for hysteria was a smart slap across the face. Kildie pointed with a trembling finger.

'That was a bloody flea!' she shrieked. 'I saw it hop onto my leg from the rug! Oh my God!'

Gran looked disgusted. 'That's quite enough language, Kildie!' she said sharply. 'Pull yourself together!' She sat down and made herself comfortable. 'For goodness' sake. You've seen enough of those in your time, my girl. Had 'em in your hair and all! Just fetch the Keating's and be quiet!'

It was too bad, too awful. Kildie knew she had come to the wrong person. She should have waited for Jim. She trailed out to the kitchen for the Keating's and shuddered at the state of the sink. If she'd married Bill he would have let Gran come to live with them. And in any case, Kildie would be a widow now. In black. Bill had always liked her in black like Hedy Lamarr. She wept anew.

It did not help one bit when she learned from an ecstatic Dorothy that Jim had called in on his way to Prestwick and had actually been at the Green when Kildie was catching fleas at Gran's. And what was more, it sounded as if Dorothy and Jim were like they'd been all those years ago in Dymock. Enclosed in a very special bubble.

Lizzie watched Chas sitting in the middle of Gran's ferns letting them tickle his face.

'He's only three,' she said to Gran. 'Why Winnie wants him to go to school so soon beats me!'

'She's worried about him. Thinks the other children will be good for him.' Gran did not take her eyes off the boy. He was welcome to sit there but if he started to thrash about . . . Not that Chas thrashed about much. He was too docile. That's what worried Winnie.

'I'm not so sure. He's so good with me. But when anyone comes—'

'No other children come, Lizzie,' Gran said firmly. 'And if the school is willing to take Chas I think you should be glad. It will give you more time with Edward.'

'Oh you begin to sound like him, Ma!' Lizzie picked

443

some grass and looked at it carefully. 'But he won't spend that time with me. He . . . he's too busy.'

They both knew what she could not say. Gran leaned back in her old wicker chair. Sometimes she was so tired she wondered how she would go on for another eight years. Perhaps Walter would no longer hold her to that promise.

She said, 'Lizzie . . . you know I love you, don't you?'

Lizzie looked up, startled and also frightened. Gran rarely used the word love.

'Of course I do, Ma. Just as I love you.'

'If you found out . . . something about me. Would it make any difference?'

Lizzie relaxed. Did Ma really think she and Sarah hadn't twigged that they had been born before Pa popped the question? Poor old Ma.

She said, 'I wouldn't care what you'd done or hadn't done, Ma. You have been the best mother anyone could have had.'

'And you know your pa and me . . . we were happy?'

'Oh yes, Ma.'

'It was because we took each other for what we were. We never tried to change ourselves or each other. We never felt imprisoned – nothing like that.'

Lizzie said, 'I know. And I know what you mean. I must accept Edward . . . as he is.'

Gran closed her eyes against the sudden burst of sunshine. Chas crowed.

'Edward loves that child. As much as you do, Lizzie.'

'Maybe. He isn't with him like I am. Caring for him.'

'He has to work, child. And – at last – he loves his work. He's found the bit of himself that is like his father. He wants to dig his hands in the earth and get to know it.'

Lizzie laughed. 'Oh Ma, you say such things. He comes home dirty and muddy, I agree. But I didn't mean that. He . . . he goes off. Drinking and things.'

'But he wouldn't if you had time for him. And if Chas is at school you won't get so tired. In the evenings you can go for walks. He can show you his plans for the Grange gardens—'

'And leave Chas in bed alone?'

'I'll come over.'

'You're not up to it.'

'I'm up to it.' She looked down the garden. 'He's my great grandchild. Don't forget that.'

'How could I?' Lizzie laughed. 'You're forever reminding me!'

Gran managed one of her slow smiles. 'No. I'm reminding myself,' she said cryptically. Then she said, 'Lizzie, before you go, could you see if there is anything in my hair?'

'Anything . . . ? Ma, you don't mean—'

'Kildie thought she saw something. But she does so much pretending!'

Lizzie hesitated, then she said, 'All right, Ma.'

They all came to Dymock that Christmas, even Marcus and Kildie. The Squire and Lady Alicia graciously let them have some rooms at the Grange and invited them all to the Boxing Day party, the first one since 1938.

But if they hoped that life would return to those times, they were disappointed. Nobody pulled their forelocks any more and even Jim, who had always been so respectful, was heard to say that some of the rooms should be allocated to people who had been bombed out.

Lizzie played the piano and Winnie danced with Chas, whirling him around until he screamed with delight.

'See? He can behave like a normal child!' she said to Holly.

Holly had brought Tom Jenkins to the dance and she said, 'If you're worried, Tom would examine him you know, Win.'

'I'm not worried!' Winnie was as aggressive as ever. 'I've got Ma and Gran to do my worrying for me!'

Holly smiled. 'What does your father say? I can see he's the proudest grandfather ever!'

Winnie laughed. 'He says if he wants a hundred percent guarantee that something will grow, he gets Chas to plant it for him!'

'He takes after Gran then.' Holly looked round for Tom and saw him dancing with her mother. 'I was hoping Gran would let Tom give her an examination—'

'You trying to drum up business for him?' Winnie put in.

'Seriously, Win. She's well into her eighties—'

'Surely you haven't forgotten she's got to live till she's ninety?'

'I haven't forgotten. It would be nice if she could enjoy it though, wouldn't it?'

They both looked at Gran who had been allowed a seat of honour next to Lady Alicia. She was wearing the grey outfit she had bought for Kildie's wedding seven years ago.

Holly said, as she had said then, 'She looks rather beautiful. Regal.'

Winnie added stoutly, 'Tell you something for nothing, our Hol. She looks a darned sight more aristocratic than Lady bloody Alicia! You'd never think she'd been a servant girl, would you?'

Holly said, 'Yes, you would. But she makes serving into something quite special.'

The two girls drifted across the floor towards Gran.

October 1945

Darling Kildie,

Thank you a million times for your letter. You are the only one who keeps in touch, you know. I do not feel quite such an orphan-in-a-storm when I hear from you. Thank you one million and one times!

Dear heart, it is simply wonderful that this dreadful war is over. I don't care what people say about Mr Truman, he has saved more lives than he destroyed. It was just the same with poor Mr Chamberlain. He bought us precious time and all he gets is vilification! But it is the same with everything and everyone. You say you feel left out by the family, yet you are the one who holds it together. You cannot see this because you are too close to them. You must take it from me, darling, that your trips to Dymock to see your Aunt Lizzie and your efforts on Winnie's behalf are terribly important. One day I will explain a great deal to you and you will realize I am not being simply a sentimental – and very proud – mother!

Never mind Jim and Dorothy. They do not mean to ostracize you, my precious. They are simply wrapped up in each other after their long separation. You tell me that Holly came to you for a weekend and did not go down to see them. Surely that shows you something rather important? They have made their own daughter feel an outsider, I would guess. It will wear off, Kildie. They were like that when they were first married. Dorothy will become bored again and then they will both want to come to see you.

As for your grandmother, well it sounds to me as if she is deteriorating fast. This business about the vicar finding her spread-eagled over your grandfather's grave is quite dreadful. But you must not let your sympathies run away with you. I agree entirely with Marcus. You cannot have her to stay with you – it is not your place to do so. Jim and Dorothy must bear that load when it becomes necessary. You will understand this too when I am able to talk to you. For now, take my word for it.

I am delighted you can discuss your marital affairs with me so freely, Kildie. No, of course you could not say such things to Gran or to Dorothy. I understand completely. I do not think it at all depraved, my dear. It is natural and a delight to find new ways of showing love. I cannot tell you how thankful I am that you have Marcus. You say he is obsessed. So long as he is obsessed with you, Kildie, what could be better? I think the incident with Cousin Charlie was good for your marriage. Try to keep Marcus on his toes, Kildie.

Much love, in fact all my love,
    Your doting Ma

April 1948
Darling Kildie,

Your three letters are before me, dearest! I am abysmally sorry to be so long with replies. Even now this must be short. I am having a simply wonderful time with an Italian film director! At my age! I am nearly old enough to be his mother! He says it is wonderful to be with a woman of experience!

You have hinted several times that I might marry Francis. Well, darling, I have to admit I have asked him more than once if he will make our partnership legal. We have a purely platonic friendship – yes, really darling! But it would be so much more secure if I had what Gran would call my marriage lines! Can't you imagine how relieved she must have been to get hers – crafty old so-and-so! However, Francis had one grande affaire *back in the days of Queen Victoria and since then . . . little boys. Don't be shocked, darling – though I am sure you won't be after what I gather from your last letter!*

I have to go. Umberto is trying to break the door down.

May 1948
Dear Lizzie,

Delighted to hear Chas is getting to grips with school at last. You must not worry about him being bullied, darling. Let him take his own chance. He'll soon learn to defend himself. And even if you could afford to send him to the Bluecoat School, there would be bullying there too.

I am so glad things are working out for you and Edward 'down on the farm'. Who would have thought he would have enjoyed it so much? I didn't realize I was doing you such a good turn eight years ago when I fixed the Squire for you! When I heard about the miscarriage I must admit I wished I had never lifted a finger to get you the Gatehouse. But, as Ma would say, as one door closes, another opens and you now have little Chas to look after. Just as Gran looked after Kildie for me.

Give my love to Edward if you dare! And tons for you.

PS I miss you all so much, Lizzie. Perhaps there is something

*about having a twin. I have recently had a very unhappy
liaison with a man much younger than myself and feel
bruised, physically and mentally! Yes, I am still disgusting,
sister dear!*

November 1948
Dear Jim,

'Thank you for your letter with news of Ma. No, I do not
think I shall be home for Christmas, my dear. I assure
you she is not calling for me – or Kildie – because she
wishes to see us. We are on her conscience, Jim. That is all
it is. Something that happened in the past. When she is over
this bronchitis you won't hear our names mentioned again.

Perhaps one day I will be able to explain things to you. I
will say now, Jim, I have always loved you very much. That
sounds as if I expect to die tomorrow! Not a bit of it! I am
going to live to a great age like Ma and plague everyone like
Ma. So be prepared.

My life in the States is idyllic. Strangely enough you have
met my employer and he was a friend of Pa's too. He owns
a chain of hotels and, frankly, I see to the running of them!
Of course, there are accountants and lawyers and managers
– but they come to see me, Jim. Your flighty sister has settled
down at last!

December 1949
Dearest Kildie,

How interesting that Holly is now a District Nurse! I know
Dorothy had ambitions for her – academic ones. I expect she
is disappointed but it serves her right. I'm glad she seems to
have patched up things with Jim and Dorothy. That's your
doing, Kildie. If she had not had you to turn to she would
have gone right away, I'm sure of that.

I must tell you that Francis is having papers drawn up to
sign most of his assets over to me! It certainly makes me feel
secure. But strangely enough I would still like to marry him!
I don't know why this can be, Kildie. After all, we have never
slept together and are never likely to!

449

October 1950

Dearest Jim and Dorothy,

How sweet of you to send me an invitation to Holly's wedding. Of course I know it is 'absolutely sincere' as you put it, Dorothy! I am indeed tempted to come because Holly was my favourite niece and I used to have dreams about her, would you believe! However, Francis is not at all well at present and I would not be happy leaving him for any length of time. So I will simply raise my glass on 7 November – is it rather morbid for Holly to be married on the anniversary of Pa's death? Probably Ma's suggestion! It sounds as if she is going downhill rapidly.

Anyway, will you ask Holly and Tom to get something nice with the enclosed money. I am enclosing a card and a blue garter. It seems appropriate. Isn't it fascinating that she is marrying someone with Dymock connections, even though they are quite loose ones! We cannot pull ourselves away from the place, can we?

October 1952

Dearest Kildie,

I am glad Gran is a little better. Yes, I agree with you, she is much happier pottering about at home with her revolting food and the garden and the hens. She would hate it in a home of any kind – and I do mean of any kind, Kildie. Even your house with its view and a private nurse would not do for Gran.

Darling, it is possible that you will be seeing me in the New Year. Francis has the chance of a window overlooking the Coronation route and though he is not really well enough to travel, I feel I would be a fool not to take advantage of it. You mention a party for Gran's ninetieth birthday next July. I don't think I would be able to stay on, darling. But perhaps I could call at Hill House just to see you. I think I must tell you something quite important. I was going to leave this for many years to come, but when I read again your last half a dozen letters to me, I think you must know the truth. Your feelings for Jim are not sinful, my dear. And if you truly *think they are reciprocated, then perhaps you should tell him what I will tell you. But . . . I cannot stress this sufficiently, Kildie – do not lose Marcus in all this. An affair is one thing, a divorce is quite another. And though it is many years since I saw any of you, I do not think Jim is the type to have a clandestine affair. But you will know this much better than I do. We will talk, my dear. Definitely.*

I am amazed to hear that Holly is pregnant. From what you told me in one of your letters I thought she had married Tom Jenkins for companionship only! I remember some of those old Dymock characters vividly and I might have guessed no-one from that God-forsaken place would take kindly to celibacy. Sex was the only thing that kept them from dying of boredom. Did you hear the terrible tale about your loving mother and Alf Matson? That is something else I will tell you, dearest. You will be very amused. There is so much we can talk about. I am tempted to suggest that you should come back with me to see something of America. But I know Marcus would never agree.

Sarah signed herself as usual 'your doting Ma' and sealed the airmail envelope slowly. She had hoped to keep the family secret to herself until after Emmie's death, but her duty as Kildie's mother must come before any peculiar sympathy she might have with Emmie. Kildie seemed to be working herself into a state bordering on insanity; she was as obsessive about Jim as Marcus was about her. Sarah had no way of knowing how Jim felt about it all, but it sounded like an unnatural triangle. She sighed sharply. Why couldn't everyone live as she and Francis lived, without jealousy, with true freedom? How would it hurt either Dorothy or Marcus if Jim and Kildie had an affair? They weren't properly related and, in any case, Kildie knew enough not to get pregnant at this stage in her life. All this fussing and fuming was so unnecessary.

Sarah smiled wryly. She was well into her fifties now and conceded to herself that age might have a great deal

451

to do with her philosophical pragmatism. People weren't chess pieces to be moved around advantageously.

She heard Francis' bell which meant the doctor had been shown out and Francis would like some tea and company. She took her letter and went into the hallway. The doctor was smiling professionally as he took his panama from the maid.

Sarah gave her the letter. 'Mail this for me, Mary. And bring tea on to the linhay.' She turned to the doctor. 'The tablets as usual, Henry?'

He shrugged. 'If you think they help.'

She returned his smile incredulously. 'Surely you are the one who knows that?'

He raised his brows. 'Surely, my dear, we both know what is the matter with Francis? There are no tablets to cure him. The ones he uses will help with the pain. For a time.'

She felt as if he had punched her in the midriff. She opened her mouth to breathe.

He said almost curiously, 'He has told you he has cancer of the colon?'

She shook her head dumbly.

'Sarah, I am so sorry. He said he would tell you eventually. I imagined by now—'

'There must be something . . . an operation?' She wanted to scream at him. She could not manage without Francis.

'I would have tried. He refused. He is, after all, in his mid-seventies.'

'But . . . simply to sit and wait . . . it is unthinkable!'

He sighed and put his hat onto the back of his head. 'Sometimes, it is much the best way. The people who fight . . . I have seen it. Often.'

'But – but – Francis! He'll find a way – he is clever, he works round things. He's probably willing the damned thing away right now—'

The doctor's smile returned. 'I wouldn't be surprised,' he said on a sudden jovial note, so obviously humouring

452

her she could have screamed again. 'I wouldn't be at all surprised!'

He slid out of the door. She watched him cross the foyer. His car was outside. It was open with low doors and he swung a leg over one of them easily. She hated him for being young and lithe and healthy.

She crossed the hall and went through the living-room and on to the linhay. The pool had long been private to their enlarged apartment, and Francis sat by it in a long old-fashioned steamer chair, studying the myriad surfaces of the water as if they contained messages to be read.

She squatted by him.

'What do you want to do?' she asked.

He turned his head, slowly like a tortoise, and surveyed her.

At last he said, 'I would like to go back home.'

She said, 'Are you able?'

'If you will be there. All the time.'

'Of course.'

He sighed and smiled. 'You could have held me to ransom.'

'How?'

'You could have insisted on getting those marriage lines of yours.'

She said nothing. She held her lips together but still they shook.

He said quietly, 'We'll be married in London. If that's all right with you.'

She breathed carefully until the tears had subsided, then she said, 'The funny thing is, I don't care about that any more. I think I love you, Francis!'

It was his turn to control his mouth. Then he said, 'Thank you, my dear.'

TWENTY-THREE

1953

At the end of February 1953, Lizzie took Chas to school as usual and started back down Middle Lane. Chas was eleven and much too big to be escorted to school; Lizzie made the excuse that by walking past the cottage six times each day she could keep an eye on her mother. Really, she hated Chas going to the village school where he might easily be bullied. She thought the Squire should pay for him to go somewhere 'a bit better'.

She glanced back at the cottage as she rounded the first bend of Middle Lane and saw Mrs Ball opening the gate and going round to the back door. Ma would not take kindly to that. But Lizzie was pleased. She hadn't time to call in as usual that particular morning. Kildie was coming for one of their discussions entitled 'What to do about Gran'. It would be a complete waste of time, as usual, because Jim would not hear of her going into a home, Dorothy was still working so she could not go to the Green, Lizzie could do nothing while she was looking after Chas, and Kildie . . . Kildie was the obvious choice. But Kildie was strangely unwilling to take Gran on now that she was not quite as clean and fussy as she had been.

The best of it was, whatever they decided between them, Gran would use her power of veto, as they said in the United Nations. Lizzie bit her lip: there were no two ways about it, Gran had become one of the most awkward old ladies she had ever met.

She heard the shout just as she reached Applecross. It was unmistakably Mrs Ball's high-pitched shriek. Lizzie was frozen in her tracks for a split second, then she turned and began to run back the way she had come.

It was a stroke. After a few days in Gloucester Infirmary Gran could talk again though her voice was quite different from her old one. Her legs would not support her so they took her to Westbury which had been the old workhouse and was now the County Council's pride and joy, a nursing home for the elderly. But Gran knew that it had been the workhouse and the shame of it nearly killed her.

Kildie said, 'Dearest Gran, you shall come to Hill House. Don't worry. We'll get a nurse in and you can look out at the view and feel like a queen.'

But Gran looked into the dark eyes and knew that Kildie would have to be very nice indeed to Marcus to get him to agree to this. And Kildie had to tread carefully these days because Marcus might well be having a fling with Winnie. And if he was, then Kildie would be even more determined to have a fling with Jim however often she was reminded that Jim was not only her uncle but practically her brother. Gran wondered when it would end and how she could end it before she died. And some days she did not care. But other days she did.

Jim and Dorothy drove down in Dorothy's little car. They leaned over her; Jim's grey eyes, Dorothy's blue ones.

'How is Holly?' she managed to ask in her new rasping voice.

Jim said, 'She's all right, Ma. It's a little girl. Holly wants to call her Lydia. After the bush. Do you remember?'

'Course I remember,' she said irritably. 'D'you think I've gone daft or something?'

'No, Ma.' Jim smiled with relief. 'Listen. Are you comfortable?'

'No,' Gran said. 'I'm not getting any proper food and I think I've got a bedsore.'

Jim looked to Dorothy for help.

She said, 'I'll see the matron, Gran. Don't worry.'

'They say one thing to you and do another to me,' Gran told her. 'It's always the same in the workhouse. Always was and always will be . . .' She knew she was rambling and clamped her gums together. That was another thing, her teeth were missing.

Dorothy said, 'Kildie said—'

Gran said, her voice suddenly strong, 'I don't want to go to Kildie's, Dorothy! Don't make me go to Kildie's!'

'Gran, we won't make you go anywhere.'

'But you'll leave me here, won't you?'

Dorothy hesitated. 'It's not that we are leaving you, Gran. You need to be in a place where you can have constant care and attention—'

'You've never liked me, Dorothy!' Gran lifted her head from the pillow. They had not pinned up her hair and it hung in half a dozen frail wisps down her neck. 'You thought I was dirty right at the beginning 'cos of that spider—'

'Gran, don't talk like that.'

'It's true! And when Mr Edwards brought old McKinnon that St Stephen's Day, you kept giving me funny looks 'cos I waited on them all. That's what I was put here for, Dorothy!'

'Oh Gran . . .'

Jim said, 'I'll have a word with the matron while you say goodbye.'

Dorothy threw him an angry look. He was disappearing as usual. Leaving her to make the decision about Gran. Why should it be left to her? She had a good job and Kildie was swanning around in that enormous house with nothing to do all day!

Gran said urgently, 'Doll, promise me you won't send me to Kildie's!'

'It's not up to me, Gran.'

'Jim and Holly . . . and you. My family. My real family . . . the girls are nothing to do with me . . .' She was rambling again.

Dorothy leaned over the bed. 'Listen, Gran, it's

Saturday today. We'll come tomorrow. We'll all come. Together. Have a proper chat.'

Gran's eyes looked up pleadingly. 'I can't stay another night, Doll! Don't make me stay another night!'

'Gran, stop it. You are perfectly comfortable. Try to relax. Eat the food they give you—'

'Slops!'

'Until we find your teeth perhaps slops are the best thing.'

Gran did not look up again. Quietly, she relapsed on to the pillows. Dorothy said, 'Just till tomorrow.' She leaned over. 'Good night, Gran.'

She walked down the ward with a firm tread so that Gran could hear her till the last moment. She felt angry with them all: the staff, the family who were being so absolutely hopeless – especially Kildie – even Gran herself for suddenly becoming the same as everyone else, losing her stoical courage at the last moment.

Jim came out of the matron's office. He was smiling but Dorothy knew only too well it was forced.

'Doll, everything is all right. We can relax. She's in the best possible place and they can guarantee a bed for the rest of her life.' He fell into step by her side. 'They say it's the same with everyone after a stroke. In a few days she will have settled down and be bossing everyone around—'

'I doubt that,' Dorothy said tightly.

'Oh Doll, please. If she won't go to Kildie what can we do?'

'Have her with us, of course. It's obvious.'

'She wouldn't come.'

'Oh yes she would.'

'But how could we manage? We can't afford a nurse like Kildie could. And with Holly pinned down with a new baby we've got no-one to look after her.'

'I could look after her. I don't like what is happening in the schools. It would be no hardship to give up teaching.' She looked at him. 'I did it before.'

He looked utterly miserable. 'You did it for my sake then. And it would be for my sake now.'

'No, it wouldn't. It would be for Gran's.' Suddenly Dorothy wanted to weep. She said, 'Jim, go on down to the car. I'm going back to say something to her. I can't let her go through the night thinking we don't want her. Go on.'

She almost ran back to the ward. Two nurses were just pulling up the sides of the bed to make it into a cot. Dorothy paused, horrified. No-one had said that Gran had to be penned in each night like an animal in a cage. One of the nurses spoke in a brisk, hard voice.

'It's up to you if you won't take your food. You know what will happen. You will die.'

Dorothy wanted to shout to them, 'She can't die! Not till her birthday! Not until she is ninety years old! She made a promise—'

But she was already moving rapidly down the ward to Gran.

She said in her school teacher's voice, 'We're taking my mother-in-law with us now. If you could arrange for the relevant papers to be signed in the office.' She whipped down one of the cot sides, put her arms right round Gran and lifted her into a sitting position. 'Jim's had a chat with the matron, Gran, and we all think it's better if you come home tonight.' She looked back. Jim was coming down the ward to her. He had not left her to go to the car after all.

'Jim, if you could just wrap Gran's coat around her while I put on her slippers.'

Matron glided up to them and told them how terribly unwise it was – still only the beginning of March – to take a person of such great age out of doors.

Dorothy said, 'Mrs James thrives out of doors. Perhaps we can drive past the house, Jim. Pick up some things and let Gran see the fern garden.'

Eventually they got away. Dorothy went into the cottage and picked up blankets and an armful of night clothes, hairpins and – still in their glass, apparently missed by everyone – teeth. Through the window she saw Jim hoisting his mother to the veranda with a sort of fireman's lift and sitting her down to look at her ferns. Dorothy found she was weeping loudly though she did not know why. If Gran got pneumonia now and died tomorrow it would be Percy Jenkins all over again.

Mrs Ball was by the car twittering anxiously. Dorothy told her what was happening and asked her to tell Lizzie. Between them they reloaded Gran and propped her up with pillows. Jim drove as fast as he could through the darkening day. 'I feel as if we're three fugitives escaping from gaol,' he said only half jokingly.

Dorothy said, 'You can have Holly's room, Gran. It looks over the garden. You'll be able to watch Jim put in the beans in another few weeks.'

Gran did not reply and Dorothy wondered if she was already dead. But when they reached the Green her voice rasped from the pile of pillows and blankets. 'I came here not long ago, didn't I? I can go over to the woods to get some firing tomorrow.'

Dorothy said, 'That was ten years ago, Gran. We've got plenty of coal now.'

Jim was on early turn. He had left home before it was properly light and emerged into a windy March afternoon anxious to get home as soon as possible and relieve Dorothy. Gran had been with them for three weeks and the first flush of their dramatic 'rescue' had died away, leaving them wondering whether they had done the right thing. Dorothy wanted to go and see Holly who was making heavy weather of her baby, and she could not leave Gran until Jim got home. He pointed out that if Gran had not come to them, Dorothy would still be at school and unable to see Holly anyway.

She snapped back, 'Well, I'm not at school, but I still can't go and see my daughter, can I?'

It was useless trying to make her see reason. She was

tired and fed-up; they were all tired and fed-up. Things would get better. He told her this and she darted him one of her looks and told him not to call her Doll.

He walked round the building to get his bike from the yard, and there was Kildie waiting for him. His heart sank.

'I must talk to you, Jim.' She had lost more weight and her mass of dark hair seemed thinner somehow. She would be forty in two years' time. Kildie, forty. He could accept that everyone else in the world was getting older; not Kildie.

She tucked her hand into his arm. 'Let's go up to the station refreshment room. Like we used to.'

She made it sound as if they'd gone on a regular basis. He could remember just the once.

'Kildie! It's nice to see you – we wondered why you didn't come down!' He pulled her to a halt. 'My dear, I must get home. Sorry. Dorothy wants to go to see Holly. Why don't you drive out? Ma is wondering why you haven't been to see her.'

Her face became tragic. 'How could I? It was so obvious . . . I felt just terrible. What must they have thought at the Westbury place? That I was some kind of unfeeling brute? Jim, I know it was Dorothy's decision, but how could you take Gran away from me like that? How could you do that to me? I thought you loved me, Jim. We have been closer than brother and sister. I thought—'

'What are you talking about, Kildie?' He felt a sense of weariness that was almost suffocation. She had met him like this before with stories of Marcus' cruelty, Marcus' infidelities, Marcus' lack of understanding. She always said, 'If I didn't have you, Jim, I would go mad.' He realized that when he had tackled Marcus all those years ago, he had declared his loyalty and she had relied on that loyalty ever since. But that was then. So much had happened. For one thing she was still with Villiers. Sometimes he wondered if she *was* a little unbalanced. But he did not want her worrying Dorothy with her complaints. After all, she was his niece, his responsibility.

She put a hand to her heart. 'You know what I'm talking about, Jim! You are more than an uncle to me – you are my brother! My God, how can you ask a question like that?'

'I meant, what are you saying about Ma? We took her away from that place because she was desperate to leave. How did it affect you?'

'I'd made *arrangements*! Surely they told you that? I'd booked a nurse to come in – got a bedsitting room all ready . . . They must have thought I'd backed out or something! Gran wanted to come to me and you whipped her out of there without so much as a . . . It's all right, Jim. I heard that it was Dorothy's decision. The matron told me. But still I thought that you . . . But you cannot risk a row with Dorothy.'

Jim looked at her and knew she was lying. Marcus had not wanted an old lady in his house and neither had Kildie. He nearly told her that it had not been anyone's decision except Ma's. But then he couldn't. She was so vulnerable; still, in so many ways, a little girl.

He said, 'Look, Kildie, come and see her. The longer you stay away the more difficult—'

'I can't. I'm not well. I shouldn't be here now, really. Marcus thinks I'm in bed. I've been in bed ever since I heard that you'd kidnapped Gran.'

'Kidnapped? Kildie – for goodness' sake—'

'If you're not going to have tea with me like the old days, I'm going back home to bed right now.' She waited, obviously thinking he would cave in.

He said, 'I think you'd better, my dear. You are obviously most unwell.' And he turned into the yard to pick up his bicycle.

That same afternoon, before Lizzie went to school for Chas, she and Edward were summoned to the Grange.

Squire Richardson and Lady Alicia took them into the morning-room where the remains of a very homely lunch was still on the table.

461

'Staff,' murmured the Squire.

'Cannot get them,' Lady Alicia enlarged. 'And that is one of the reasons—'

'Just a moment, m'dear.' The Squire sent her a warning look. 'Cart before the horse and all that sort of thing.'

'Ah yes. Quite.' Lady Alicia indicated chairs by the window. They settled themselves and looked across the lawn to the ha-ha and then the cows. Lizzie hoped they would not be too long. Chas would come home on his own and if he did it once there would be no reason at all why he should not do it again.

The Squire stood behind Edward's chair and put a hand on his shoulder.

'You know of course, my boy, you are my heir.'

Edward and Lizzie looked at each other. It was such a bombshell they said not a word. So often they had anticipated this moment, steeling themselves against disappointment. There was a cousin in Stirlingshire . . . perhaps Lady Alicia had relatives tucked away somewhere.

Lady Alicia smiled. 'Of *course* you knew, Edward. We have always treated you as our son. Especially since Edwina and – and—'

'Especially since you were orphaned,' the Squire concluded bluffly. 'We had our difficulties, certainly. But in the last ten years you have amply repaid us, my boy. The land is in your blood. Absolutely in your blood.'

Unexpectedly, Edward reddened with sheer pleasure. He tried to speak and could not. He patted his uncle's hand which was still on his shoulder and felt ridiculous when it was removed quite quickly.

Lady Alicia took up the batting again.

'We have been talking, your uncle and I, and it seems to us a great pity that you have to wait for your inheritance. This big old house—'

'Rattling around like peas in a drum,' interpolated the Squire. 'Plenty of room for all of you. And Mrs James.'

'Yes.' Lady Alicia turned to Lizzie who was now pop-eyed. 'Your dear mamma. That is why we wish to broach the subject – put our thoughts into action – as soon as may be.'

The Squire waxed enthusiastic. 'A Deed of Gift. That is what is needed. It will help with the rotten death duties later on – not for a long time yet, of course – and can have in-built clauses about care and accommodation for your aunt and myself when we – er – become—'

'Decrepit,' said Lady Alicia firmly. 'Let's not mince words, my dear. We too shall become as Mrs James has become.'

Lizzie said, 'Ah. Yes. I see.'

Edward babbled, 'I can't tell you how grateful . . . Lizzie, it will be wonderful for Chas. And Gran can be upstairs and keep an eye on everything—'

'And I can do the cooking,' Lizzie said.

'You are such a wonderful cook, dear. What a splendid idea!' Lady Alicia enthused.

Lizzie looked at the two of them grimly. They were getting old and had no servants, the crafty old devils. On the other hand, it would all become Chas's one day. And Gran would get such a kick out of living at the Grange.

Lizzie wondered who she could recruit to help her with this great place. Mrs Ball had a couple of daughters in the village. And perhaps Winnie would know of someone who would live in and do the rough.

Gran said, 'Don't be daft, our Lizzie. What would I do in the Grange? Perhaps later on, when I can help you out with a bit of laundry or something—'

'Ma, the Grange is going to be our home. It will be your home.'

Gran smiled, 'Never. It's where the Squire and his lady do live.'

'Listen, Ma. Edward will eventually be the Squire. And I shall be his lady.'

Gran continued to smile. 'That's as it should be, Lizzie. You were always different. A throw-back. Ladylike. And capable with it. You'll take to it like a duck to water.' She leaned back on her pillow. 'How things do work themselves out if you let them,' she said, obviously talking to herself as she did so often these days. Her eyes began to close. 'It's just Kildie. She's the one now.'

Lizzie followed Dorothy downstairs. 'Winnie tells me that Kildie is having some kind of nervous breakdown,' she said when they were in the living-room. 'That's why she hasn't been to see Ma.'

'Really?' Dorothy looked surprised. Jim had not told her of his encounter with Kildie, but word had got through via Winnie that Kildie considered Gran to have been kidnapped.

'I rather thought her nose was put out of joint and she was waiting for someone to go up and apologize and be all sympathy!'

Lizzie laughed. 'So you heard about the kidnap, did you? Honestly, Dorothy!' she sobered. 'She also thinks Winnie is having an affair with Marcus. As if Winnie is interested in him.' She sobered more. 'As if she's interested in any man!' She shook her head. 'No, I rather think if she *is* having a breakdown, she's talked herself into it! She's heard from Sarah who is coming back to this country, no doubt with an American accent and a great deal of money! Let Kildie tell *her* all about it!'

Dorothy thought of Kildie at nine years old. Beautiful and intelligent. She said sadly, 'Ah well.'

Lizzie went on, 'Try to talk Ma into coming to the Grange, won't you? It's just not fair her being with you all the time.'

Dorothy was touched. But she still shook her head.

'Leave it till after her birthday,' she suggested. 'You'll be a long time settling in. Perhaps in the autumn.'

Lizzie nodded. 'Thanks, my dear. This so-called gift is merely a ruse to get an unpaid cook-housekeeper, you know!' She smiled. 'I'm determined it shall work in our favour too, however. Chas can go to the Bluecoat School and have all his friends home for the holidays. And you must come and see us whenever you feel like it. I've never forgotten how you took me in that time when the raids started.'

She pecked Dorothy's cheek before climbing into the farm truck next to Edward, Chas wedged between them. As Dorothy said that night to Jim, 'Who would have thought that Edward and Lizzie could be so happy – so settled so – so—'

Jim said, 'So aristocratic?'

They laughed. Dorothy had been going to tell him about Sarah's imminent arrival in this country, but decided against it. Their moments of togetherness were few and far between now and she wanted nothing to spoil them. She wondered whether he still saw Kildie when he was on early turn. He was often late home.

Gran's birthday dawned warm but sunless.

After Holly had done her hair she and Dorothy set up a trestle-table across the bed and laid it with finger rolls and jellies and a cake made by Lizzie with candles in the shape of a nine and a nought. Gran sat up in her blue shawl and held Lydia while Jim took photographs. Tom arrived late from the hospital and said portentously, 'In my opinion, madam, you are actually fifty-five and a half!' and then he kissed her and said, 'That's for my dad. And that's for my Uncle Percy. And that one is for my wicked grandfather, Old Man Jenkins himself. And that one is for me!'

Gran held on to his hand and said, 'Eh. You're a good one. Old Dymock stock. She did better to come back to old Dymock stock, did our Holly. Never mind Charlie – nothing in that. And that chap from across the water – Bob whatever his name was – calf love! Bill Masters might have done, but he was always Kildie's. No, she was waiting for you, I reckon!'

Holly went bright red and Tom cocked one eyebrow and said, 'Old secrets, eh? I'm glad I came today!' And then he went and stood by Holly in the window and clamped his arm around her shoulder as if he would hold her from anyone else in the world.

Lizzie and Edward brought Gran a tiny ermine cape – 'It's to be worn as a bed jacket, Ma,' Lizzie insisted. 'You've got something to live up to now, you know.' She kissed her mother and said, 'I've made you a new nightie, Ma. I smocked it all by hand.'

'Like your wedding nightie then,' Gran said. And it was Lizzie's turn to blush.

In the kitchen Jim beamed at Dorothy. 'She's in fine form.'

Dorothy poured tea as if she were in a canteen. 'You know why.' She looked at him. 'You remember the promise?'

'Of course.' He took the tray. 'She's strong, Doll. She'll go on plaguing us for a bit longer I think.'

'Maybe.'

Kildie arrived after the cake had been cut. She was supported up the stairs by Winnie and Marcus.

'Gran . . .' Tears fell on the table, the sheet, the shawl, the ermine cape. 'Gran, I thought I would be too ill to see you. And on your birthday too – oo—'

Gran gave her a hanky. 'Give me a kiss when you've dried off, Kildie,' she said. 'It won't take long. It never does.'

Kildie let Edward find her a chair. They were all crammed into Holly's bedroom like sardines into a tin. Kildie gave Jim a soulful look. He returned it with a rallying smile. Marcus glowered. Winnie looked sardonic.

Gran said, 'Lizzie and Edward have brought me this.' She displayed the cape. 'You know they'm landed gentry now, do you?'

'I heard.' Kildie fiddled with the bedspread. 'We haven't actually bought you a present. As such.' She looked up at Marcus.

'Thought a cheque would be more useful,' he said, his dark eyes looking at no-one. 'Help out with all the expenses. Et cetera.'

Winnie said, 'Bed socks from me, Gran. Hand-knitted. We're going to have a really cold winter according to the almanac.' She put them on the bed. 'If you dare tell me you don't want them I shall put them both over your head, so be careful!'

Gran did not smile. She said, 'You're all so kind. It's living with him. I know that. He was kind. Always kind.'

Nearly everyone smiled but felt relieved when the sound of a car came through the window.

Dorothy said disbelievingly, 'My God . . . it's Sarah!'

They could hear her running through the house, taking the stairs much too quickly for someone in her fifties. Winnie chuckled. 'Just like before,' she said. 'At Grandad's graveside. She's a bit premature, isn't she?'

Winnie's utter lack of taste was ignored as Sarah entered the packed bedroom. She seemed to create a whirlwind in the confined space. Her New Look skirt was almost to the ground and it whirled around her as did her too-black hair and long hooped ear-rings.

'Darlings – darlings – how lovely to see you all! Oh Ma, hello – you didn't think I'd come, did you?'

Gran was obviously surprised. 'Well of course not! I thought you'd gone to Americy to stay! Why *have* you come?'

Sarah laid a long finger, enamel tipped, on Gran's inverted lips. 'Our secret,' she whispered. Then she turned. 'I've come to tell you all: I'm getting married!'

Everyone stared. They had not seen her since the beginning of the War. They had all aged; she had not.

She said, 'Well? Congratulations are in order, you know!' She held out a hand on which a large diamond glinted. 'This is the engagement ring, just to prove I'm serious!'

They responded awkwardly, artificially. It was Winnie who said, 'Well? Who's the poor sod of a victim?'

Sarah didn't mind. She laughed, made her fingers into a pistol and pretended to shoot Winnie. Then she put her head on one side. 'Pa knew him. He's been my protector,

467

my patron, my employer since I was seventeen. Now it seems sensible – to tidy things up.' Sarah met Gran's eyes defiantly. 'It's Francis Passmore-Williams,' she said.

Nobody made a comment. If Jim remembered the name he said nothing. They were all watching Gran and Sarah. It was as if the two of them were alone in the room, Gran propped up on her pillows, Sarah sitting on the bed looking right at her.

Gran said, 'Is he the man who told you I was not your mother?'

There came a sound from Lizzie rather like a yelp. She squeaked, 'Sarah?'

Jim started forward but Gran held out a hand to stop him.

'Not you, Jim. You belong to your father and me.' She went back to Sarah. 'Well?'

Sarah said, 'Yes.'

Lydia in Holly's arms began to cry. Tom took her gently and crept out of the room, squeezing past Kildie and Marcus without them seeing him.

Gran said quietly, 'You cannot marry him, Sarah. He's an evil man.'

Sarah shook her head impatiently. 'I thought so too. I wanted to protect Pa from him. Oh . . . he liked young boys. I suppose that is . . . wrong. Sinful?' She gave a brittle laugh. 'It's not unknown, Ma. Maybe if Pa hadn't beaten him to it with my real mother, he'd have been all right.' She smiled at herself. 'I still call you Ma, you see. Funny, isn't it?'

Lizzie tried to speak again and Edward suddenly put his arms around her and held her to him.

'Sarah . . .' Gran spoke very slowly. 'You cannot marry that man.'

'My God. He said it would be a shock to Pa. Not to you! Ma . . . I know everything there is to know about Francis. I am marrying him because he is dying and he wants everything sewn up legally.'

'Then there is no need for a wedding ring.' Gran leaned

back on her pillows as if surrendering to an enemy. 'The man is your father, Sarah.'

At first there was no reaction from anyone. And then Kildie began to weep noisily, and Lizzie said loudly, 'But that means . . . that means—' and Winnie put a hand on her arm and silenced her. Edward enfolded both of them. Jim glanced at Dorothy, then Holly. They moved in and stood together. Only Sarah continued to stare as if she had known this truth all the time and yet had been unable to recognize it.

She said slowly, 'Go on, Ma.' She looked around. 'Shut up, Kildie.'

Gran said, 'I can only tell you what I think happened. None of us knows for sure. Only Elizabeth. That was the name of your mother. Elizabeth. Your real mother.' She took a breath and said very softly, 'I have thought about it. Often. So often. She was the love of Walter's life. When she died . . . he was broken for a long time.' There was a long pause. She was looking back, seeing Canon James' son in those far-off days before the Great War. She took another breath. The silence in the bedroom was thick and hot.

'Elizabeth sent him packing in ninety-eight. Her new lover was in the Church and might be forced to marry her to keep his own respectability. But when she told him she was pregnant, he cast her off. Denied everything. So . . .' She touched Sarah's hand gently. 'She went back to Walter and passed the pregnancy on to him.' Sarah looked down at the gnarled hand on hers and did not move. Gran said, 'It is what girls had to do then, Sarah. Otherwise there was only the workhouse.'

Sarah said, 'All right, Ma. But how do you know? How can you be certain she wasn't lying? You just said that you worked all this out by yourself.'

Gran leaned back on the pillows and closed her eyes. 'Your father . . . Walter . . . often wondered. But it did not matter to us. We loved you. You were our daughters.' She opened her eyes suddenly and there was the old gleam of grim amusement in their greyness. 'You were more my daughters than his! When we fetched you from your foster home . . . everyone in Dymock thought you were mine. I was proud of that!' She closed her eyes again. 'When Walter died I needed you – needed you to be my girls and Kildie, Winnie, Charlie, my grandchildren. But Adrian Frost thought I was living under a burden. That I needed to be freed. The births were registered by Walter who had entered his name as the father. But there had been a priest with Elizabeth when she died. Walter had gone to see him. To thank him for . . . last rites. Things like that.'

Holly looked down at her hands. They would always be red and rough from her nursing days. Rather like Gran's. She swallowed.

Edward said over Lizzie's head, 'I don't understand how my father comes into all this.'

Gran looked across to him and smiled faintly. 'He was a good man, Edward. That is why I know you are right for Lizzie. You will look after her, won't you? Don't let her work too hard in that great place—'

Lizzie whimpered and Gran stopped herself and breathed carefully and went on.

'He came to see me. It was just after the funeral. I told him things . . . about Walter and about myself. He wanted to talk to that priest. I told him not to. But . . . some time afterwards . . . he sent me a letter. Heaven knows how he'd got it – priests are supposed to keep their own counsel, aren't they? But Elizabeth had confessed to that priest just before she died and he wrote it down and signed it and Adrian Frost sent it to me.' She moved her head. 'It's in my bag. Inside the lining.'

There was a little silence then Sarah said, 'So. Elizabeth made a fool of Pa all those years ago—'

Gran looked surprised. 'A fool? Oh Sarah . . . She did him a great honour. She gave him her babies. She trusted him to find a way of caring for them. She chose their father and she chose well. You cannot deny that, child!'

Sarah said, 'Ma . . . *he* chose well. He chose you.' She

tried to go on but could not. She put Emmie's hand to her face.

Kildie's voice was loud and accusing and overrode the murmurs that were breaking out. 'Why didn't you tell us before? Why didn't you tell us you weren't their mother or my Gran! And when you found out about Grandad – why didn't you – why didn't you?' She was gasping. Marcus gripped her hard.

Gran looked across the room. Her grey eyes were sad. 'Don't you know that, Kildie? Ah . . . I did not want to lose any of you . . . that is true. But more important than that . . . I wanted Jim and Dorothy to be happy together. And you would have spoiled that if you'd known. It was important for you to think Jim was a close relative, Kildie.' She struggled up on her pillows and leaned towards the girl. 'Don't you remember when they met first? They were meant for each other, Kildie. You knew it then. But as you grew older you wanted more and more of Jim.' She tried to reach out her free hand and began to shake. 'Kildie, please don't – please don't—'

Quite suddenly, Jim took control. He moved away from Dorothy and Holly and went to his mother. He was smiling, edging carefully around the trestle-table, holding her up, pushing her hair from her forehead as if she were a child.

'Ma . . .' There was even a small laugh in his voice. 'Dear Ma. Don't you think I could have a say in this? I won't pretend I don't know what you mean . . . We're all trying to be truthful now, aren't we? But there was never any real chance of Kildie spoiling things for Doll and me—'

Kildie cried out at that but Gran ignored her and said fretfully, 'Don't call her Doll, Jim.'

Jim went on, 'We must have something rather special to get through the War and the things that happened then. Something special like you and Pa had. D'you remember me catching you canoodling in the kitchen the day Doll and I were married?'

471

Gran said, 'He was silly like that. He said silly things. He said his eyes were glad to see me . . . I was only a servant, Jim. But he respected me. He could see I was starved for love and children and motherhood . . . he gave it all to me, Jim. And when he went I wanted it to stay the same. It was all I could do for him then. Do you understand, Jim?'

He kissed her gently and cradled her against his shoulder.

'We all understand, Ma.'

And it was then that Kildie collapsed into hysterics and was removed from the room by Marcus.

They were all at the funeral, even the Squire and Lady Alicia. Mrs Ball wept noisily and then apologized profusely.

Holly glanced at Kildie. 'Not at all, Mrs Ball,' she said. And even Kildie managed a wan smile.

Afterwards there were sandwiches and tea and cakes at the Grange. Chas electrified Lizzie by asking loudly, 'They said at school I'm a bastard. What's a bastard, Nanny?'

Lizzie looked at Winnie helplessly. Winnie doubled over with laughter.

'Oh Chas,' she gasped. 'Don't worry about it, darling. We're all bastards!'

He smiled, well pleased with the success of his remark, determined to use it again at the first opportunity.

Winnie said, 'Ma, stop looking as if the earth had opened up! He's growing up. It's great?'

'Win, I really can't see how you can be so cheerful. Gran has just died and she wasn't even Gran!'

Winnie put an arm around her mother and said robustly, 'What difference does it make? It's like she said, if it hadn't been for all that old, old business, she wouldn't have been married to Grandad and you and Sarah wouldn't have grown up happily . . .'

'Oh . . . You!' Lizzie pecked at her daughter's cheek. Winnie was what they called a career woman. She was beautiful too. Lizzie said, 'You make the whole of life sound like a game of consequences!'

Winnie looked at Kildie and thought of Charlie. The game of consequences had gone sadly wrong there.

Chas moved across the room to where his baby cousin was being nursed. He adored Lydia and hoped he might be allowed to hold her. So he looked up at his Uncle Tom and Aunt Holly and came out with his party piece.

'I'm a bastard,' he offered. 'Did you know?'

Tom stooped and looked him in the eye. 'It couldn't happen to a nicer chap,' he said.

'Is Lydia a bastard too?' Chas asked.

'I don't think she is, actually. So don't swank about it too much. We don't want her to feel different.'

'Gosh no!' Chas was suddenly fervent. 'I'm going to look after her,' he said. 'When I'm grown up I'll marry her and let her live in the Grange.'

Aunt Holly nodded gravely and indicated one of the heavy old chairs. He sat on it and she placed Lydia on his lap. He beamed happily.

She said, 'Tom . . . it's the strangest thing . . . I think I am loving you more and more each day. Is that possible?'

'Oh yes. It's a medical fact, you know.'

'I don't want to know about the chemistry. Don't tell me about the chemistry of it!'

'I thought chemistry was your thing? You told me Miss Joliffe said—'

'Tom, be serious. Just for once.'

'I am always serious. Especially when you think I am not. Our long courtship—'

'Friendship. We were friends.'

'We still are. It makes good growing ground, does friendship.'

'Tom – I asked you to be serious!'

'Holly Jenkins, how can I convince you? I know – your beans. Your precious kidney beans. You plant them on May the first, yes? They make friends with the earth. Yes? Then they start to climb. They need the sticks – otherwise they'd flop all over the place . . .' He made flopping motions which included crossing his eyes. 'But when they're supported and nurtured . . . up they go—'

Holly was laughing in spite of herself.

'Tom – I want to tell you something!'

He put an arm around her. 'Hol . . . Gran is somewhere. And she's still planting beans.'

Holly put her forehead against his shoulder for a moment. Her eyes were closed.

She said, 'I'm pregnant again. Lydia will only be just over a year old. And we've no money.'

He was still, his arm tightening around her.

Then he whispered, 'Oh Hol. How wonderful . . . how *wonderful!*'

She said, 'But darling—'

'Listen, Hol. Did your grandparents have any money when they went to Dymock first? They were practically disowned, weren't they? And they had two little girls and then your father . . . did it matter to them?'

'No,' she said, her voice muffled against the jacket of his suit.

Tom said, 'Chas, old chap, we're going to have another baby.'

Chas said, 'Will it be another—'

Tom interrupted firmly, 'No. And what did I just say to you?'

'Sorry, Uncle Tom.' Chas smiled. 'I mustn't swank about it, must I?'

'No!'

Dorothy, who had not cried once since Gran's birthday, felt her eyes water when they told her about the baby. Jim was exuberant. Kildie said, 'Oh, we shall still be away when it's born, Hol. I'll bring back loads of presents though!'

Marcus was taking her on a long cruise. She was already making her present list. Silver bangles for Sarah and miniature ones for Lydia. Tooled leather for the men.

Maybe something small for Jim though. She had avoided Jim since the birthday, but perhaps . . . when she came back . . . she could call at the Green when she knew Holly was there . . . And now, a new baby made it easier still. Babies were so – so universal. She thought suddenly of Charlie and looked over at Winnie who was looking at her. If only . . . if only . . .

The long summer evening was darkening and it was time to go.

Lady Alicia said, 'Don't thank me. It was an honour. Your mother . . . someone very special. And in any case, Lizzie is chatelaine now, you know! She has this wonderful woman from the village to help, but she virtually runs the place single-handed.'

Sarah said to Lizzie, 'I would stay the night, darling, but Francis is sinking fast.' She pecked Lizzie's cheek. 'I know you don't want to see him, Lizzie, but he's really happy about you. It . . . it's all . . . sort of . . . vindicated his life. In a funny way.'

Lizzie said with unusual sarcasm, 'Oh well, so long as he's happy—'

'Darling, it doesn't make any difference to us. Pa is still Pa. Ma is still Ma. When I knew about Ma I tried hard to get her out of my system, but I couldn't.'

Lizzie shook her head helplessly. 'I'm still at sixes and sevens. I'm putting everything into this place. Trying to . . . find myself, I suppose. But I don't feel I've *got* anyone any more!'

Sarah said, 'You've got Edward.'

'Have I?'

Sarah smiled. 'You always had him. You didn't know it. Maybe he didn't know it. But you did.'

Dorothy said, 'Well. We'd better go, Jim. Where's the white charger?'

'White charger?'

She smiled. Her eyes were as blue as ever, her hair only a little faded.

'You know, the one you use when you come to rescue people.'

He did not smile back.

'Are we all right now, Dorothy?'

She took his arm and led him down the steps of the Grange to where her small car waited for them.

'I wish you wouldn't call me Dorothy,' was all she said.

THE END

SWEETER THAN WINE
by Susan Sallis

The quarrel had begun many years before – in 1850 on a West Indian sugar plantation – but although Charles Martinez and Hanover Rudolph had been dead a long time, the resentment and grudges of that old enmity still separated the two most important families in Bristol. The Rudolphs and the Martinez disliked each other intensely – until the Michaelmas Ball of 1927.

There, Jack Martinez, handsome roué and gambler, danced with spoilt, precocious Maude Rudolph and a spark was kindled. The two young lovers, scandalizing respectable Bristol, forced the families to unite and an uneasy truce was formed in time for their child to be born.

But there were others in the feuding families who were to be drawn into the subtle, confusing, and emotional bonding. For Maude had a brother, a tense, silent, moody man called Austen, who still couldn't forgive the Martinez family, even though he thought Jack's sister, Harriet, the loveliest and most gentle girl he had ever seen. As the families fused, blended in the most tragic and unexpected ways, so Austen and Harriet found themselves trapped in a complex union of passion, lies, and frustrated love.

0 552 14162 3

DAUGHTERS OF THE MOON
by Susan Sallis

The twins were born in war-torn Plymouth in 1944, two little girls whose parents – touring actors – didn't altogether want them. Their unorthodox childhood, first as evacuee babies in Cornwall, then at boarding school, then living with their Aunt Maggie, made them grow up uniquely self-sufficient. They didn't need anyone else. They had each other.

Miranda was the vibrant, flamboyant one, determined to be an actress, determined never to conform or be dull and conventional. Meg was quieter, more self-effacing. But it was Meg who always knew when anything bad was happening to Miranda.

As they grew up, the bond between them held – until Meg went back to Cornwall to buy a house, to paint, to fall in love. And for the first time events conspired to drive a rift through their special relationship. Their lives shifted – for Miranda found herself trapped into domesticity, and Meg – feeling herself betrayed – had to seek a new path that ultimately took her to unexpected success.

But the link was still there, in spite of all that was to happen, in spite of violence and tragedy, and finally it led to happiness that came when they had ceased to expect it.

0 552 13934 3

AN ORDINARY WOMAN
by Susan Sallis

When Rose was four the scandal broke about her head. She was really too young to understand what was happening – only that her mother was in disgrace and that they were leaving Aunt Mabe in America and returning home to England. The following May, Joanna – 'Jon' – was born.

Rose and Jon were totally different. Jon was vivacious, fun, liked a good time, and always got what she wanted, even when what she wanted happened to belong to Rose. Rose was reserved, controlled, never wanted to leave her home or Gloucestershire, and was – well – an ordinary girl who grew into an ordinary woman.

But as Jon raced from disaster to disaster, from one violent relationship to another so Rose, in her quiet way, salvaged the family, held them together, pasted over the cracks of tragedy and emotional upheavals whilst at the same time fighting her own personal crises.

It was much later – when the children were growing up, when life at last seemed tranquil and settled, that Jon precipitated Rose across the Atlantic and into the most extraordinary event of her life. When Rose finally returned from America no-one could ever again think of her as an ordinary woman.

0 552 13756 1

A SELECTED LIST OF FINE NOVELS
AVAILABLE FROM CORGI BOOKS

THE PRICES SHOWN BELOW WERE CORRECT AT THE TIME OF GOING TO PRESS. HOWEVER TRANSWORLD PUBLISHERS RESERVE THE RIGHT TO SHOW NEW RETAIL PRICES ON COVERS WHICH MAY DIFFER FROM THOSE PREVIOUSLY ADVERTISED IN THE TEXT OR ELSEWHERE.

☐	13992 0	LIGHT ME THE MOON	Angela Arney £4.99
☐	14231 X	ADDICTED	Jill Gascoine £4.99
☐	13686 7	THE SHOEMAKER'S DAUGHTER	Iris Gower £4.99
☐	14139 9	THE SEPTEMBER STARLINGS	Ruth Hamilton £4.99
☐	13872 X	LEGACY OF LOVE	Caroline Harvey £4.99
☐	14138 0	PROUD HARVEST	Janet Haslam £4.99
☐	14262 X	MARIANA	Susanna Kearsley £4.99
☐	14045 7	THE SUGAR PAVILION	Rosalind Laker £5.99
☐	14002 3	FOOL'S CURTAIN	Claire Lorrimer £4.99
☐	13737 5	EMERALD	Elisabeth Luard £5.99
☐	13910 6	BLUEBIRDS	Margaret Mayhew £4.99
☐	13904 1	VOICES OF SUMMER	Diane Pearson £4.99
☐	10375 6	CSARDAS	Diane Pearson £5.99
☐	13987 4	ZADRUGA	Margaret Pemberton £4.99
☐	13636 0	CARA'S LAND	Elvi Rhodes £4.99
☐	13870 3	THE RAINBOW THROUGH THE RAIN	Elvi Rhodes £4.99
☐	12375 7	A SCATTERING OF DAISIES	Susan Sallis £4.99
☐	12579 2	THE DAFFODILS OF NEWENT	Susan Sallis £4.99
☐	12880 5	BLUEBELL WINDOWS	Susan Sallis £4.99
☐	13136 9	ROSEMARY FOR REMEMBRANCE	Susan Sallis £4.99
☐	13756 1	AN ORDINARY WOMAN	Susan Sallis £4.99
☐	13934 3	DAUGHTERS OF THE MOON	Susan Sallis £4.99
☐	13346 9	SUMMER VISITORS	Susan Sallis £4.99
☐	13545 3	BY SUN AND CANDLELIGHT	Susan Sallis £4.99
☐	14162 3	SWEETER THAN WINE	Susan Sallis £4.99
☐	14230 1	MISSING PERSON	Mary Jane Staples £4.99
☐	14118 3	PRIDE OF WALWORTH	Mary Jane Staples £4.99
☐	14118 6	THE HUNGRY TIDE	Valerie Wood £4.99
☐	14263 8	ANNIE	Valerie Wood £4.99